# TRAP, PREY, LUST

*A Novel*

By Carolyn Shanti

Published by
Filament Publishing Ltd
16, Croydon Road, Waddon, Croydon,
Surrey, CR0 4PA, United Kingdom
Telephone +44 (0)20 8688 2598
Fax +44 (0)20 7183 7186
info@filamentpublishing.com
www.filamentpublishing.com

The right of Carolyn Shanti to be identified as the author of this work has been asserted by her in accordance with the Designs and Copyright Act 1988.

ISBN 978-1-912635-03-0

Printed by 4edge Ltd

This is a work of fiction, inspired by real-life events. Names, characters, businesses, places, events, locales, and incidents are either the products of the author's imagination or used in a fictitious manner. Any resemblance to actual persons, living or dead, or actual events is purely coincidental.

*"Their suffering, far from going to the grave with them and ending there, is passed on to future generations...The sickness remains in the soil."*

Misha Norland, Author of *Signatures, Miasms, AIDS*, Yondercott Press Abergavenny, 2003

# CONNECT WITH THE AUTHOR

www.carolynshanti.com/

www.twitter.com/CarolynShanti5

www.facebook.com/carolyn.shanti.5

https://www.youtube.com/channel/UCQPcPRa5F-qtA2B-aeKlBZA

# ABOUT THE AUTHOR

Carolyn Shanti is the author of *Trap, Prey, Lust*. The novel is based on the true story of her own childhood, where she was brought up in a wealthy and privileged family in England.

A secluded and idyllic mansion, surrounded by acres of private property, was where she spent her childhood years. It was also a place of dark shadows and sexual secrets.

Her father, a prominent businessman in the fashion industry, was a member of a well-known occult society. As a young child, Carolyn suffered ritual sexual abuse and was raped, not only by her own father but by members of the society. She was 'groomed', and the use of mind control techniques were put in place to work against her remembering the abuse or the perpetrators of these acts of violence.

It was on a trip to India in 2013 that she started to have memories of the abuse. She was so unwell that she sought the help of Dr Rajan Sankaran, a renowned holistic physician, homeopath and international speaker. In gratitude for his help, she has dedicated her book to him. For four years, she was under his care at his clinic in Mumbai and has now almost completed her healing. It has been a long and arduous journey.

In *Trap, Prey, Lust*, she has narrated her own story of childhood abuse in the form of fiction. Her wish in publishing this book is to demonstrate the seriousness of the issues that we face in the sexual abuse of women and children, the cults and secret societies that support these crimes, and the cultures that often condone these practices.

# DEDICATION

The book is dedicated to
Dr Rajan Sankaran
with love and gratitude

Carolyn Shanti

# CONTENTS

# Dr Sankaran's Analysis of Carolyn's Case.

I took Carolyn's case to discover what her individual experience was in the various situations that she had experienced. With her cooperation, I uncovered the deep pattern in her that underlies all her experiences. Based on this understanding, we chose a homeopathic remedy that matched her experience exactly. The remedy we chose is called Mancinella. It is made from one the most poisonous trees in the world, but in ultra-dilute doses called homeopathic potencies, it is capable of curing the specific pattern that Carolyn had deep within her.

Carolyn mentioned that all her problems and symptoms had come out of a childhood situation which involved ritual sexual abuse by her father. Twenty years before the consultation, she had had memories of this abuse, causing a collapse, and for six months she had been unable to do any work, taking complete rest. But she had then gone into a complete state of denial.

Her father, a successful businessman, was a member of a private club that was dedicated to the practices of occultism involving the predators wearing Ancient Egyptian dog masks. They also used blood in their ceremonies. The house in which she lived was full of darkness.

These issues were all hidden in her deep core – the feelings of terror and panic, someone coming from the back and capturing her, the fear of being tortured.

She had times of being out of the body whilst having memories of sexual abuse. She experienced floating, pins and needles down her arms, feelings of panic. Then she can laugh again and relate to the world. The pace of the case is intense.

In taking her case I tried to understand what her experience was at various levels. At the sensation level, her experience was one of claustrophobia; a fog that closes in on you, holds you down with hands over the mouth, strangling you, no freedom, tight, constriction, a contraction feeling; the opposite of which is expansion, freedom, space, going out into the open air, walking.

Her most frequent fears and terrors were of being tortured, being held down, tied, tight. We chose the remedy Mancinella, since it had the images as well as the sensation of the Euphorbiaceae family to which Mancinella belongs.

In Homeopathic literature, the perception of Mancinella is described as the following delusions:

- Delusion – she is possessed
- Delusion – persecuted
- Delusion – swimming in air
- Frightful dreams of ghosts and spectres
- Fear that something will happen
- Anxiety – control over the senses is lost, somebody is possessing me
- Eeriness and weirdness, black force, evil spirits

The sensation of the plants belonging to the botanical family Euphorbiaceae can be described as follows: tied, bound, trapped, gripped, tight held, difficult to move, unbound and escape

Carolyn was prescribed Mancinella 10 M, which was repeated a few times in the next few years. This helped her very much. Later, she needed the remedy chocolate for a state of attachment that came up in her relationship to me as her physician and other significant people who had come into her life.

## Carolyn's sharing of her own case:

In the first of four years of the treatment with Mancinella, I experienced a sense of the patterns within me emerging and coming to the surface of my consciousness. But I was not in a state of awareness. It was more as though I was besieged by the patterns; for example: nightly terrors, memories of abuse, being trapped, held down, tortured. All the most terrifying and threatening patterns were the first to emerge. I had to experience them repeatedly, as the action of the remedy started to dilute them gradually over time. Then I would not react and could see the patterns for just what they were.

During long sessions with Dr Sankaran, I would talk about my experiences. As the months went by, the patterns were not nearly so strong. Then, other less disturbing patterns would emerge, and I started to become much more aware as an individual as to what I carried in my own consciousness. I attended Dr Sankaran's retreats, where for five days through various exercises such as meditation, drawing and creating music, we would as individuals and as a group see and understand our patterns and how they drove us, causing reactions in both ourselves and the outside world.

But no healing journey is in a straight line, and it was only in the last four weeks that the worst part of the trauma appeared before me. On finishing the book, I felt in some ways this story had happened to someone else. I still could not own it completely. I became ill suddenly and unexpectedly, and my path to health was one of finally acknowledging the terrible truth of what had happened to me as a child.

As I owned the whole incident, I felt all the pain of rapes, my father, the other men, the terror, the shame, the self-punishment and worst of all a dreadful feeling that somehow it was all my own fault. These feelings are so typical of victims who have been sexually abused. I cried for days but then felt that I had finally reached the bottom and that now there was only the way upwards to healing and light. My heart is full of gratitude now for everything that I have received, the true understanding of myself and the chance that was given me to heal.

I thank all those people who have come on this journey with me and supported me in every way.

Carolyn Shanti

# FOREWORD

I am seeking to understand the collective insanity of our world that has developed over centuries of human history and its expression in the extremes of sexual practices, abuse, and the possession of souls.

We need to come to terms with the madness within us; the roots and patterns of our souls over lifetimes; and our fictitious sense of self, in which we have become trapped.

Only then can we really experience true suffering with understanding. In this way, we move on through to the silence and the peace within us, which as human beings is our true heritage. I have researched the extreme sexualization within our cultures, erotic fantasies and delusional states. Our modern world is an expression of the fornication of culture and the men and women who are exploited within those cultures.

I look at the consciousness in which we live, the sense of self and holding patterns and roots housed within insane thought forms and sexual expression and ideologies with which we identify. These deeply embedded thought forms mean that we inhabit a conceptual reality cut off from our deepest selves.

Our sexual expressions have become corroded and corrupted and are displayed in our craving for the erotic, pornographic and incestuous. Our collective unconsciousness holds still within our genes and cellular memory, the most carnal of sexual images and exploitation. Of all this we are to a major degree, completely unaware.

The Mancinella and the Upas tree from Java (Antiaris Toxicarea) form a mythology written about by Blake, Coleridge, Byron and Erasmus Darwin. Their writing is based on the notion that poison lies within the mind. *Trap, Prey, Lust* details the delusions and obsessions of the gothic culture and its literary works and its impact on a society waiting with bated breath for furthering of their fantastic fantasies.

Carolyn Shanti, October 2018

# SPELL 1108

*The Deathless one, with many forms, doorkeeper of the First Gate.*

*He feeds on the evil ones who know not how to pass through the gate.*

## Spell to pass through the gate:

*"That which is before him is my protection from his hand.*

*I know how to ferry the self-existent one across to the other land."*

*From*
*'The Wandering of the Soul'*
*Text translated with commentary*
*By Alexandre Piankoff*
*Bolinger Series XL. 6*
*Princeton University Press*

# The Golden Rosary of the History of Padma (Sambhava)

'On what we practise now dependeth our future: As the shadow followeth the body, karma followeth us. Each hath perforce to taste what he himself has done.'

*From the Golden Rosary of the History of Padma (Sambhava), 2 chapter 1x. Quote from Tibet's great Yogi Milarepa, A biography from the Tibetan, Edited by W.Y.Evans-Wenz.)*

# PROLOGUE

Farlingham Park, the ancestral home of the first Countess of Rigby in Shropshire, England, looked more like a small cathedral than a house. In 1810, it had been cleverly designed by an architect who, following the Gothic traditions of symmetry, made sure that the measurements and calculations would create a certain kind of disposition within the human brain to sexual fantasy and delusions of the Gothic culture.

It was very much a showpiece. And it was the headquarters of the first Hexagon Club, a club given over to meeting the lascivious sexual appetites of the landed gentry and aristocrats, the wealthy and the famous. There were grotesque gargoyles on all the buttresses, their long tongues hanging out to collect rain and sunshine alike. All through the night, people would come and go in their dark and magnificent coaches, also with their tongues hanging out, hoping for a glimpse or to tongue the half-clothed who would adorn the silk-covered sofas and bedrooms in all manner of compromised positions with their partners.

They would come as spectators or as willing participants, impatient to shed their clothes, to seduce and be seduced. There was no end to it for them; they lived the Gothic beast in all his magnificence. It was their dream, their delusion, masks pulled tight, their long noses sniffing what was before them, of the delicacies on offer.

The vast halls of the mansion were divided into small rooms with great lengths of raw silk. Brocaded, tasselled cords would draw the silks apart, revealing velvet lounging sofas for private use. On these, naked couples would recline. Young, nubile women would walk with their breasts bare and bejewelled, as they wandered through the public and private areas offering cocktails, aphrodisiacs and endless toys and diversions.

And so, Farlingham Park eventually became a mansion of evil purposes, misguided intentions and ruinous consequences for the men and women involved. These were not the days of sexual pleasure, but of sexual ruin.

Amelia, the Countess and mistress of Farlingham Park, was brutally murdered in 1820 in the attic of the mansion; thereafter, her husband Sir Ashley Cooper, who was physician to the Royal Court of George IV, boarded up the house, where it remained desolate and haunted by strange spirits for almost two hundred years.

# PART ONE

Anna Carrington stood with her cousin Casey in the marshes near Casey's parents' house in Cambridge. Casey, so small then, was wearing green rubber boots and a short skirt, her thin white legs wet with the rain. They wore pullovers and raincoats and were far out in the marshes, away from everyone. They were both nine years old, and although they lived close to each other just outside Cambridge, they did not see much of each other. Casey was too quiet for Anna, and there were always shadows under her eyes. Anna found her frightening in a way, and her bedroom seemed very silent and full of secrets.

Casey seemed to avoid her parents, especially her father who was a diplomat and frequently away in Argentina.

They were both moving further and further into the marshland. Suddenly, Casey stepped into a bog. She started to sink and after only half an hour, the rubber boots were barely visible. Every time she struggled, she sank deeper. Anna screamed out for someone, but they were over a mile from the house.

Casey talked non-stop to Anna now, saying she did not care if she died; she hated her life so much. In those moments of terror, she told Anna almost everything about her life, except about her stepfather. Anna was shocked at the way Casey talked

1

and the desperation that she felt. She shared with Anna that her sleep was so troubled, she was tired all day, that she could not get a grip on her life. She experienced terrible nightmares and stomach aches. Next year, they were sending her away to boarding school in the north of Scotland. She vowed that she would never come home again.

At that point, a Land Rover appeared from the edge of the woodland. Casey's parents owned so much land that they had managers and rangers to look after it. They were immensely wealthy. The ranger saw immediately what had happened and stepped in with ropes and a harness. This was evil land. Casey fell apart after she was rescued; and then, when they reached the house, her stepfather ordered her to be taken to her room by the maid.

Anna thought this was odd, that he did not embrace or console his daughter or go with her. Casey's mother was away for the weekend. Casey's stepfather had suggested that Anna come over to keep Casey company. He had then taken Anna into his study and called for tea.

Anna had for years completely forgotten that day. But one day, it would surface from her memory for the first time, like a sharp shard of glass, into her consciousness.

Lord Oliver Pemberton was someone that Anna had hardly spoken to. He was a member of the House of Lords and a diplomat. Anna was a bit in awe of him, as she had sat for tea with him in his study that day. He was tall and thin; his strange eyes were very pale blue. A beautiful-looking man, she was both repelled and attracted by him. He had beautiful hands, slim and elegant; the nails perfectly manicured.

By now, she had shed the rubber boots and was sitting in the easy chair opposite him with her socks on and her short skirt, a kilt as she later remembered. She had a slice of Victoria sponge in her mouth and was trying to drink her tea in a ladylike manner. Lord Pemberton was talking about his friendship with her own father, that had gone back a long way. They did not talk about Casey at all.

The tea was finished, and an uncomfortable silence now pervaded the room. They had run out of conversation. Lord

Pemberton said that she must have been frightened by the experience earlier with the bog and marshes. In the half-light, he had asked her to come close to him. He had already got up once to turn the key in the door. But Anna was unaware that she was locked in. No one would be troubling them now.

Anna, who never received any physical affection from her own father, found herself walking over to him. The room was very dim now, and there was no move to put on the lights. The fire in the grate flared up for a moment, revealing Lord Pemberton's remarkable eyes. Anna found herself sinking into those eyes; and soon, she was sitting on Lord Pemberton's lap with his arms around her. For the first time in her life, she was lulled into a sense of security and love. In the warmth of the fire, her small body relaxed into a daughter's love for a father. She arched her back and lay further back in his arms. She felt so sleepy, it was hard to keep awake.

It must, she remembered many years later, have been a long time that they were like this, together, in such a loving embrace. She was asleep and then woke up when she felt his hand on her knee, stroking it and moving down to her feet. He kept stroking her, wrapping his long fingers around her toes. She found it hard to stay awake as he ran his hands gently along her legs.

Lord Pemberton was well aware of what was happening; he had added a little something to Anna's cup of tea when she was not looking. She had started to become very drowsy in his arms. He just wanted her in his lap, no more, but it had gone further; he could not control his lust for her; it was too late when he realized what he had done. But she had been drowsy; surely, she would not remember. Anna was extraordinarily beautiful; her full red lips were half open; she was responding to the love and warmth that she would never receive from her own father.

"It is time that I took you home, Anna. It is late; your father will be wondering where you are. It is hours since you came back from your walk."

He spoke softly to her; after all, she was still a child and destined, as soon as she came of age at sixteen, to Fabian. These were the rules of the Fraternity and the Hexagon Club.

Fabian had made it very clear to him that both her father, Professor Richard Carrington and any other man in the Fraternity were not so much as to touch Anna. She was refused boyfriends, and every attempt would be made to keep her virginity intact for the day she would belong to Fabian. Without disturbing Anna while she was with him, Lord Pemberton had taken a picture with a concealed camera in the oak panelling, of Anna lying on his lap and him hanging over her. At least he could treasure this forever. It was one of many pictures he had of young girls and, of course, many pictures of himself with Casey, his stepdaughter.

After taking Anna home, still tempted to hold her hand again in the car, he returned to the house. It was veiled in darkness; and one by one, he heavily climbed the old staircase to his own daughter's room and slowly opened the door. She was asleep but, in his urgency, he woke her up and held her in his arms. His longing knew no end. There was no doubt he would have to satisfy himself elsewhere. She was still too young.

But Lord Pemberton had raped Anna. He had sexually awoken her when she was too young. She had no memory of it. The next day, she had high fever for two days; and from then on, she had started a perilous onset of masturbation leading in later years to almost continual urinary infections and gynaecological problems. She craved what Lord Pemberton had awoken in her; and when finally Fabian seduced her, when she had reached sixteen, there was no end to her sexual desire and obsession for him.

Anna had struggled for years; she had been harmed at such a young age that she was almost entirely unconscious of what had happened to her and ever after; she had moved into the mists and fogs of a woman's existence, without ever being able to lead a normal life as a woman. She was caught in a net so vast that even she, with all the knowledge that Fabian gave her, did not understand what the net was or that she was tied within it forever. It was as though she, like 'The Sleeping Beauty', fell asleep for a hundred years.

It was to be a long time before the spell was broken. She herself knew of no spell nor how it was to be broken.

# 1

*(Anna Carrington has now married Sir Justin Bowlby, an eminent heart surgeon, in London. She is thirty-two and known as Lady Anna Bowlby. They live in a house called The Beeches, near Grassock Oaks in Kent. The year is 2010)*

"Anna, Anna, you are so distant." Anna could still hear Justin's words ringing in her ears, He had said it twice while he was making love to her. She remembered it all, his touch and his despair that she wasn't really there for him. Now, his words were an ache inside her. Her back ached from the tension of trying to fulfil her husband's sexual needs.

And now she heard the crows again outside the windows, their black shadows staining the glass. However many they shot each week, still more came to haunt the house. It was believed crows lived in the void; they were outside time. They brought omens with them, but Anna felt that they brought a message of death and entrapment to her. John, their gardener and chauffeur, would carry the carcasses across the lawns and burn them in the woods beyond.

She moved in her velvet monogrammed slippers now, to the bathroom. Justin had given her the slippers last Christmas at their house in the South of France. He had said that they were regal, suitable for a queen. Yes, she had been a queen in other lifetimes. There had been crows then in Egypt and much worse.

But she turned away now from the crows to look at her own body and stood facing the full-length looking glass in the bathroom. Slowly, she let the silk robe slip from her body. She watched as it fell away, revealing the delicate line of her shoulders and the gentle curves of her belly. Her fragrance was one of gardenias, her favourite flower. She ran her fingers over her belly and breasts, anxious that there might be a line or mark on the translucent whiteness. But there was nothing; it was like silk still.

After soaking in a bath of fragrant oils, she put on a single strand of Japanese pearls held around her neck by a clasp of diamonds; a sapphire on a long golden chain fell between her breasts. It had been Fabian's gift to her all those years ago when he met her as a young woman, when he had exerted his privileges over her. She remembered the long days and endless nights. There had been marks on her body then – yes, marks and bruises, physical and emotional.

Her lustrous black hair she now coiled heavily around a single tortoise shell pin, a pin she had acquired on an exotic trip she had taken to Japan visiting one of the wild clubs she frequented. Her sexual secrets on these trips were always safe, as she was part of the aristocracy; whatever people thought about her they would never utter a word, except perhaps in the privacy of their families. She walked slowly across to the window, measuring her steps and looking out at the lawns and lake beyond with expressionless grey eyes. The eyebrows were finely arched, her mouth full, often a deep red against the pale almost alabaster skin of her face. Anna was beautiful; everyone said so.

The bathroom was dedicated to her good taste. She soaked her hands now in the water held in the basin that had once been a jardinière. They looked strange somehow underneath the surface; looking dead, creating unwanted memories.

This was a morning when she had time for herself. She loved this bathroom; it was so nurturing, and the gold taps on the sunken bath felt reassuring. For her, the world was not a safe place. She glanced again out of the window and saw a black cat running across the lawn. Was this a lucky or unlucky sign? She couldn't remember. It worried her. This was Anna: silent, brooding, unable to express her real feelings about anything. After all, she had been trained that way. She had been her father's favourite, but it had come at a price.

She had been seduced by her father's friend Count Fabian Roth at sixteen years of age; then, he had suddenly abandoned her for eight years after being with her for two. She had become completely shameless with this one impossible and unattainable man who continued to devastate her life and cast an everlasting shadow on her marriage. Memories of lovemaking with him still left a faint hint of raised colour on her pale cheeks.

Anna remembered, long ago when she was sixteen, being in the attic room of her huge family home outside Cambridge. The door had opened, revealing her mother, Lucille: beautiful, demure and looking always like Lauren Bacall. It was her mother from whom Anna derived her good looks: her ephemeral beauty, the full lips, wide eyes and the tapering long and exquisite legs.

Her mother had entered her room and sat down on the bed, eyeing her daughter. They were to have guests that day, an American senator from Washington. Anna was completely unaware that she had been promised to Fabian almost since he saw her soon after her birth. He had immediately fallen in love with her. He was the one to take her virginity; there had been a ceremony and then the surgical removal of her hymen, a week earlier. It was all part of the family tradition. Anna had thought this was normal. She had no idea of the family to which she belonged, and the secret sexual practices performed over centuries securing the older daughter in folds of entrapment and surrendered to a male chosen by the father.

Her father had carefully groomed her, creating a system of mind control suitable for her, to prepare her for the day when she would come of age, her maidenhead offered to his best friend. Of course, he was careful; he had been paid an inordinate sum of money to give his daughter away to Fabian, one of the richest men in the world. A hand-picked group from the

Fraternity watched the ceremony of penetration and deflowerment on the special bed used for the occasion. The group wore masks so that Anna could not see who they were. She had been trained never to speak of these things outside the family, and she never did. To her, what happened to her that night was normal; she was told that these rules and customs went back centuries. Strange things occurred during the ceremony. She was placed in certain positions on the bed. She could remember nothing else, but after that she belonged only to Fabian. She had no idea what had happened to her from such a young age. She was encased now in the family mysteries, protected, coiled within, never to escape.

Lucille was totally aware of her husband's sexual wanderings and the carefully kept secret of the Fraternity. She and Casey's mother, Antigone, turned a blind eye to the sexual appetites of their husbands and their rendezvous with the many young girls across numerous continents. Lord Pemberton was renowned for his excesses. Nothing stood in the way of the needs and wishes of the Fraternity. Lucille's own father had been a member in previous generations. It all went back to the early nineteenth century, probably even earlier. Lucille was brought up to expect a certain amount of bondage and sexual activity as a young girl. She had also been groomed. She knew that Anna would be going the same way; and if Fabian had not done it already, he would be grooming Anna for the prize, to become his beloved whore, to be used by him and anyone else that he chose.

It was still early in the morning and Justin had already left for the hospital. She had felt him kiss her as she still drowsy and heard the sound of the Mercedes over the gravel on its journey towards the gates. When Anna had returned to the bedroom, Julia, her maid, had left the breakfast tray on the table near their bed. Again, the night flooded back to her. She blamed herself for her lack of passion. Feelings were a problem.

The mail was neatly stacked between the coffee and the silver hot water jug. She glanced at the invitations. She and Justin were invited everywhere. One letter stood out from the rest. It was distinctive because of the family crest, an engraver's handiwork – a falcon, the foot of the falcon clamped down on the head of a snake, a cobra. It seemed strange, out of place, somehow. Something stirred and then subsided in her memory. She opened the envelope with a paper knife, its handle carved of black onyx. Inside the envelope was an invitation inviting them to a weekend event at the home of the Countess of Rigby in Yorkshire. Farlingham Park was the name of the house. "Very grand," thought Anna. It must be near Jane's house. She thought of Jane now; Jane who had been her best friend for so long, since their days up at Cambridge.

Anna had never heard of the Countess of Rigby, let alone Farlingham Park. "Probably one of Justin's friends," and she carelessly threw the invitation onto his side of the bed. The phone started to ring but then stopped. Julia had no doubt answered it, knowing how little Anna liked to be disturbed in the mornings. It rang again. This time she picked it up smartly with a slice of toast in the other hand.

"Anna, darling, I'm sorry to call so early, but I must talk to you. I had such a strange dream last night, really unnerving. Do you mind? I have to tell someone..." Jane's voice dropped to a whisper, not sure now of Anna's response. It was, after all, still very early in the morning.

Jane Crosby-Nash was one of Anna's closest friends. Anna didn't encourage closeness, but in Jane's eyes they were close. Years ago, they had been up at Cambridge together. Jane had done expectedly well with a double first in philosophy. After Cambridge, she seemed to drop out of life in England. She had gone to Egypt. It had been five years; she never spoke much about it but came back thin and far too introverted, according to Anna.

Anna had tried to forget her own experiences of the inner magic, what she had learned at sixteen from Fabian who had so cleverly seduced and left her in no way compensated for all the power he had given her over her physical world. He used to call her 'The Great Wife', a name given to the pharaohs' chief consorts in Ancient Egypt.

Jane had come back almost as though she had never left. She married Fairfax Crosby-Nash, a barrister in Lincoln's Inn, within a year and settled down to what seemed like a pretty conventional life in Chiswick; but there was a side to Jane about which Anna always remained curious.

"Are you there?" whispered Jane.

"Yes, of course; why don't you tell me?"

"I was in a carriage pulled by black horses along a narrow road. Suddenly, we turned into an entrance to a country mansion; there were huge iron gates. Inside the carriage, there was a man opposite me, but the corner of the carriage was dark, and I couldn't see him clearly. The carriage gathered speed along a driveway lined by an avenue of overhanging trees. I was holding up a small mirror to look at my face. It wasn't my face now but someone else's.

"As I looked into the mirror, I caught sight of someone through the back window of the carriage. The rider came closer. First, I saw the black horse. The horse's beauty fascinated me so much that it was a while before I looked at the rider. When I did, my legs went numb. The man had the face of a jackal or some kind of animal, yellowed and swathed in black cloth. I remember it was so wet with the rain that the cloth clung around his sharp features. His eyes pierced me. Then he lifted his finger and pointed at me. Time seemed to stop. I felt all the life go out of me. I glanced away for a moment and when I looked back again without the mirror, he had gone. I woke up drenched in sweat. Fairfax is away, and I am all on my own at the house. Anna, I was so scared. Do you think it's a warning?"

There was a long silence at Anna's end of the line. She adjusted the phone from one ear to the other; she pressed the phone too hard against her face when she was concentrating, and it always left a mark. She yawned.

"So, is that it?" asked Anna flatly, pretending to be bored.

"What do you mean 'is that it'? Don't you think it's totally amazing?"

"What is totally amazing?" replied Anna, feeling nervous.

"God, Anna, don't these experiences and dreams affect you?"

"I hardly ever dream, and when I do I never remember them. Once or twice I did remember, and I tried to forget it as

10

quickly as possible. Anyway, how do you feel now that you have told me?" asked Anna.

"Well, it's strange. I still have this heavy feeling, and I can't help but think the dream is ominous." Jane's voice was reduced to another whisper as she confided. She, like the Ancient Egyptians, believed in the prophetic power of dreams. She had also recognized the likeness of the animal-headed man to Seth, the God associated with violence, chaos and disorder.

Jane did not really mind that Anna appeared to have no real interest in her experiences or dreams. Anna was wondering why Jane was having this dream that was really her dream; she had had the same dream now for some years, but she was not going to tell Jane this. She already knew now that she herself was a reincarnation of the lady in the carriage, Amelia, the first Countess of Rigby, and that not only had she been brutally murdered but that she had been the wife of Sir Ashley Cooper, physician to King George IV.

More she did not know. But Jane was in this somewhere, perhaps the same incarnation. But who was she, and why were they having the same dream? Anna dared not share any of these experiences with Jane; she feared Fabian's reprisals, as she knew they would come. Never could she share anything about her family; it was strictly taboo. He knew everything about her, the thoughts and the dreams. No, she dared not involve Jane.

Jane knew somehow that Anna was lying and had her own connection and lines of knowledge about magic and Egypt. Jane thought that Anna pretended she was something other than who she really was. She suspected that Anna had been brought up in an environment full of fear. She had found things in Anna's bedroom by mistake while looking for a scarf. There were some relics, miniature statues of Egyptian gods. Then there were other items of regalia for rituals and magic. Jane had never known before that Anna knew how to practice magic. She wondered if Anna had let her into the secret on purpose. In the very back section of the drawer, there was a many-stranded whip with long and plaited tails; the laced leather sported beads at the tips. There was also a photo of an older man, so extraordinarily handsome with black hair, with his arm around Anna. On the back, it said Switzerland and a date that made the photo at least fourteen years old. She wondered who the man was whose picture was left so close to Anna's personal things.

This conversation was too much for Anna at nine o'clock in the morning. Besides, her scrambled eggs were getting cold, not to mention the coffee.

"Well, Jane, darling, I really must go. Why don't you and Fairfax come over for bridge one evening? Justin has been getting home early from the hospital, and the evenings are so lovely. We can have drinks on the lawn, then go into dinner and have a few rounds of bridge afterwards. Oh, and Sidney Henderson is coming over from France in a few days." Anna was trying to steer Jane's mind away from her impending sense of doom. She hoped that reminders of the day-to-day world of Grassock Oaks would soothe and coax Jane back into the mundane world.

"Who is Sidney Henderson?" asked Jane, aware of Anna's tactics of distraction.

"You must know Sidney; he is the hottest thing these days in interior design, all exotic gothic and extravagant classics. He is a magician, and everyone is after him." Anna was wondering what ideas Sidney would have for 'The Beeches'.

"So how is he connected to the world of medicine?" asked Jane, curious about what seemed a deviation from the doctors and politicians that usually graced themselves on Justin and Anna's elegant sofas.

"Jane, stop being a bore. We met him and his gorgeous wife, Moira, in Nice. They have a villa near there. We met them last summer," concluded Anna, determined now to end the conversation. She already had her finger on the intercom to summon Julia to bring more coffee and toast. It was one of those mornings when she ached for Fabian's company. It was not to be. But he always wanted her. She could not concede to the terms of his demands.

She was, after all these years, still devoured by her love for him. She remained aloof but sooner or later, she would give in to him. Justin would suffer, suffer even more – Justin, who had never really been close to her but always longed for greater intimacy. It was never really going to happen. It was like a three-cornered hat.

"OK, Anna, I'll call you later in the week. Oh, by the way, I saw Justin was written up in *The Times* yesterday for his new heart surgery techniques."

"Yes, he's amazing, so clever." Anna said goodbye. She decided that in the future she absolutely wasn't going to take any calls before breakfast. The phone rang again. Julia picked up the phone this time.

"It's your mother," called Julia.

"Tell her I'm at the stables." Anna could not believe that Lucille would call her this early in the morning.

Anna and Lucille kept a discreet distance from each other. Lucille was aware that her daughter was living in a torn world, that Anna had no really clear memory of what had happened to her in her childhood, of the sacred mating ceremony with Fabian, or the people who had been there in their masks, watching. Anna was aware that Lucille kept many secrets from her about her life, secrets about the family that would never be disclosed over centuries. Anna was to remain in a cocooned prison, never really knowing who she was. No, distance between mother and daughter was a necessary evil in both their lives.

Julia gave her a certain look, which implied that Anna's mother would not believe that she was out riding this early. "Well then, tell her that I am still asleep and that we had a late night," said Anna.

She heard Julia tell Lucille; Julia was, after all, adept at keeping Anna's mother at bay. Finally, more eggs, fresh coffee and toast arrived, and Anna sank back exhausted onto the down pillows encased in their white lace slipcovers with the blue monograms. She wanted to be left alone. Out of the corner of her eye, she caught sight of the black embossed coat of arms of the Countess of Rigby on its stiff linen paper. It was already a warm summer's morning, but she found herself shivering. She still could see in her mind's eye the animal-headed God in her dream, Seth. Then she thought of Anubis, the deity whose association was with the Western Desert – home of the dead

– the God of Death to the Pharaoh alone, and the presiding deity of embalming. She soon fell into a fitful sleep again, half awake, half asleep, her black hair spread out on the pillows; she was always so tired. Justin had remarked on it; he wanted her to have some blood tests. As she fell asleep, she went back again to another lifetime. Memories surfaced battling for recognition to define who she really was now.

She had been back to that other lifetime before, when she was the Pharaoh's wife in the Hyksos Dynasty. The Hyksos people practiced horse burials; their chief deity, their God, was the deity of storms and the desert. And his name was Seth. It was a wonderful reign but then it ended in disaster. The magician had brought the asp to the Pharaoh, but it was not his time to die. It was a trick. The Pharaoh locked the magician up as punishment in the King's Tomb and let him die. He removed every image of the magician from the city. Anna knew that Jane had been there at court too; she was not aware of why. Of course, Jane knew that she too had been there, but she never mentioned it to Anna.

There was so much fear between them both; although, in many ways, they were close. They went horse racing, visited art galleries and had tea in some of the poshest London hotels. They were part of the Cambridge set and spent time with their friends in old mansions in the country and smart London houses in Hampstead. Anna envied Jane's trouble-free idyllic childhood. She could never share her own childhood with Jane; it was such a fog to her and full of danger and terrible secrets.

Anna remembered her time with Anubis, the God of Embalming. In their magic practices, Fabian had taken her to these other planes of existence. She knew that Anubis alone supervised the internment of the mummies, performed the opening of the mouth ceremonies and conducted the souls to the fields of celestial offerings. She wanted to forget it all. It all happened to her so long ago; sometimes she thought it had all been a dream, nothing more. She wondered, though, who it was giving Jane these dreams. Could it be starting all over again? Would there never be any resting place for her? It had to be Fabian who was never going to let her or her friends alone again. He was starting to get to Jane. She too was soon going to be in danger. Anna felt these things long before they happened. But how could she warn her without revealing who she really was in her past life? It had become terrifying to her. She was trapped and truly alone. And then the sex; she was the sexual prey, he the hunter. It truly terrified her.

Anna was concerned about being with Fabian again. There had to be rules this time. There had to be conditions; yet everything within her longed for him. It had been so many years, and he had taken everything from her at such a young age. But she was now afraid that he would try to do her harm again, since she only recently refused him one more time.

She did remember now when she was sixteen that he and an American senator had taken her to her father's stables, tied her up and raped her. But she had no idea that she had been promised to Fabian for years and nor was she aware that somehow her own father had seduced her mind, controlling her and preparing her for this sexual servitude. She was never allowed any male friends. Her father had brought her very expensive clothes and took her to fancy restaurants in London. It was as if she was so often his date, her mother well in the background. She was vaguely aware that somehow all was not right within her; she had strange tastes later, after Fabian had bonded with her. Fabian had in the private clubs shared his sexual privileges over her with other men. It was as though she was under a spell. Partially, she was aware of her life and sexual habits, but it was as though she was always somehow in a dream, never really coming to full consciousness. She was driven but unaware. Fabian had given her drugs on occasions, nothing serious or heavy, but just to take the edge off things, so that she would not think too much about what she was doing.

At times, she felt as though she had become a whore. But there was always this fog around her and she could never think clearly. It was very strange; she did not understand it. Sometimes, when she travelled to Europe and went to clubs, she would end up with one man or another, craving for exotic sexual experiences. She would often do it for money; it was a high for her. But she could never get enough and always, she longed for Fabian as though he was her very own being.

She got up and moved to the wardrobe and took out a box from a drawer, covered in dark blue sequins. She looked inside at the fine silk pouch. Nestled inside was the black silk thread that would just slip between her legs and then up around her shoulder. Fabian had given it to her some years ago. The magic started within her, and she remembered the nights that she had slept with Fabian; in one of those hours of lovemaking, was the night that their child was conceived.

She had worn the sacred thread, around her shoulder and between her legs, and there was no end to her arousal with the fine thin silk. It had a movement almost all its own, like a black snake. Fabian knew exactly the magic of this thread and how to pull and twist it. It had a kind of coiled mouth that would move over her to bring her to sexual heights she never thought possible.

But Fabian would hit her, then she would only cry out for more as he twisted the thread this way and that. Anna could bear the thoughts no more; even thinking of him and the thread created panic of being overpowered by him yet again. She could not get the images or sensations out of her head or body. She had become obsessed and it frightened her. She would never get out, was a prisoner in a chain of longing and loathing for what he did to her. There was too much pain; he made mistakes and she was the one who paid for it. Tears ran down her face as she closed the box. She felt the cord would be her death. She felt it still between her legs and felt faint at the thought of those hours with him, the heightening of her senses, the passion. It had lasted for days, those long hours of lovemaking, the unbelievable joys of tantric sex. She would depart to other worlds, going up through her skull. Pangs of guilt had hit her when she realized she had conceived; it was Fabian's child, not Justin's. How could she live with this and deceive him? But somehow, she did, almost convincing herself at times that Giles was Justin's child.

Fabian was a polo player and knew how to train young fillies. Sexually, he had trained Anna so that she had become an expert, but always at a price. She completely surrendered to him. She never questioned what he asked of her.

Of course, she already adored him, so absolutely stunning in every way. She always felt unloved, as though there was something wrong with her. Never did she have any idea how beautiful she was and so, she accepted his tantalizing embraces, the quick seduction. She did not realize it had gone too far, and she had completely opened herself to him. She was shameless. He taught her everything she would ever need to know about the erotic arts. She gave herself fully, but he hurt her so badly that she would never ever give herself completely to anyone else. Every afternoon, he would come to the silent house.

He asked too much of her and in her adoration, she allowed him to do things to her that she later regretted. It was as though he cast a shadow over her soul and put his poisoned seed within her. He possessed her and then she was unable to belong to anyone else. It was as though he was always inside her, in her head, in her body.

And then there were years of silence. He had told her she was his and that there would never be anyone else. She saved herself and then after eight years, she gave up. He never came to see her, and her heart was broken.

Then she married Justin who had been at the medical school at Cambridge. Justin adored her. This had already been arranged years ago that Fabian would have Anna and then a suitable marriage would be found for her. She would continue with this marriage and still be Fabian's mistress. She would hear her father talking about Fabian frequently, but he never came to the house again. Her father would meet him in town. He and her father, it turned out, were collaborators in sexual intrigues with families that she would never at the time realize was possible. It was a web of which she was now a part. But it was years before she would ever come to know that she was just one of the young girls with whom these men took their pleasure. It had broken her life. She would never know normality but a kind of perversion.

Her cousin Casey lived in Cambridge in the middle of the marshlands and the dark forests. Deep down, Anna felt something awful had happened to her cousin in that elegant house of secrets.

# 2

Jane lounged in the green hammock slung between two apple trees in the garden. It was one of those idyllic English afternoons; the mellow sun was warming, and the air filled with the scent of flowers and newly mown grass. She was thinking of Egypt: the dust storms and the Nile at Cairo, the network of canals and drainage shafts, and the high banks looking like brown threads projecting like veins on a hand above the surface of the land. Then there were the trees: Phoenician juniper, Eucalyptus and Poinciana. She remembered the smells and noises, the chattering of the brightly-garmented young women toiling in the fields.

Why would Seth come in her dream? She hadn't summoned him, although she knew how. Was Anubis warning her? He along with the other gods had helped her when she was performing her initiation rites to enter the first gateway. She remembered his symbol, an ox hide spattered with blood and borne on a pole. He was the warrior who wore the coiled cobra, the symbol of Kundalini and the sacred serpent power. She had become an enemy of the cult members of Seth. She still feared Seth, his black wings beating about her, trying to prevent her entry into the hidden mysteries. Now she wore the snake's head talisman to protect her from the servants of Seth, Rerek and

Apep. She had spent five years in Egypt with one of the most legendary spiritual teachers. Ancient Egyptian culture was so interwoven with the cult of the dead; this had been her main area of study, to enter the chambers of the dead and receive the living mysteries into her soul.

Jane had explored her past lives in meditation. She had in one lifetime been Anat-Har, the ruler of the House of Life, the temple and libraries of the Pharaoh. Later, she had researched the dynasty, from 1640 BCE, at the family seat in Avaris. Together with Pharaoh King Khamudi, the fifth Hyksos King, she had murdered the magician Ya Qub-Hat. She had been part of the royal family of the Seventeenth Dynasty of the Hyksos Kingdom. King Khamudi's wife was Nehesy, 'The Great Wife' and the Pharaoh's chief consort.

She had researched the Akashic records for all the information that was encoded in the non-physical plane of earth's existence, otherwise referred to as the astral plane. Her memories were at times misty and confused. Perhaps, she had covered up some of the more painful experiences. She wondered if she had been connected to Anna and Justin in that life. She knew Anna was closely connected to Ancient Egypt, but she did not know how. For some reason, they never discussed it. Fear came between them, always.

Her reaction when she had to return to England had been to hide in a set of circumstances, like a chameleon. She took up with the Cambridge set from where she had left off; people like Anna and Justin Bowlby. These were the people who had built a comfortable world with strong financial and social structures. All she had to do was to emulate that world and pretend there was no five-year gap. She had found a husband who would take care of at least most of her identity issues.

Fairfax Crosby-Nash was a successful barrister who was so wrapped up in his own work that he would never notice her lack of direction. After they were married, she took on the role of devoted wife and ran the house in Chiswick with incredible care. She entertained her husband's friends and took pleasure in the house. She would avidly read novels and magazines, wrapping herself in mundane stories and news. But the life she had created wasn't working, and she couldn't dull herself completely from the times she had experienced in those years away. She felt a deep sense of frustration, as though her real life had not really started. Who was she fooling and why was she hiding from herself?

She rolled off the hammock and went inside the house. It was surprisingly cool. To walk into Jane's house was an invitation to a life of bygone eras – dark floors and upright long-backed chairs. Rooms led into one another through narrow double doors. It was a feast of oil paintings restored to their original colours. Portraits of Jane's ancestors hung on the walls. There were kings such as George III and George IV whom her ancestors had served. The house itself was Georgian, tall with three floors and attics. For some reason, she avoided the attics. High terrains in a house filled her with fear, as though some memory was there just out of reach of her conscious mind. It filled her with dread.

A fragrance of dried lavender flowers filled the air in every room. Jane looked like a woman from centuries gone by. Her extravagant red hair was in such contrast to her delicately pale skin. Anna's father, Richard Carrington, had warned his daughter that women with red hair were dangerous. It was not until much later that she realized the secret society of which he was part, shunned women with red hair as if they embodied the Devil himself. Anna had been shocked but was unwilling to let go of her friendship with Jane. She told her father she intended being friends with Jane, and Richard let the matter drop. He rather regretted saying anything. He was always afraid somehow that Anna would remember what had happened to her, the control of her mind. Richard was not an unkind man, but he was totally taken over by his sexual appetites and longings and was deeply committed to the Fraternity and his friends within it. No one in his public life would have any idea. He frequented the Hexagon Club in Mayfair on numerous occasions with his friends, Fabian and Lord Oliver Pemberton.

Jane's eyes were a deep violet, like round violet mirrors looking out on the world like a Holbein painting. On entering the house, you would hardly remember you were living in an age of cars and computers. She had planned the house that way. She preferred other centuries. She heard the phone ring, one of the few reminders that she did, in fact, live in the twenty-first century.

"Jane, it's Catherine. We've just arrived at Heathrow. The flight was great. The children can't wait to see you. We must run now; our car is waiting. See you soon, darling."

Catherine, her sister, hung up, leaving her in another world of memories. She noticed that her maid, Fiona, had put some letters on the table, near the front door. Picking them up with a cursory glance, she leafed through them. At the other end of the house, she heard the soft strains of one of Vivaldi's concertos for clarinet. The music stirred her as she walked through to the library. Her own cello, which she now rarely seemed to play, stood in a corner of the book-lined room. She looked down abstractedly at one of the letters.

The invitation was black embossing on cream linen paper – strange heraldry, a bird with its feet clamped down on a snake. It reminded her again of Egypt. It was an invitation from a Countess of Rigby to a weekend event at Farlingham Park for Mrs Jane Crosby-Nash on the fifteenth of July. Not an invitation for Fairfax, she noticed. She was to go alone. She did vaguely remember the name, some socialite written up in *Hello* magazine, some months ago. Briefly written up, it was a short mention only of some accident that had happened to one of her family.

Jane sunk into a low love seat in the library; the music had moved to a haunting allegro. She stared again and again at the invitation still in her hand. She could recall nothing really of this woman. Her memory was blank, but she was intrigued. There was no phone number, just an address and RSVP. Two hours had slipped by unnoticed. The Vivaldi had become silent. She heard a car draw up.

"Hello, darlings, it's so good to see you," cried Jane on seeing her sister and her two children. Catherine and the children piled out of the car. Marcus, just ten years old, ran to meet his aunt, with Lucy in tow, while Catherine looked as elegant as ever in a dark green suit. Her blond hair was short and chic, a Paris look, thought Jane. Jane looked down at her own long moss-coloured robe, Evangelina – the designer dress she picked up, she could not even remember where – creating smocking and ripples on her neck and wrists.

Catherine, like Jane, was a very private person living alone with her two children who were now at boarding school just outside Paris. Catherine lived in Antibes. Her husband Louis, whom everyone had adored, was killed in a skiing accident just over a year ago. His death had been a mystery to them; there were never enough details available. Catherine had not been satisfied with the explanations given about his death. Louis had been working closely with a man called Count Fabian Roth, the famous Count Roth. Catherine had met him once in London at a dinner party and had immediately disliked him. She had asked Louis not to work for him. For once, Louis took no notice of her and from then on seemed to live a life of his own, away from the family. Catherine could see the change in him, but she could not understand what had happened to him.

Louis seemed almost under a spell. Their business dealings had not been going well and then the Count had invited him away for some winter skiing without Catherine and the children. Louis had insisted he had to go for business reasons, but Catherine was against the trip. Despite her protests, Louis flew to Switzerland and stayed at the Count's castle in a remote part of the Alps. The next thing they heard was that an avalanche had killed Louis while he was out skiing. Catherine saw the body after they had found it in the snow. His death looked unreal, as though he were asleep. He looked as perfect in death as he had in life. He had been a beautiful man in every way: handsome, clever and a wonderful family man, until he had met the Count.

The children ran up to their rooms in the attics. Jane led Catherine to her own sitting room on the second floor. There were sofas at each of the long Georgian windows. Jane rang for some tea to be brought up. Cedric, her Irish wolfhound, sat at her feet, his grey body stretched out next to her.

"Well, how are you?" Jane never quite knew what to say to her sister; they inhabited such different worlds.

"I'm painting again, now the children are away at school. It's better that way; I just don't have the emotional energy to be with them all the time. Anyway, they love it at school with so many other children to go on trips with all the time." Jane could see Catherine was still trying to convince herself that it was the right thing for them. After the death of their adored father, it must be hard for them. Jane felt it was better not to share her own views about boarding schools with Catherine. After all, the family decisions were up to her sister, and she rarely asked for Jane's advice.

Jane really loved her sister and could see what Louis' untimely death had taken from her. She had remembered him well, his sweetness and devotion to the children. And yet he had seemed like a man with another life, as though his thoughts were on something else, some other interest. Of course, she had not seen him that much, as she had been in Egypt most of the time. But it had intrigued her as to what was really going on with Louis.

"What are your plans these days, Jane?" asked Catherine, bringing Jane out of her reverie about Louis.

"Well, nothing really, the same routine. We see Anna and Justin at weekends, down at Grassock Oaks. It's so gorgeous there in the country, and the house and grounds are like stepping into another world. More tea? This cake is one of my specials; I know the children like gingerbread, so Fiona is taking some up to them. Where was I? Oh, yes, I have been remodelling the garden." She carried on in some detail.

Jane had taken great interest in the garden; it soothed her nerves, and she had been planning an elaborate Jacobean garden with herbs and shrubs. They had also had several small pools dug up and stocked with goldfish and lilies. The latest project was an ornamental maze on one of the lawns; it was to have hedges in dark yew. To Jane, it had a mathematical and symbolic significance. She did not choose to explore this with Catherine. Neither could she tell her sister about the nightly dreams that haunted her. She had been going over and over them in her mind while listening and talking.

She realized she had drifted off again and that Catherine was looking intently at her, expecting an answer to the question she had just asked. She repeated it, looking slightly irritated at her sister's lapse in concentration.

"What are you and Fairfax doing for your winter holiday this year?"

"Fairfax is interested in going to Cairo and then down the Nile," answered Jane, wondering how she would feel on revisiting Egypt again; perhaps it was too soon. Still, if she didn't visit the pyramids, it would probably be all right; she would just consider herself a tourist.

"Won't it be a little hot?" asked Catherine.

"I like the heat, but it is not hot in winter. Besides, there are some places that I would like to revisit, and Fairfax hasn't seen the insides of the pyramids; he'll probably do that on his own." She wondered whom she was trying to convince.

"It would frighten me to go inside one of those things. I read once about some of the people who went inside the first pyramid to be opened. They all died very soon afterwards, and no one ever knew why," replied Catherine who was starting to look anxious.

Jane had good working knowledge about why they had died; after all, she was an authority on the subject, although practically no one knew it, not even Anna. She was not going to elaborate. Weariness started to overcome her; it was the constant strain of inhabiting a world that nobody could really understand. Sometimes, and only sometimes, Jane wished she had remained spiritually unconscious, living in the world of the mundane, like other people. Jane raised her arms and pulled her long red hair up and back, twining it and knotting it on top of her head. She closed her eyes.

Fresh tea arrived, and Jane and Catherine moved onto safer topics. They always strived for greater intimacy with each other; but sooner or later, they would find themselves hastening for other shores. It had been like this for as long as Jane could remember. Catherine was still sitting stiffly on the sofa, her long legs tapering off to her neat feet in the Ferragamo shoes. "She never really relaxes," thought Jane.

## CHAPTER 2

Dusk and then darkness had descended in Chiswick, and the lights that remained on in the house started to go out one by one. Hours ago, Fairfax had returned home from the city, having had a drink with Justin Bowlby on the way through Southwark.

# 3

Sir Justin Bowlby was indeed revered and highly respected in the field of cardiac surgery. He sped along the motorway into London. This was his usual journey every day to St. John's Hospital and then on in the afternoons to the clinic in Harley Street. He was forty-two years old, and he wore his sleek blond hair longish. Sometimes when he was making a dramatic gesture, a strand of his fine hair would come loose from the suave style and fall onto his forehead. Justin, like Anna, was very stylish; some said he was all style, but that was unfair. He wasn't superficial at all; inside him, there was a deep insecurity. It was a kind of wound that wouldn't heal. He was only partially aware of it. He had lost something along the way in his passage to fame. Some hidden fear or emptiness plagued him. Something was missing.

Outwardly, Justin made up for the missing piece in fame and success. As he walked into St. John's, he looked like a god. People always remarked about his confidence and strength. Everyone turned their heads in his direction as he entered the hospital; he had been careful to select the most exquisite rose from his garden before he left the house. The dew had still been resting on it, early in the morning. He wore this now on his lapel. He wore a suit with a silky sheen and a dove-grey shirt with wide buttons down the front. He hardly ever wore a tie; he couldn't stand them. They would make him feel that he was choking. Anna used to tease him about it saying that he died by being strangled in another lifetime. But Justin didn't believe all that.

Although he turned everyone's head, he was one of those people who were admired from a distance. Even with medical colleagues, he never really became involved in intimate conversation. He would talk about all sorts of things; he would have people to the house, but it was hard to get to know Justin. He didn't really invite it. His family had all been doctors and surgeons for generations. The untimely car accident and death of his parents when Justin was only thirteen led to a highly sensitive nature and anticipated sense of loss with everything in his life. He had no siblings or cousins, which in many ways had given him a lonely childhood. Emotionally, he was not demonstrative and found it hard to trust other people. His uncle had taken care of him through his boyhood, and he was encouraged by him to study medicine at Cambridge where he had met Anna. And being with Anna had been an essentially lonely life too. Her secrets and his reclusiveness, maybe it was not such a good match.

He made his way through the hospital corridors; the old part of the hospital had its face to that timeless river, the Thames. The modern additions, coronary units, operating theatres and research units had all been added later, and not with crude incrementalism like some of the buildings in London. No, St. John's flowed easily between the old and the new, like the flow of the river beneath it.

On passing the chapel, Justin found himself facing the usual question on this part of the journey to his office. Who or what was God anyway? He had never been able to come to grips with this problem, either from the standpoint of traditional religion, which bored him, or from the approach of modern physics. He and Jane would argue for hours on the philosophy of religion, but never Anna. It wasn't her thing. He thought of her now with a pang and wished he had not left so early; last night had not been easy for either of them. She was always remote, keeping him at arm's length. Sometimes, in his worst moments of reflection, he wondered if she had a lover. As usual, he dismissed the idea.

Justin's question of relating to something above and beyond himself gnawed at his heart as he moved on with his morning walk. But there was no place of rest. He passed the gents, then backtracked and went in. He stared at himself in the mirror; his aquiline features and thin lips looked back at him, as if to say, "Well, we are all here, so what now?" Justin looked and wondered what was behind the face, the soul. Who was the witness really? He was too pale, too many hours in the operating theatre. He should get away more often.

Then who was the one really watching? Quickly washing his hands, almost like a benediction, he looked again in the mirror. He realized Felicity would be expecting him. Doctors have their lives run by their secretaries, he thought, as he walked quickly along the rest of the corridor, strong with the morning's smell of antiseptic.

For Justin, who almost daily wielded a scalpel over the chest of his anaesthetized patients, the question of existence and its meaning often arose in his mind. Seeing the inside of the human body for the first time had been a humbling experience, even more so when the body was a live one. For Justin, a certain awe had taken up residence within him. He experienced it as a kind of belief in something far greater than himself. Sometimes, he wondered if it was because his technical focus was on the heart itself. Was it, he thought, that the heart was connected to the soul, if there was such a thing? He had read up on medicine in Ancient Egypt; he had been amazed with what the embalmers did to the hearts of the dead. In some ways, Justin felt very connected to this era in history, but he would not admit this to Anna. Also, he had no idea why this feeling of attraction or connection was there.

He sensed things about Anna that scared him sometimes, like the stuff she would keep in her wardrobe, ancient ritualistic tools. When he asked her about it, she just laughed in that lovely light way she had and said they were only relics; he did not feel comfortable questioning her further. But sometimes he did wonder about her.

When Justin was performing surgery, he was always amazed to see the heart beating away, pumping pints of red liquid through the body. On and on it would beat without ever questioning the point of its action. Sometimes, the hearts were tiny, or dull-looking, heavy things with too much de-oxygenated blood, giving them a weird bluish colour. Justin wondered what his own heart would look like if his own chest cavity were opened for public view.

And now, Justin's metaphysical dialogue for the day was ending as he was nearing the office. He heard Felicity moving around and the telephone ringing in the distance. When he reached his office, the door was wide open, revealing a picture of infinite calm within.

"Good morning, Sir Justin." Felicity was perched on a chair facing Justin's desk. His desk was by the window, not a great view of the river. Instead, it looked onto a stack of chimneys emitting black smoke in the background. He had often wondered what was burning to create that amount of smoke.

"Felicity, try and find out what all that black smoke is again, would you?" he asked aloud.

If he was sitting at his desk, a rather large non-descript desk that he had inherited from someone who vacated the office, the usual NHS cheap, standard furniture of which the hospital was filled, he had a distinct advantage over anyone entering the room and standing or sitting opposite him. He was in the shadow and they were in the light. He would observe the truths and lies that crossed their faces, colouring the emotions of people as they walked in. He also saw the pain, and there was more than enough of that. He saw patients here as well as in the outpatients' departments.

Justin was an acute observer of his fellow beings; he was shrewd and could be ruthless, if provoked. His desk was almost empty. There was a green desk lamp that shone onto an empty, crystal stem vase and a picture of Anna in a wooden frame, purchased long ago in the John Lewis store on Oxford Street. In his desk drawer, there was another smaller picture of a nine-year-old boy smiling out at him. The picture lay face down; Justin had put it there over a week ago. Last week would have been Giles' birthday.

Justin looked at his secretary.

"Coffee," she suggested and went off to make it.

Felicity had come to his office when she was only nineteen. She was now in her mid-twenties. She had been top of her class in secretarial school and Justin had been her only employer. She worshipped Justin but was wary of Anna; she didn't understand her. Felicity had arrived at a tragic time in Justin's marriage, when their son Giles had gone missing.

# 4

A week later, Justin was driving home. It was past rush hour, but the traffic was still heavy. A large truck stood right in front of him in a long line of traffic that had now reached standstill. He was out on the overpass near Hammersmith; a deadly grey area full of high-rise buildings and concrete overhangs. It was architecturally a nightmare, with nothing to please the eye. Since it was raining heavily, Justin kept the wipers on to clear a view for himself in the wetness and wind. He was travelling home, his mind already drifting off to the next day, planning surgery and thinking about his patients. Anna hadn't called him, which was unusual. His car emergency phone went off. The 'hands-free' automatically answered it.

"Sir Justin," said a nervous voice at the other end of the line. "It's Julia. I'm sorry to call you, but I am worried. It's past eight o'clock and Lady Bowlby is still not home. She was due hours ago. She asked me to be ready by four to prepare dinner. When I got to the house it was empty, and she didn't leave a note like she usually does if she is going to be late." There was a silence at Justin's end of the line. He heard the shaking of Julia's voice, always fearing the worst. It seemed his whole life had been filled with calamities. He felt tears pricking his eyes.

"That's very unlike her. Wasn't she going into London today? I met John this morning. He was driving her there in the car."

"I was about to say, sir, that John and the car are not here either. I called John's mobile but it's not working. His wife, down at the lodge, has been calling me every half hour." Julia's voice sounded even more strained.

"I'll be home in a while. I'm sure Lady Bowlby will have returned by then. Tell John's wife not to worry." But Justin was worried, very worried.

"Yes, sir, I'll do that. It seems so strange without Lady Bowlby here."

"I'll be back soon," said Justin, turning off the phone.

Someone else was also making a phone call, but it was from the South of France, from a mobile phone in Mayfair.

"We made sure the car went off the road. There was no movement at all from inside. It went down the ravine, just the spot we discussed. The dog did a good job. Perfect timing," the voice said.

"Good, just do the follow-up and make sure this hits the press." The phone went dead.

Julia walked slowly into the spacious drawing room off the hallway. Justin and Anna's house, a large Edwardian mansion, had been gutted and renovated, creating a vaulted roof with the original oak-beamed rafters. The house was surrounded by lawns and fields, and everywhere there were the dark russet leaves of the beech trees in the gardens and woods. Only an hour and a half from London, the house was close to the village of Grassock Oaks beyond. They had bought the house and nine acres of land over nine years ago. Justin had installed electric gates at the entrance to the property.

Wall and table lamps cast a soft glow over the richly furnished drawing room with its velvets and silks. A large lavish oil painting of Anna stood over the fireplace. An off-the-shoulder crimson velvet ballgown adorned her figure. An armchair in the Bergère style stood by the still open French doors leading out to the terrace. Julia thought she heard the sounds of gaiety among the canopied swing seats and the deck chairs. But the striped chairs were empty, and the sound was only the wind. Julia shuddered. It was just starting to rain, great drops landing on the crazy paving. She closed the doors and drew the curtains against the weather and her fears for Lady Bowlby. If ever there was a troubled soul, it was her mistress. But Julia never breathed a word of this to anyone.

She went upstairs to Anna and Justin's bedroom. The house seemed so strange without Anna. She went to turn down the bed and caught sight of an envelope; it had a black crest on the back of it. Carefully, she placed it on the bedside table. In the bathroom, she was straightening up the white towels that Anna always used, when she saw a white tissue on the carpet. She picked it up; Anna had used it, the mark of her red lipstick tracing the path of her lips on the tissue. Suddenly, Julia started to feel the strain of the day. She sat on the edge of the bath for a few minutes, trying not to cry, but her hands shook.

An hour later, Julia heard Sir Justin's voice from downstairs. She was still tidying up upstairs, making sure that everything was ready for the night. Anna was fussy about how things should look, what lights should be on, the temperature of the house. She always liked ease and comfort and to have things the same way every evening when Justin came home.

"Has there been any news, Julia?" Justin called out to her.

"No, sir, and the car isn't back either."

"Well, we will have to call the police." Justin moved towards the phone and put the call through to the local station. They had no reports of accidents and knew nothing that could help at all. Justin gave them all the details of Anna and the chauffeur, John. Julia came downstairs to greet him.

"Sir, would you like me to bring a supper tray for you in the drawing room?" Julia was anxious to make sure Justin had at least something to eat; it may be a long night ahead.

"Yes, that would be nice. Maybe they will be back soon. This silence is so unlike her." His mind was totally occupied with thoughts of Anna. Where was she?

Justin went upstairs to their bedroom and sat on the white linen sofa. Anna's blue cashmere wrap was hanging over the back of a chair. The smell of her delicate Chanel perfume hung in the air, filling him with longing. The house felt like a tomb. There were other times that Justin had longed for Anna in her absence; the sudden trips to Switzerland or Berlin; she said she had wanted to see friends and write about her travels. But Justin wondered about Anna; it was the kind of clothes that he found she had taken on these visits to other countries. Cocktail dresses and the extravagant high-heeled shoes, but when Justin asked her, Anne just laughed and said she had friends who had invited her to a few parties. Anna did not tell the truth in order to protect her own sanity; lies had to be part of her existence. She had got used to it, lies to her parents, lies to Fabian to ensure her survival and now Justin, to secure her privacy.

It was exactly five years ago today on the last day of June that their son Giles had disappeared, aged nine. He had never returned. Justin wondered about the significance of the dates and felt something was menacing his life and family.

Twenty minutes later, Julia came up the stairs. "Shall I leave it here for you?" asked Julia, the tray in her shaking hands. Justin had not returned to the drawing room, and she felt he should eat something. She could see that she had disturbed him. Embarrassed by her intrusion, she hung at the doorway.

"Yes, yes, that's fine, just leave it on the table." Justin tried not to sound impatient.

He sank back in the chair and looked around the room. Colours surrounded him in the gentle light of the room. Paintings hung on the damask walls – Mediterranean scenes, azure skies. Behind the sofa on which Justin sat, a Picasso etching looked down onto the room, a thin seated figure with two grey faces, in the background an open window, a white veiled curtain as though it was moving in the breeze. Another picture showed the photograph of their villa in the South of France, Anna and Justin laughing and sitting on the steps in the sunshine. But all the pictures of Giles had been removed. Neither of them could bear to see his image.

An hour later, Justin's meal still lay untouched. His mind was far away, to the time when Giles had disappeared. That day when he had said goodbye, his son had clung to him, not wanting to let him go. It was unusual. Sometimes, he only gave

Justin a cursory glance, eager to be getting on with some project or to go and play with a friend. He had been a silent and independent little creature. Justin adored him. All that day he had felt a strange sense of dread, as though something was terribly wrong.

Later that morning, Giles had come around to the side of the house and stared through the window at Anna who was writing in the library. The window was open. Giles had on several layers of clothing and a coat, even though it was June, Anna questioned him about this, but he insisted that he was cold. He told her he was going with his friend Michael through the park to the woods. She didn't question him further; after all, it was their property. What harm could come to them? Michael was an older child of eleven and was very responsible.

Anna didn't really give it another thought. That was the last she saw of her beloved son. She had been strangely abstracted that day. Three hours had gone by, and she realized that Giles had not returned home. She of course called Fabian, but he remained unavailable. She wondered if he had taken Giles. But never in all these years had he admitted anything. In a way, he had never known Giles and had of course never bonded with him. Once, when Giles was two years old, they had taken him to Anna's house in Switzerland; they had four desperate days after which, unbearably, they had to part. It was devastating to both that they were not able to be together. Fabian always exhausted Anna with his insistent demands. Sexually, he was a predator; she knew that. She could not live with him and she could not live without him. It was a tragedy that they had in some way to live with for the rest of their lives.

She had called Justin, and they had made several calls to Michael's house. His mother said Michael had left Giles at the gate to the lawns on the way to the house. He would only have to run a short distance. But he never ran to the house and no one had seen him again. Justin remembered the way his son looked. He had Anna's dark hair with deep blue eyes like his own. His skin was fine with just a few freckles around the nose. Tall for his age and very thin, his enthusiasm for life had been tremendous.

35

Justin remembered the calls to the hospital, the police who were so kind. They had dragged the ponds and the river all around the property within a four-mile stretch. They had sent men and dogs, day after day. The family never slept, one day merging relentlessly into another.

One night, Anna had become hysterical with tension. She had run out into the rain in the middle of the night in only her nightdress; she did not return. Justin had been asleep and only in the early hours of the morning had missed her and then, after a long search and with the help of John, they had found her in the woods, unconscious, with her nightdress torn. They had sent her to the London Clinic. Dosed with sedatives, for weeks she wouldn't utter a word. In time she recovered, but she never mentioned Giles. She always kept conversations within careful limits, tired easily and avoided intimacy. Justin had been shocked by the changes in her. He grieved in his own way and buried himself in his work. Now, he looked down at his hands resting on his knees. "Anna, darling, Anna," he cried to himself.

He looked at his long fingers, the fingers that sutured hearts back together and the fingers that ran a scalpel across the length of a chest wall. The hands were white; blue veins stood out from the skin. His wedding ring was a thin twist of gold. He watched his breath going in and out of his body and waited. The intercom went off.

"Yes?" he answered.

"Sir Justin, a car has just come up the drive," said Julia from downstairs.

He tore down the stairs. He had been lost in thought, and the intercom and news of the car had shocked him. He could feel his heart beating too fast. He thought of the recent literature that he had been reading on coronary occlusions.

Running down the stairway, he thought of all the possibilities. Who was in the car? Whatever it was, he would be ready. The hallway was large, ideal for welcoming frequent visitors to the house. Persian rugs lay over the polished wooden floors. As the eye travelled upwards to the rafters, a winding inner staircase revealed all the three floors. The attics lay beyond. Justin saw it all before the moment he answered the doorbell. He noticed that his palms were wet with perspiration; all the memories of Giles were flooding back. He realized before he opened the door that the news was going to be bad. It was.

"Excuse me, sir, for troubling you so late. May I come in for a moment? I'm Detective Inspector Grahams from the local station. I'm quite new to the area." He kept talking as Justin led him into the hallway. His raincoat was soaked; its soggy blackness dripped over the wooden floors until Julia rescued it and took it to the cloakroom. There was mud on his shoes. "Definitely a country man," Justin thought to himself.

As though reading Justin's thoughts, he said, "Oh dear, my shoes are very wet. It's an awful night, and I had better remove them." Julia took the offending shoes and went off to clean them. She felt it was something to keep her busy and her mind off what she felt would be a terrible evening ahead.

They did not waste time and quickly walked into the drawing room and shut the door. Justin motioned for him to sit down in one of the wing armchairs they had recently brought back from Paris.

"Sir, I will get straight to the point. I wanted to give you just a few minutes to sit down, but my visit is very urgent. There has been a terrible accident. Your wife and her chauffeur, John Grey, were found only about an hour ago." He paused, waiting for Justin's reaction. One had to be so careful with people. Justin turned pale but looked intently at him. He continued.

"They were found lying in the blue Bentley at the bottom of a ravine. The chauffeur was probably killed outright, impaled by the steering column. Your wife was in the back of the car. She is still alive, but they had to cut her out of the car. It's too soon to know . . . She's been taken to the Queen Charlotte Hospital. Of course, you know it. One of my men is with Mrs Grey now at the lodge. We can go there straight away if you like before I take you to the hospital."

He was still watching Justin. He seemed frozen in his seat for a few minutes and was very quiet. Detective Inspector Grahams kept talking, filling in the details so that Justin had time to adapt.

"The road where they went off is about an hour from here, It's on the B26 – a pretty road but precarious in places. Still, it's well marked, so it's hard to know how the accident took place. From the skid marks, I would say that the driver was trying to avoid something running across the road. No other cars reported an accident, so it must have been something like that."

"How did you find the car?"

"Well, it's odd, really. We had a call from someone who works for the local press – quite a coincidence. He said he was driving along and had parked the car near there because of some engine trouble. Then he noticed there were skid marks and torn branches, and when he investigated a little further, he saw the car and climbed down to look. As soon as he saw what had happened, he ran back up to his car and called the police on his mobile."

Grahams got up then and asked Justin whether he would like to be driven to the hospital. He had seen this calmness before. It was usually the clever ones like Sir Justin; totally calm on the surface but underneath highly strung and could go to pieces at the flick of an eyelid. He had also done his homework and knew this was a family wrapped around success, a great deal of money and a large share of tragedy. Their son had disappeared five years ago, never to reappear. The police suspected he had been abducted and then murdered. But by whom? "Was this another case of foul play?" Grahams wondered to himself. Justin was a type that could become deeply depressed. And he had known some of them to commit suicide. Grahams decided he was going to keep close tabs on Sir Justin; besides, he admired him. He was well thought of too; he was always in the papers written up for his work, even the international press. Grahams made sure he kept abreast of national and international news.

They went out into the hall. Julia emerged with a tray of tea. When Justin told her the news, she almost dropped the tray, but Justin was quick to help her regain her balance.

"You have the tea, Julia, and take care. Just rest until I get back. We may need you later." Justin was very kind. He was careful with people; he treated people sometimes a bit like patients, let them know a bit at a time to get them to adjust to things. He had noticed Grahams used the same skills. He was grateful to him for at least not rushing the news.

The black Jaguar eased out of the driveway carrying Justin safely to his wife. He wore the collar of his raincoat up, a kind of protection against the battering of this world; he knew all the possible medical and surgical procedures that Anna would have gone through by now. He offered a prayer to a God he did not know.

The car moved swiftly, but Grahams remained silent. He wanted to give Justin plenty of time and space to prepare himself for the visit. It was raining heavily now, and the outside world was only visible when the windscreen wipers pushed away torrents of water momentarily from the glass. It made Grahams think of endless, unshed tears. In seconds, the view was again occluded. Justin was forced to look inside himself, to recognize the pain and to wonder why his family had again been attacked.

# 5

Anna knew who had tried to kill her, but her first experience after the impact of the accident was darkness and silence. She was not supposed to die. It was a warning. She would feel no long-term effects; Fabian would make sure of that.

Fabian was the puppet of The Jester, a disembodied spirit. The Jester had possessed his soul since he was a child. The two had become one and Fabian had to obey The Jester's every command; indeed, one could not separate the two of them. If The Jester died, Fabian would also lose his life.

She knew that the character of The Jester was not happy with revenge upon Anna in her last life as Amelia, Countess of Rigby in George IV's reign when he was jester to the King. He wanted to wreck further havoc in her life in this present century.

And now, they had vowed revenge when she had played at remaining aloof from Fabian. He wanted her, and nothing would assuage his fury and desire. But he had the power to bring her back from the dead. She almost did not know which life was which. He had done this so many times. This accident was his doing, to warn her that he was the owner of her soul and that she had to obey him. She was his creature.

She did not know that Fabian was leading a life of degradation, that he had sold his soul to no less than the Devil, that he had read all the books that showed a life of sexual excess, sadistic practices, the stealer of souls and their bodies. He was utterly corrupted. He was the embodiment of everything evil. But she found it impossible not to love him. He had made her his. And what was worse, his soul had so been clearly taken over by The Jester. But Anna led a life of confusion, and it was always a fog in which she lived.

Giles, being Fabian's son, had been taken from her when he was nine with no warning. It was so like Fabian. She thought of the night of conception when Fabian told her that she must never link herself strongly to any other man. Anna was ashamed, but she was powerless against this man, her love so strong, her body so intimately connected to his. Their night together and his vehemence that they should have a child together had shocked her. And then he had brutally taken Giles away from her, although he never admitted it to her. It was part of the tricky way in which he lived.

The night of the conception, they played no games of violence, but she had worn the black magic thread that swept over her shoulder and between her legs, the coiled mouth on the cord bringing her to a heightened state of sexual ecstasy and longing. And then she had conceived, amidst the mantras and ceremony on which Fabian had insisted.

She both hated and loved Fabian. This was her agony. She plotted revenge but was never able to run against him. At times, he came close to physically torturing her during their nights of lovemaking together; such was his excess. But these strange practices had bound her even closer to him. He studied and then performed sadistic practices on many women, but Anna knew nothing of this. She had even lost the ability to distinguish in her own body the difference between pleasure and pain. Anna thought blindly that she was the only one. He was untouchable. His huge wealth, connections to the Mafia and aristocracy, made it impossible for the women to speak out against him; they felt their lives to be in danger.

Now, after the accident, she was experiencing a brilliant light both inside and outside her head. She found herself somehow outside the car, looking in. She saw John Grey slumped over the remains of the steering wheel column; the rest of it was embedded in his solar plexus. She put her hand to her chest with the shock of seeing him, but her hand went into thin air. She had no chest. She had no body.

Looking through the window of the car, smashed to pieces by the impact, she saw her own body, slumped in its brown suit on the back seat. There was a slow but determined trickle of blood running from her head. Her fingers were curled up into the palms of her hands as though she was a child asleep. She felt very detached. Although happy in this state, it was vaguely confusing. When she looked down at where her body should be, she was standing in a pillar of darkness.

Slowly, she felt something pull her away from the car. She was being pursued through the woods, and she found herself on a path of golden and blue light. It was not only a path, but a kind of tunnel made of webbing. Her life, like a movie, was running its events before her eyes. Scenes from her childhood – she saw her mother giving birth to her; she held an apple in her hand collected from the trees on a long summer evening in France. Then she saw her marriage with Justin and their honeymoon in Switzerland. Giles came before her eyes, the memory like the jarring of a trap door that had ceased to open. She cried as she had never cried before, in great sobs, the grief welling up again and again in her heart. And then there was Fabian. The blackness of her life stood staring at her. He told her that once she had recovered, she would have to come once more to be with him, whatever it cost her. There would be no dying for her. Not this time.

The tunnel was winding on and on; at each side there was a deep abyss. She looked down into it; mists swirled into black nothingness, and strange birds like ibises flew in the air. Holes appeared in the mists, revealing a view of the whole of the earth's surface spread out like a giant canvas beneath her.

Suddenly she was still, then she felt a sense of rapid descent, like being in an elevator. It was quite a shock, rushing through what seemed like time zones. She was entering the earth's orbit, and for the first time, she felt the impact of gravity. Then there was the sound of scraping metal. She was inside the car in her body, and they were trying to get her out. She felt so weak but was aware of the voices and the hammering outside the car. The door was apparently jammed. They were using blow lamps and crowbars. She could see the blue sparks of the lamps falling around the car like spent fireworks. She did not want to be here. This was the story of her life. She always had the sense that she wanted to be somewhere else; she knew the place but could never describe it. She had been there on a journey to the netherworld, but then it was snatched away from her before she had learned how to return on her own. She wanted her life back. She was imprisoned in every way.

Later that night, Justin could not sleep. He had been to see Anna at the hospital, was amazed at how unscathed she was and was appalled at the death of his chauffeur. After he had spent time with her, he had gone to spend an hour with John's wife in the cottage. She had been given something to help her by the GP, but he wanted to make sure she was not alone.

Now he reached over to the bedside table for his new sleeping pills. They were to help his nights of sleeplessness. He wondered how much longer he could go on bearing the frustration with Anna. He had always been faithful to Anna, but he now suspected that Anna was leading a double life. The loss of their son, these strange incidents and her frequent trips abroad made him realize he knew nothing of the woman with whom he lived.

The tablets kicked in straight away, but instead of real sleep, Justin found himself in a dreamlike state. It was as if he were in another lifetime. He could see and hear everything clearly. First, he was labouring to walk in hot sand, a desert, endless and eternal. The sand went on forever. Just when he felt he had to give up and die, he found himself in a building.

He found himself creeping along an endless corridor. He seemed to be a pharaoh. He saw his name written everywhere, but he could not quite make it out. He was wearing the Egyptian garments of a king. He was trying to get into what seemed like his queen's bedroom; the door was locked against him. It was hot, and he was sweating and deeply agitated. He went around the corner to what must have been another small door that led into a cupboard within her chambers. He let himself in and heard voices in the bedroom. He could see through a hole in the cupboard door, but the occupants of the room were unaware of him. And there in the room was one of his advisors, Salitis, his political advisor in that lifetime, but Justin was not aware of this.

And here was a woman more beautiful than anyone he had ever seen before. Her long raven black hair lay strewn loosely across a pillow. Her eyes were open, brilliant blue, and her skin was dark. His eyes followed her smile and then, he looked down at her naked body, taking in the curves of her belly and hips.

He saw bedclothes strewn everywhere. His queen was lying there naked. A man was kneeling in front of her. She was wearing a black thread over her shoulder that ran down between her legs creating a fully uninterrupted circle. This thread and how it was being used was so erotic that Justin was more aroused by this than anything else. The cord was hissing like a snake between them.

But Justin had already gone. Anna, still out of her body, came to Justin in his sleep at that very moment. She removed the memory of his past life; except, she was unable to erase one thing, the black thread and who was wearing it. It was the one thing that Justin remembered when he woke up many hours later. It was Fabian who had power and control over the knowledge of the black thread, not Anna. He already had power over Anna.

Justin woke up later than usual. His first thought was of his dream and the black thread that the woman had worn so seductively around her body. He remembered watching it fall between her legs. Then the awful realization came to him that he had seen this thread before. He got up too quickly, banging his head against a beam in the low ceiling as he moved in his pyjamas to where Anna kept her things in the wardrobe drawer. He cursed.

The drawer was stiff and hard to open. He had been inside it once or twice, looking for things for Anna. He had seen the sequined box but had only opened it once. It looked like threads inside. Now he pulled out the contents with shaking, furious hands. There, it came into his hands, the long circle of magic, the black thread – the same as he had seen in the dream. He felt aroused now at the erotic memories of the thread. It was silky and warm in his hands. There was a coiled piece that obviously fitted where he had seen it used in his dream. He thought of Anna using it and could feel his own sexual feelings even more strongly now as his fantasies overtook him.

Justin had read about the black thread, one rainy afternoon, in one of Anna's books in her library. It was a magic mating circle to obtain the highest arousal possible in tantric sexual intercourse, to move the coupling partners to the nether regions where all senses are heightened to such an extent that they force the soul out of the body for a brief instant, creating unknown ecstasy and taking them to unseen worlds. It is also used for practices of tantric conception, bringing special powers into the foetus.

He could not believe he was handling this thread that was worn by his wife. Whom did she wear this thread with? Certainly not with him. With her own husband, she was unable to achieve any proper intimacy, or only for a brief minute, as though nothing could make any difference to her frigid body.

Justin groaned, holding the thread in his shaking hand. He lay down in a kind of agony and rolled over and over on his back, confused in his mind, wondering all the while about who Anna had been enjoying this sexual ecstasy with. He felt cheated and betrayed.

Anna was asleep, unknowing now of Justin and what he had found out.

Fabian had always made sure that she only had partial knowledge and power in the magic. Then she was not aware of what she did not know, which was a dangerous situation to be in. Now she would also not be aware that Justin knew about the black thread and her infidelity. It would change her marriage with Justin forever, and she would not know the reason why. Fabian's threats were becoming a reality.

Behind all these actions and experiences of both Anna and Justin were the play and malevolence of The Jester and his puppet Fabian. The Jester knew how to break down the fabric of life and destroy people within their own games. He was tweaking the threads of life, and they were becoming loose. It was a dangerous game, the players confused and unable to control anything that they thought was theirs.

# 6

On the same day as Anna's accident, her cousin, Casey Pemberton, stood in her New York kitchen trying, with little success, to open a tin of cat food. She didn't have the right equipment and was frowning at the offending tin opener. The cutting edges, so worn down now, had ceased to be effective. She paused and gazed out of her window on the twenty-fourth floor of the Manhattan apartment block.

All she could see was a series of black water towers sitting on the roofs of the adjacent buildings. They looked menacing. It was raining, and spots of water threw themselves onto the windows only to be dashed off again by the wind moments later. She looked down at what she was wearing, having little recollection of what she had put on that morning. Very soon, she would have to make an exit to meet with her agent, Daryl Hubert. She was bare-legged, except for cowboy boots with their fake zebra fur on the top edge. They were her social killing of the month, although it was the usual hot New York summer. She didn't care that they were winter boots; she liked them. Then there was the short denim mini-skirt and the pink T-shirt with white frosting. She could almost hear her mother saying, "To think we sent you to one of the best English private schools; really, Casey, can't you grow up?" The voice went off into nowhere in Casey's brain. But it was true; Casey was English and had been known on occasions to wear cashmere sweaters and a string of pearls over a good Scottish tweed skirt. She was just playing another kind of game that morning.

She flung the hopeless can opener to the other side of the room in total disgust. It lay miserably in the corner of the kitchen only too aware of its offence. Casey's cat, Mimmy, a grey long-haired Persian, snarled at the opener. Casey fumbled around in six different drawers and finally found a brand-new electric opener, but the can had been so badly mauled by the previous opener that nothing happened. Another tin was found from the hundreds that stood against the wall. Casey said a prayer and put the tin and the new opener into magnetic union. It worked. She slid the cat food onto a brown plate with lurid red designs and placed it in front of Mimmy. The cat took one sniff at it and walked off into the other room. Casey threw the empty tin at her in exasperation.

With that done, she went to her bedroom for some makeup. She heard the music of Coldplay coming from outside. It was her favourite band, and she adored the lead singer. Even so, she was not in the right frame of mind to listen to them so slammed the window shut to cut out the sound.

Casey was indeed agitated; it was days since she had heard from her best friend, Maxine. They were always in touch, and it was now five days since she had heard from her. She had started to worry. There was nothing but an answering machine at her number, and the mobile did not even ring. She had even called Maxine's father, Senator Alistair Cleveland, an ambassador in Washington. He had not heard from Maxine either. He knew there had been some plans to travel to Cairo on a story and perhaps Paris, but he presumed she had returned. Maxine did have her secret moments and unexplained trips, but Casey would have expected to hear something by now.

Casey was late. She stopped thinking and grabbed a purple silk trench coat, made, it had said, from a discarded parachute. Then she slipped on some gold leggings, a black designer top and her boots and headed for the door, picking up her briefcase, credit cards and mobile as she spun out.

The rain had abated, but she grabbed a taxi and took it up to Bar 24 on the East Side.

"How's your mother, Casey?" laughed Daryl. Casey's mother was always a bone of contention in her life.

"Shut up, Daryl." She poked a finger into his ribs.

"Casey, darling, I have great news. This calls for a celebration. Can you guess?" taunted Daryl pulling his fingers through his dark hair. He had one of those styles that constantly fell forward and so with one hand and a shake of the head, he was constantly pushing it back off the face. Everyone did it; it was an affectation that summer. Frankly, it annoyed Casey.

"No, I can't imagine," replied Casey feigning ignorance.

"Antoinelli's in Milan want to hang three of your pictures in their gallery this fall. They will pay for everything – the shipping, your trip out for the opening and all the incidentals. Considering the size of your pictures, that's a real coup. It means you are really getting famous." Daryl smiled at her.

Casey became silent; it was her dream to have her work hung in a gallery like this. But she felt not just elation but something else as well. Her life was changing, taking on an unexpected form. In the back of her mind lurked a new reality that she dreaded. It was strange to feel this way.

"Which ones do they want?" Casey showed no reaction.

"Mainly the Myling period," answered Daryl, wondering why Casey wasn't as pleased as he thought she would be at the news. He put an arm around her.

"Please," she said, indicating she wanted the arm removed.

The Myling period had been a serious time in her life. It was a period when Casey was going through Jungian analysis with a man called Oyoto Myling, a Japanese Jungian psychoanalyst who practiced his own brand of Jungian thoughts on the Upper East Side. He was highly skilled and enabled Casey to look at much of what she did not want to face about her involvement in her family. Dreams and nightmares had emerged from the debris of the past. Her stepfather, Lord Oliver Pemberton, haunted her. She had never enough space as a child. She was too physically close and bonded to him, leaving her mother outside the circle in a dark vortex of hatred for not having saved her from the attentions of her stepfather and for not loving her enough.

She remembered the secret passages of her mind and how she had at first fought her stepfather when he wanted the intimacy of her body. She had been too young. But it went on for years. Her mother had been strangely absent, as though she did not want to know or did not care. Casey both loved and hated her stepfather and strangely, seemed unavailable to everyone else. She just could not give herself.

Actress Flo Eddings glided into the restaurant with Bruno Bentalli, a young film director, on her arm. They made straight for Casey's table.

"Aren't you going to England soon, Casey? I thought you were going to see the gallery that's showing your works of art," asked Flo.

"Another nudge from destiny creeping up on me," pondered Casey. She thought of the remote house near the Cambridge marshes, where her mother and stepfather still lived. She remembered the day Anna had come over to the house and when she herself had almost been sucked completely into the bog on the marshes. She remembered that she had been sent to her room and it was Anna who was invited for tea in her stepfather's study. She wondered about that day. She saw little of Anna after that.

Her bedroom at the back of the house had been dark, its leaded window covered by ivy. In winter, the cold stiff leaves would tap on the outside of the windows at night. In summer, the leaves would creep silently into the room and grow onto the window sill. She remembered how she loathed their intrusion, the hated ivy. Sometimes, they would cut it back, but they never could cut her stepfather back. He was like ivy growing into her being, destroying her while she was trying to grow, holding her in a strangling embrace, never letting go.

His long fingers were never still on her counterpane, always searching, penetrating her reality – busy fingers, menacing fingers. Eyes, like ice on fire, stared at her, robbing her of her privacy. Her head was full of nightmares, chased by birds, lost in deserts and darkness. And then she would start weeping, long and lasting. He would leave on business trips to Argentina, and she felt she could begin her little life again. But then he would return. Over and over it would happen, robbing her of her childhood; always she would hope that this was the last time, but it never was. He wanted her forever, to possess her. She was under his spell. When he was gone, her body ached for him, but deep within herself, she hated him for stealing her life.

"Yes, I'm going this month actually. I'm going to the gallery, but I'm also planning to go to Shropshire. The Countess of Rigby, Emma Rigby, has invited me to her house," stated Casey blankly.

"How do you know her? You are such a recluse, Casey. I'm surprised you are going to something like that," said the lovely Flo, looking frequently at Bruno who seemed unfortunately mesmerized by Casey. Daryl was not even listening; he was working out the costing of Casey's shows. He did, however, notice Bruno's interest.

"I met her last summer in Nice. She has a chateau further north. I was introduced to her; she is almost beyond description. Radiant, that is how I would describe her. She is beautiful. But it's the inner radiance that grabs you. It's strange, really, this kind of magnetism in people. She was so kind and seemed to take an interest in me. I can't think why. She said that she would be entertaining this summer in England. She invites a lot of socialites and famous people; I mean, people who are really producing things – scientists, research doctors – those kinds of people..." Casey trailed off, aware of Bruno staring at her.

"I have heard of the Countess of Rigby. The family is famous, or should I say infamous. There was a mysterious story surrounding them a few generations ago. My mother said they practice, or used to practice black magic, Egyptian magic," said Bruno.

"Oh rubbish! I've never heard anything so ridiculous. You must have got them mixed up with some stupid book. Anyway, I don't believe in all that stuff. She's just a really nice woman." Casey was livid at Bruno's suggestion. He made her so angry, but she didn't know why, and she wasn't going to let him find out how she felt.

Flo was having an attack of the giggles; she was holding Bruno's arm again, looking into his eyes. Suddenly, Casey felt irritated by the restaurant and this whole social scene; she wanted out.

"Seen Maxine, Flo?" asked Casey.

"No, we haven't met for weeks. Come to think of it, I haven't seen her around. I saw Allan Walker though; he said she has been covering that story of a new film in Cairo, the one Anthony Jackson is producing. She skipped off to Cairo to do some research, just for a few days. But that was a few weeks ago. No, come to think of it, I have not seen her since then." Flo looked thoughtful.

"It suited her to look like that, instead of all this fluff she was caught up in," thought Casey.

"I know she went to Cairo, although I didn't know the story. Maybe she was delayed over there for some reason, but she usually calls me; even her father hasn't heard from her," Casey replied. The group fell silent as they thought of Maxine – wild, brilliant Maxine: her black hair and chiselled features, long-limbed, gaunt, restless. She attracted everyone's attention and had carried off award after award already, at twenty-eight, for her contribution to political journalism.

Then Maxine had changed her focus, shifting it to more bizarre social issues – murders, the disappearance of people, cults, kidnapping. Her latest story was covering Anthony Jackson's new film. It was to be based on the pharaohs' journey after death to the regions beyond, the cult of Seth and its strange relationship to the death and rebirth of the pharaohs. Jackson had announced that he had found the source of power and sacred secrets related to spells and the journey to the afterlife. The secrets would come to life in the film. It was as though Maxine wanted to live on a razor's edge. Loving...living wasn't enough for her. It was as though she wanted to taste death itself.

"Daryl, I must go; there are things I need to take care of," said Casey picking up her bag.

"See you, Casey; I'll call you tomorrow when I have done all the paperwork and the faxing to Milan. Then the contracts will be ready for signing. By the time you go to England, everything will be ready for the shows in London, Paris and Milan. Then all you must do is to sit back and enjoy it," concluded Daryl.

Casey left the restaurant and wrapped her trench coat around her, as if to keep out the Devil. It was raining heavily, and she was hungry, but she did not want to stay to eat with this crowd. She was not in the mood.

As soon as she arrived at her apartment, she ate a stale croissant and cheese in the kitchen and then she checked her answering machine. She had three messages. One was from her mother in Cambridge. The next was from Jane Crosby-Nash in London. The third message was from Jack.

Whenever she received a message from Jack, she got a sinking feeling in her stomach. The message was blunt; a photographic shoot was taking him out of town. There was no doubt about it; Casey felt abandoned. It was a perfectly valid reason for not seeing her; it always was. Why did she feel this way?

Again, she remembered Oliver, her stepfather, the intimacy he demanded from her, starting when she was only six years old. Then he would go away for weeks on end. Her fear of him had turned to longing once again. She remembered her time at the boarding school, the loneliness as she got older, never being one of the crowd. She would call out for him during her times home in the holidays in the first year. He would say, "Just a minute, darling, I just have a report to finish." But he would not come. She would wait and wait. In fact, as she neared the age of eleven, her stepfather seemed to become less interested in her and left her alone. His visits to her room waned and then stopped. She was abandoned. He abandoned her for two long years.

Her thoughts wandered again around the territories of her childhood. Her mother, Antigone, was always engrossed in her own world. Wife of a successful politician, she would cater to his every need, with little time for Casey. She was also a don at Oxford, always immersed in her books. It had seemed a convenient move for her parents to pack her off to a remote boarding school in Scotland. After all, everyone went to boarding school. Her stepfather returned to her bed again in the holidays two years later. Her mother was constantly away. Casey did not leave school until she was seventeen, but then there had been her terrible sixteenth birthday. She would never forget it. By that time, she was so encased in her own walled world of suffering and so deprived of human love that for years no one could get near her at all. It took analysis to undo some the damage. By that time, she had directed all her energy into her paintings.

Again, she had little contact with Oliver after she left boarding school. She went through art school in London as strictly as she went through boarding school, living on her own in Chelsea. But she had had affairs, many of them, always looking for love. Her desires knew no bounds, but her choices of partners would always be unfortunate. She would fall in love with men who were unattainable, married or worse. She did not understand her sexuality and felt that somehow, she had learnt something that other people would not understand. After that, she became a lot more careful about who she saw and set up better boundaries for herself. She dated rarely, but overall her relationships were not successful. She had such a poor sense of self-worth.

And then Oliver came back into her life; it was gradual at first. He would come to the apartment at Primrose Hill that he owned and where she now lived in London. It was unexpected. She was surprised, but she was intensely bonded to him from such an early age; it seemed quite natural for them to be together again, sexually. But there was nothing natural about Oliver. Casey had been his lover since a young age. He knew all about young girls, how to capture their imaginations and their sexuality with his clever hands and mind. Casey had always been under his spell, although there were times when she had fought him but not for long. He had introduced her to the most bizarre and difficult of sexual practices. He was a well-known paedophile, not only in London but also abroad. He was immensely wealthy and could have what he chose. He was serviced at Fabian's establishments and successfully managed to avoid scandals, paying for what he needed.

But Casey, in the end, felt as though she was not only losing her mind and her body but her soul as well. So, she left abruptly for New York. Now he was a constant ache inside her, and she knew that when she went to London this time, it would start again: the ritual abuse, the terror, the hypnotic trances he put her into. He was a drug that she could not do without. The New York experiment would fail and again, she would be inside Oliver's trap, his prey forever.

An hour or so after these memories and realities had surfaced, Casey, still hungry, was having a cup of tea. She had nearly eaten a whole packet of biscuits. She heard a thump on the front door. She ignored it, and then the thump came again, this time more insistently.

"Who is it?" yelled Casey, irritated that her privacy had been invaded. "And how did you get past the security system?" she added, still angry with the intruder, whoever it was.

"Casey, it's Randy." A little voice yelled from the other side of the door. "My mom's been taken to the hospital again and there is no one at home. Can I come in?" continued the voice.

"My God," thought Casey, "I only have to think of a nine-year-old miserable child and here comes one knocking at the door." Randy and her mother lived in the same block as Casey, and she had become friendly with the child. She unbolted the door, and in walked Randy in a fluffy, blue faded dressing gown and a pair of beaten-up Mickey Mouse slippers.

"I found her on the floor when I got back from school. She was so pale and sick. I thought she was dead, so I telephoned the ambulance," said Randy. "They came and took her to the hospital; just the same as usual." Randy's nonchalance at these events always appalled Casey. But she knew the trick, the cover-up; she had been like this herself. When her parents had told her that her dog had died, she had merely said, "Oh, really!"

Randy kicked off her Mickey Mouse slippers and lay down on a faded green bean bag that sat in a heap on the polished floor. She lay like that for half an hour, then she looked around the room.

"You don't have much furniture, do you, Casey?" she asked. "I like that green painting over by the window. What is that called? It's so big. Oh, I'm so hungry; can we get something to eat from the deli?" Casey picked up the phone and placed an order for the Blue Star Deli downstairs. They ate and then called the hospital. Randy's mother's condition was unchanged.

"She is going to die soon, isn't she?" asked Randy as Casey was getting the bed ready. Casey didn't answer. She didn't know what to say. It was late and since there was only one bed, Casey slept in her usual place and Randy lay at the other end. She lay across it like a log, her feet sticking out at the other end. Above the bed, high up on the ceiling, was a canvas of blue, full of light and stars. The moon looked down on them from the canvas. It seemed to draw them up into the sky away from the earth.

"Is God in the sky, or is he here with us, like close, all the time?" asked Randy. Casey wondered where God was; she really didn't know. She had read a book once that said 'God is closer than your own breath'. She watched her breath go in and out of her body for the first time. After a while, it felt exhilarating, as though she had found some bliss inside her own being.

"Hey, Randy, try breathing like me and watch the breath as it goes in and out."

Randy tried it; she imagined her breath to be pink, light, soft and glowing, entering her small form. She thought of it running around her body, having a quick look at everything, checking out the inner scene. She started to feel that the light inside her was a kind of Disney World.

"Casey, I feel so light I could float into the sky and just stay there looking down at my body. Sometimes I feel that I belong everywhere in the universe, inside the flowers, up the trees, in the lions at the zoo. Then I look at my hands, and I know I am inside me as well."

A few minutes later, Casey looked down at the end of the bed. Randy was asleep, her small body loosely covered by the bed clothes. Long strands of hair fell across her face. She looked almost deathly. There were dark shadows under her eyes.

Casey left her asleep and went into the next room. She wanted to call Jane. She had left it a long time; it had been hours since her call. She dreaded it all.

"Hi, it's Casey. What's happened?"

"Casey, I thought you would be over here by now. Something's happened. Anna had an accident today; we've been up half the night. The car went off the road into a ravine. Her chauffeur was killed." Jane was talking fast.

"And Anna?" asked Casey, bleakly.

"She's recovering, no damage at all, except bruising and a cut on her head; she's slightly concussed, of course. It's a miracle," concluded Jane.

"Or a spell," added Casey.

"A spell?" Jane drew breath.

"Yes."

"What do you mean?" asked Jane.

"Something to frighten Anna, to warn her," replied Casey.

"What makes you think that?" asked Jane.

"Well, she told me some things that happened to her once. I think she is bewitched," said Casey.

"By whom?" asked Jane.

"Oh, I don't want to go into it now." Casey wanted to get off the phone.

"When are you coming?" asked Jane, knowing not to press.

"Maxine has disappeared," said Casey, not answering the question.

"When?" asked Jane, shocked.

"Jane, I have to go. I'll call you tomorrow."

Casey slipped back into the room where Randy was sleeping. So, Anna had had another encounter with death – Anna, lovely and beautiful, who hung always so close to disaster. Casey wondered if she ever came back from the dead. Someone or something troubled Anna deeply. Casey could feel it. She was so unapproachable, so she could never ask. One day, she remembered she had walked over to Anna's parents' house when Anna was about sixteen. A black Porsche had pulled up with windows shaded in grey. Anna had stepped out. Casey heard a man's voice. The car pulled away. She remembered seeing Anna's face; it was completely vacant. There was a bruise on the side of her neck. She just ignored Casey, as though she was invisible.

Casey climbed into bed beside Randy and slid into a dream world inhabited by the house in Cambridge. The place was filled with cobwebs; it had long been deserted. Someone was calling her from the long tunnel of webs. It was Anna.

# 7

"So, you are lunching with the Countess of Rigby, Anna?" Sidney Henderson raised one eyebrow on what was otherwise an impassive face. The face was long and drawn. His now silver hair stood out at odd angles from his head. He had on a black shirt with a rather strange-looking wing collar. But then Sidney was at his best with everything Gothic.

Sounds of clinking glasses and champagne bottles in ice buckets were coming from the lawns where groups of Anna and Justin's friends were standing, enjoying the summer evening and the first streaks of pink clouds moving into darkness across the sky.

Anna's mother had just left the group and had gone into the house to check on the arrangements for dinner. Her daughter breathed a sigh of relief that she had gone. Lucille held the secrets of Anna's childhood but would never disclose anything to her. And so, there was this uninterrupted tension whenever they were together. It was a silent collusion between them to never reveal the secrets of the family or the Hexagon Club.

Anna stood in the centre of the group; no one would have thought that three weeks earlier she had emerged from a near-fatal accident. She stood radiant in the long slim line of a black sheath dress. Dark braided hair framed the translucent skin of her face. Blue veins appeared on the surface of her neck. The dress was strapless with only a thin veiling of black lace over her arms and shoulders. Sidney stood beside her. She looked radiant. She had been laughing but now her face was sombre with troubled thoughts and grief.

The designer, world-famous for his Gothic interiors, felt himself to be at home in this group of friends. But he was acutely aware of the change in Anna's mood.

"Well, yes, we were thinking of going. I think it's a pretty big function. Why the interest, Sidney? Do you know the family?" asked Anna. A slight frown crossed her unlined face.

Jane joined in the conversation. "I received an invitation as well, but on my own, without Fairfax; it seems so mysterious, and in the middle of Shropshire too. We have the house nearby, such a coincidence." She looked at Sidney, waiting for an answer to Anna's question. Everyone was aware of the house where both Jane's parents had died, her mother of a dreadfully painful bone cancer and her father really from a broken heart, one year later. His books, now famous across the world, lived on without him.

"It's funny you should mention it," said Sidney. "Yes, Moira and I have met her. She lives in the South of France. We got invited to one of the gatherings at her house – beautiful place. She is what I would call 'an enchantress', She puts on these elaborate parties for socialites, big affairs. Then for months, she becomes a complete recluse and doesn't see anyone at all. I was going to do some work for her, but it never really came to anything, and the connection we had kind of petered out. Casey met her too; I think they kept in contact. The Countess liked her paintings and was going to promote her work in the South of France.

"There is a strange history attached to the family in England and France from way back, of course. The family received its title and privileges, and the house was built in the reign of George IV. The King loved the family, and Sir Ashley Cooper was his physician. There were some very peculiar stories attached to the family. Some say that they belonged to a cult; of course, it was the whole Gothic era then. The family were sorcerers of one kind or another, but Sir Ashley's brother, John Hargreaves, was very powerful. Amelia, the first Countess of Rigby, was his mistress. Then Amelia was murdered; a letter apparently reached her husband that had been found in the bedroom of the King – rotten business really."

Silence fell on the little group. Anna started to shiver. Her alabaster skin was tight on her cheek bones. How could she shut Sidney up so he did not reveal any more about what had been her past life. The air was becoming close; they heard thunder, but there was no rain.

Anna asked, "Well, Sidney, what about the house in France? What was it like, and why should she have wanted you to work on it? Surely it was already in order."

Sidney was aware of Anna's tactics in diverting him from talking about the family and Farlingham Park. He noted this, and Anna's pallor and shivering in the black dress. He wondered about her secrets and tears.

"I walked all over the house," continued Sidney. "It was a cold place, enormous. One wing that I visited had oil paintings stretching along vast corridors. There were paintings of French courtiers and English royalty – mostly early centuries, fourteenth and fifteenth. It was quite impressive, I must say. But how did you come to be invited to Farlingham Park, Justin?" he asked. One of the waiters was topping up his glass.

"Oh, she is a friend of Anna's, I think," said Justin, "one of the people she knows from the villa." He continued looking at Anna, weighing up every word, every move. She looked very gaunt now, looked frightened even. Was this because Sidney was talking about the first Countess of Rigby? Her beauty still captured him, but he no longer trusted her. Anna had felt a shift in the way he spoke to her after the accident. She could not understand it; she would have it out with him later, she thought. Justin would never show his rage. He remained polite but aloof.

"Darling, I don't know her at all. I thought she invited us because of your work," said Anna, taking Justin's arm. "Didn't we discuss it some weeks ago?"

"We are going for a weekend to someone we don't even know! We have accepted now so we can't back out. Really, we must check these things more carefully. It could be a terrible bore, except that Jane has been invited, and without Fairfax," said Justin, giving Jane a humorous wink. He pulled his arm away from his wife. They all saw the gesture and were amazed. This was a different Justin they were seeing.

Everyone noticed how roughly Justin was speaking to Anna. He seemed obsessed by her movements and was overtly critical and questioning. The others could not understand it; he was usually so loving and gentle with Anna.

"I would think carefully about going, Justin, I've heard some peculiar stories around families like these; people have had their lives turned upside down for no apparent reason. This life we lead is in a delicate balance; if you start messing around with people in touch with these forces, disaster could be around the corner." Sidney was looking perturbed. Justin and Anna had had enough tragedy, more than enough.

Sidney's wife, Moira, came to the rescue. "Such morbid conversation! Let's change the subject and have a little gaiety; after all, it is Anna's birthday. You are far too serious sometimes, Sidney. Why do you have to have these deep conversations all the time? Justin and Anna are only going away for a weekend, and Jane will be there too. What harm could possibly come to them?"

A butler was approaching. "It's actually time for dinner," said Anna, seeking further distraction from the conversation which was now making her feel ill.

Later that evening, a quartet of musicians came to play in celebration of Anna's birthday and more guests arrived. It seemed everyone was there that evening: her mother, cousins, friends, neighbours. It was one of the last happy nights that Jane would remember in years to come. She found herself wanting to capture every detail. She saw Justin several times that evening. It seemed his face, and not Anna's, bore the scars of the recent accident, the trials of their marriage and the disappearance of their son Giles. Jane wondered what it was about Anna. There was always that detachment, that other worldliness about her. Somehow, those close to her suffered great tragedy, but she was never really touched by it herself, except with Giles. The accident in the ravine was a perfect example; her chauffeur had met a violent death, but Anna emerged from the whole thing virtually unscathed.

Justin did take on Anna's pain. She never asked him to; he just wanted her so much. When they made love, she would captivate him to a point where it was almost unbearable for him. But when they were close to a real union, she would not let him penetrate her feelings. He was always standing outside her, somehow denied access to what he most desired. She had stayed just beyond his reach now for so many years: beautiful, tantalizing, radiant but not attainable. He never gave up; he kept trying. But now he hated her for her betrayal. He thought again of the black thread. He wondered with whom and what she did sexually with the black thread. It was beyond imagining. He found himself both aroused and disgusted by his own thoughts.

Later that night, Jane and Fairfax were driving back to Chiswick. He said, "Travers came to see me today; the house in Shropshire has become available again. He wants to know if we want to have more tenants."

"No, I don't want anyone else there. I'm going to completely redecorate it and make it a place I can go away to and be on my own. I can write there, take Cedric for walks." Jane was talking fast, as though some train of thought had set up a reaction that involved plans he was not aware of at all.

"But I thought you didn't like the house; last year, you couldn't bear the idea of using it," said Fairfax.

"Well, I have changed my mind, that's all. I'm entitled to do that." Jane was not giving away any secrets.

"Could it have any connection to the fact that it is close to the house that the Countess of Rigby owns? Really, Jane, I have never seen you suddenly so enthusiastic like this about any of your properties before." Fairfax was looking at her as she lay back on her seat. The purple velvet of her dress spread around her like a queen. He wondered how much he really knew of this wife of his. But Fairfax was patient; he didn't have to know all the answers immediately.

Jane's mind was elsewhere. She was back in her childhood which she had spent in the house they had just been discussing, remembering the secret garden that she had kept to herself. The whole place was wild and old: gardens, courtyards and walled gardens, stone-flagged corridors and high-beamed ceilings. Her father had taken her there for long periods after her mother had died, and they nursed their grief together. She loved her father, and he had done nothing but encourage her in her childhood. But he did not outlive her mother for long. And then she had been terribly alone.

Scenes returned to her that she had left unopened in her memory: the smell of lilies of the valley and the crushed lavender between the palms of her hands, the sound of Elizabethan music and her father's love for the harpsichord. She would hear the gentle tapping of the keys, as his hands spun out the music as she lay on the lawn by the overgrown fish pool. She used to lie down in a gingham frock on her stomach, looking at the fish winding in and out of the weed. Then there had been the autumn when they would go into the garden and catch the huge leaves falling in the wind and rain from the chestnut trees. Her father had told her that she could have a wish every time she caught a leaf before it reached the ground.

Wild with laughter, they would run this way and that, judging the wind and wondering which way the orange leaves would dance next on their way to the ground. Her father's name was Clement: tall, thin, surrounded by books. She remembered his bed, the double bed that he slept in alone, always on the same side as when his wife and her mother had left them, her body buried in the frozen Shropshire snow in the same churchyard where they had been married. Yes, his bedside table was stacked with books gathering dust in the late September days. He would read to her from the books he was writing, and she had stared in pride at the books he published one after the other in their bold print and their colourful covers.

She sighed to herself as they entered the gates of the Chiswick house. She spoke very little as she went to bed, still wrapped in memories of the house, a house that had meant too much to her. She made up her mind to go there. It had been so many years. Yes, she was ready now. She wanted to be near Farlingham Park, wanted to see it. She thought again of the jackal-headed figure, the spell, the incantation and the thousand small jewelled scarabs running through her fingers.

# 8

Justin was on a ward round at St. John's, a few days after Anna's party. He wore his best pinstriped suit for the many meetings that he had today. For a moment, he wished he were somewhere else. He felt his life closing in on him – the surgery, endless lists, administration, meetings, troubles with Anna. He thought of other possible lives away from this, where he could breathe freely and be himself.

He stared at the muddy river beneath the buildings. It was flowing rapidly this afternoon, like his mind, hating all the distractions of the day that took away any kind of time of his own. A few tugs were pulling a barge along the river, creating a soft wave of water along the banks. The sun, so rarely seen in the last week, was glistening over the water. He thought of Anna and their villa in France: the blue glazed tiles in the bathroom, the den where he kept all the family photos, pictures of undergraduate days at Cambridge, cricket. He remembered the first time he had met her – the white silky dress and her cold, grey eyes. How much he had loved her then.

"Sir, we are going to see Stephanie Arnold now." Dr Allan Greenberg, his senior registrar was speaking to him. Justin could feel his stomach knot up again. He had slight indigestion from a lunch taken in the private dining room with Sir Rupert

Spence, the Dean of the hospital. Sir Rupert had looked at him over the top of his glasses with their expensive tortoiseshell frames. He wanted Justin to go on a visit to Saudi Arabia. Justin had declined.

"But, Justin, this is such a great opportunity, both medically and politically. Besides, we would gain so much knowledge about theatre design; they have used the best architects in the world. There is nowhere else you can see a set-up like this," Sir Rupert continued.

"I'm not interested in where they put the taps. It's simply not my forte. Why don't you send someone else?" Justin was irritated by the suggestion of having to take yet another break from attending to the long list of patients awaiting heart surgery. He suddenly saw all the lines of harassed faces, the anxious wives and husbands along the hospital corridors, "Besides, I'm too busy to go, Rupert."

"I really would like you to make this trip. How about the first week in July?" Sir Rupert drilled on as though he had not heard Justin at all. Justin was beginning to feel nailed.

"Take Anna with you; it will do her good," was Sir Rupert's last remark. Justin could have strangled him. How dare he bring Anna into this! It seemed they had no private life anymore, the tragedies all over the newspapers.

For the first time, Justin began to be aware of Allan Greenberg in front of him. "Sorry, who did you say we are seeing next, Greenberg?" asked Justin apologetically.

"Sir, it's Stephanie Arnold. She has a private room in the children's ward. Stephanie is nine; her father is Paul Arnold, the famous violinist. He's a friend of Lady Bowlby. There is a hole in the aorta, very small and very inaccessible. They are aware of the danger that she is in. I would say that it's operable, but most risky." Greenberg spoke quietly. He had been to Anna's party. He was an affable man, soothing, thought Justin, as he allowed himself to be cajoled away from thoughts of the Middle East and the infuriating Rupert.

In the children's ward, Justin's first view of Stephanie was of the sunlight hitting her blond hair as she bent over a scrapbook containing rather crookedly cut-out pictures of horses. Hours seem to pass by, as he looked at her, drawn by something just out of reach.

She was very thin; her large brown eyes were framed by hair that had been tightly braided on both sides by an overzealous nurse. Justin felt he wanted to undo the braids. He could see the hair was pulling too much on the scalp. He resisted the temptation; it would seem silly. After all, he was her doctor. She had on a loose-fitting night shirt in brushed cotton with line after line of nose-to-tail sheep printed on the blue material. Her long arms hung by her sides and she sat in perfect repose, cross-legged at the end of her bed.

Justin introduced himself.

"I'm happy to meet you. My father says you are the cleverest doctor in the world," said Stephanie, solemnly.

Justin felt the blood run to his cheeks. He noticed that Greenberg noted the fact. For some reason, this little girl moved him. Her medical situation was extremely serious. Any surgery was going to be a risk.

"Where do you live?" he asked, appalled at the mundane nature of the question. He was tongue-tied and self-conscious in the little girl's presence. Why, he wondered.

"I live at school a lot. My mother is dead now, and my father travels all the time. I spend the holidays with him, wherever he is." She was staring at him with her round eyes.

"Are these pictures of your horses?" he asked, knowing full well they were not. But she rescued him by taking a serious interest in the question.

"No, not really, but they are really sweet. Do you like horses?" She really wanted to know. It was amazing; she was interested in whether he liked horses. He thought about it; yes, he did, in a way. He visited Anna's horses at the stables at their home, even if he didn't ride them.

"My wife has two horses," said Justin, wondering if she would pull back at the mention of his family. She didn't, and they went on talking about this and that. It seemed like he was in the room for hours. What was keeping him? He never spent long with patients. Ward rounds were usually kept to cut-and-dried business. There was never enough time to be there with people, really get to know them. It was the part of his job that he disliked the most – not enough time to get to know his patients.

Justin told Stephanie about her medical situation as best he could, and the likely tests that she would have to undergo in the next few days. He felt a deep sadness when he thought of the pain that she would have to endure. Her small arms would be bruised from all the blood tests. He knew the routine; his mind dwelt on it.

"Why are you so sad?" He was aware of her voice. Everyone else had left the room. They were alone. Before he had time to answer, she said again, "Don't be sad; I won't feel anything, I don't feel things, if I don't choose to feel them."

Justin stood in a sort of neutral territory. Instead of saying anything else, he removed the rose that he customarily wore on his lapel. He had picked the yellow rose this morning when he left the house. He handed it to her and went on to catch up with Greenberg,

Later that afternoon at about five o'clock, he called Anna. He pictured the garden and the house at that time, the rooms full of the scent of flowers and the garden warmed by the afternoon sun.

"Hello, darling, how are you? I'm just finishing off here. I should be home in a couple of hours. Felicity has just left for the day. What's happening this evening? Are Sidney and Moira coming back later?" Justin waited for her reply, always gauging the mood.

"Sidney has been at some tower all day, designing round rooms," said Anna dryly. Justin guessed she found this amusing.

"But they are coming back later," she continued, "and we are supposed to have some bridge tonight – dinner at the usual time." She didn't extend the conversation, and he was about to hang up.

"By the way, Justin, I was cutting some roses an hour or so ago. I picked them up rather carelessly for Julia to arrange. A thorn went right into my finger, quite deep. Do I need to do anything, darling, you know, tetanus and all that? I can't remember." Her voice was soft, pleading, almost like a little girl's.

"No, I wouldn't worry about it. I'll look at it when I get home. Bye."

It was at that moment, for some odd reason, that Justin felt that someone was watching over his life. He could not have said why. It was just a feeling; yes, watching over his life for some time now from a distance, maybe even from another country far away and yet intimately involved in his life with Anna. He also knew that there was absolutely nothing he could do about it. He tried, as he drove home, to remember the fairy tale about the thorn that pierced the princess' finger. Was the thorn placed before the finger for some reason? There was something happening, but he had no idea what it was. Was it Sleeping Beauty? But try as he might, he could not remember. It was a kind of fog that he moved in these days; his memory was terrible.

# 9

Jack's leather coat lay on one of the few chairs that existed in Casey's apartment. In the hallway, there were several long ornate mirrors. You could see the coat reflected several times. Randy was at school; her mum was still in the hospital.

Casey was talking to Jack about Anna. She noticed he had lost weight. Always an ambiguous relationship, they were never really at ease with each other. Jack's face was in a shadow. His fingers drummed on the edge of the chair. It annoyed Casey, as did his looking at his watch every five minutes as though he had somewhere to go; she felt diminished by it.

"Maxine is still missing. Yes, I know you are going to say that she is always missing, but Jack, this time it's different. I mean, I just feel it. She hasn't answered my calls, which is unusual. She always calls me, even when she is out of the country. Also, they haven't heard from her at the magazine either."

She went to get some coffee from the kitchen. Her head was aching with all the worry. Jack wondered whether something was wrong. He liked Maxine, but Casey was really close to her. He felt Casey was changing; they were drifting apart. They hadn't really discussed it. Casey hated any kind of separation. She always overreacted. Now was not a good time to discuss their future. She could get hysterical at separations.

He remembered Fabian had mentioned this when he had agreed to make the arrangements to date Casey. The money he had been offered to seduce her was huge, and he needed the money, so he took his chance. But he felt guilty about it too. Casey was very vulnerable and had been subjected to some hideous sexual situations in her childhood. But she was a good lay, so he went on with it. Fabian had then mentioned to Jack that he required photographs of Casey in the nude. This was a bit of a stretch, so double money was immediately put into his account. He went on with it all, doing everything that was required. Casey had no idea of the real set-up. She had been glad to have Jack for a while, to try and get away from Oliver. But Jack's embraces were never the same. She wanted her stepfather again desperately.

Casey returned with the coffee. Mimmy, the precocious cat, had taken Casey's seat so instead she sat on the floor. Jack wondered why Casey seemed to cater to Mimmy's needs so much. He would have shoved her off the chair, instead of just sitting on the floor.

"I think that we should go around to the apartment. I have the keys and the doorman knows me. Coming?" she asked.

"OK, I'll come, but suppose she is there, we will look pretty silly. Let's call her one last time," he suggested.

They tried but still the same message played back to them.

Maxine's apartment was on the Upper East Side of Manhattan, off Madison Avenue near 62nd Street. They took a cab uptown. The traffic was jammed. They nursed their Starbucks coffees in their hands. They looked at the crowded streets and shop windows of the bigger stores.

Maxine's father, Alistair Cleveland, was an ambassador in Thailand, and there were generations of wealth in the family. Maxine's apartment was vast. The doorman showed them up in the elevator. He knew Casey well. He said Maxine was away but usually she said when she was coming back.

"Not like her at all; always lets me know when she will be coming back, laundry, dry cleaning, the maid," he mumbled, half to himself, and held the doors open for them. All these things had to be taken care of on the Upper East Side of Manhattan. It all went with the territory.

The door of the apartment opened. It was a shock. Instead of the usually beautiful and ordered apartment filled with antiques from all over the world, everything was in chaos, and had been thrown around the room. Drawers had been pulled out and their contents lay in heaps on the floor. Flower vases and lamps had been overturned; two had smashed against the white marble floor, bits of glass everywhere. On the elegant French bureau was a mass of papers that had been ripped from the desk. Filing cabinets spewed their innards on the floor. Maxine's French fountain pens lay crushed on the floor, computers pulled apart, hard drives shoved open, USBs everywhere. The wall safe that lay behind one of the paintings hung open at a peculiar angle as though it had been wrenched off its hinges. Casey and Jack ran into the bedroom. Covers and sheets lay in disarray, and Maxine's clothes, or most of them, had gone. In the bathroom, the cabinets stood all open. Bottles had been pulled out and dropped onto the floor. Christian Dior cosmetics and perfumes were strewn everywhere. Many bottles had broken. All the other rooms were in the same state. The kitchen was the only place relatively intact. The place smelled of Indian incense sticks made with the essence of Mogra that Maxine always burned in her home.

Casey and Jack sat on the study floor in stunned silence, finding it hard to believe what they were seeing.

"We should phone the police, of course," said Jack at last, breaking their shocked silence.

"No, that may not be the best idea, and it could put Maxine in more danger." Casey was thinking hard.

"But we have to do something. We can't just walk out of here and pretend that we haven't seen all this. It would be absurd," replied Jack.

"I wonder what she would want us to do. I think we should call her father, but not from here. The place may be bugged." Casey got up to leave. This was the beginning of the change in her life she had recognized earlier, the 'something' she had dreaded. She was saying goodbye to a life; she would never be the same again. She looked at Jack; suddenly, he seemed like a stranger to her. Her feeling for him was gone – the longing for what was always hoped for but would never be, gone.

"Who would have done this to Maxine?" Casey was not aware of her friend's research, not aware that she had stumbled on the Fraternity, the Hexagon Club and all their dark secrets. Headquartered in England and shrouded in secrets, Maxine had come across the group quite by chance while doing research for Anthony's film. Men belonging to the Fraternity reared their daughters according to certain codes of practice. They were groomed; subjected to mind control, drugs and hypnotism; carefully guarded to be deflowered, their hymens removed, and their virginity taken at the age of sixteen. The Nazis also removed the hymens of women before they entered into arranged marriages in the 1940s.

She had discovered that they followed the practices of gurus such as Albert Getter, whose followers practised every kind of sexual perversion from Ancient Egypt and the Gothic era and beyond to the present day. The God Seth and his sexual codes led men into deviant relationships with young girls, women and same-sex relationships. Practices moved from the Egyptian culture through to medieval times and beyond. The erotic papyruses of Ancient Egypt showed clearly cave drawings depicting anal sex; one of the authorities even said these images were of one of the few Egyptian queens. The origins of the Fraternity went right back to the first Hexagon Club. Its headquarters were at Farlingham Park, the ancestral home of the first Countess of Rigby, Amelia. And sodomy was no stranger to them either.

The father would offer the virginity of his first-born daughter to his best friend within the cult. The members stopped at nothing, and it was thought that the more advanced the sexual activity and the younger the girl, the better chance of becoming a god of one's own universe.

Casey, of course, had no idea that members of the Fraternity were in her family, that her stepfather and Anna's father were very high up in the cult. She had almost no memory of her early years; she only remembered the terrible early relationship with her stepfather, and the first time he had trapped her in her room and had intercourse with her on the darkest day of her life. After that, she quite quickly had become addicted to him. He controlled her mind for many years, and she had become his, body and soul. His slave, there was no sexual practice that she would not do for him. As a child, he sought her night after night, holding her in his arms, his longing never assuaged.

Lord Oliver Pemberton was wealthy and privileged and was sexually addicted to young women and girls. The Fraternity took care of all his needs, and he was one of his best customers at the brothel in Mayfair and the weekly orgies at Thackeray Hall. He had never been found out, except there was a close shave with one young school girl in Hampstead, who told on him and what he had done to her. She was hushed up and ridiculed, and after Lord Oliver had given an enormous sum of money to the school to build a new science library, the child's parents were politely asked to perhaps send their daughter to another school.

His mother Agatha, an immensely wealthy tobacco heiress from one of those vast mansions in Newport, Rhode Island, set sail for England in her early twenties, determined to marry an aristocrat. His father Randolph, was indeed an aristocrat but became penniless, having lost all his money in gold explorations in South America. It was a perfect match; they married in style and lived an expensive life in Bloomsbury. But Randolph, despite his young son Oliver and his lovely wife Agatha, became deeply depressed and committed suicide by shooting himself in the mouth in the library of their home.

Agatha shut up the house and they moved to Cambridge. When Oliver had just started as a day pupil at a private school near their home, Agatha found loneliness too much for her and took Oliver to her bed every night. This strange, exotic and incestuous relationship went on for years. Finally, Oliver left for Oxford University, hardly ever seeing his mother again. He hated both his parents for depriving him of a proper childhood. From a young age, he developed fantasies about young girls. His whole life was lived around this deep pattern of sexual longing. Even Lord Fabian was shocked by Oliver's excesses but was paid handsomely for procuring young girls for him, so was only happy to oblige. Agatha, still deeply in love with her son, mourned him. On her death, she left him her vast wealth and all her estates. He was one of the richest men in England.

Oliver had it all sewn up; he believed himself to be untouchable, and his Harley Street doctor took care of any mishaps he had with the girls. Money took care of everything. Every so often, the police would question the family, but they were too high up in the social ladder and therefore untouchable; the questions led to a dead end.

Maxine was in danger, as she now held on her hard drive details of some of the members of the men in the Fraternity and could expose them to the press. Whoever had come to her home had been looking for those names and her record of them.

They closed the door on the chaos and took the elevator to the lobby.

"Everything all right?" asked the doorman.

"Yes, fine," said Casey as they walked out to 62nd Street. Jack went off to a photo shoot and Casey took a cab home. She felt something had broken inside her. Unbeknown to her, another car also took off from outside the apartment and followed her home.

Casey opened the door to her home and stood in the hallway. Jack had left his coat. She stared into the mirrors. "Mirrors," she thought. She remembered that someone once had told her the story about a dog. The dog had stood in front of a mirror and saw a dog like itself barking back at it. The dog continued to bark and bark and became so terrified that in the end, it lay down and died of fright of its relentless pursuer. Casey felt she was entering the house of mirrors, spells and witchcraft. Anna was not the only one in danger now; they would all be involved in the spells surrounding them. But she did not know what the danger was; it was invisible, reaping its revenge silently and wrecking all their lives.

Casey continued to stare at herself. In the last hour, her face had aged and changed. It would never be the same again. She couldn't go back; she was no longer there. Something was beckoning. Her face filled her with wretchedness; she had suffered too much. Deep down, there was a terrible chaos inside her, her childhood taken from her at too young an age.

She remembered the first time her stepfather had full sexual intercourse with her; it was night time, the house completely silent. He had crept into her dark bedroom, locking the door. Seizing her hair, he pulled her roughly onto the wooden floor. Ripping her nightdress off with one swift movement, he forced his way inside her, as she lay there screaming at his brutality. His tongue dug into her mouth. His vice-like grip brought bruises quickly to her arms and thighs. She was bleeding, her bottom lip was bruised. He was neither gentle nor patient. She felt ripped apart, seared by the indescribable pain. She thought he would never stop. He was like an animal. When he had finished, he left her there on the floor, unlocked the door and left; she could hear his footsteps going down the corridor. And then it was night after night for as long as she could remember – those footsteps, the door opening, knowing what was to come. She remembered waiting terrified, the panic, as he came again into her room. For weeks he was brutal until he turned her. Once she was in his trap, he was loving, but it had taken weeks.

She slowly became hooked on the endless cycle of pain and pleasure, the teasing and the slow seductions. His training of her had gone on for many years. He knew exactly how to make her his prey forever; she was in his trap now, never to be free.

The persistent ringing of the phone brought her out of her reverie.

"Hello, darling. Why haven't you called? I've been worried about you. Are you all right?" Casey's mother, Antigone, was calling from England. Casey felt that it was too late now for Antigone to worry, far too late.

Antigone, living in the lonely house in Cambridge, mostly on her own since Oliver gallivanted here and there, was reminded of the sins of both her husband and her daughter, perhaps her own sins too, in letting what happened in her own house to take place. She had known about the Fraternity. She and Lucille would meet occasionally to share the burdens of their lives, but they were bound by secrecy. In the dead of night, Antigone would hear her husband Oliver leaving their own marital bed and walking down the cold corridors in his slippers to Casey's bedroom. She knew that he would again force Casey to have sexual intercourse with him.

But within a year, Casey wanted it and then it became the norm. Antigone knew that Oliver had turned Casey. The experiment with their daughter had been a success. Antigone would watch Casey flirting with her husband; she was insatiable. Then there were the days when she would come home and find the house unusually silent, but then the door of Casey's room would slam, and she would hear Oliver running down the backstairs to his library downstairs. It was terrible for her. She was encased in everlasting grief – the loss of her husband who rarely had sex with her anymore and the betrayal of her own daughter. She developed eventually her own sexual tastes and interests far away in Oxford. She became part of it all; her husband had turned her too, and she became a full practicing member of the Hexagon Club. Antigone had entered a frozen space then from which she would never emerge. The guilt was enormous that she had not run to protect her daughter. It was forbidden by the Fraternity to obstruct the passage of the initiations.

Sometimes he had taken Casey, drugged in the back seat of the Jaguar, to one of the Fraternity meetings. There, he would share his beloved stepdaughter with the other males; eventually she would remember, many years later, her body put in the shape of a cross, spreadeagled on a board. Oh yes, years later, almost every memory would surface: the gynaecological surgery, the infections, the pain. Casey would remember the dim lighting and something being waved in front of her eyes, round and round and the words 'do not remember, do not remember'. There was a chalice of blood, and the people there wore strange masks, like dog heads. She remembered then being tied in certain positions and turned over, the blood from the chalice flowing onto her. There were incantations being sung.

One after the other, the men would come and lie on her, their organs shoved in her mouth and between her legs, over and over till she left her body and was looking down at herself while they defiled her. They penetrated her anus, each taking a turn and then there was nothing of her left for them and they would stop. She frequently left her body and when eventually she did have her memories, she would faint often, her arms becoming a sensation of pins and needles and then numb. She would lie for days in her room, silent, recovering. Her abdomen would shake uncontrollably with the shock and release of memory. But that was many years later.

Antigone had turned a blind eye. They all did, these wives, to the monsters to whom they were married. As young girls, they had suffered the same fate but were powerless against it. Doctors were sometimes called in, but they were all part of the endless circle of secrets. There was no escape for the mothers and none for the daughters for generations. All the families were from wealthy, high-born and privileged backgrounds, whose secrets were utterly safe. Their wealth and privilege could buy them out of anything.

"Yes, Mummy, I am fine," she said in her matter-of-fact voice that she had cultivated for her mother from the age of ten. It was all right if she said that everything was fine. On rare occasions, she thought her mother really did want to know if she was all right, But once when she had told her the truth that she was in an absolute mess and totally miserable, her mother had abruptly changed the subject and had started talking about the new curtains for the drawing room, so Casey had deduced that her mother did not on any account want to know how her daughter really was.

"Oh good. You heard about Anna, darling, didn't you?" said her mother.

"Yes," said Casey blankly. With the phone cradled between her neck and her shoulder, Casey made some notes on her laptop. She was making plans about Maxine.

"Must go, Mummy, I'm late for a meeting; I'll be in England soon, the middle of June at the latest." She wanted to hang up.

Her mother's voice was trailing off now with unexpressed feelings and resentments that she had borne over the last thirty years. Their conversations were always like this. Her mother's voice started in an enthusiastic tone, almost hysterical. Then it would drop a little at a time and then fade, the depression that was there becoming more and more evident. At this point, Casey would always feign an excuse to get off the phone.

With a sour feeling in her mouth, she made three phone calls. Then she went to the bathroom. It was a mess. She put all the face cream and makeup into a plastic bag. She added the toothpaste that she usually either forgot or that emptied its contents all over her luggage.

The phone rang again.

"Darling, I forgot to mention there was a phone call for you the other day." Her mother's voice was strong again.

"Who from?" asked Casey abruptly.

"Well, it was from someone's secretary; oh dear, I think I forgot the name. Let me go and get the piece of paper. Yes, here it is. The Countess of Rigby, she wanted to know if you would be staying at her house for the weekend in July." There was a pause.

"I have to go. There is a car waiting for me. I'll call you soon." Casey hung up.

Casey emerged from her walk-in closet transformed, dressed in a black Armani suit, her hair neatly drawn back from her face, fully made-up. She looked as though she had stepped out of *Vogue*. Casey was a chameleon. Now she walked out into the hall with its resplendent mirrors and surveyed her image. She was encased in a walled world; much of her past she could not remember now. She made a last phone call to a messenger service to have Jack's coat picked up from the doorman. That was the end of Jack, she thought. But Jack's photographs had already been sent on to Fabian. The deed had been done. Casey was completely unaware of their existence. In one arm, she carried her luggage; with the other she swooped up Mimmy and rang the next-door bell. A friendly arm reached out and grabbed the cat that Casey proffered.

"Sorry, can't stop, Richard. Cat food's in the kitchen. Randy is staying with friends till I get back."

"Limousine service," the doorman announced through the intercom.

"I'm on my way down. Can you send up the elevator?" She was ready.

Looking around the apartment, she wondered what her life would be like when she returned. Then she carried her cases to the hallway, the computer and briefcase, and got into the waiting elevator.

Already it was dark outside; the smells of New York's night air hit her with a memory of other exits from the city: traffic jams, tears, mists swirling around the top of the high-rises, Coldplay and then Mozart concerts at Carnegie. The night air brought it all back. She entered the limo, its windows darkened against intruders.

It sped off into the darkness, into tunnels and overbridges. Another car followed behind at a safe distance. Casey had an enemy, an enemy who did not want her to discover the whereabouts of Maxine Cleveland. But there was much more.

Reaching for the car phone, Casey called Daryl.

"This is Daryl on tape. Leave your name and number."

She let the line go dead. Who knows who was picking up Daryl's messages these days? She wasn't about to let anyone know that she was out of town.

The limo ploughed on into the night. Casey thought again about Maxine's apartment, the broken vases and the smashed bottles. Then she remembered the night that they first met. It was a full moon night in Connecticut. The party was wild, someone's mansion. The place was full of journalists. Maxine was the centre of attention, acclaimed for an article on Castro's personal life that had hit the press and stunned the world with images of his love life yet untold. Maxine had a way of getting inside other people's lives.

On that night, Casey had walked into a room upstairs. She had heard someone cry out. She found a man, half drunk, trying to pull Maxine onto the floor. He had his hands around her neck. Casey had come in just in time. She told the man to get out with so much force that she was even surprised at her own power. Maxine's dress was torn and one shoulder of it had pulled right away from her breast. Her long black hair was untied and had fallen all over her face. Maxine was tall, suntanned, stunning and now in tears. Casey had driven her home to her house, and they had spent the next two days together. They became such close friends that often they would think the same thoughts or have the same dreams.

Casey lay back in the seat of the car. She realized that she was aching all over and had a sore throat. That was the last thing she wanted. She had to remain alert. How were they going to find Maxine?

She was in the airport and was picking up her ticket.

"Window or aisle seat?" asked the stewardess.

"She wants a window seat," said a voice behind her.

"What the hell are you doing here and how did you know I was at the airport?" Casey was mad.

"I have an in-line to your computer. It came up on mine over two hours ago. Then my phone rang, and the line went dead. I knew it was you." Daryl was standing too near, his eyes summing her up.

"What are you going to Washington for, Casey?" he taunted.

"Well, that is pretty impressive," she said, stalling for time. She hadn't wanted anyone to know that she would be in Washington. Neither did she believe that Daryl had tapped into her computer. Why was he here? She felt a strange unease come over her. Was Daryl mixed up somehow in Maxine's disappearance? Was he too an enemy?

"So why are you here, anyway, Daryl?" she asked.

"Well, rumour has it that you are getting up to here in a situation that you know nothing about," answered Daryl, indicating his neck region with his hand in a cutting motion. "And you are my client, not to mention friend," he added.

But Casey's mind was gone. She felt at this point in her life that she didn't have a single friend and that from now on she was going to have to be on a razor's edge with everyone. She had stepped through a door and there was no going back. For her, neither Daryl nor Jack were there anymore; the cards had been reshuffled and a new deck was being dealt. These people, so much a part of her life, were part of a dead game. She turned on her heel and walked away. The flight was being called, and she was the first to board.

At the other end, she was picked up by Ambassador Cleveland's chauffeur. The car was not followed. They, of course, knew already. They knew where everyone was: Casey, Stephanie, Anna and Justin, Jane and Maxine. And then there was Anthony. The pieces in the game were being carefully positioned. Seth was the ruler and instrument of chaos and disorder. Everyone's life now in the group was in some kind of chaos. Each person was living a delusion of one sort or another. It was being masterminded by the God and his powerful minion, The Jester.

# 10

Anthony Jackson, son of Clinton Jackson, the shipping magnate, had kicked off his shoes and put his legs onto the chair in front of him. He was halfway across the world from England, in the Western Desert, burial ground of the pharaohs.

A dust storm seemed to be brewing. The horizon looked dark, and the temperature had risen steeply in the last hour. Markh trees, leafless, thorn-less affairs with their bare branches and slender twigs, stood like sentries outside the hotel. One or two women walked back to their shabby houses dressed in black, with their headdresses and scarves waving in the wind. Kites and hooded crows sat on railings and fences waiting for the storm. Anthony looked at the water and saw a crocodile slide on its flat belly to deeper waters and disappear. "Not a good sign," he thought. The crocodile was one of Seth's symbols. Whoever came across it would feel the chill of an evil omen.

It was nearing the fifteenth of July, astrologically the old New Year, the Julian calendar observed by the Ancient Egyptians. It was the day of the dawning of the Dog Star. It coincided each year with the rapid rising of the Nile. The date jogged his memory and then his mind went blank.

He was now at the edge of the desert, checking out yet another location. The chair that supported his long legs was in a small hotel along the banks of the Nile. It was a part of the river that was slow and sluggish and stank of dried fish and decaying guts. A very ordinary hotel, more for the locals really, but there was an endless supply of beer. The Egyptian beer could be as intoxicating as the famous wines for the special festivals of Bast, Sekhmet and Hathor, where people would traditionally get more than drunk in times of worship of these goddesses. Sekhmet was a deity of the sun.

Tonight, he had hired a group of camel owners and their men to take him into the desert to see the dunes by moonlight. He was exhausted. He didn't know why, but he felt drained by something inside him. Life was not quite the way he had imagined it when he had pictured taking on the movie. Since he had arrived in Egypt, it seemed that things had slowed down inside him. Sometimes, he wondered whether they had stopped altogether. On one level it intrigued him, in another way it was terrifying.

Personally, he was not happy at times when he had leisure. Immersed in his work, he experienced moments of great exhilaration and contentment, but when alone, he was restless and felt life to be meaningless. Materially, he had everything he could possibly want. Every dream he dreamt was realized the moment he thought of it, and yet it left him empty. The gods had made him sit under a wish-fulfilling tree but had withheld the meaning of life and the secrets of creation. It felt sometimes as though he was being tortured, shut out from anything but a one-dimensional reality filled with endless wealth and pleasures.

The imagined secrets hung over him like the grapes over Bacchus, never to be attained but always desired – the fragrance and promise so near and yet so far, impossibly out of reach. Now with the movie, it would be different. He was so close now. He had been excited by Maxine's visit. She seemed to know so much about the secrets of the pharaohs, the magicians and the sacred power of the Kundalini – the Serpent Power, as it was known. She was strangely excited about her impending trip to Paris. She had come across a cult called the Hexagon Club that was directly traceable to a cult dating back to the nineteenth century. They based their magic on Ancient Egyptian ceremonies and initiation rites. She felt she had found the leaders of this cult. He had pointed out the possible dangers, but she wasn't perturbed. They had agreed she would come back to Cairo after her research was completed. Maxine was extraordinarily optimistic about the outcome of the movie; she felt it would bring about a breakthrough in consciousness never seen before in the twenty-first century.

Anthony had not matched Maxime's enthusiasm for the myths about the exotic sexual practices of the Ancient Egyptian pharaohs; he was far more interested in magic and the power to become immortal and to taste the afterlife. They had many arguments when Maxine would say that the extremes of tantric sexuality was in itself a path to enlightenment. But it left Anthony cold and his own experiences now were of the upper chakras and not sensuality of the lower chakras. He was worried for Maxine, in the grip of her research about the cult of the Hexagon Club. These would be dangerous people. She was strong but there was a vulnerability to her that worried him deeply. She seemed in a way so driven.

Now when he stopped thinking about all these things, he felt a shift of consciousness take place. The gatekeeper had at last opened another gate. "Which one would open next?" he wondered. "The gate of the divine or the rasping gates of hell?"

Anthony went upstairs to his room. It was still light outside, but dusk was beginning to descend – still no storm. He had some hours yet, before he was due to go out with the camel drivers. He was alone here. The rest of the crew were back in Cairo at the Adelphi Hotel. As he reached his room, a deep despair filled him. He lay down on the narrow bed. The despair deepened; it was almost tangible. It was moving in waves across his chest; it was becoming hard to move. The best he could do was to lie still and let it pass. He waited. The pain wasn't attached to any thought, but it was intense. Night descended on the Nile. Dozing a little, Anthony awoke to find the pain gone.

He was out on the dunes now with the camel drivers, just the sound of a few animals like the Egyptian fox and camels moving across the sand. The scene spoke to him professionally.

It was the biggest movie that he had made. Being in the desert at night was like being on the face of the moon. Something within him was stirring. He was looking for possible filming and scenes for the camera crews at night. Everyone was excited; they talked of nothing else.

Back in his room, the window open to the full moon; he quickly fell asleep. He heard in his dream a voice calling him. He found himself alone on a beach. As he walked, he saw a speckled cobra coiled up on the desert sand. It wound around itself three times. He knew when he passed it that it would jump up and bite him on his neck. His steps dragged along, heavy as clay. He thought the snake was asleep, but as he was passing it awoke, flew in the air and bit him on the right side of his neck. At first, he thought he was being poisoned; his whole body was filled with heaviness. But this was a new energy, a sensation that he had never felt before; it moved into him bit by bit, reaching the ends of his fingers and toes.

At last, the dust storm hit. Anthony pulled the windows and shutters closed and retreated into the world of the dead pharaohs and to the remainder of the night.

# *11*

Jane was alone at her family home in Shropshire, standing in the walled garden. The wall was symbolic of the closed emotional space that she had shared with her family. She was an only child but was very close to her parents. Creative and gifted, they shared an inner life rich in fantasy and adventure. Jane had never lost that sense of peace and joy. She looked across the lawns to the empty fish pond. The garden seemed a wilderness to her now, paths lost and the topiary, once clipped to strange shapes conjured up by her father, grown wild into the size of trees. She thought it was just like Sleeping Beauty's castle. Brambles were everywhere guarding the entrance to the secret places, and the smell of wild flowers came from every direction where they had scattered their seed. There was complete silence. After the London streets filled with traffic, it was sublime. She wondered why she had ever chosen to go south.

She heard Cedric barking; the sound seemed far away in her reverie. He was always around leaping downstairs, staring imploringly into her eyes. He was a complete snob, regal and aloof, totally ignoring people if he chose. He would do this by averting his eyes. It was uncanny really and it was disconcerting to people. Sometimes, they would try to pet him to get his attention, and he would cow down to avoid their touch. Then they would be most offended, and Jane would come to their aid with some excuse or other. Fortunately, he liked most people, so it was only the odd occasion.

The barking increased, rising to rather a shrill sound for Cedric, and she ran into the house. There shouldn't be anyone around. She felt a sense of foreboding. Was someone spying on her, knowing that she had arrived? She felt chilled as she entered the cool long corridors of the house, the ancient flagstones worn in places by the tread of others from centuries before. The house was Elizabethan. As she walked the length of the house, she thought she heard the singing of falsetto voices. 'Eliza, Eliza', she remembered the song that had heralded Queen Elizabeth I's arrival everywhere she went. It followed the queen along the river, the barges alight with a thousand lamps. It announced her arrival at great houses, her horses thundering over the turf. Yes, thought Jane, Eliza had visited her house, had stayed several nights with her ancestors – Queen Elizabeth, her pages dragging her ermine train through the snow. Her footprints had lain in the snow, and the skates of a thousand people at court had cut figures into the ice on the ponds and frozen rivers of their land.

The kitchen door was locked; Cedric was on the other side of the door. He had locked himself in. He jumped all over her and then she let him out of the back entrance, so he could go and roam in the woods.

Jane noticed she had lost weight; she looked down at the waist of the jeans she was wearing, tugging at them and seeing the gap. She had on a shirt belonging to Fairfax, in pale blue cotton. It was soft to the touch. She noticed in the mirror in one of the downstairs bathrooms that her face was starting to take on an angular appearance. The red hair cascaded well below her shoulders. She remembered that they used to burn women with red hair. It was a popular belief that they were witches. Jane thought she looked like a witch. Violet eyes, the hair; all she needed was a broomstick. Anna's father did not like Anna to be friends with someone outside their circle, and especially a woman with red hair. It was not until years later that Jane understood why he had said this to Anna. At the time, it had confused her. She heard a tapping suddenly on the window and nearly jumped out of her skin. It came again, and then it stopped. She stealthily left the bathroom and crept around the outside of the house to find the window. But there was nothing there, so she returned to the wall garden, shutting out all possible intruders.

It was almost dusk, and the sweet aroma of flowers filled the air. The bees flew around hoping for a last drink of nectar before the heads closed for the night, encased again in their own beautiful worlds.

She sank into an old deck chair; the wood had long since shed any kind of paint. She found her thoughts returning to Egypt. She remembered her conversation with Casey in New York. What did she know about Anna that she herself did not know, and what was the spell to which she had alluded? Sometimes, she wondered what curses she had activated within her when she had finally fled the tyranny of the pyramids, the narrow dark corridors and high ceilings breaking apart her psyche. She had been so naive when she had started out. Her search starting with a mathematical formula she had come upon by chance at Cambridge. But Seth's evil form had somehow always hung over her, taunting and menacing, confusing her brain. Would she ever recover from the danger of delusions so inherent in the quest for the spiritual?

Her evening was filled with thoughts of Farlingham Park. She thought of the power of alchemy. What was the real meaning of it? It was like a transformative mantra. She heard the name of the mantra she had used repeatedly in Egypt, but she just could not really remember the real meaning. It eluded her. She only heard its sound.

The next day, Jane rose early and went down to the kitchen to find some food. She was starving, having forgotten to eat the night before. She hastily boiled a couple of eggs and slipped something onto a plate for Cedric. Today was the day. She hadn't told anyone she had decided to go and look at Farlingham Park. It excited her; she felt that something important was going to happen. It would be easy to find, and she could maybe wander around the grounds if no one was there. As soon as she had eaten, she gathered a few things into a basket; maybe she and Cedric would even have a picnic at Farlingham Park. She couldn't wait to see it. She wondered why she was so excited. It was good that no one else knew. Justin and Anna would not approve of this and Fairfax, well, he would think she was crazy. As for Sidney, one would not even want to mention it to him.

She took the Lancia and put the roof down so that Cedric could be in the open air. It was a perfect, perfect day. The map lay on the front seat and she took a cursory glance, knowing exactly where the Farlingham Park was in relation to her own house.

But by early afternoon, she still had not found it. They had been on several walks and had eaten their picnic. It seemed that she was going around in circles. Jane simply could not understand it. It was supposed to be just outside a village called Copthorne. She felt confused, could not remember things, as though someone was tampering with her brain. She had tried every road that led out of the village, asking a few people, but no one had heard of it and didn't seem to even want to talk to her. It was a strange, rather quiet village, she thought. Then along a road not exactly in a village, more like a group of houses nestled together, she found a shop.

Jane decided to go in. It was a small shop, typical of villages in that area, a place where people buy postage stamps and small children get candy and long strings of liquorice.

"Excuse me, but I'm a bit lost. I have been trying to find a house called Farlingham Park. It is supposed to be near here. Do you know it by any chance?"

The grey-haired middle-aged man on the other side of the counter looked at her for a while before he spoke. She was slightly unnerved by him; she wondered if he had even heard the question; perhaps he was deaf.

"Do you know..." She didn't have a chance to finish.

"Yes, I heard you the first time," the man said. "What do you want to go there for?" His reply stung her.

"Well, I have been invited there and I want to find it." The words were out, and she wondered why she had told him this.

After all, it was none of his business. She was glad she had left Cedric in the car and closed the hood. He would hate this man. There was something about him.

"It's up the road ahead; take a left. You will see the black iron gates in front of you. They are covered in ivy."

Ivy, iron gates, what was it? Why was her head swimming? The dream, of course, the dream, the one she had told Anna – the carriage. It was all coming back to her. He was observing her.

"So, you do remember what it was like then? Don't you remember me, Jane?" He was moving towards her now. But first he went to the door. Slowly, deliberately, he pulled down the shade. The window would now show 'Closed' on the other side. He bolted the door. The trap had been set and she had fallen into it.

She edged away from him. Her breath was coming in gasps, and her heart was beating fast as he drew nearer. Yes, she knew this man. His face had changed into that of another from a different life. Somewhere, he had been in the dream. Was he associated with her death? She remembered Egypt. Only there had she experienced this kind of power wielded against her, Seth, this man was serving Seth; she was sure of it. He had Seth's energy written all over him. She was terrified. Sweat was trickling down her back and she was dazed and confused; she was now out of time and space.

He was on her now, pushing her to the floor, pulling at her clothes. Her head hit the floor as his hands moved to pull at her jeans, pulling at the shirt. He ripped the zipper and grabbed her as she tried to tear at him with her free hand. He was tugging at his own trousers. She hit out at him, but her energy seemed to have left her. He lay on top of her, suffocating her. She tried to scream but no sound came out.

"I've wanted you for a long time, wanted to beat the life out of you. You and your little group, we hated them all. I will get you, every one of you." He breathed into her face. The acrid smell of stale cigarette smoke filled her nostrils, making her want to vomit. He forced his tongue into her mouth. His fingers dug between her legs, slowly gaining entry to her, the other hand at her throat. Her shirt was ripped. She kicked at him in the air.

Now she remembered, Farlingham Park. They had all been there in that previous lifetime, hence the dreams. She had lived at Farlingham Park, but as whom? She had been part of a circle of magic, practicing the dangerous ways of the Ancient Egyptian priests. They had performed a ritual; it had involved salt. Why salt? She just could not remember. Her mind was going... Then there had been the Hexagon Club. She remembered that and then all the magic, the strange sexual practices. Her head was spinning; she was unable to think. Then who was this man? And why did he hate her?

An unmistakable sound rent the air. The shop window flew out and exploded into a thousand pieces. Jane found herself in her original spot just inside the door asking directions to Farlingham Park. The man on the other side of the counter was patiently listening to her when he noticed she was staring into space as though she was seeing something. She was back in the present time.

"Are you all right?" he asked, obviously concerned.

"Yes, I think so. I feel rather faint," she answered.

"You look as though you have seen a ghost. I'll ask my wife to get a cup of tea. That will fix you up, and plenty of sugar." He went into the back.

The tea did settle her. He was right, but what had happened? She looked at her watch and her mouth fell open. It was two hours since she had entered the shop. She remembered checking her watch before she left Cedric, a reflex action.

"Well, perhaps you could give me the directions to Farlingham Park." She was ready to go.

"It's up the road ahead; take a left. You will see the black iron gates in front of you. They are covered in ivy." He was looking at her; these were the same words that were said before. She felt her memory jog again, and there was a pins and needles sensation in her arms.

She summoned all her energy to leave. The door opened, and she noticed that the glass had recently been replaced. Shivering, she made for the car. Cedric was whining to get out;

another sign that she had left him for over two hours. He jumped out of the car before she could stop him. He was running towards the shop, barking ferociously. She grabbed his head and pulled him away. He was frothing at the mouth. She looked down at her shirt and jeans. The zipper was broken, wrenched apart. Her shirt was hanging loose outside and torn. So, it did happen. But she was still confused. There had indeed been a time warp, a dangerous thicket of experience. She still could not remember about salt. She had just met The Jester in disguise. It was a dangerous place to be in.

Her enthusiasm for visiting the home of the Countess of Rigby had driven her to investigate ahead of time. Preparations were not complete, and she had inadvertently slipped into another dimension. It could have cost her life. Why had she been so naive and stupid? The Jester would have had it that way; he wanted her dead. It was just a question of time. His revenge had lasted for centuries. She and her friends and family had been pursued over the hills of time. It was never going to be over. They were all powerless against such evil.

When one steps close to the divine, timing is critical; one false move and a poor sense of balance could lead one to fall into an abyss from where there would be no rescue. To enter heaven, one must navigate the portals of hell; The Jester had all the moves ready for her. He wanted to trap her in the ancient web forever. He had been responsible for the deaths at Farlingham Park, but whose death? It was not hers. She started to remember some strange visitors at the house; it was so long ago now, but they were from the court. A thin figure of a man, strangely dressed, had spent days there, but why? As much as she tried, it was not possible to recall anything else.

Jane drove up the road. There, indeed, was the mansion, looking like a small cathedral, all buttresses and long elegant lines, the house of which she had dreamed, with its iron gates, the grotesque gargoyles, the long driveway, and the pointing finger of her dream. She knew this place, not only in her dreams but in life. It was familiar to her, as though it had been her own house. And there was the gatekeeper's cottage, now unoccupied. But the gates were closed; in fact, they were padlocked. She stood outside. She could perceive nothing and no one. In sheer frustration, knowing that she could never tell anyone, she burst into tears.

She remembered some things now: the death, her loves, being pursued as though by madness. The house became desolate after the death and became almost a ruin for over two hundred years.

Jane drove home; she felt so shaken by the day. She made some coffee and then went into the living room and lay on the sofa. It was then that she remembered her lifetime in full at Farlingham Park. It was there in every detail. Amelia, the Countess of Rigby, had been her sister. She knew suddenly that this was Anna's life and death. She remembered all the duplicity, the Hexagon Club and the nightly orgies, the worship of the Gothic beast, the terrible cravings, lust and longing of those days. It was truly demonic. Anna was the queen of this empire, Jane no more really than a horrified onlooker.

It was like a giant jigsaw where one or two pieces had been missing. Now the full picture was coming into place. Jane was aware now for some reason that Anna had also had knowledge of this lifetime, her death and torture, but she had never revealed this secret to Jane. Now Jane's past life was surfacing; it was like a dream, yet she was there experiencing that fateful evening. An image emerged fuelling her memory, like ripples of water taking her far below the surface now into the lake of her past life memories.

As Jane came out of the past life and memories of her time at Farlingham Park, and her sister's murder, her thoughts went immediately to Anna who had lied to her; it was Anna's dreams she was having at night, not her own. Anna had deliberately let her think that the dream of the avenue of trees, being in the carriage and pursued by the hooded figure of death, was hers. It was Anna who had looked into her mirror and seen Seth. Why had she lied? Who was she protecting? Jane now knew that Anna had already remembered she had been Amelia, the first Countess of Rigby, in that lifetime. Jane was terrified as to what the situation could really mean for them. They were in shadow play where they saw images of themselves projected onto the walls of their lives. There was no way out. The filmmaker would eventually remove the images, and their lives would no longer exist. Why had Anna not confided in her? Somehow Jane felt that Anna must be really on the side of the enemy, a servant to Seth perhaps, and involved in all his trickery.

Who was giving her these dreams? Who was this man whose photo she has seen next to Anna's personal things in the drawer? What was the meaning of the whip with the tasselled thongs, the redness of stains as though from blood? What was Anna doing? Who was she really? Jane felt shut out now from what she had thought to be a close friendship with Anna.

Jane could not use her logical mind to perceive these new realities; she would have to wait. She also realized that she could not approach Anna. She was going to be on her own now for a long, long time.

# *12*

"They used to bury their dead in a crouching position," said Anthony authoritatively.

"No, they didn't. That was the Celts," said his co-director Richard Abrascus.

"Look, it's like this." Anthony bent down into almost a foetal position.

Richard looked at his friend with a smile on his face. Anthony always made him think of some Greek god; sometimes he hardly looked human, so tall, with sea-green eyes and a mane of black hair tied back behind his head. His eyes always seemed to focus a little beyond everything he saw, as though he knew something that no one else knew. That and his talent won him a great deal of success.

"You are not looking, Richard; don't get caught up with looking at me. Listen to what I'm saying. You must get the gist; it's important." He went on demonstrating.

"They crouched like this, because it would protect them in their journey to higher realms. This position protects the chakras, the subtle energy centres of the body. In the Middle Ages, these were depicted as the wheels of fire; in the Tarot, they are painted like wheels, pentacles, representing eternity. The wheels are the true gates to enlightenment. Look at all the research that Maxine did on the first Hexagon Club. They had access to the secrets. They knew what they were doing."

Little did Anthony know about the Hexagon Club, that it was a left-handed path leading to not the upliftment but the destruction of souls in the fire of sexual depravity and eventual ruin. He looked at Richard with a sense of detachment. Would he ever get as excited as himself about this movie, this journey to the centre of the pyramid? A pyramid that was relatively unexplored, holding the secrets of the pharaohs and their serpent power, or so it seemed from their research.

"I still think that the Egyptians were buried lying down. Think of all the museums we have been to and the thousands of photographs of mummies. They are all lying down, Anthony."

"They were not all lying down. They were the ruling classes. They had to carry all their wealth with them and their protective luggage, wooden boxes full of hundreds of miniatures of the workers. Imagine, the labourers were not even mummified, and the courtiers scantily dressed in thin linen, unbleached and slung around them carelessly. People were often buried in a hurry, depending on the position of the moon and flow of the Nile. The peasants were buried in a crouching position, because that was the position in which they could best protect their kings and princes. No one can put up a fight in a prone position," he finished, triumphant.

Both men laughed at the ridiculousness of the argument. They laughed because they felt strong, invincible and far from the danger of death and disease. They sat in what was called the Hanging Gardens of the Adelphi Hotel; tiered gardens filled with flowers, palms, and sublime orchids. A white canvas umbrella hung, shading the table. Waiters hovered nearby. But the shadows were becoming long; the sun had had its heat for the day. They looked at each other, filled with a sense of their destiny of how great the movie was going to be – maybe Oscars for them both. They had it all mapped out, nothing could go wrong.

A week previously, Anthony had returned to Cairo. Soon after, the camera crew arrived and Richard had flown in from Los Angeles so they could direct the movie.

They fell into silence as the evening drew in, each reviewing their own feelings about the death ritual of the Ancient Egyptians. Anthony was also thinking about his dream of the snake bite. He had seen many such cobras depicted on the wall paintings of the Ancient Egyptians. Jung had written of the snake in his books, about the unconscious mind of man. Jung had written about the bite as the beginning of man's journey to enlightenment. For Anthony, the dream had changed him; somehow, he seemed to see things differently.

On the one hand, he was more alert, more conscious. Yes, there were times when he seemed to be drowsy, as though some new force was running in his veins. He found himself a little less sociable, wanting to spend time alone, and then he would fall into a state of what he assumed was meditation. It was powerful. He would sometimes see a blue light, vivid, for a few seconds in front of his eyes. He thought of sharing his experience with Richard but somehow there was never the right time for the conversation. Perhaps he wouldn't understand. Yes, it was best he kept it to himself.

Richard left soon after their discussion. The next day, they were going to view the pyramid. It was a small one, but only one section had been opened and not to the public.

Anthony returned to his suite, and there was a knock on the door. "Yes?"

"It's Sean," came the voice from the other side, an English voice. Anthony let him in.

"Vince just called from London with odds and ends. The manuscripts that we want are proving incredibly hard to get hold of. Mostly, they are in private collections. There are some messages as well." He thumbed through some papers. "There was a call from the South of France, Emma Rigby, known as the Countess of Rigby. She actually called herself and spoke to Vince. He said she had the softest voice; he was tantalized by it, said it soothed him so much he almost fell asleep."

"What did she want?" asked Anthony, impatiently. He had heard something about her but couldn't remember what. Somehow, he knew it was connected to Egypt.

"Oh, nothing much! She wanted to invite you to a special thing she has arranged at her country house in Shropshire."

"In Shropshire? But I'm in the middle of a film in Egypt! I can't just go waltzing off to England. I suppose it's soon." He looked at Sean – straight out of college but with a mind like a razor blade. Anthony had picked him because he had a First from Oxford and because he knew nothing about the film industry but plenty about applied mathematics.

"I can't go, Sean. Send a message, a nice message through Vince in London. God, he must be out of his mind."

That night, Anthony could not sleep. Something was bugging him. What was the connection between Emma and the pyramids? Was he in danger? Why had she invited him to Farlingham Park? He had heard of her, of course, but from whom? Was it Maxine who had mentioned her? When he finally did fall asleep, he saw in his dream – no, it was not a dream – a house with long windows and grey brick stood before him. It was built like a cathedral. Huge gargoyles looked out from under the roof. Walls ran from the house to form courtyards and gardens. There was a lake and woods. It seemed enchanting to him, very Gothic. He was coming down a long driveway, walking from side to side as though he was drunk. Rain created mud that swum around his feet. The house still basked in the sunlight. Anthony's steps were getting slower and slower.

A carriage was coming; he could not move to get out of the way. The horses, all black with plumed headbands, were at a gallop. Then he saw the strange animal-headed God Seth astride a huge stallion; he was galloping towards him. Anthony cried out, but his voice was lost. The horses and carriage were nearly on him, and he had slipped and fallen in the mud. He woke up covered in sweat, in fear of his life. His room was in darkness. He felt he was going to die.

Anthony had read that Seth was depicted with an animal head. He represents everything that threatens balance and harmony in Egypt. The brother of Isis and Osiris, he was the God of war, chaos and storms. He was devilish and created endless chaos and confusion in the minds of men. He had, according to myth, sodomised his nephew, Horus.

Anthony was also dreaming of his own past life at Farlingham Park. But for him, it was just a dim memory. In fact, in this lifetime, he was James Wetherby, the editor of a medical journal. He had accompanied Sir Ashley Cooper many times to Farlingham Park. Wetherby had relentlessly sought out The Jester, because he suspected that he was depriving King George IV of Sir Ashley's ministrations as a physician. The Jester wanted Wetherby dead, because in a previous life he had been part of the death plot against The Jester in his past incarnation, as a magician to the Pharaoh in Egypt. Wetherby had met Amelia too before her death. But Anthony had no recollection of names. To him, it was just a fog of memory.

Unknown to Anthony that day, The Jester had been behind the carriage in which sat Amelia and Jane, in their former life. He had seen the same God of Death and Destruction that Amelia had seen in her mirror – Seth, The Jester's own lord and master. Anthony's memory of being almost run over by the carriage was his own delusion and the overwhelming trauma of the past life experience. But it was in London that the poison was delivered to Wetherby's office that would end his life. It bore the stamp of Sir Ashley and so Wetherby had swallowed it thinking it was a potion for him after some recent discussion with Sir Ashley about his health. He died some three hours later. It was The Jester's doing.

The poison was from the infamous Upas tree from South America, one of the most poisonous trees in the world. Pushkin's poem 'Ancha' describes the tree as standing alone in the world. Only some black whirlwind dares to disturb the poison tree, he says. The tree itself becomes pestilential, and where does this contagion stop, he asks.

It was then as he lay dying that Wetherby knew that The Jester was not only killing him but also had murdered Amelia. He had been aware that Amelia had a lover who had enchanted her. She had lain with Sir Ashley's own brother, John Hargreaves. Sir Ashley felt that the Hexagon Club had put a curse on the house and all who lived there, but it was really the King's jester who had caused the nightmare. He was the magician of delusion and bestial sexuality. The Upas tree, the poison that brings down pestilence upon his victims, was The Jester's weapon. It seeped into man's heart and soul, causing utter destruction and death. It turned a man's mind to the demonic.

Sir Ashley could hardly bear to think about Amelia's death; she had been wearing a black thread. He knew about these threads from the club; they were toys of lust. He feared the Hexagon Club and its members and ended his membership. It had brought about ruin and destruction to his family. What had they been thinking of to allow these forces to enter the house? After Wetherby's death, Sir Ashley had the house boarded up and the gates padlocked. But then soon after, he too was killed by The Jester. The house became deserted and feared by everyone for miles around. Ghosts, it was rumoured, haunted its ramparts.

Anthony was unaware of all this and of his life as Wetherby, and it was to be Emma that told him the full story of his past life and the dangers of the present time. The Jester wanted him dead again. It was Emma's protection that saved him.

Sean was in another room at the Adelphi. He was immersed in measuring yet again the dimensions of the passageway from the Queen's to the King's Chamber in the pyramid. Huge maps were everywhere, and he was calculating in royal cubits. The measurements from floor to ceiling did not vary by one sixteenth of an inch – a miracle in numerological exactness. He was now considering the Northern and Southern burials of the pharaoh. The Southern burial was for the 'Ka' or spirit of the pharaoh. This was where Anthony wanted to work. Every pharaoh performed a ceremony of regeneration every thirty years, so they could remain young forever. Anthony wanted this very power.

Anthony now knew the chambers and where their secrets were held. The burial place of the 'Ka' had to be aligned with the celestial North Pole – the dead king ascends to heaven to join the indestructible stars. Sean figured the spells they had found in some of the manuscripts were connected to each stage of the pharaoh's resurrection. Anthony wanted the secrets of the magician for the pharaoh's journey to the next life. He wanted the secrets of eternity. If he were a magician, he knew he would enable the deceased and the living to pass by the various guardians of the netherworld. Anthony wanted the magician's secrets.

But the magician, now in the form of The Jester, had other ideas. Sean knew there was a spell already in force against Anthony. It spoke of driving off a crocodile that draws near to take away a man's magic. The crocodile is one of Seth's symbols. The pyramid contained 'the House of Life'. Here were the magician's secrets, his images of wax from which he made himself repeatedly. If these secrets were found, he would no longer exist in anyone's form.

Sean's thin legs in white jeans were wrapped around the chair that he was sitting on. He wore a black turtleneck covered in white paint spots. The rest of the paint was on a complete replica to scale of the pyramid that Anthony and Richard were filming. Sean was making sure that Anthony would never find the House of Life, but the House of Death instead. In Sean's notebook was an image of the animal-headed God, Seth. No one really knew what animal this was. Sean bowed to him and then erased Anthony's name from all the documents he had. The spell of erasing the name meant that Anthony would cease to exist. "The word is the deed, saying makes it so," he said over and over again into the face of Seth.

The Jester wanted to make sure that Anthony never found the House of Life, but only the House of Death. Sean had created a false map that would lead to Anthony and Richard's certain deaths, once they were in the pyramid.

# 13

Maxine was covering the unusual story of a film director, Anthony Jackson, turned mystic, who had uncovered some ancient secrets of the pharaoh's magician. He had stumbled upon the whereabouts of the secrets by chance. The Kundalini, secret of rejuvenation and of entering the netherworld while still living, was one of the possibilities. A power lay in the temple they were about to film. For a world with an appetite for the Holy Grail, the magic world of Harry Potter and the possibility of other lifetimes, the press was hot on Anthony's heels. Maxine was close behind.

Maxine's research had gone far and wide and had led her to Paris. She had uncovered stories of an occult group called the Hexagon Club, its roots in the cult of Seth. The cult had been very widespread, and drew on sacred religious rituals practiced during the pharaoh's time in Egypt. A papal bill had been issued condemning the cult and declaring that all women who were found to be witches would be burnt at the stake. In those early centuries, fear and paranoia had swept like wildfire throughout the European continent. All manner of people had been accused of witchcraft and were either imprisoned or burned at the stake in the centre of the towns. Most cults and their activities were forced into hiding, and the prophets of the day were only allowed to speak or write of their secrets in the most veiled terms. Women were accused of stealing men's powers through the sexual act, and women generally became suspect, and in men's eyes, dangerous. Even a look from a woman to a stranger could become a dangerous thing leading a man to fall into the clutches of the Devil. Men preserved their semen, avoiding sexual activity except with their wives, and ran to church every day for the masses. Fear and delusion were widespread.

These cults, their occult power still intact, had survived to the present day. The Hexagon Club was the most powerful. The paths of the cults were often guided by the richest, most influential families and their power and practices had spread to many countries in the Western world. Maxine had the facts, but she was also an innocent with no real idea of the power of these groups, what they could do or the danger that she could be in.

Drugs, sex, incest, deviant sexual practices and even human sacrifice had been practiced among these groups. In Western terms, they could be seen as worshipping the Devil himself. In Ancient Egypt, it was the God Seth.

Maxine had already stayed in Paris too long. She had opened her eyes wide and asked questions in dangerous places. An irresistible pull had led her to track down more and more people who could lead her to knowledge of the cult members. She wanted to have a first-hand experience of the Hexagon Club. She could not be satisfied with anything less. It was to be her downfall, and who was to know that she would be enmeshed and bound by the present-day President and owner of the club, Count Fabian Roth.

She was invited to a party that was being held outside Paris. She had a feeling that this would bring the answers for which she was searching. She had become wild, her need to be on the razor's edge again, pushing her into dangerous situations.

She caught a train to a small place called Valancin. She was alone. The village seemed deserted. Tall houses with their shutters closed stood on either side of dark winding streets. It was summer. The trees were burnt as though by some fire, the branches bare, a cold chill was in the air. There were no children playing in the street; no one was around, A rat, the only living thing she saw, ran across the road in front of her, making her jump. She walked on, eventually rounding a bend in the road. In front of her was an avenue of shar, pointed Cypress trees.

At the end of the trees was the mansion. The place was enormous, but most of the windows were shuttered and the house looked boarded up. The garden was a ruin; the long grass blew carelessly in the chilling breeze. Maxine was starting to doubt whether she should have come when the door of the house, a solid oak structure, opened to reveal a woman in her forties, glamorously dressed; on her head was a platinum blond wig.

Other people had already gathered in the house. It was a smart set; people whom she recognized from the press, politicians, society hostesses. There must have been over a hundred people in the elegant drawing room. Maxine was swept into the room as though pulled by an invisible energy. But she felt isolated. The other people across the room were political figures, but there was something strange about this crowd. It was as though they all had a common purpose. When they realized she did not share it, whatever it was, they just walked away. There were meaningful glances between people. This wasn't just a social gathering; they were here for a purpose. But what purpose? She was soon feeling an outcast in this group.

Maxine felt out of her depth; no one else spoke to her, and people moved off into other rooms in the house. She went upstairs, looking for a bathroom, walking silently along the thick-piled red carpet. As she was turning into the bathroom, she heard a moan from one of the rooms. The door was closed. She listened outside. There were whisperings, incantations, strange music like a Gregorian chant, then moaning, shrieking, like one of deranged ecstasy. Voices were whispering in her ears from some other sphere, then silence. She heard someone coming and moved away from the door into the bathroom.

The bathroom was a large room, decorated in red-embossed wallpaper, and the floor covering was the same rich red carpet that was in the passageway. Reclining chairs covered in red velvet were set along the walls. There appeared to be no windows. Two small chandeliers dimly lit the basin with its ornate gold taps. On the other walls were some Egyptian paintings of young priestesses. Maxine felt overcome by a strange energy; she felt like sinking into one of the chairs, but instead, she remained standing.

Maxine turned her head away and then looked at herself in one of the French mirrors. It was a long mirror, and she took a good look. Shocked by her reflection, she did not see herself. She was staring into the face of an Egyptian priestess, one of the women from the pictures on the wall. She was in a state of complete disarray. Her dark hair was long and matted and was stuck up high with long ebony pins. An almost transparent robe of black silk had been cleverly pulled sideways, away from her body, by the man standing behind her. Her breasts hung heavy and bare.

She was now naked beneath the gown; her belly was pressed against the basin. She was half bent forwards now clutching to keep her balance, her knuckles white. The man behind her had every advantage; she felt the expertness of his touch on her skin. Then he forced her harder over the basin, insistently pulling at her hair and dragging her head backwards. Her spine was tight, unable to move.

In a strange series of movements, the man whom she could not see overcame her. She found her body moving with his, as he found the vulnerable place between her legs. She offered no resistance as would have happened in real life. It was like a dream. Her energies spiralled higher until she felt herself orgasm, her body cascading somehow back into the black fabric of the gown. It was like an image from another world. In that moment, she knew that she had become something else and would never return to who she had once been. It was as though in that one penetration of her, complete and absolute, he had taken her very soul.

And then he was gone, she was looking at herself again, her own image. She was sore and bruised. The past reflection vanished into nowhere. She was drenched, beads of sweat stood out on her forehead. Her skin, always suntanned, had become pale, and there were dark circles under the eyes. Her hair was dull and lifeless. She stuck out her tongue. It was covered in a yellow film. Still reeling from the shock of the first image and the pain caused by the man behind her, she threw up into the basin.

Maxine tasted the sourness of her own bile. She was too thin. Her arms looked like scarecrows' in the black cocktail dress. Tomorrow, she decided, she would leave for America. She had lingered too long and now she was in danger. Anthony's counsel to her had been right. She should have known better than to enter this kind of power. She knew already she was lost. Someone was playing with her mind, watching her. She could have cried at the way she looked.

She crept out of the bathroom and heard the front door slam. Someone else had arrived, but late. Her stomach turned over. The house seemed too dark, kept that way, she thought, by people who had too many secrets. Her body still hurt and, aroused, she felt violated by unseen forces. She was aware that she was still on a sexual high. This was an initiation. Her father always pressured her not to lose her virginity before marriage. Slowly, she walked down the curving staircase, the banister polished walnut. The end of the banister at the bottom of the staircase ended with the head of a wild boar carved of the same wood, its claws clasped around the body of a snake. Yes, she remembered this banister; it was in the paintings and diagrams kept in secret at the first Hexagon Club housed originally in England, at Farlingham Park. Her own past life memories were returning.

Her first view of Count Fabian Roth was the back of his dark navy suit. His hair was black and longish, falling straight and some few inches beyond the collar of his shirt. The first thought that came into her head was Seth. When he turned around, she noticed his eyes were also black. He looked immaculate, impeccable. Maxine found herself breathless. His eyes took her in, penetrating her soul.

"So, you are Maxine." He smiled and bent a little forward in a mock bow. "I have heard so much about you, and you are becoming quite famous. Your journalism is, I believe, bewitching us all, is it not, Madame Roche?" He turned to his hostess, the woman in the blond wig.

His every move flowed effortlessly, a man whose power and word were never questioned. Maxine felt the strong energy. His eyes held her and took in every detail. She instantly both adored and hated him. He was both the sweet one and the cruel.

"Maxine, allow me to introduce you to Count Fabian Roth, one of our leading international industrialists. He owns many of the steel industries across Europe." Madame Roche paused, summing up Maxine's responses.

Maxine didn't say anything. She felt completely drained of energy. She walked away across the room to the sofa and low easy chairs in front of the fire. Most of the lighting in the room was from small table lamps with yellow silk shades. It was subdued. The crowd that had been there previously seemed to have gone. It was a huge fireplace, the fire glowing and warming. She stared into it. Someone offered her a brandy. She rarely drank but she accepted it. Time had stopped still, and she had long forgotten who she was at all. She drank another brandy, not even remembering who had given it to her.

Her breasts felt sore, the nipples still pointed, her body strangely on fire. The Count was standing a short distance away from her in conversation with various people. But he would turn and look at her, his eyes devouring everything about her, knowing everything. He thought about how long he had waited for this moment and the secret small album he had kept of her photographs: pictures of when Maxine was a little girl, then ten and then fifteen years old, her sixteenth birthday and then more recent pictures from the South of France. Oh yes, he had waited a long time, planned this moment. He felt intoxicated; the scene in the bathroom, yes, she had felt him take her, had seen herself in the mirror as the Egyptian girl.

Yes, he thought Maxine was still a virgin, had been carefully prepared by her father for Fabian alone. Maxine had never slept with a man. Her father had forbidden it. Already, her mind had been programmed and guided all those years ago. She thought nothing of it really, never compared herself to other girls. After all, Alistair, her father, another leading member of the Hexagon Club, had taken Maxine there when she was a child. Like all the daughters, she was subject to mind control. No wonder in her adult years, she was drawn to such a place and this very party. They had done nothing to her at the club, maybe a dalliance here and there, a soft touch, nothing to sexually awaken her, no question of a deflowerment.

But in her mind, maybe she had perhaps seen too much. They had taken her into the rooms of the club, let her watch the sexual partnering, the young underaged girls being deflowered by older men. This could have created in her an appetite for the bizarre, for living on a razor's edge. None of this she remembered, not until many years later. Her father was an expert groomer. Maxine had no idea of what had been done to her from the time she was a small child. Even her meeting with Casey had been arranged; Lord Oliver was a good friend of Alistair. They set up the meeting suspecting the girls would develop a close bond; after all, they had both been programmed at a young age. But Casey's path had been so different, and Oliver had secured Casey for himself. He hardly let her out of his sight. Some said he was obsessed by his daughter.

Maxine sat mesmerized by the fire and the alcohol; she was sliding into a space she knew was both comfortable and dangerous. She had no idea of the danger she was in. She had had too much success too early and now, she was becoming a pawn in a much bigger game.

Already it was past midnight. The drawing room was almost deserted. She stayed alone, slumped in the velvet chair. The Count lifted her up and helped her with her coat. Then they walked out of the house and into the waiting car. The chauffeur closed the doors. She offered no resistance.

"I'm taking you to the chateau, my home, Maxine," he whispered to her. Her hands looked so white against the dark blue of the coat. She didn't hear him; she had fallen beyond sleep.

The car moved off into the night. She did not wake up again until the first light of dawn when they had reached the South of France. The black stretch limo was standing in front of modern electric gates, waiting for a signal from the house. The gates opened revealing an exquisite scene. The driveway wound ahead of them. Vast lawns gave way to a wide lake in which swam black and white swans. Two peacocks stood motionless on the green expanse, cautiously watching the new arrival. The chateau was surrounded by water and stood with its green copper roofs majestically overlooking the surrounding countryside. Tall pointed turrets looked this way and that. Behind the chateau in the distance was a slowly moving river with several ornamental bridges. A central drive led up to the entrance of the chateau. It was lined with marble statues of nymphs and mythical figures. Two huge statues of elk hounds stood outside the entrance and doorway. She had never seen anything as grand or as beautiful.

"Where the hell are we? Why didn't you take me back to Paris? What is this place?" She tried to get out of the car but it was locked. He gently restrained her.

"Maxine, I want to show you my home. Of course, you can go when you like, and I will arrange for you to leave for America, if that is where you want to go." His voice was soft, well-modulated. He saw her relax a little.

The car drew up to the entrance, crunching on the tiny white stones of the driveway. Maxine felt stiff and sore, as though her body was not her own anymore. Her head ached from the alcohol and she longed to lie down. The house inside was as sumptuous as the outside: cool greens, silks and light. He took her up to the room that he had decided would be hers. It was on the second floor. It was decorated in pastel blues and overlooked the river. One of the ornamental bridges was visible. There was a four-poster bed with trimmings of the finest white gossamer lace. There was a suite of rooms for her and a bathroom.

In any other situation, she would have been overjoyed to stay here but now, like this? And then it was as though he had read her mind.

"Maxine, you are not well. We wanted to bring you here for a rest. Just see it as part of the Parisian hospitality."

"I don't want to stay here, I want to go back to Washington," she said, but she was already feeling exhausted.

"You should rest now. I will have some breakfast sent up to you. Now you are tired; you will think differently when you have rested." He slipped out of the door. She was alone, trapped in this beautiful room. Then she went into the bathroom. She still had on the black cocktail dress. Her mascara had rubbed off her eyes onto her face, and she looked a total wreck. Washing off all traces of makeup, she put on the silk nightgown, winding it loosely around her. When she came back into the room, there was a breakfast tray, flowers and a newspaper, the *New York Times*. "Oh God, Casey, where are you?" she thought. She opened the paper seeing things so familiar and yet so far away. It was torture.

Down a hundred or so stairs, Fabian was on the phone.

"Call the hotel. Tell them Maxine has had to leave Paris unexpectedly and that they should have the things sent to the house in St. John's Wood. I have everything she needs here. No, there isn't anything else. Has Sean called from Cairo? Yes, send him the instructions that I had prepared; tell him he must follow them exactly. I don't want any mistakes. Get someone out there to track his movements and then get him out of there afterwards." He slowly put the receiver back.

He had made sure Maxine would sleep well all that day and into the night. He had added something to her coffee. He wanted her rested for the night. He again climbed the wide staircases. Ancestors looked down on him from the paintings on the walls. Now he was on the second floor where Maxine was already asleep.

She lay across the bed, not even in it, the silk robe still wrapped loosely around her. He smiled. Her head faced him, the delicate line of the jaw, her lips slightly parted, full lips, beautiful breasts. The light lace curtains were drawn across the windows shading it from the sun but creating a delicate blueness around the room. He sat beside her studying her. He eased the silk gown away from her body caressing the soft skin, as his hand trembling with desire moved slowly downwards, lingering and then moving on. Then he stood up and left the room. At last, she would be his. He had waited so many years for her.

Maxine slept on into the night unaware of the Count's frequent visits to her. When the moon was at the highest point in the sky and the lace of the curtains failed to keep out its luminosity, he came again to her room.

Maxine, still half asleep, still drugged, found Fabian seated beside her. The gown no longer covered her. He moved quickly to lie next to her. Curiously, she felt no resistance, as though this moment had been made for them forever. He rested himself against her belly, massaging her and arousing her. He stroked the large breasts and slid his fingers into the crease of her buttocks. She cried out then, wanting him, but he made her wait. He teased her, made her put on a mask; but she ripped it off wanting to see all of him. Never had she lain with a man. She felt that she had belonged to him forever. And so, in a way, she had.

"Where is she?" asked Alistair Cleveland. Casey and Alistair were sitting by the empty swimming pool at his house in Virginia. The dead leaves from the previous winter still lay in strange designs at the bottom of what was usually, in the summer, an expanse of turquoise blue water behind the opulent residence. A light summer wind blew around them as they sat in silence. The pool, as empty as it was, became a reminder to Casey of the emptying out of her own life. She didn't feel she had a life. Maxine's apartment in New York, the splintered glass, the fractured vases, had broken her own psyche into too many pieces. She didn't answer Alistair's question; it didn't even seem like he was expecting an answer.

Later that day, she walked into the woods; the silence of the trees enveloped her. Her feet made no sound upon a ground made soft by winter after winter of pine leaves lying upon each other, becoming the very soil out of which, the trees were growing.

Casey had no idea that for decades, Maxine's father, Senator Alistair Cleveland, now at the dizzy heights of his own career in American politics, was a long-time member of the Hexagon

Club. The group included her stepfather, Alistair, Anna's father, Professor Richard Carrington, and many other high-ranking and wealthy men. Count Fabian Roth orchestrated this group, saw to their needs and procured the young women and girls. These men would meet every few months at Thackeray Hall in the country where young girls from twelve to twenty-one would favour them with sexual pleasures and normally out-of-bounds activities. These men thought nothing of their sins. They were firm friends and extensively shared their sexual exploits and tastes with each other. During their time away, they would sometimes work a girl as a group, shutting themselves away with just one girl at a time, securing their lustful tastes. Occasionally, but not often, they would sodomize each other making the bond between each other even stronger. They had seen and heard Seth at this work of bestiality back in Ancient Egypt. He even came in their dreams, titillating their senses with orgiastic ceremonies.

But Casey knew none of this except the devastation of her deflowerment by her stepfather that had happened so long ago. There was always a part of her that yearned for him; even thinking about him created an arousal in her. She remembered he was insatiable and could not get enough of her. Almost every night, he would come to her room in the dead of the night, his hand over her mouth to prevent her mother from hearing her sobs and young orgasms. But then she wanted him, was obsessed and longed for his visits. He had slowly and carefully turned her into his creature.

# *14*

Stephanie was now out of hospital; she was dancing slowly, rhythmically around on the same spot. It was her tenth birthday and she was wearing one of Anna's huge hats with a brim that almost entirely hid her face. The hat had a little pink lace edging. They were all by the pool at The Beeches. It was a hot, overcast day. Anna had known Paul Arnold at Cambridge and had invited Paul and Stephanie to their house several times. Stephanie was building up her strength for surgery in a month's time. Sidney and Moira had arrived back from the South of France. Jane was staying with Anna. She had not told anyone what had happened to her.

It was late in the afternoon and Fairfax had just arrived from Chiswick.

"I'm worried about Jane, Justin. Ever since she came back from Shropshire, she seems to be in another world," confided Fairfax before they all went in to get changed for dinner.

Justin heard the anxiety in his friend's voice. "Yes, she is a bit remote, but she's often like that, you know, kind of dreamy, thinking about something miles away. Why? Leave it, Fairfax, it may just come out during the conversation. You know, we're going to the Countess of Rigby's big do next month; maybe things will resolve themselves then. I know she is excited about it." Justin was as usual comforting and supportive to his close friends. He was very fond of Fairfax. Sometimes, he wished he himself could confide in him, but it never really happened. They would meet for drinks after work or sometimes played squash together. And then there was bridge playing at Grassock Oaks.

Later, they were all dressed for the birthday party and sitting round the long table in the dining room. It was unusually warm so the windows were flung open, allowing the cooler evening air to enter.

Jane had taken up her cello. She had brought it with her and now accompanied Paul on his violin. Anna was seated at her new piano, purchased for her birthday by Justin. They had played Mozart serenades and Chopin's *Nocturne No. 20 in C sharp minor*. Its haunting melodies had moved them all. And then the music finished. There was silence.

And then Sidney's voice came from the depth of his chair. He was seated far in the corner in a wing-backed chair, upholstered in midnight blue velvet. His white, wiry hair was standing on end as usual. He was looking much older lately.

"Jane, I've always wanted to ask you. What you were really doing when you were in Egypt? Were you there for most of the five years away from England?"

You could have heard a pin drop. It was a question that everyone had wanted to ask, and no one had ever dared. But tonight, Jane, for some reason, decided that she was going to tell everyone everything. It was time, and she was tired of the pretence in trying to lead two different lives at once. Justin looked across at Anna summing her up, watching her reaction to Sidney's question. These days, he hardly ever touched her or came near. Her pale skin looked so smooth above the sea blue chiffon of the dress. Her beauty haunted him, but she was defiled now. He still felt the ache for her. It had to be dismissed. He thought again of the clasp on the black thread. "How was it used sexually?" he wondered.

"The first two years I was in Cairo doing doctoral studies in Pyramidology. There were things that intrigued me, more esoterically than scientifically. There was some force or forcefield that the Egyptians were involved in that I wanted to know about, to experience. No one had the answers for me. The paintings, the symbology of the pyramids, told the story of a master race who had the powers of the gods. They believed they could do anything. All the burial ceremonies, everything, pointed to one fact, that they were in touch with the power of Kundalini." Jane was dressed in black this evening, her long hair braided down her back; the hair back from the face made her look younger. She reached for her wine glass, whilst still leaning over the cello.

"But the Kundalini is a very dangerous thing. People have died trying to awaken it. If it goes into the wrong channels of the body, it can give you many infirmities, make you feel you're on fire. It has also been used for the black arts and secret sexual societies such as there were in Ancient Egypt." Jane felt a hundred years of words were coming out of her now.

Sidney was watching her intently.

"It is only dangerous if it is awakened in the wrong way or used for dangerous purposes, to harm others, for example. It is the energy that makes the human being into a god. That is why the Egyptians were so careful and had elaborate rules for their initiation chambers," continued Jane. She was enjoying this experience. Finally, it was time to share.

"But what was the connection with the pyramids?" Justin looked at Jane fondly. He was also still staring at Anna, wondering what she was thinking.

"The pyramids held initiation chambers for the awakening of the Kundalini; they were immensely powerful places. That is why when they were first opened and people walked into these chambers, some of them died soon after. It was like walking into an unprotected spiritual nuclear power station." She was about to go on when Julia entered the room and told her she was wanted on the phone.

It was Catherine from the South of France.

"Jane, I had to call you. Things are happening here; I feel afraid. It's as though someone is peering into my life; I can't explain it. I think I am in danger. The other day, Fabian Roth came here."

"Really, what for?" asked Jane.

117

"He came here two days ago, just unannounced, He had someone with him, a beautiful American girl, tall, black hair, but very young. There was something about her; she seemed so radiant, so attractive, but her eyes looked glazed in some way. Anyway, she did not come into the house; she walked a little in the garden. He came into the house, said that he had found some of Louis' papers and thought I might want them. Then he said that if I ever needed any help, that I should contact him. He gave me a card and said they were leaving for Switzerland and then London in a few days. Then they left. It was eerie in a way, just arriving like that. The car was one of those very large Mercedes, black with tinted windows." Catherine waited.

"What did he look like? I don't think I ever met him," asked Jane, playing for time.

"Oh, he is quite devastating to look at. He has dark colouring, sharp angular features. He has black hair, very straight. There is a little scar on his wrist and another scar on his chin – small, you would hardly notice. He is tall and thin, always a good dresser – no casual clothes but suits, things like that. We went to several of his parties. There was always a set around him, his people. I hated him. Then there were the stories of his women, real scandals but nothing ever seemed to touch him. They would sometimes call him the 'Trickster', I mean, the people that didn't like him. He had a lot of enemies. The women were too scared to speak up, but there was talk of rapes. I think a lot of money went to keep things quiet."

"Catherine, as the children are at school in Paris, why don't you come over and stay at Chiswick for a while?" Jane was very protective of Catherine; it had been very hard for her, losing Louis.

"I will certainly think about it. Somehow, I feel I am in danger here, the sort of danger that Louis was in. The papers that the Count brought were all old papers that Louis never used. Fabian asked me if Louis had given me any list of names. He said that Louis was doing some research into the names, genealogical research. I haven't a clue about the names. He was quite insistent, said he needed these names and if I found them to send them to him and then destroy them."

"What were those names? We should have them here?" Jane tried to sound relaxed, but these names were going to be essential to them all. The names would be from the times at Farlingham Park. It could give them a lot of secrets about the deaths and the Hexagon Club.

"I can't remember off-hand; they are upstairs; one of them was John Hargreaves, James Wetherby, I think, and George IV. I must go, Jane; I've got a long-distance call coming in. I'll be in touch soon."

Jane returned to the room. She did not tell them about her conversation with Catherine; it was not the right time. But they could all see that she was distracted. They were lingering now, waiting for Jane to resume her experiences in Egypt. The conversation went on around Jane and Sidney Henderson mainly. The others were listening intently. Jane was starting to tell them about her own initiation. The room was so silent, you could have heard a pin drop.

Stephanie was upstairs in bed; it was late for her. Earlier at dinner, before the music, they had cut the cake and given her presents, Anna's hat was at the end of the bed. She adored Anna, but she was also curious; Anna didn't have any light around her. All the others did, wide light, but not Anna. She couldn't figure it out.

They were all in the drawing room, sitting on the sofas and chairs. The curtains were drawn; they were drinking coffee and eating the chocolates that Sidney had brought from the South of France. Anna was tired. She was half listening to Jane, but her mind was also on the phone call that Jane had received. Only Justin had not shared his fears about someone watching his life.

"Why did you come back if you had found what you wanted, Jane?" asked Moira. She knew as much as Sidney about esotericism; it was their hobby. It was usually Sidney that was talkative. They had never had any experiences, only read it in books. They were fascinated by Jane's story, but wary.

"Daddy, I can't get to sleep. There is someone outside the house walking up and down." Stephanie was standing, hanging over the banisters, looking down at the hallway below. Justin and Paul got up. Justin put on some shoes and went outside. It was quiet. There was no one around that he could see. Then he went over to the pool and looked there. It was deserted. He walked around the whole estate. In the stables, he found one of the doors open. It was always left shut, but it was flung open. Then, he heard footsteps. They sounded like they were on the other side of the house. He ran around the back of the house. He got there just in time to hear the gates at the front of the estate close. Then he heard a car take off. He went back to the stables. One of Anna's horses had walked out into the yard. He fetched the halter and led her back into her stable and then went back to join his guests.

"Yes, there was someone, and I have a feeling they will be back. Someone is watching us, Anna. I felt it before, but I didn't want to alarm anyone," said Justin.

"Anna, what really happened, I mean, just before the accident?" Sidney looked at her. They all looked at her. She looked shocked.

"It was a dog, a black dog that came out of nowhere. John tried to avoid it, but the car went out of control. Why are you asking? Do you think someone was trying to kill me?" She laughed. Her laughter seemed strange, out of place somehow, as though she was removed from it all, as though she didn't care.

The incident somehow had broken the evening up. They tried to settle down again. They wanted to hear Jane, but the closeness had gone, and people seemed to be distracted and tired.

Stephanie lay awake in her room; she wanted to say goodnight to Justin. She looked at the end of the bed. There was a blue light. She often saw it. The light was her real home – one day she would go there.

Justin put his head round the door; then, when he saw she was awake, he sat down on the bed.

"It's time you went to sleep. You need to rest and here you are all day running around the gardens in Anna's hats and shoes. What are we going to do with you?" Justin teased her.

"Why doesn't Anna have any light around her?" She stared at him, waiting for a reply to what to her was a straightforward question.

"Why doesn't she what?" Justin looked back at her, baffled. She was always ahead of him; he could never reach her. She lived in a world of which he had no understanding at all.

"Well, everyone has a light around them. It's kind of a bag that everyone stands in. It's kind of a protection, an energy field. Everyone has one, but sometimes the colours change. If someone gets very angry, it all goes red. But, Anna doesn't have one. I saw a dead person once who didn't have one either. Do you think that Anna is really dead?"

Justin sat back on the bed; he leaned against the wall. He didn't say anything.

"Justin, you have a son, don't you?" she continued.

"Our son disappeared; we assume he is dead," said Justin.

# 15

Fabian was in the west wing of the chateau, in his library. He fingered one of the yellow-paged books in front of him. They smelt musty. His days were filled with intrigues, webs being spun all over the world. There was not a place now that he did not touch. He turned the page and saw a photograph of a boy; the deep-set eyes looked out at him. Giles was ten years old when this picture had been taken in South America. The memories of Justin and Anna would be dimmed by now.

He bent over the heavy oak desk. He always had a mirror on the desk, a woman's mirror, ornate, delicate. Now he couldn't remember who had given it to him. His face looked back at him; the dark hair hung in some disarray across his face; the black eyes were cloudy; the skin bore a yellowish pallor. He was thinking of his favourite book, *The Picture of Dorian Gray*. Like Dorian, his sins were taking a toll on him and so was his ordeal with Maxine. But unlike Dorian, it was his own face that was showing the horror of his life rather than a portrait. But he liked the book; he likened himself to the evil Dorian, who stopped at no sin, if it met his fancy. His obsession with Maxine was causing him to make mistakes. His lips moved as he read the spell for possessing the soul of another human; over and over he read from the pages, its meaning hidden in the Latin text. The room smelt of sulphur as he worked. He bit his lip as he pondered over the next move. He could taste the blood. Next door was the anti-room; it had no windows and was always in darkness. More volumes of books could be seen in the candlelight, then the high altar with its magnificent red candles, the chalice, pieces of hawthorn bush. A statue of the winged Seth stood high overhanging the room. He wanted a spell that would make Maxine forget herself and become one with him forever.

The room was small and shrouded in velvets; at the side stood a glass showcase. The case was about four feet square with a door and a gold lock. He went over and stared inside. There, on a black velvet cushion, was a court jester's hat, hundreds of years old and almost threadbare in places. It was cleverly fashioned into three peaks. The peaks were made of cloth, red, green and yellow, On the tip of each point was a silver bell. The Count took a key from the pocket of his grey silk trousers and opened the lock. Ceremoniously, he took out the hat and with great care lifted it onto his head. To anyone looking, it was as though he was putting on a crown. His lips were working with the spell that he was repeating over and over to himself. The hat fitted closely to his head. He had assumed a completely different expression, a kind of fixed look. It was as though he had become somebody else. A dark silence surrounded him in the padded darkness. He stayed there for fifteen minutes as though listening for something or someone. His expression did not change. Then he removed the hat, shut it back in the case, locked it and left the room.

He made his way to the drawing room. His personal assistant Henryk had brought in the tea; they were expecting guests. An elaborate arrangement of silver teapots, tall and ornate, stood by the gold-rimmed china cups. Henryk was tall and willowy. His figure bowed like a thin bent rod hovering over the tea, waiting for the Count. The phone rang on the desk at the far end of the room. Long windows led out onto the lawns beyond. English cakes stood on elaborate tea stands.

"Count Roth's residence," said Henryk, watching the Count sit down on one of the long green sofas. "He looks ill," thought Henryk to himself.

"Sir, it's the Iranian Consulate. They want to discuss the arms deal in South America. They seem quite upset; think you have cornered the market." Henryk waited for a response.

"Tell them I am out and that I will call back tomorrow. Get a name though; we don't want to be chasing all over the Middle East, do we, Henryk?" The Count was restless; he kept moving around the room. "We want to keep them waiting. Of course, we have tied up the market, so we want to keep them hopping until they offer the right price. Meanwhile, we have other things to do: Cairo, Washington, London, Kent, Shropshire, and our own cellars. Did you know about the cellars, Henryk?" The Count gave him a sharp look.

Henryk bowed slightly in response to the question. He didn't quite like to verbally acknowledge something that was not really his business. He poured some tea. After Henryk had left to fetch the sugar bowl and spoons, he entered the room yet again.

"Lady Eunice Cousins and her husband, Cecil, are here, sir."

"Show them in, of course, and you can bring the rest of the tea now. Can you also fetch all the papers we need for this little matter?" He sat back against the softness of the cushions. Of course, he thought to himself, Lady Cousins and her husband are looking for Maxine. Alistair must have asked them to check up on her. Just as well he had put her in the cellar. She was getting too arrogant and fighting him again. He wanted her away during the visit.

Maxine sat motionless in the cellar of the chateau. She had little light and what there was came from a small slit in the wall. It was not daylight that came through onto her but the beam from a naked light that shone from the room beyond. Her cell was big enough to hold a mattress, bucket and a washbasin. The walls were slimy with the dampness from the lake. She had been there now for one day; it must be that long; she could hardly remember what everything outside looked like. She decided to try and open an old tin of sardines. It was days since she had eaten. Trying to prise the can open with a brick, she knocked over a glass jar of water, her only water.

"Damn," she said. Now she had the added risk of cutting herself on the stray pieces of glass that she would not be able to see. It was her only water supply, and she knew that whatever she refused to do, she must drink. She had to prepare herself for what was next.

There had been many frightening and totally bizarre situations that had presented themselves since her arrival at the chateau. The first one was when she had woken to find the Count in her room at three o'clock in the morning. For days, she had reeled from this, her body pivoting between a state of ecstasy and painful humiliation, her virginity gone. There were days when she wanted to throw up, and her tongue would make strange movements in her mouth. She wondered if they were signs of possession. There were days she wanted him to make love to her. At these times, she was filled with a terrible and unrelenting longing. Other days, she hated him and would keep up a terrible silence. There were days of little conversation, when they would sit in the darkness of some room together, a communion of energies. Then he arranged for her to be shut in the cellar. There was no reason; it was just the way he was. It was as though he was operating from a realm of ideas to which she had absolutely no access. She knew that she was normalizing, that she was beginning to go through a stage that all prisoners go through where they start to see the frenzied antics of the captors as normal, to accept the situation. Maxine had slowly stopped thinking about leaving. She found herself thinking about the Count, brooding. Her defences were breaking; she could feel that he was starting to own her. He was inside her.

She had no idea how much later it was that she heard a key grating in the lock of the cellar door.

"Maxine, where are you?" He whispered her name softly.

"I'm here. Shall I come out with you now?" She was always careful to give him the power in the situation.

"Yes, yes, come onto the lawns; it's so late in the afternoon. It's so beautiful out here." He waved his arm in the direction of the lawns.

He led her out. The grass was freshly cut. A table was prepared with a large green and white and green-striped canopy over it. On the table, set on a white cloth, there were silver dishes of fruits, a banquet just for her – fresh strawberries and cream, damask napkins. He had thought of it all, blue china bowls, plates and teacups edged with gold. He led her to a comfortable chair, a swinging seat, soft with cushions.

"But your dress, darling, look at your dress; it's covered in stains. Go and change; there are dresses in your room." He waved his hand irritably.

The truth was that he could not bear to see her looking like this. He closed his eyes in horror at his life. It was a terrible existence, but what could he do? He had sold his life so many years ago and there was no going back. Only death could free him.

It was late now, and the sun was fading. Maxine came back out to the garden; she walked slowly, dressed in a long Edwardian dress with pearl buttons from the neck to the ground. The dress was made of the finest gossamer lace. Her hat, broad-brimmed, was secured upwards by a single cameo brooch. She looked radiant; her dark eyes and translucent skin were pure nectar to him.

"Do you like your room?" he asked. The question caught her off guard.

"Yes. Do you live in the house all on your own?" She wanted to know more about him.

"My family has lived here for generations. My parents brought me and my sister up in this house. It was an idyllic life, but they were away so much."

"Where is your family now?" she asked. He was looking away off to the right, towards the lake.

"You know there is no one here except us. Henryk and all the others have gone home. We have the whole place to ourselves." He was thinking, planning now, how it would be for them.

"But your parents?" she asked again, not wanting to anger him, but curious.

"It's a long story. They were away a great deal. They had houses in many different countries. Sometimes we travelled with them, sometimes not. It was an interesting kind of life but very isolated. My parents had certain ideas. They didn't want us to mix with other children very much. There was just my sister Emma and myself. They felt they were part of a chosen race, you see. They wanted to pass that power and that teaching down to us."

"What kind of teaching?" she asked.

"They felt in a way that they had become gods. They had studied certain esoteric doctrines. They wanted to make sure it stayed in the family. They really had a power no one else knew about. They would practice all kinds of rituals here in this house. The practices were Egyptian. We knew the secrets of the pharaohs. Maxine, you must never tell anyone else about this." He looked at her, concerned, and wondered if he had told her too much.

"What kind of practices, and what happened to them?"

He looked tired tonight – kind of spent, in a way.

"Another time, I will tell you. One time they were in Germany. They never returned. I tried to find them. We never knew whether they had decided to stay there and break contact with the past or whether they were murdered." Fabian was lying to her. He told her that he could not discuss this with her now. Of course, he could not tell her about the Hexagon clubs now.

What Fabian did not share was that his parents had long ago resurrected the Hexagon Club. He was privy to the secrets and their sinister hold on his own sexuality. From a young age, Fabian knew no sexual normality and developed habits and tastes way beyond his years – this fractured part of him. And so, he was open to the macabre ministrations of The Jester, who then took over his life, piece by excruciating piece, dismantling him, till there was little left of his own soul. But his parents had in the early years been his teachers. His mind had been led into their pathways for what they wanted him to become – a guru and head of thousands of such clubs around the world; places where the cherished super race would sport and create the new sexuality, the sex of the Gods. And then, the new age of children would be born, the secret sexual patterning already in their genes.

In its great years, the club was cleverly resurrected for German Nazi officers, resident in France and Germany during and after the war. His parents had eventually been murdered in Germany by members of the Reich who survived the end of the war and lived on to preserve the culture. They were taken and hanged when he was only still a young man. It was some years before he and his sister Emma had left the chateau after the terrible incident, that terrible day that he hardly wished to remember.

As a child, he hardly knew of the club's existence, but he was conditioned by his parents who had run this club for so many years. His parents had left old manuscripts for him about the club. All the practices were laid out for him, the rules of the club, how the daughters were to be brought up, what their sexual habits should be, the grooming and mind control, and the rules laid down for surgical procedures to remove their hymens. The young girls were taught complete submission to the male's sexual needs and demands. In turn, they were trained to be Nazi whores. There were ceremonies to be observed, tight rules of conduct and absolute secrecy. Family members and children were not to mix with other people outside the club; it was forbidden. If they disobeyed these rules, they were threatened with punishment and even death.

It was now almost dark. They lapsed into silence. A single peacock stared at them from across the grass.

"Maxine, you haven't eaten any of this wonderful food; eat now," he scolded her.

She smelled one of the fresh gardenias lying on the table. She was thinking about her family, her father, Casey, her dead mother. She had almost forgotten what they looked like. They didn't seem to matter anymore.

It was no coincidence that she was thinking about her father. He was in the outskirts of Paris, driven by an embassy car in the late part of the afternoon. He had been told that this was the last place that Maxine had been seen in public. She had been at a party with Parisian socialites.

He arrived at the deserted house, alone, in the afternoon, convinced that he would find some clues to his daughter's disappearance. The overgrown garden perplexed him; it looked like a hideout rather than a place where well-known people frequented. He walked slowly up the path. He was trying to remember; it was something he had read about, a place like this. Maxine had shown it to him in Washington over a year ago. Now, the house was not only completely empty, but the door was boarded up. Two boards lay across each other and were driven to a resting place by four enormous nails. He remembered later how bizarre this looked. He sat on the steps and put his head in his hands. Tears fell from his eyes in his despair at the loss of his daughter. Fabian had told him that he would take Maxine from him; she had been promised, but he could hardly bear the reality of it happening. And where had he taken her? This was the lead in Paris that he had hoped would bring something; now his way to her was barred. Heavily, he got up and walked back along the path. The embassy car drew off towards Paris. The streets were empty.

Fabian led Maxine back into the chateau from the gardens. It was twilight, the witching time and the last sound of crows circling the trees faded as they made their way inside. One of the crows had flown to sit on Fabian's shoulder. He took Maxine up the staircases to the top floor where he opened the doors to a most magnificent room. He placed the crow on a perch in the far corner of the room. It sat there in its blackness, sombre and brooding.

Two fireplaces stood, one at each end of the room. The room was only dimly lit with candles; white satins, silks, brocade – thick white fur skin rugs covered the floor and furniture. In the middle of the room was a bed with soft pillows and lacy linens. Around the room, the walls were hung with mirrors, all sorts of mirrors: antique baroque, large, small, square, round, and one stood on a wooden stand in the centre of the room by the bed.

They looked at each other. He was watching her and offered her red wine. He was aware of her heightened senses. He kissed her on the mouth, the wine trickling down into her and then down her throat. He knew exactly how to arouse her. Their lips were wet with the redness now. Already there was intoxication of the moment. Both unclothed now, she bent her head and then ran her lips expertly down the entire length of his body until every part of him was throbbing with the pleasure of her tongue.

"Lose yourself in that feeling, just let go. I will do everything, Maxine; just let me take you to that place. I know what it is like, pure heaven." He stood with her in front of the long mirror. They saw themselves reflected. There was only one universe now; she knew there was only him, and she wanted the complete abandonment to him. There was no other way.

He stood in front of her. Then she could not wait for him to put his hands on the secret places of her body.

"Now I am going to dress you," he whispered.

She looked at the contents of the box; her mind went numb. He took a wig out of the box, long black hair, tangled. He put it on her, slowly pinning it up away from her face with long bone pins. Of course, she remembered it all — the night of his first coming into her; she had been bending over against the basin and he was behind her.

Now he pulled the robe around her, the lose folds of the silk revealing the curves of her body. She looked like the priestess that he wanted her to be. He moved his hand along her spine from the base to the top of her head. It was as though he was awakening a new energy, like cascading water. He touched each vertebra; it lit a new fire in her, sweeping her whole body beyond anything she had ever experienced. She cried out with the intensity. Then he quickly took her in his arms; she was so open, so ready for him now, no resistance. He wanted her.

His lovemaking was so intense; and as she finally opened to him, a storm of passion was unleashed in her. They went higher and higher into the tantric realms of complete merging with each other and the universe. They used their breath to bring their souls out of their skulls and into the cosmos.

Afterwards, she lay exhausted, hardly hearing his words, filled with the void of abandonment. And later, dressed, he bent over her and covered her with the rugs that lay around her. Again, the crow flew to his shoulder.

He made his way with the bird down to the study. Seth often took the form of a crow, and Fabian knew this visit and it sitting on his shoulder was a good omen. Anna had had the crows at The Beeches shot; but as he had warned her, it was a dangerous thing to do and it would only anger Seth. At last,

Maxine was his. He heard a familiar laugh as he turned the corner of the study and the sound of a tinkling bell.

In Geneva that night, Lady and Lord Cousins were dining late.

"We will have to call Alistair in the morning. There was no sign of Maxine at the Chateau. Strange man, I thought; so nice about Maxine though, so concerned about her disappearance. Poor Alistair, he must be half out of his mind. I'm glad that Casey is staying on for a while. She's leaving for England though, at the beginning of July," said Lady Cousins.

# 16

"Scalpel and protractors, please," said Justin.

The lights were fully up in the operating room. An hour earlier, Stephanie had been rushed from her home in Chelsea; with her condition now becoming urgent, they had to do the surgery immediately. A valve was leaking. Her father, Paul, was waiting outside. Now six surgeons clad in green gowns and masks stood over her body. The rib cage had been cut away to expose the heart. He thought of last weekend when they were all in the country together and he had held a buttercup under her chin to see if she liked butter. She had laughed at the buttercup and asked Justin why he didn't just ask her if she liked butter.

Beads of perspiration stood out on Justin's brow as he proceeded with the surgery.

"Clamps," said Justin. The major incision was made, the decisions finalized.

They closed the main vessels to the heart and set up the artificial circulation system.

"The heart looks in good shape, sir, better than the X-rays suggest," said Greenberg.

Justin was intent on reaching the suturing point that he had just made after removing the debris from the incisions behind the heart cavity. He saw the damage in the valve. It was so small and inaccessible.

The final moves were made, and all the suturing was done. They would wait before putting the rib cage back. They all looked at each other, elated that it had gone so well. The team moved off to the side of the room for a short break and to allow the situation to stabilize. There was a holiday-like atmosphere in the operating room.

Then everything went quiet. Six pairs of trained eyes stared at the machines attached to Stephanie. The heart rate had not only slowed down but had stopped.

They all stood over her body; Justin administered adrenalin. Still there was no movement. They were massaging the heart, willing it to live. They were in despair.

"You've lost her, Justin. There is nothing you can do now," said Dr Nicholls, one of Justin's colleagues.

Justin did not reply. He was still massaging the heart, giving it all the love and strength only he knew how.

"Justin, it is too late. There is no way she is going to survive now." Nicholls moved close to Justin, wanting to lead him away from the table.

The team was starting to move away. They knew the signs, and they didn't want to prolong the agony or Justin's obvious pain. No one was really close to Justin to understand his feelings. He was aware that they wanted to leave, pulling at their gloves, wanting to be gone from the intense sense of failure in the room.

"Justin, you know the score. Even if the heart started again, she would be brain damaged. What sort of a life is that?" Nicholls was closer to Justin than the rest of the team; they had been friends for years. He looked him in the eye while he was talking.

The room was deathly quiet. Justin stopped massaging the heart and walked to the other side of the room. He sat down for a few minutes. Justin briefly looked up and saw a woman's figure bend over Stephanie for what seemed like a minute and then was gone. What he heard was his name being called.

Suddenly, the room became alive again. "Justin, the heart has started again, on its own, Also, the oxygen levels for the heart and the brain are registering as normal. It's unbelievable!"

Nicholls helped Justin who was feeling quite overcome with what he had just seen and heard.

The rest of the surgery was like a dream for Justin. The others had taken over the last part. He was a doctor, but he was in a state of witnessing, that it was just a role he played. He was in a deep place of rest and silence that he had never known before.

Two hours later, they had finished. All vital functions were strong, the rib cage back in place.

Paul was waiting anxiously in the Relatives' Room. After letting him know that Stephanie had come through successfully, Justin walked quickly down the long corridors to his office. It was Felicity's day off. He wanted to get away, not to see anyone. He went into the inner office and sat on the blue sofa. Suddenly, all the weeks, months, even years of pent-up feelings, just let go. He sobbed for Giles; he cried for Anna and himself, the terrible sudden death of his parents, sobbing like a small child, on and on. He could never remember ever doing that. All the pain he had ever felt gushed up with the tears. Afterwards, he lay exhausted. He knew that his life would never be the same again.

# 17

Maxine flew to Washington. Fabian drove her to the airport. They parted in silence. He could have put her on one of his private planes, but he didn't want to arouse suspicion. Together they concocted a story about where she had been. She was not to mention Fabian to anyone. She landed in Washington at night, and her father and Casey were there to meet her. They were emotional, tearful, but she was dry-eyed. She didn't have it in her to shed tears. It was as though a veil had come over her life. She thought only of Fabian. She knew that to meditate on him was important; it would facilitate the process he had begun within her.

He was training her already to do his work. Eventually, she would be submissive. As with Anna, he would share her with other men. He thought of the eventual parties, the sex, the Hexagon Club. He was aroused at the thought. Yes, Maxine would learn to love it, pressing the boundaries, turning her too into his whore and his accomplice. She would be the supreme whore, his high priestess. He imagined her spreadeagled and bound on the great baize-covered tables.

Her father saw her as remote in the days to come. He put it down to tiredness, but there was something changed in her, a sadness, somehow. She had lost her light-heartedness and her joy. He knew too that Fabian would have taken her virginity now, the sacred hymen removed; sexual secrets once held in her vagina would now belong to him and him alone. These were the workings of the Fraternity. Casey found Maxine secretive and evasive. She had no understanding of what had happened. There was a wall around Maxine that no one could penetrate.

Fabian travelled to South America. There his people greeted him. His company and the main residence for the organization's activities had been set up long ago. Giles gave him a greeting like a son. He had even forgotten that his real parents were in England. Fabian was a guru to them all. He initiated; he directed, while they clung to his every word, his every movement. But Maxine knew nothing of this.

Then he flew back to Switzerland to the castle where Louis had spent his last days. Louis, Catherine's husband, had made too many mistakes. He was out of line and didn't pay him homage as he should. And then there were the women. Once Fabian had turned Louis onto the Hexagon Club, he just could not get enough of it and was becoming a nuisance to everyone. The Jester had wanted to get him out of the way; he was too closely aligned with a family that he wanted, for his own reasons, to destroy. And always, The Jester was pushing him to worsening deeds, evil deeds and excesses.

Steep crags of black rock stood out from the mountain top. On the highest point of the jutting face stood the castle. Gothic lines of windows and doors interrupted the wet line of the black walls that had been chiselled out of the rock centuries ago. The castle, its history lost in mystery, stood out alone from the surrounding landscape of mountains and waterfalls that gave way to the valleys beneath. So high up, it attracted few visitors. If anyone saw the castle, they would not have been drawn by a sense of beauty, but more repelled by its haunting darkness.

Sidney had come here once for a week. It was some years ago, to give advice to Fabian on the interior design. Of course, he would never have breathed a word about it to Anna or Moira. Fabian tried to turn Sidney to the left-hand path, the path of Seth, and idolatry. Sexually, he tried to ensnare him, but Sidney would have none of it. He even refused Fabian's money and vowed he would never come under Fabian's shadow again.

High up in the castle was a room that was completely round. The roof was a dome where once an artist had depicted in complete fresco the dance of Salome and the actual beheading of John the Baptist. Windows that went the entire length of the room allowed one to stare out onto the sheer drop below. In the middle of the room, on a thick-piled white carpet, stood a desk carved out of a single walnut tree. The feet were shaped into the claws of a dragon. Grey silk shades hung around the room on various lights.

It was almost dark outside, but the curtains were not drawn. A huge Dobermann lay on the carpet in front of Fabian's desk. Fabian was pacing the room when a call came through.

"Your little princess Stephanie came out of surgery," said the voice at the other end.

"He won't be pleased," said Fabian. "What else?" he snapped.

"We have a man in Cairo; he is following Sean to see that all the right moves are made," said the person at the other end. There was fear in the voice.

"And Jane?"

"She is staying with Justin and Anna."

"Good, we have to wait, no moves yet. Do you understand?"

If the situation had been his doing, he would be pulling the strings slightly differently. But it wasn't really his game; well, it was, and it wasn't. He thought about the relationship between him and The Jester, and about his parents who had initiated him into the Hexagon Club.

When he was five years old, he had experienced a dream. In the dream, a jester had walked towards him at a fairground. He had waved his jester's stick and all sorts of pretty and interesting things appeared. The Jester beckoned to him and had given him the stick. He had waved it and all the things that he desired had appeared before him. Then the dream faded. Fabian had been fascinated and amused, but he never told anyone.

Then the visits, in one form or another, had become more frequent. Initially, they were related to dreams. Fabian would wake up sweating and his heart thumping from the excitement. After a while, he would come at night just before Fabian would go to sleep. The Jester would sit on his bed. At first, his visits were short, but then he started to stay longer. There was a strange excitement that Fabian felt at the visits. The Jester revealed many secrets and illusions to him. He showed him the Ancient Egyptian spells, secrets and sexuality.

The relationship was a strange one. He always felt closely bonded to him, as though he was part of himself, somehow. There was an intimacy and communication that simply did not exist in Fabian's other relationships. In a way, it was a sexual bond; with him he had his first sexual experiences, heady and almost beyond his body, the tantalizing awakening of his own sexuality. At times, The Jester would stare into Fabian's eyes, making him drowsy and feel that he was merging with everything around him. He was losing himself. It was a time of great bliss when this happened. He would be sad for days if The Jester did not appear.

He was a boy given to too many fantasies and desires. He wanted all sorts of powers. The Jester promised him all the things that he desired. He taught him how to say magic words and to perform small spells. For a long time, it was a game between them. Then for weeks, one summer, The Jester disappeared. He just vanished. Fabian was beside himself. He felt abandoned.

It was one summer that he was almost entirely alone with his sister, Emma. His parents were in Germany again with the Hexagon Club soirées. Before they left, they prepared him week after week. His first sexual initiation involved incantations and sexual magic. His lessons were those of how to unleash the supreme creative power through diverse and carnal sexual patterning. This power could not only create an ordinary foetus but a magical child of god-like potential. He had to learn extreme discipline in all acts, to maintain absolute control of himself and his prey. He had to learn how to trap.

Fabian learned in those short weeks that we can all become gods through the sexual acts. He learned from his father the importance of the orgies. The orgies have the potential to create liberation and thus to imbibe within us the qualities of gods. His father told him that if the Hexagon Club was again brought to life in England, orgies had to be one of the chief ways to give initiation to its members. His father told him that forbidden desires must be exercised and satisfied, every taboo rendered without fences, enjoyed, consumed.

It was then, at the end of these weeks of training, that Fabian had been taken to a darkened room in the dungeons of the chateau for the ceremonies. Huge torches flared throughout the night. The orgy was set in place. A mask of Seth with its headdress of an unknown animal, was placed upon his head, and then Fabian was part of the sexual ceremonies and initiation rites. All other Hexagon Club members who were there wore long-nosed masks. Fabian had to move through his own lust and revulsion; what he had thought as forbidden, he was forced to experience. He became the seducer and the seduced; he experienced both the shame and the exultation of power alike. Every act was performed upon him, until he learned all the possible repertories of sexual practice. And then, in turn he took his cue from the room full of people and he had his way with many of the tempting young girls and more; there were no limits. He was both frightened and exhilarated.

This was the last of his programming; after that he would be left to The Jester. From then on, Fabian's sexual appetites were secured within him as part of the programming. His parents had learned all this from the Nazis and the mind control practices in the concentration camps. But for Fabian they used pain as much as ecstasy and pleasure in creating the god that their son would become. His teaching would soon be complete.

After the initiations, his parents had been often away in their own mysterious world, a world of long shadows and strange aspirations. Fabian remembered whole summers and sometimes winters when he and Emma were left entirely alone except for a few servants. He remembered the summer that he was sixteen. Emma was just two years younger. They rarely saw any other children and lived in a world of their own. There was no end to the games they devised and the fantasies they enacted. He remembered Emma's beauty, her wild straw-coloured hair, and the brilliant blue eyes. Her body was small and thin, with a face of even and exquisite bone structure, such a delicate smile, and such fullness in her lips.

One morning, after a restless night of strange nightmares that filled him with endless desires, just out of reach, he went to find Emma. He was still full of the experiences of the initiations from The Jester. He couldn't find her all morning. She seemed to have vanished. It was a glorious day, and he made his way out to the cornfield. There he saw a track in the corn. He knew Emma had been there and was probably now out in the middle of the waving corn, lying down. He followed her, first picking some wild redcurrants from the bushes and putting them in a small basket. He crept slowly into the field, wanting to surprise her. The corn was high. Already it was so hot. He walked on and on. His mind was on fire, and he thought about the dreams from the night before. Finally, he found her lying on a rug, her bare legs stretched out. She had on a white muslin dress.

"Fabian, how did you find me? I was hiding from you today," she whispered, still sleepy, her eyes half-open and shielded from the sun by her arm.

"I saw the track; I knew that you had come here. It was easy, Princess, and look what I brought you." His voice was uneasy; he felt unnerved by her beauty and his lack of assurance. She was still lying down; he knew she had the upper hand. She wanted to taunt him.

"Feed me the fruit," she commanded like a real princess. One by one, he stuck the small fruit into her mouth until it was quite full. The skin around the lips was stained red with the fruit and some of the drops had appeared as though out of nowhere on her dress. "Now, you lie down, and I will put them in your mouth," she spoke as she propped herself up on one elbow. He lay on his back and parted his lips to receive the fruit from her hand. She shoved the fruit into his open mouth.

The sun was so hot; he became drowsy with it. Then, as she fed the fruit to him, relentlessly, into his mouth, his mind filled with the fantasies from that night and the stories The Jester had told him. His mouth was overflowing with red fruit; the juice was running out of his mouth. He was becoming sexually aroused, thinking of what he had done at the orgy and his initiation. He had the power and he wanted to use it.

"Fabian," she was bending over him, laughing, but unaware of what was happening to him. "You look like you are dying, like blood is running out of your mouth!" She didn't say anything else, but they lay down on the rug and went to sleep.

Who knows what their dreams were, but Fabian woke to find his sister sleeping on her back; her white muslin dress was creased, and her lips were red from the fruit. The magic was gone, and he felt that he wanted her. She was going to be his prey and he the hunter. Frustration, lust and hatred filled his mind. He wanted to let her know how he felt. He kissed her roughly on the cheek and she awoke immediately. He was filled with longing. He saw the downy hair on her arm. He saw her now as his prey. He was going to put her in a trap now.

"Stop it, silly," she said in the dismissive tone that she sometimes used when she was addressing him. This made him even madder. This time, he did it again, kissing her on the mouth. A cloud moved across the sun and Emma felt chilled. She tried to pull away, but she was trapped under his arm. He laughed at her; the game had become serious. If Emma were to break free, he would trap her again. There was something he wanted, some recognition that he wanted from his sister. They struggled like this for another hour. He chased her further and further into the corn. Her dress was torn. His mind was in chaos. There was a side to him that he didn't understand. Fabian looked at her torn dress. He was frightened by the sense of a new kind of arousal in him. Then she tripped and fell. He was startled and stopped in his tracks.

"We'd better get back," she said.

"Yes," he did not have a thing to say; he was angry and confused. All the way back they were silent, each of them reeling from the events that had overtaken them.

Heaviness hung in the air; it was an unusually hot night. They were in their rooms; the chateau was dark. He lit a candle in his room. He had an altar, just a simple affair with a small cup of silver and some old bones. He wished again and again that he had real power. His parents had given him the power; now he wanted to use it. He remembered his initiation again, and it fuelled the sexual longing that he felt for his sister. He lay awake in his bed, missing The Jester. His mind dwelt on his relationship with Emma.

An idea came into his head. He got out of bed and went to the mirror. Standing in the middle of the room, his eyes looked back at him, the olive skin completely without blemish, the lips full. His dark hair fell now almost to his shoulders. He thought he looked like a god. He was captivated by his image. He was naked. He adored his body, his manhood that stood out from him in all its wonder. The idea sprouted inside him, growing, maturing. He savoured it; he thought it was a message from the gods that he felt were always standing around him. He pondered for an hour or more. He became an embodiment of the idea. He became the embodiment of the hunter and went out of his room and walked down the staircase to the second floor where Emma's rooms were looking out onto the river at the back of the chateau. He was, he knew now, stalking his prey.

The door was not even locked; it opened easily, soundlessly. She lay across the bed; the sheets had fallen off her. He stared at her nakedness. In the darkness, he took off his own nightgown, his lust growing with each minute. She was still asleep. Emma awoke at his first touch. Then came his violence towards her, as he held her down and lay on top of her. She was now indeed trapped.

"No, Fabian, no! You're hurting," she screamed loudly. The sound carried along the corridors to the servants' quarters. Then there was silence.

It was one o'clock in the morning when Emma's screams again rent the air as thunder crashed outside. The servants rushed into Emma's room, as the first lash of rain hit the open windows. They found Emma in her bed naked, her brother lying across her, the sheets covered in blood. Fabian was skewered with a paper knife that hung at an odd angle from his wrist.

The next day, their parents sent orders from Germany; Emma was sent away to be with her parents. Fabian was the next day sent to his uncle in America and then on to military school for six years. But his longing for the young Emma had created a poisonous wound. The longing for a young girl's body, to possess it, to defile, never left him, and he sought to find the image wherever his went. He was possessed. The Jester had watched it all. Now Fabian was truly his. His parents had secured within him their secrets, and it was to be the death of the boy that they had known.

The memories receded as Fabian arose from the sofa to set a light to the large logs and sticks in the hearth. He never saw Emma again. His parents were dead in three years, killed off as if they were vermin by the Nazis. The club went again into hiding. But Emma was still in his life, a rival to his power. Sometimes he wondered whether he had even had a choice about his life anymore. The Jester had entered his life unannounced when he was five years old. He had never left. Now it appears they were one and the same.

After that night with Emma and when he arrived in America, The Jester had returned suddenly one night. The relationship was re-established. It went on for years until it reached a point where he felt that he could not have lived without him. The Jester satisfied all his now almost insatiable appetites for power, wealth and sexual excitement. The more he had, the more he wanted. The most beautiful women in the world were at his beck and call. But there was a price and there were scandals. He was rumoured to have strange tastes in bed.

Then the game with The Jester became deadly. He started to ask him to carry out certain tasks for him. At first, they were easy things. Then the demands were much riskier and complex involving illegal activities, even murder. One night, Fabian refused a certain request. He had become hardened, but there were still certain things he did not wish to do. The Jester gave him a terrible look. Fabian started to sweat and felt his life force starting to ebb away. His limbs felt weak and he couldn't think. Again, he started to question the relationship and why he had become so involved. The Jester kept giving him that look, eyes searing his being, and Fabian became weaker and weaker. He thought he would die. He remembered all the training that his own parents had given him, but it was not enough. He had no choice now but to surrender his entire life to The Jester; otherwise, he would lose his own life forever. As soon as he surrendered, his life flowed back into him and The Jester smiled a smile of triumph. At last Fabian's body and soul were his, ready to carry out his commands at any cost.

# 18

The sun was already hot. It was an orange ball of light, huge in an azure sky. Anthony was reminded of the Ancient Egyptians and their worship of the sun, Ra. Everything they did was based on the idea of linking the earth back to heaven. Already they had seen the dangers of the deep separation between the two, and they foresaw that increasing materialism was driving a wedge between man and God. All the rituals that Anthony had studied, the manuscripts sent over by Vince from England, pointed to their belief that man had to know God to understand the meaning of existence. On the dark side, Anthony was aware of the evil entity Seth who would laugh now at the great man-made toys that ruled the minds of men, that created depravity in the private being of their worlds. Yes, it seemed that Seth ruled the world, creating the wars, the constant chaos that now seemed to reign everywhere. Man had the opportunity to become god but what kind of god was he to become? It seemed that there was a choice. It was told at the point of death, that one could proceed at death beyond karma to the moon, the sun and beyond, without ever returning to the earthly plane. The Ancient Egyptians also knew that beyond their own age, in time, man would forget God; so they created the pyramids as a reminder, as well as having them being the last station on their way to the other planets. For Anthony, his journey to the pyramids had become already his personal journey to something for which he longed. He felt now that he was very close to discovering the secrets that he knew lay in the pyramid. But Anthony did not understand the dark forces that lingered and fingered his own reality. He was suffering also from the delusion of his own power that somehow the secrets of the pharaohs would indeed become his.

This morning, Anthony could hear the haunting sounds of the morning prayers from the turrets around the city. He and Richard were doing laps in the pool on the roof terrace before breakfast. It was exhilarating, feasting on the open air and the sun. Today, they were planning to go to the pyramid for three days, to camp and to set up the location for the movie. The movie was about the Egyptians and their real secrets, the world of Kundalini, the serpent power, how the pyramids were really built, the secrets of the magician Anubis and the cult of Seth. It hinged around the life of one of the pharaohs, his struggles and his final death, killed by the asp held in the magician's hand at the appointed hour, then the magician's incarceration in the King's tomb and his journey in death to the other planets and beyond.

Anthony was lost in this world of the pharaohs. For him, it was a constant meditation. He wondered if already he had received his own initiation for the awakening of the Kundalini and he thought that in time he too would become a god. For the next three days, he and Richard had to focus on the pyramid they were going to use. There were still areas that seemed very unclear, such as where the entrance to the King's Chamber would be located. There would be some danger in navigating the pyramid, which in parts was relatively unexplored. They had Sean's numerological studies and now, there was a map to go on.

"That's twelve laps. I've had it and I'm ravenous. Let's get breakfast and then go," said Anthony.

"Sounds fine to me. I think Sean is coming up to go through some of the last-minute details. He was up till midnight last night. I know he had some late calls come through," replied Richard.

Sean arrived; he seemed restless and kept pacing round the table.

"I really think you should wait, Anthony. I haven't finished some of the calculations," he said, anxious about the trip and his own instructions from Switzerland and Fabian over the last few days. Too much was being asked of him. He was scared and now he didn't have any choice. Suppose something went wrong? He was going to be all on his own except for only one other person.

"Ready, Richard? I want to get out of here." Anthony ignored Sean.

Richard was aware of the edge in Anthony's voice. This was unusual. He had never known Anthony to be like this. He was always calm, but now something else was driving him. Things always flowed with Anthony. But Richard had his own agendas. He mustn't get too distracted by Anthony's part in all this. Anthony went down to the rooms with Sean.

Richard was alone now on the roof. Before he went to his room, he looked over the edge of the balcony. They were so high up here; the whole of Cairo had spread itself before him. The buildings, old and new, were all crushed in together. It wasn't an entirely happy marriage, but the overall view was breathtaking. He could understand why Anthony was so obsessed with this movie.

If you had seen Richard from the back, which someone did at that moment, you would have seen a man as tall as Anthony's six foot two, blond, very short hair and a pair of broad shoulders. He stood there, alert, with his feet apart. "Trained in combat," thought the observer, and he was right. Richard had other missions. The movie was a camouflage for him. Richard picked up his jacket and went down to his room.

The observer also left the roof. He had a phone call to make to Switzerland. Everything was on schedule. Sean and himself would drive to the pyramid later and enter by another door. Then afterwards, they would take a flight to London, their next stop.

The car was packed and pulled out into the congested Cairo streets. Car horns beeped constantly. Within fifteen minutes,

Richard and Anthony were on the major highway to their pyramid. Anthony lay back in his seat, silent.

He was reflecting on his experiences that morning. Earlier, he had taken a shower. He was planning to read some of the film script, but he felt a force pull him into a deep state of meditation. It was so deep that he lost all sense of his body, as he sat cross-legged, leaning against the bed. He hoped that no one would come in. He watched his breath go in and out until it was so still he didn't know whether he was breathing or not. Then he saw a light behind his eyes; it was white and then blue. At first the blue disk was large, but as it moved away from his forehead, it became a small brilliant dot of light before him. The light and its colour were indescribable; the sight of it filled Anthony with such a sense of bliss. Then he had sensed a taste, like honey, at the back of his tongue, as though something was trickling from the roof of his mouth.

"Anthony, what's up? The driver has asked you three times for directions." Richard was staring at him. Anthony seemed distracted.

Anthony jerked upright, aware that he had been totally lost in the thought of the morning.

"He wants to know where we are going, how to get there," said Richard.

"If only I knew," mumbled Anthony, laughing to himself.

"What do you mean, if only you knew?" asked Richard, losing patience. "Don't you know where the pyramid is?"

"Oh, the pyramid, of course, I know where the pyramid is." He issued an impressive set of instructions to the driver. "Vince is trying to get hold of some more manuscripts. There are some secret documents on the burial of the dead and some other vital maps and information that we need. The problem is that they are in a private collection. He has tracked someone down, though, who lives in London – a woman pyramidologist called Jane." Anthony was looking at Richard.

"When did he go to London? I didn't know he had left." Richard looked annoyed.

"He left a few days ago. I thought I had told you. I spoke with him the other day."

"No, you didn't tell me," said Richard. He was clearly annoyed.

Like most people, who are repeatedly not told things and then left out of the picture, Richard was becoming suspicious of Anthony. The open relationship which they had enjoyed was becoming occluded by something else. In his room while collecting his things, he had looked at the photograph of his wife Cher and their two children, Barnabas and the little one, Ruth. He had looked at them and felt uneasy. Why did Anthony want to go to the pyramid for three whole days alone? He wondered if there was another agenda. The film industry had brought them close, but he wondered what he was up to this time.

Anthony took a silver cigarette case from his shirt pocket and slid a Russian cigarette out. It was bound in black paper. He put it between his lips and lit with a match from the Adelphi Hotel. The safety and assurance of the Western hotel seemed far away. Richard was looking out of the window, also having thoughts of his own – second thoughts, maybe.

The driver was gathering speed, sure now of his directions. Buildings gave way to an occasional gas station. The desert was before them, miles of nothingness. Anthony suddenly thought of the Murray River and the land north where he had travelled to the centre of Australia, the same feeling – nothing, Nothingness made you turn within, to your own sense of mortality. Perhaps that is why the Egyptians thought so much about their death. They were surrounded by nothingness.

Then suddenly the top of the pyramid appeared on the horizon. As they approached, they saw a truck parked at the entrance to the pyramid. Ron, the cameraman, was unloading some of the equipment they would be taking inside. The pyramid was not for public viewing and so the place was deserted. A ramp of scaffolding had been erected by the crew. The entrance they were to take was twenty feet above the ground. They were instructed to set up and then leave the area. Richard had thought this was unusual planning, but he went along with it.

Anthony wanted to make a last-minute call to London. He needed to speak to Vince. Something about the documentation of the death rituals was worrying him. There seemed to be a missing pathway. The energy lines did not match up in the chamber that held the most interest for him, the Chamber of the King. Vince was staying at Claridge's. He thought about it now, the comfortable sofas and the wonderful room service. Checking his watch, he realized it was still too early to call. He called Sean instead, but he wasn't available. Anthony thought it was odd; he had agreed to wait in his room as a sort of standby.

Anthony emerged from the limo.

"You guys can start moving the equipment in but hurry up; we want to get inside as quickly as possible." The edge was back in Anthony's voice. Richard felt he was trying to control something inside him that had gone out of control. Richard took off his sunglasses and slowly wiped them clean with a striped handkerchief from his pocket.

"What's the plan, Anthony?" he asked, carefully putting his glasses back on.

"Let's get back in the limo and look at the maps; at least the air-conditioner will be on."

The driver was reading the local newspaper. They both got in and pored over the maps. It was brilliant. Sean had put in every conceivable measurement that they needed. Some pathways were going to be too narrow to climb into; others were just about all right.

"This is incredible. The man is a genius," exclaimed Anthony. "We will make our way down this passage." His finger pointed to the immediately descending passage near where they would enter. It was very narrow but led to a chamber with a highly elevated roof. "We will haul the stuff down into this main chamber and then split up for a while. I want to investigate the lower chambers. It's a dead end and used to be an initiation chamber." Anthony looked at Richard.

"How did you know that?" asked Richard.

"Numerology, sacred geometry – initiation chambers have to comply here with certain measurements." Anthony was confident he had enough information at his fingertips to make this movie. It was going to tell thousands of people about the secrets of divinity, never released in such a public way; about the King who was a guru to thousands of Egyptians. The King in Ancient Egypt was the person who would secure the mortal's path to heaven.

"What do you want me to do?" asked Richard.

"Well, it may be an idea for you to work upwards towards the Queen's Chamber, then above again to the King's Chamber. The passageways are so narrow, the walls very steep. There is a labyrinth of passages. It will take a lot of care not to get lost. We need to connect ourselves to each other somehow." Anthony stopped abruptly.

"I can't understand it. There is a whole section of the map here that simply is not charted. In fact, it is blank. Sean hasn't filled it in."

"You are right," replied Richard. "It kind of fades into nothingness, right in the middle of the map. What was he doing to omit such an important piece of information?" Anthony put his head in his hands.

Anthony felt his brain was going to putty. His inner and outer experiences didn't seem to match. He was overcome several times a day by a strange exhaustion, and then quite suddenly he would feel alert and full of energy again. Some of the books he was reading said this was the experience of the early initiates of the serpent power, the Kundalini. Anthony was intrigued, but he could not plan how he would be feeling at any given moment.

The crew finally had everything in place inside the pyramid. The truck and the limo left at the same time, leaving a pile of dust in the air. The place was now deserted. Anthony and Richard entered the pyramid. What they found was completely unexpected.

# 19

Jane was standing with her Givenchy umbrella over her head, poised against the torrential downpour that was hitting Knightsbridge at that moment. She was trying to find herself a taxi to get to Claridge's in reasonable time for tea. She was meeting a man called Vince Lowell to discuss some Ancient Egyptian manuscripts that she had in her possession. They were very rare documents. No one in the last six years had shown any interest whatsoever in the documents. And now Vince Lowell had written such a nice letter on behalf of an American film director, Anthony Jackson. She had responded to the letter out of curiosity. The letter was very esoteric and full of numerological data on the pyramids. A part of her was longing for the experiences of the pyramids again, at least to be able to discuss them with someone. The letter had come at the right time.

She adored Claridge's. It always swept her up into a cocooned and nurturing world that she associated with her grandmother. Even the drawing room for tea was decorated in the colours and style of her grandmother's house in Chelsea. She went to the ladies' room and had the umbrella and soaking raincoat removed from her to be whisked away somewhere to be dried. She immersed her hands in the basin of hot water that had been prepared for her. Lastly, she sat in front of the mirrors with their gilt edges; beneath stood glass-topped dressing tables with silver brushes and bowls of face powder. She did the best she could with her damp hair. She was dressed from head to toe in black velvet; it was her mood today reminiscent of her life in Egypt. She felt excited about meeting Vince. She went into the lobby to where in winter there would be a log fire, but today it stood empty.

Vince hovered at the doorway of the tearoom but seemed somehow to recognise Jane immediately when he saw her sitting in a side corner of the room. He introduced himself to her.

"Thank you so much, Jane, for your notes on the Egyptian manuscripts. They were of great help to Anthony. But I have some grave news about him and his assistant director, Richard Abrascus. They have disappeared; we are all so worried. They were meant to go into the pyramid for three days, and after five, we still have not heard anything from them. A search party has been combing the pyramid, but there are so many passages and still there is no sign of them."

Vince was sitting opposite Jane on the brocade sofa. Jane was in a leather chair. She thought maybe it would be nice if she went and sat next to him. The high-backed chair was pressing into her back. Their tea now sat before them untouched as Vince filled her in on the details. He was one of those Americans who spent many years in England. It had given him a slight English accent that softened the once strong American East Coast voice. He was a New Yorker; everything spoke of it. In conversation, he could be pushy but then he would sit back on the sofa relaxing into a laugh about his American style and behaviour. Jane found him delightful, and, of course, they had so much in common.

As he called one of the waiters over to freshen their now almost cold tea, he whispered to her, "You will stay for dinner, of course. It's late already and we still have a lot to discuss. Why don't you come and sit on the sofa; you look awfully uncomfortable?" He must have read her mind and she liked his assertiveness. He put the invitation for dinner in such a way that she didn't want to say no. She found herself rehearsing the phone call to Fairfax to let him know that she would be late. She reached behind her head and untied the bow holding her hair. The redness fell around her, released from captivity. She wondered to herself if she was flirting, but it was as though she had met a long-lost friend. She had moved now to be closer to him on the sofa. Vince started to look at her intently. His dark eyes fixed on hers and then held the gaze. She wanted to stay to tell him everything about herself, the past, the time in Egypt. Finally, the fresh tea arrived, and they ate some of the dark fruit cake they had ordered.

"I'm leaving for Cairo tomorrow," said Vince.

"How are you going to find him? Don't go on your own; it could be dangerous." Jane was genuinely concerned.

"Let's go up to my suite before dinner, and I will show you the documents that we already have and why we need yours. Did you bring the maps and documents on the pyramid, by the way?" he asked.

"Yes, but I need to put a call through to my husband, Fairfax. He will be worried if I am late." She wondered why she was doing this and spending so long with Vince.

"It's all right, Jane. I am really quite safe to be with." He laughed as though he read her mind again. He was haunted by Anthony's face suddenly, as he led Jane up the grand winding staircase of Claridge's to his suite. He knew Anthony was alive, but he was in grave danger.

"What's wrong?" asked Jane as she saw him hesitate halfway up the stairs. His face had become pale.

"It's Anthony. I feel his presence very strongly, as though he is telling me that their lives are in harm's way, that something has happened to them."

Vince had a beautiful suite at the front of the hotel There were two bedrooms, bathrooms and a large reception room. Papers were spread all over. A butler came in with drinks and then left. He spoke again to Jane, now an avid listener to what he was going to say.

"Anthony is trying to penetrate the mystery of the pyramids. He is so naive. Sometimes in his enthusiasm, he doesn't realize that countless others have tried to capture and know the secrets of the universe. Not yet does he realize how hard the path is and how many trials there are. You know that, Jane. My teacher said that at times spiritual life is like walking barefoot over broken glass." Vince sat down solemnly in one of the chairs. Jane sat down as well, opposite, the documents spread on the table between them. Something caught her eye.

"Yes, please look at them. I'm going next door to change for dinner." He went off to the adjoining bedroom.

Jane was pouring over the sheets of the once scrolled paper in front of her, when Vince returned from his bedroom. He was wearing a black suit instead of the tweedy jacket that he had on before. He walked over to her and sat opposite to her again. His cologne was delicious. She loved the subtle aroma.

"So, what have you found?" he asked.

"I'm very familiar with the structure of the pyramid here. I studied many layouts like this. You see these chambers? They all have replicas either above or beneath them. They are always sealed off and unless you know of their existence, you can get lost. Sometimes, there are many fake doors. Then there are defences all over to guard the entrances to the tombs. One false move and you could incarcerate yourself. I hate to say it, Vince, but it is possible that Anthony has got lost or incarcerated, or both. He will die if that has happened; Richard too, for that matter, unless someone who knows what they are doing gets them out."

She looked down again at the documents; she had also put her own maps spread out on the wide table. Vince came and sat on the wide arm of the chair, and as he did so, she felt him slide his arm around her. Then slowly he was pulling her towards him. His hand held her face and he kissed her, gently at first, and then when she didn't resist, his mouth became more forceful. She found herself aroused in a way that she hadn't felt for years. Then the phone rang. Vince got up and went back into the bedroom to take the call.

She got up, still reeling from the effects of his embrace. Suddenly she grabbed her coat and headed for the front door of the suite. She could still hear Vince on the phone; it sounded like long distance. She could not risk staying with him; the attraction was too strong, and it was time she went home to Fairfax.

Out on the street, she asked the doorman for a taxi and went straight to Lincoln's Inn Fields to find Fairfax at his office. It was too late, and he was already gone for the day. She felt silly as she could have called him first. Then, she took a taxi to Primrose Hill and sat in a café for an hour thinking about what had just happened. Her mind, usually calm, was running on fast forward. Maybe she shouldn't have just walked out like that and left Vince, but she had felt so overwhelmed. Fairfax would be home by now. She again felt stupid sitting in a café near Casey and Lord Oliver's flat. She had only gone there because she knew the area. She felt so lost and indeed her mind was in a turmoil. Since Egypt, all her attachments to the outside world had been broken. Her path was an inner one. For years now, she had been prepared to just pack a suitcase and leave any minute. When she went to new places, she always felt lost. She was not so connected now to the outer world.

She decided to call Anna, who, she felt, somehow understood her – not the details, of course, but the overall picture. Anna's silences always helped her get through whatever it was that was gnawing away at her. She found a reasonable phone booth at the end of the street. She did not want to use her mobile.

"Oh, my God," she thought, remembering that Vince had her fax and home number. She hoped against hope that he didn't call the house and speak to Fairfax.

"Anna?" she waited for a reply.

"Jane, where are you? Fairfax just called to see if you were over here; he's worried about you." Anna's calm and distinctive voice was coming down the line, giving her reassurance about the world of Grassock Oaks that she so wished was real.

"I think I am going to Cairo tomorrow." She had realized before she said it that this was what she was, in fact, planning to do. It had to be very soon to help find Anthony; in a way she felt that she already knew him. She had the knowledge to help rescue him, probably trapped in the pyramid.

"What on earth for?" Anna sounded astonished by the suggestion.

"Well, it's all about some documents that I have on the pyramids. Anyway, there is a man in London who I met today that needs help. A movie maker, called Anthony Jackson, and his co-director have disappeared. They were inside a pyramid." Jane's voice trailed off. She was not making much sense to Anna who was shocked at the sudden call.

"Then you had better go. Fairfax will probably think you are crazy. Who is the man in London? Anyone we know?" Anna, as usual, had honed in on the real reason why Jane had phoned.

"He's called Vince. I was just with him at Claridge's." Jane's voice had become a whisper, she noticed to herself. Anna had also noticed.

"And?" asked Anna.

"And, yes, it wasn't what you think, but it could have been. Oh, Anna, I feel so guilty. I mean, I didn't ever envisage that happening. I was really swept away. In the end I walked out while he was on a long-distance call. I feel awful," she finished.

"Jane, get yourself into a taxi and go straight home and have a hot bath. I will call Fairfax and cover for you somehow. Yes, I'll say you went late night shopping in Oxford Street and couldn't reach him so called me instead, and that you got stuck in traffic. Oh, that won't do. He will have to know why you are going to Egypt. You had better tell him the truth that you were meeting someone at Claridge's about a trip to Egypt."

Jane put the phone down, relieved. She called Fairfax to say that she was on her way and had gone to meet him at the office but had been delayed.

Back in Chiswick, Fairfax stood at the door with a fax in his hand.

"Darling, this just came for you. Are you all right? I was worried. Anna called and said that you have had an interesting meeting, that you may have to go to Egypt. How exciting! I wish I could get away!" Fairfax kissed her on the cheek. No, Fairfax did not excite her passion. Dear Anna, always paving the way for her, covering her tracks.

The fax read as follows:

*"I quite understand your early departure today and think it more than a possibility that you will come to Egypt tomorrow to look for Anthony. I know that you are one of the few people that can help. Why didn't you tell me about your ordeal in Shropshire? Did you think that I didn't know what you went through there? Be in touch soon. You have my details. Best wishes, Vince."*

"How on earth did he know about Shropshire?" thought Jane.

# *20*

"**A**nna?"

"Who is this?" She had just bathed; her skin still slightly damp; a crimson floral silk robe hung around her casually, as she went into the bedroom to take the call.

"Anna, don't play games; you know who it is," he said.

"I'm sorry, but you will have to tell me." She wasn't going to give him the satisfaction of knowing that even when the phone rang she somehow knew, after all these years.

"Anna, don't play games with me." His voice was angry. She could feel it,

There was a silence at Anna's end of the phone that seemed to go on forever. In that time, she found herself removing the ribbon that she had tied at the back of her hair. The hair fell loosely now, down around her shoulders. She breathed heavily, her perfume filled the room. She ran her long fingers through her hair as she spoke. It was soft and silky.

"So?" she said.

"Anna, I wanted to hear your voice; I never see you." His voice sounded just the same.

"I asked you not to call here. You know that I can never see you again. It's not easy." She had sat down on the chair near her desk. The modern version of a quill pen sat on the desk;

she fingered its black feather in her fingers. It was so smooth, so sensual, somehow. It reminded her of something that Fabian used to do to her.

"I want to see you, Anna," Fabian said.

"Impossible," said Anna, her gaze still on the feather. She was already aroused; she could feel it under the redness of the silk.

"Please, Anna," he was being nice, of course; he hadn't always been nice. She remembered his rages, his violation of everything that she had held sacred. He had taken everything from her, possessed her so completely. There was not a part of her that he had not enjoyed and captured. When she wanted to end it, he would not let her go. She fought.

He had told her that if she left him, she would carry a curse into her life, that he would take everything that was precious from her. She didn't believe him then, but it was true; she had never really been able to give herself to another man. He had ruined her. His whole being had penetrated so deep inside her, and he had taken her to a netherworld and beyond but had never let part of her come back. She thought then of how he had trained her, the subtle suggestions, in the ties and sharpness that he used in the unravelling of her body and mind. She inwardly groaned at the remembrance of these things: the mating ceremony with Fabian at sixteen, the sexual rituals, the surgical removal of her hymen, the guests with their hideous masks. And what else had been done to her in those early years of childhood? The path to her memory was blocked. When she felt and thought of these blocks, she would become overwhelmed and dizzy. It was best not to go there; she was not supposed to remember.

She shuddered now at these things – the Hexagon Club, where she had been drugged, worked over until she could not remember who she was anymore. And yet, part of her wanted it again: the highs of endlessly pushing the sexual boundaries of pleasure and pain; when pain, ecstasy and longing became one; when one could not differentiate the pain and pleasure; the dangers of skin or flesh resisting. And always more: longing, tearing at her legs, inside her, her womb, then outside her, a long, low drumbeat of intoxication. She had not known when or how to stop. Fabian only knew how to put an end to it before she was in real danger.

"No," she said; she wanted to mean it. She knew that she didn't mean the 'no', that it was always an implicit 'yes', and she knew that he knew this as well. She could feel her body responding to even his voice after all this time – the tell-tale feelings of arousal. After five years, he was still that deep inside her.

"We miss you at the club; it is not the same without you, so many of them asking for you." Fabian was unleashing memories for her, of the club men.

"Lord Oliver was asking for you the other day too. He wanted to meet with you too." Anna's mind stirred then, the memory of the marshes in Cambridge, just nine years old, of sitting on Oliver's knee, his blue eyes. She had been asleep. Did something happen then? She had been ill after that. Anna's mind as usual went into fog when she tried to remember anything about her past or childhood. And then after that day, there had been the aching longing in her, the hand rubbing against her genitals, thinking of him, those blue eyes, the frequent urinary infections and stomach aches. She wondered now, if Oliver had done something to her. It would have been so easy for him, while she was asleep, enchanted on his lap.

Many years later, on one of her first visits to the club, Oliver had come over to her, kissed her on the lips, sliding his hand around her waist and then onto her bottom. He had never forgotten Anna, and after Fabian had divested himself of her as his prize, he hoped that Anna would now come his way. He still remembered that afternoon when Anna was nine, the young girls lost in the marshes; just a little way, he had reached just a little way into her young body where she lay there in his study. But Fabian came over to them and removed Anna. Oliver knew now that he would never be allowed to tread on this sacred ground. He would have to find his pleasures elsewhere.

Anna had last seen Fabian just before Giles disappeared. They had gone to a sumptuous house in London for an afternoon and evening. Their passion still knew no bounds; they did not know how or when to stop. For hours it went on. She remembered everything, the positions, the toys. She couldn't even go home that night or the next to have Justin see her like that. She looked pale, ravaged. Fabian had wanted her to stay back to be with him. He hit her hard across the face when she refused. Then they started making love all over again. Finally, she left and went away for a few days. Her body had ached for weeks. She hardly remembered who she was. After that, she felt that a part of her had gone with Fabian to Switzerland forever.

"Darling, don't you remember, I never forget? It is like a constant fire that never goes out. I need you, Anna. I must have you with me." He was pleading with her now.

"I can't leave Justin, I just can't," said Anna. She meant it.

"Anna, meet me in London. I am here for a week or so." He was so persistent. The memories made her weaken, her body remembered. Justin could not arouse her passion like this. She was a woman that already belonged to another man, but it would be a life of death. Whichever way she turned, death seemed to laugh in her face. Often, she had thought that Jane's dream of an omen had been meant for her. Whatever her choice, it meant a kind of no-life. Her mind was made up.

"No, Fabian, I am not going to see you. I cannot bear it." She was going to put the phone down.

"Anna, you will regret this. I will have you, Anna, one way or another. You are mine and you know it. You took the initiation of the black thread. You wore it and we became one in the magicians' circle. Without me, you cannot have a life; you are dead, Anna, dead. You will regret your decision, Anna, you will. Your days will be dark; I will tear Justin away from you. Even your own life will be taken from you." Fabian's voice was insistent, penetrating her ear.

Then he hung up. She didn't know where he was. He wouldn't try her again, she knew that. He was ruthless, always had been. There was nothing that he would not do to get what he wanted. She felt her life, what there was of it, had just gone out like a thin flame of a candle. Now it was only a question of time.

The phone rang again. She didn't answer it and it wasn't him, of that she was sure. The machine started to answer the call. She lay on the bed covered in the red satin robe, lying on her side, pulling her legs up towards her belly in a foetal position. She ached for him; her body moaned. The red of the robe was like the surge of blood within her, moving inch by inch towards her lover.

An hour later, she awoke. She still lay there thinking – a plan was developing inside her. She decided to call Jane to see how her own plans were going. Then she would go to the club without Fabian. She was getting restless, but she wanted to cut Fabian out of her life. She wanted the highs now without the attachment to Fabian. She wanted her freedom.

"Hello, darling, it's Anna." She thought she sounded bright, perhaps a little too bright.

"Anna, are you all right? You sound awful!" Jane was packing.

"No, I'm all right, just a bit tired."

"I'm leaving this afternoon. Vince went on ahead. He will meet me at Cairo Airport this evening and take me to the hotel where the film crew is staying. It's the Adelphi; I have never heard of it. Here is the number in case you want to reach me."

"Take care, Jane. I presume Anthony is still missing?" Anna asked.

"Yes, I am afraid he is. We will be going to the pyramid almost as soon as I arrive. We are taking a crew of demolition workers and various other experts with power tools and so forth. He is probably lost and trapped in one of the chambers."

Anna did not, after all, talk about herself to Jane; she never did. Jane would be shocked at her life, the knife edge that she lived on. She thought of the club now, how she would dress up in one of those revealing cocktail dresses, don her emeralds for the night ahead. She knew her power and that she could have whatever dalliance she wanted. The stakes would be high. Justin was away and she could have what she wanted.

Detective Inspector Grahams drove slowly up the drive of The Beeches. He had forgotten how beautiful the garden had been, and it was a week or so since his last visit. In his mind, there was still a question mark over the whole incident of Anna's chauffeur and the accident in the ravine. Things were not adding up.

"Hello, Julia. I think Lady Bowlby is expecting me. We had a two o'clock appointment." The house seemed very still; perhaps she had forgotten.

"If you would like to wait in here," she pointed to the drawing room, "I will tell Lady Bowlby that you are here."

"She did remember, then?" he asked.

Julia gave him a sidelong look. She knew Anna was still upstairs; she hadn't seen her for hours, come to think of it. She wanted to stall for time a bit in case Anna was sleeping. She was always so tired, thought Julia to herself.

"I'm sure she remembered that you were coming, sir; she always remembers things." Julia saw him sit down. Today, he didn't have his country shoes on; in fact, he was dressed in a dark suit. No longer did he have the look of a local detective but looked as though he had just come down from Scotland Yard. His pipe wasn't in his pocket. Julia went upstairs to Anna's room.

"Yes?" Anna asked, as Julia knocked.

"Detective Inspector Grahams is here, Lady Bowlby. Will you be coming down?" Anna still hadn't opened the door.

"Tell him I will be down in ten minutes or so; say I have been resting. Get him some tea, will you, Julia, and some magazines or something." Anna sounded as though she had been asleep.

Dressed in charcoal grey silk slacks and a black shirt with a Chinese collar, Anna looked immaculate as on all the other occasions he had seen her. "Lady Bowlby, I am so glad to see you. Thank you for your time; there are still some things that I need to clarify with you." Grahams was an acute observer of his fellow human beings. She was nursing a grief, though, not only related to the loss of her son, but something else hung around her presence – a kind of constant nagging worry. He felt it had been there for a long time.

There was something so deeply erotic in this woman, but she was disturbed, possessed by something just beyond her reach. He could not fathom her depth. But she was the epitome of elegance, perfect legs, beautiful and manicured hands. The lushness of her hair, that when uncoiled, he suspected would fall well below her shoulders. Yes, she was a born seductress; she had the skill of the burlesque about her. She titillated. Right in front of you, she could remove her elegant silk clothes, one by one to the sounds of soft music and the fizz of champagne. Yes, Anna was intoxicating.

Anna sat down on the sofa opposite him. He stared at her: her hands with the red enamel on each nail, the gold bracelets on the slender wrists and a large solitaire diamond ring next to her wedding finger. She was used to his gaze, the male gaze; men always stared at her. It did not disconcert her; they could never get enough. She felt she had Grahams in the palm of her hand.

"What can I help you with this time?" She was making the point that she thought his visits were unnecessary. He was too probing, wanting to know secrets that she would never tell. It was futile for him to come. He couldn't save her, no one could, and it was too late.

"Have you ever felt that someone is trying to destroy you?" said Grahams, He went straight for the mark.

"No, I can't say that I have." She wasn't going to give long answers. She wanted this interview to end as quickly as possible.

"Someone who is jealous of your husband's success, your money and privilege?" he continued.

"No, there are plenty of people who have the money and success that we have; no." Grahams had a knack of getting through the cracks; she could feel him banging away on her psyche.

"I am sorry that I have to ask all these questions, but it is really for your own protection. Let me explain. You see, you said that the accident was caused by a black dog running across the road. We have checked, you see; no one in the area owns a black dog. Funny, isn't it – all sorts of other dogs, but not a black one? Are you sure it was black? Was it a dog or something else?" He looked at her. He was trying to be nice, but she didn't warm up to him. She kept herself remote as only she knew how.

It irritated him; he wanted her to confide in him, confide the secrets that he knew she held to herself. She aroused him, and it threw him off centre.

"Can I get you some fresh tea?" She completely ignored his remarks or questions about the dog. What could she say? They couldn't possibly accuse her of causing the accident. It wasn't her fault. She knew that it was an attempt to warn her, to harm her. She wanted the conversation to end.

And then Grahams agreed to go. He knew that they had to accept the story and they didn't want to incur the displeasure of Lady or Sir Justin Bowlby. He had lost; so, in the end the police would drop it. It would become an entry on the file to gather dust in the office. So many of these rich and famous people got away with murder.

"Give my regards to Sir Justin." He put out his hand and she graciously took it.

"Of course! Julia will show you out."

She started to turn away. She heard Julia talking to him as he found his way to the car. The car started up and then stopped. He was coming back into the house. "Damn," she thought, "what does he want now?"

"Sorry, Lady Bowlby, but do you remember John, your chauffeur, mentioning anything about the car needing work? We found that some of the wires around the engine had been severed – only a few. It could have been the impact that caused it, but it was also possible that they had been cut by someone with malicious intent." Grahams was watching her closely now.

"No, I have little to do with the car. I don't remember anything," she said.

But it was the first time that he had seen her lovely eyes widen in that way. This time, she did hear the car leave.

# 21

Anthony had his hand on a large lion carved from lapis lazuli. It was very smooth-edged. The Egyptians had wanted everything to last, so there were no hard corners. He had found the lion in one of the tombs that stood open. Lions protected the world of the spirits.

"We'll never get out; there is no exit!" Richard lay back on the floor of the King's Chamber where they had been for the last three days. They had no communication with the outside world. Anthony had chosen not to take any mobiles in; they wouldn't have worked anyway. Richard had been angry about it; he thought they should have carried some safety devices.

"There has to be a way out. They always had a secret entrance. At least we have some food and there is some air. If there is air, there must be a way out," said Anthony, determined to stay optimistic.

They had entered the pyramid three days before. They were supposed to be leaving today. The passageway they had come into was lined on either side by twenty identical huge statues in black of Anubis, the jackal-headed God. The passageway was much larger than they thought, but they felt overwhelmed by the energy in the pyramid; it seemed to affect their ability to think clearly. It was as though a thousand eyes were looking at them, the dead still alive occupying what was now perhaps a heavenly rather than earthly world. Richard felt his hair literally stand on end as they walked past some of the burial chambers. The mummies were wrapped and then put in a series of sealed coffins, one inside the other. The outer coffin had every available inch covered in exquisite designs of different animals, hieroglyphics and birds. The face of the occupant was painted also on the outside where the face would have been on a real person. The eyes were made of glass and looked real. When Anthony and Richard walked past, it appeared as though the eyes stared at them from their lidless sockets, surveying the intruders.

They had been doing well. The map was helpful, and their last ascent led to the King's Chamber from the Queen's Chamber. They had mapped out all the filming that they wanted to do. The hieroglyphics containing the power of sound – it was the power of sound that made the world function. It was the power of certain sounds on the chakras that made it possible for a man to become a god; Anthony was realizing the possibilities of becoming a god. Treasures of vital scenery lay open to them; it seemed they were getting lucky. Then, as they both entered the King's Chamber from a long narrow corridor with a fifty-foot ceiling, they heard a noise like thunder coming from the end of the tunnel. Having no idea what it was, they stayed waiting in the King's Chamber. Within no time at all, they saw an enormous stone rolling at great speed, coming towards them. It hit the entrance of the tomb and stayed there, a plug that fitted the entrance perfectly, effectively incarcerating them. That was three days ago.

Richard groaned; he had a fever, probably brought on by the strange energy in the tomb.

"We have to find a way out of here. It's our only chance; come on, Richard, think! We only have enough water for another day; then we are really in trouble!" Anthony was inspecting all the surfaces of the stone, looking for a lever or a hole. There was nothing. He felt that things were not right somehow; it wasn't just the stone at the entrance but a feeling that someone wanted them out of there. There were forces that he did not understand. Suddenly, he found himself looking at the coffin in the middle of the floor.

"That's it, Richard!" he said. "There must be an entrance under the coffin; I just know it. The coffin hides the entrance; we have to move it!" Richard looked at him as though he were mad.

"How would anyone move that? It's so large!" he said, still lying down. He was thinking of his wife and children. Waves of panic were rolling over him, drowning him in a fear worse than he had ever known. He had the feeling that the people who hated him had finally caught up with him; he had plotted so long against them and now they were reaping their vengeance in this tomb. He couldn't confide in Anthony who had no idea about the other aspects of his life. He felt himself as dark, hopeless; it was all coming to an end.

Anthony bent over him and helped him up. He was aware that it was too much for Richard; he was slipping into a delirium. He gave him some brandy which helped for a while.

"Come on and help me," said Anthony.

But Richard was looking awful, very pale and whispering, "Get me out of here, Anthony, for God's sake!" He stood up for a while and tried to walk to the other end of the tomb. His steps started to falter again; he sank down onto his knees.

Carefully keeping his eye on the statue of the King who was buried, Anthony said a prayer to it, asking for help. Then he turned to the serpent carved along the wall, the now-familiar Anubis head and to Osiris who was the ruler of the netherworld and King of the Dead. To all of them, he muttered his prayer asking for help. He felt renewed. There was no way that he could lift the coffin, but a stone slid sideways easily beneath it. A hole appeared, revealing hundreds of scarab beetles carved in red jasper, cascading out onto the floor. He felt them in his hand and thought of their meaning – the symbol of rebirth. It seemed a good omen and now even Richard started to look more hopeful. The gods were on their side and he knew it. And then they saw the hole just as

Anthony had predicted. They gave silent thanks for their rescue.

The hole was not huge but was like a chute leading to a passageway below. They squeezed through and slid six feet on their stomachs. A long corridor flanked by coffins and pillars ran to the right and the left and at their feet were boxes of shawabty, miniature carvings of workers who were sent with the dead kings to help them with whatever tasks were needed. Anthony put a small one in his pocket for luck. They saw a light at the end of one corridor. It went on and then off. It was impossible to distinguish whether it was daylight or not. They decided to walk towards the light. They both had their own light but the other in the distance seemed brighter, somehow.

Anthony was starting to worry. He thought that he kept hearing laughter, not happy but a kind of demonic sound from the other end of the corridor. He felt uncomfortable again as though something was wrong.

What happened next was so fast he had no time to avoid it. Richard was walking ahead, filled with new vigour from the escape. He started shouting something to Anthony who was only a few feet behind. It was dark but Anthony was close enough to see a hand come out from what seemed like a wall and push Richard down a deep shaft that had literally opened under his feet. There was a deathly silence.

"Richard, Richard!" he yelled but there was no sound, no hand, and the laughter had gone. There was only silence. Richard's light had fallen with him and so Anthony only had one flashlight and he was all alone. He tried to climb down after Richard. But there were no footholds. Calling down was no use either; only his voice echoed back at him.

Anthony, shocked and shaken and getting no response from Richard, wandered this way and that until he came, by remote chance, to the very chamber that Sean had most wanted him to avoid. It was a curious place with symbols and signs all over the walls. There were boats in rows along the wall. Anthony knew that the boats related to the solar aspects of afterlife. Even with the flashlight he was able to make out small statues in the vessels, wearing crowns and carrying rods with bent ends. He was fascinated to see these and reached up to look more closely when he noticed the instruments for the 'opening of the mouth' ceremony.

As he stared at the hieroglyphics, knowledge started to come to him: the secrets of leaving the body, seeing suddenly inside his own body and again the nectar dripping onto his tongue. The statues, he knew, served to bestow regeneration on the deceased. He reached out and touched a large jewel on the crown of one of the boatmen. As he did so, he saw the door of the chamber move and then close. He rushed over, but it was closed tight. He was trapped yet again.

"Oh God, don't forsake me now." He thought of Richard. Someone must get them out sooner or later.

Feeling a strange burning sensation, he looked around the room for his bag but realized that he had given all his water to Richard. He felt as though he was on fire. Sweating, he took off his shirt and lay down on the floor. After a while, he lost all sense of his body and then it felt as though a whirlwind was hitting him, hurling him into the cosmos. Ghastly dreams and demons visited him, waving their arms above their heads. Nightmare after nightmare enveloped and bombarded his psyche. He saw demons with erect phalluses, huge and ugly, penetrating humans and skeletons. He saw before him the ancient evil practices of sexual deviance, then the seduction of Horus by Seth – sins that he had only heard half-whispered about Ancient Egypt. Seth winged around him with blackness; and in his mind's eye, he remembered the sexual images used by the Hexagon Club, realizing to his horror that the rumours were true. His mind was wide open and at last he saw that there was going to be no way out of this. His life force started to ebb. He realized at last that someone or something had programmed all their minds a long time ago.

He started to remember his former lifetimes in Egypt. He saw himself as the Pharaoh's priest wrapping the dead magician in the fine linen cloth. Then he was a Pharaoh sitting on a throne in the golden sun and heat. A blue sky was overhead; eagles circled in the air above him. He had plundered the tombs and laid waste the burial chambers of the dead. He saw his greed, his cruelty to others and eventually his own death. His body was beaten by his enemies, and his flesh hung out on stakes for the cormorants to feed on. Then there were monsters that tried to suck the life from him, and he was pursued by strange sexual desires. He felt he wanted to die. The vision was so awful; maybe, this was what he deserved, his karmic retribution. Then he screamed at the top of his voice.

"I'm in here. Help me, help me!" but no answer came.

He knew that if he did not leave the chamber soon, he would die from thirst and from the deadly energy that sucked even at the marrow of his bones. He realized that this was one of the initiation chambers. It was for senior initiates, who perhaps could have withstood the lashes of energy, but it was killing him; he was not strong enough. He thought of all the movies where people had escaped, but this wasn't one of them. He had been lucky before but not this time; he lost hope. Then he screamed again and prayed to a God he did not yet know. He prayed for his life, for his soul – on and on, until exhausted; he fell into a deep sleep.

He slept for what seemed like forever. When he awoke, it was to the sound of drilling. He thought it was more of the nightmarish experiences, but this time it wasn't. Then in through the drilled hole walked Jane Crosby-Nash and Vince Lowell.

"How the hell… Richard, where is Richard?" he cried.

"Anthony, Richard must be dead. He fell over thirty feet. I'm so sorry," said Vince.

Anthony knew nothing else until he awoke at a private clinic on the long oasis of a tree-lined avenue in the suburbs of Cairo.

# 22

Sidney Henderson was sitting in his striped, silk pyjamas and dressing gown, having breakfast. His white hair as usual stood on end. It was a magnificent day, and he looked from their terrace at the sun-drenched town of St Paul de Vence. He and Moira had just arrived back from a stay with Anna and Justin. Moira brought fresh coffee and croissants to the table.

"You were asleep, darling; we just had a call from Anna. Jane has rescued that film director, Anthony; the other man was dead though, fell over thirty feet down a shaft, but they could not find his body." Moira put down the coffee in a silver jug on the glass table with its white linen cloth. The cloth was embroidered on each edge with bunches of primroses. It had, Moira seemed to remember, been a wedding present. She noticed that Sidney was very quiet this morning.

"Anything the matter, dear?" she asked. The paper lay untouched on the breakfast table.

"You know, all these things started to happen to Anna, Justin and Jane after they received the invitation from the Countess of Rigby. I don't like it, not one bit. There is trouble brewing. I warned them; perhaps I didn't say enough to warn them?" Sidney looked up at his wife. She looked so relaxed, dressed in a simple cotton dress. She wore a string of pearls around her neck. She always wore them. It was always he that saw the complications in things; she only ever saw simplicity and beauty.

But Sidney was deeply troubled. He remembered, in nightmarish sequences, his trip to meet Fabian for the first time in the castle in Switzerland, over ten years ago. He had told no one of this journey, not even Moira. Fabian had showed him all the designs that he wanted for the castle. It already looked like a Gothic horror story; it was shocking to Sidney. Then one evening, Fabian took Sidney into a room in which there was a strange hat, the kind of hat a court jester would wear in the Middle Ages. Sidney was overcome with a strange energy and Fabian's eyes were looking right into his own. It was as though he was losing consciousness and he was terrified. He had screamed at Fabian to get him out, but Fabian only laughed in this face. And then as Sidney fainted, he felt Fabian's hand reaching for his genitals. He woke again, realizing that he had been drugged, his lower body and legs were almost numb, and Fabian was standing behind him. Sidney's trousers were already gone, and Fabian was easing his own body closer to Sidney's rear. He was in no doubt that Fabian was planning to sodomize him.

And then crows flew out of the glass case and attacked Fabian. They came from nowhere, as though summoned by some outside force. Fabian suddenly lost his balance in the shock of the moment, giving Sidney time to grab his trousers and run out of the door and escape through the castle gate.

Somehow, hours later, he found himself at the bottom of a ravine; he had walked for miles until he found a place of safety. He never told anyone but was now absolutely terrified that his friends would have a similar fate in store for them, or even worse. Sidney thought Fabian was indeed the Devil himself. The horror of that night has stayed with him all those years. And this anxiety gave such a vehemence to his conversations with his friends, a vehemence that they truly did not understand. He was deeply on edge with anxiety. He was trying to warn them.

"Well, I thought you told them everything you knew. Is there anything else, Sidney? You know she only invited them for the weekend. It's not long, you know. Aren't you taking it a bit too seriously?" Moira sat down to have breakfast with Sidney. She knew he wanted to talk about it, and it wasn't going to be a short conversation. She could always tell when Sidney was getting started with something important. But Sidney said nothing about his own experience; he couldn't.

"You see, Moira, I didn't tell them everything. After all, people must live their own lives. You've met Jane's sister, Catherine. Her husband Louis worked for a man called Count Fabian Roth. Louis died while on a business trip with him. The family was never happy about the verdict of his death; they felt that there had been some misadventure. The Count is rumoured to have very strange tastes. He comes from a family of occultists. There was even talk of vampires in the family back in the nineteenth century.

"Well, there is nothing to prove it all, of course. In ordinary life, he has business interests, of course; owns a fair bit of the steel industry in Germany. The Count, however, is the brother of Emma, the Countess of Rigby." Sidney was slowly spreading his croissant with the morning's butter and marmalade. Moira was looking at the table cloth, thinking. Sidney was hiding something from her, she was sure of it now.

"Apparently, they never see each other. Something happened; no one really knows. But why would they not meet? It must have been something major. There are all these connections, Moira. First, Anna and Justin lose their child, Giles – so heartbreaking! Then Louis, Catherine's husband, dies mysteriously. Next thing we know, everyone seems to have an invitation to the Countess of Rigby's, ten days from now. A month ago, Justin's chauffeur is killed and Anna escapes death by sheer luck, it seems. And now, Jane is in Egypt rescuing Anthony Jackson. His co-director falls down a shaft and gets himself killed. No one seems to be adding this up except me." Sidney waited for an answer. Moira knew he wanted one.

"I know Inspector Grahams suspects something," said Moira, anxious to at least add something.

"Oh, Grahams, Anna can't stand him; she told me so; always around there asking questions. Justin thinks he is marvellous though. It's odd; they usually agree on things. Perhaps Anna is hiding something, and Grahams touches a sore nerve. What would she have to hide at The Beeches? No, it's impossible, or is it?" He finished off the coffee and looked over the balcony. There was a sheer drop beneath. Sidney had no head for heights. He wondered about Anna. Who was she really? There had been a large photograph of her encased in an elaborate silver frame on Fabian's grand piano at the castle. Sidney had not met Anna then, but when he did so, he remembered the photo, and it was not long before he was starting to piece things together. Although until much later, he was never completely sure that Anna and Fabian were lovers.

"Let's go sailing today, Moira. I feel like having some fresh air. Let's forget about London and working for the day." He walked over and took his wife in his arms. They would soon be celebrating their silver wedding anniversary.

Moira was used to the sudden change in Sidney's thoughts and actions. It was what made him brilliant, kept people on their toes. But she knew that he would continue to mull things over, even on the boat. He was like that; once he had an idea, he would not let it go.

A week later, Jane brought Anthony to London, and he stayed with her in Chiswick. Vince stayed in Cairo to oversee details of the production. Anthony looked worse than anyone she had ever known go through an initiation chamber. For days in the clinic, he seemed to be in another world. It was obvious to her that Anthony had already awakened his kundalini with the dream of the snakebite. This had meant he was more susceptible to the energy in the chamber than anyone else. So, the effects had been more devastating. The clinic was, of course, unaware of the kundalini, but they were concerned that Anthony's brain scans were abnormal; they had shaved his head to do repeated tests. His eyes did not react properly to light. They suspected a tumour. Jane wanted him seen by a specialist in London; she didn't trust Cairo, and the language was always a problem. Being near Vince was also making her anxious. Nothing had happened between them, but only because they were so focused on Anthony. Once, they had almost spent the night together, but Jane had in the end extricated herself and returned to her own suite at the Adelphi. Fairfax called her frequently; it was a reminder of who she was and where she belonged.

Richard's body was sent back in a wooden casket to Los Angeles. His wife and children had stood open-mouthed at the news of his death. They had no idea that Richard was even in Egypt, let alone inside a pyramid. His wife thought he was in the Balkan states. There were a lot of unanswered questions, and Anthony was not in any state to answer. Richard had led a double life; he had been paid to keep secrets.

John Grey was also in a coffin in the local churchyard of Grassock Oaks. His wife moved away from the lodge within a few weeks and went to live with her sister up north. Justin made sure that she would be comfortably off for the rest of her life; John had served them well as a gardener and a chauffeur. But his wife always wondered why it was Lady Anna's life that was saved and not John's. She never really liked Anna; there was something about her that she did not trust. She remembered John said that she used to frequent a club in Mayfair; it was an unmarked door, but John had questioned the doorman who told him it was the Hexagon Club. The doorman only raised his eyebrows when John wanted to know more. But, always curious, John had done further research and was shocked beyond belief at what he found out. And then one night he had entered incognito, got in somehow, but was then discovered and interrogated. But John had seen enough in one hour, incredulous at the club's sexual offers of gratification. That one hour, at the wrong time and in the wrong place, had cost him his life. He had been found out and the knowledge of the Hexagons would die with him. They had simply got rid of him. There would be no scandal now.

Maxine had returned to Washington to make a short visit to her father. Casey did not return to New York but flew to England to visit her mother in Cambridge. She had work to do with her shows in London and Milan. Then she was planning to go to Shropshire to stay with Emma. Randy's mother had died of leukaemia, and Casey had been tasked with looking after her now that her mother was gone. She was going to bring Randy to England to live for a while. Randy was very excited about this. She had heard so much about London and the red buses and could not wait to get on one.

Maxine slept for days on her return to Washington. Her father thought she looked strange. In some ways, he hardly recognized her; she was so changed. He didn't press his questions and Maxine did not stay long. Her apartment in New York had been cleared up. Fabian had gone through all the contents that were important to him; then, his men replaced everything as it was; the glassware and cosmetics were new. But he had not found the names he wanted; he took all her other research on the Hexagon Club. She didn't really notice the changes; she was adjusting to a new world where Fabian was a constant presence, even when he was not with her. She experienced a lack of feeling about anything except for him; he was the centre of her life; that was just the way it was. She did not care about her research now; after all, she and her family were all on the same side, in the same family of Hexagons.

Fabian had met with Alistair; they had spent the weekend together, playing polo and celebrating. Fabian had given Alistair the rest of the money he owed for selling Maxine to him. The Hexagon men, the Fraternity, often sexually enjoyed each other, and this weekend was no exception. They were, after all, a celebrated brotherhood; Seth, their master, had taught them to couple with each other. It was part of their practice, the legacies of Seth in Ancient Egypt. They bonded in their lust and their extravagant sexual habits. Fabian shared the most precious of sexual secrets with Alistair of how he took Maxine's virginity. Alistair wanted to weep and remembered all the photographs he had sent Fabian when Maxine was still a young girl. He wanted Maxine for himself; it had been a terrible sacrifice for him to give her away. In some ways, he wished Fabian were dead, and he was filled with murderous rage.

Fabian had told him that it had all gone to plan. There had been a ceremony; Maxine had fought a little on the road to becoming submissive, but Alistair's training of her mind as a child had been perfect. And now, Maxine was Fabian's property, not ready yet for any activities out of the fold. That would come. She would, like Anna, be his whore; she had been groomed well. She had to be drugged on occasions to perform some of his sexual requests but overall, it was good as far as it had gone. He saw himself as home and dry. Maxine was beautiful in every way. He could honestly not get enough of her.

Maxine had indeed been a virgin, and he himself had surgically removed her hymen while she was drugged and asleep. It was an easy procedure. The released secrets stored in the vagina came immediately to him. He knew these secrets now; it was key to ownership of her soul. Penetration was the key to most of the higher occult practices. Semen and its retention were key to higher knowledge. Alistair was at least happy that his side of the bargain was secure. And now, whenever he was in London, he enjoyed the delights of young women on offer at Fabian's establishments. It was heady stuff. Alistair was on a permanent high with it all.

Fabian had given Maxine certain instructions about what she should do while she was in America. There were people to see and things he wanted her to report to him. She never questioned his commands. She had merged into him and now they were one entity. There was no pain at the loss of her inner self.

Fabian had business in London; he did not repeat the phone call to Anna. Despite herself, she was often thinking of him, but there was no contact. She threw herself into the house, spending time with Justin. She had her own plans.

Everyone was, in a sense, waiting for something. It was only a few days before they were all due to go to Farlingham Park. They were all making their own preparations. The game had moved on, and the players were positioned accordingly. They, as Anthony suspected, had no real choice in their lives now.

# PART TWO

## *CHAPTER 23*

Lord Oliver Pemberton surveyed the room at the Hexagon Club with his ice blue eyes. He did his flies up and his belt two notches tighter than usual. He was rapidly losing weight. There had been some bleeding – not a good sign.

She lay across the bed, her red hair curling down her back. The firm buttocks, so recently enjoyed by him, were scarcely covered by the black satin of the sheet. On the bed lay a long tapering rod of leather, tightly braided, ending in a thin strand sporting one red bead. It was called the Unicorn.

His rage was immense. He changed his mind about leaving and again undid the belt, unzipped the pants and removed his clothes. He was now positioned on all fours on the bed, she was kneeling behind him, the long mane of redness running down her back. She took the Unicorn in both hands and beat him till he cried out with the pain. Ejaculation for Oliver had become an immense problem. And now his climax was coming; he was sure of it now. The whip was sound; finally, he was tipping over the edge. The relief was immense. As he lay down, the feelings of spentness had come now. He was flaccid again, waiting for the next time; almost immediately, he wanted to start the sport again. It was always that way; he was never satisfied. But he would have to leave it today.

His appetites gave him a terrible reputation at Hexagons, of roughness and lengthy assaults on his sexual prey; he could never get enough. Sometimes, he had to take two girls with him into the room. He dressed and left a wad of one hundred pound notes by her side. Money was no issue for him; he was one of the richest men in England. She had her back to him, face averted, as was the custom at Hexagons after a sexual encounter. She felt disgust and loathing for him. He had often asked of her the most degrading and perverse practices to be performed on him. Even she, who was such a professional, was sickened by him. She had to comply, always; it was her job. Oh yes, Oliver was becoming a liability to both himself and his human sacrifices.

His mobile had messaged him that Fabian wanted to see him in the Mayfair office. The brothel asked an initial membership fee of the tidy sum of five million pounds. Once paid, you could have what you wanted, and everything was on offer. And then, there was Thackeray Hall for the overnight orgies. Oliver attended these on every possible occasion. The girls were from all over the world. The younger the better, as far as Oliver was concerned.

The Hexagon clubs flaunted their wealth and sexual favours. Titled and rich men roamed the universe like so many scavengers, looking for the next toy, the more elaborate out-of-bounds sex, and under-aged girls. There was an endless search for a better, more expensive orgasm, and the nightly rates for a whole evening with one of the girls was sometimes as high as twenty-five thousand pounds.

Oliver was wondering why Fabian wanted to see him. He went upstairs; Fabian was out on the balcony under one of the sun umbrellas. He was looking at an elaborate centrefold, which he showed Oliver. They both smiled. Fabian had secured the young girl now for the Hexagon playgrounds. They were all going to enjoy the goods. "But not Oliver," thought Fabian.

"Oliver, we need you to go to South America. This death at Hexagons is creating a bit of a problem. What were you thinking of, to let this happen, and to such a young girl, Oliver? I don't know how we are going to cover this up? We need you away for a while. You also need a check-up, Oliver. You are losing weight, and I am aware that you are not well." Fabian was setting Oliver up. "We have you booked on a flight this afternoon. Please take it; you will be met the other end. Your destination is Montevideo, and then out to the country." The phone rang, breaking the silence, the drop-dead silence.

"Goodbye, Oliver, take care, I must go now. I have booked you into a private hospital for tests; after that, you will go to my villa." Oliver did not like being ordered around, but he owed Fabian favours, human-trafficking debts for innocent people that he had damaged. Fabian had covered for him, paid off members of Parliament, the police, doctors. He knew that Fabian had never forgiven him for sullying Anna when she had only been nine years old. Somehow, someone must have told on him. In fact, it had been Lucille who had inspected Anna on her return to the family home after Anna and Casey had got lost in the Cambridge marshes. Indeed, actual penetration had happened with semen in evidence. Anna had been in disarray, distressed. She had a fever for days. She had obviously been drugged, as she had no memory of it, but it had damaged her irreparably. Lucille reported this to Fabian, who had paid an inordinate sum for Anna's deflowerment, but not until she had reached the right age, according to the scriptures of lust that all these families followed. Yes, Fabian had been very angry with Oliver.

Oliver took a car to the Primrose Hill flat, the home where he and Casey still lived together, when he was in London. For years they had this place, where he enjoyed her body repeatedly. Neither of them could stop it. It had become an addiction for them both. It was a wrench to leave the place. He wondered when he would return to see his beloved again; he longed for her, and it was she that he loved the most in his life.

Casey had never really been able to leave him, the root of attachment still so strong inside her from such a young age, entrapment lodged in her vagina. She was still lost in her dream of him. Sometimes, when he was not there, she would awake with a terrible longing for him; it was in the seat of her belly, all over her body. He was as important as breathing to her; she could not live without him. Oliver had indeed cast a spell over her with his seed inside her many years ago. She was, it would seem, trapped forever.

Oliver panicked. He was shaking, in a daze, in shock. His life disturbed him now; there were no exits, no places to run. The good life had caught up with him. He took a small suitcase, some razor blades, his small pistol and, last of all, the box of narcotics that Fabian had given him before he left. He was hooked on cocaine, his favourite drug. It made him feel like a sex god, invincible, the drug being something of an aphrodisiac for him. Long term though, it had given him erectile dysfunction, and ejaculation was now so difficult that securing this one, unattainable thing had become a nightmare.

One week later, Oliver was recovering from all the tests at the hospital. It was not good news. Fabian was right; he was seriously ill. He was now resting at Fabian's villa. It was a heavenly night, and he had had one last swim in the pool. He told the staff that he did not want to be disturbed; in fact, he sent them all home. He took a large brandy and soda and surveyed the table in front of him. On it rested the box of razor blades, the gun and the narcotics. The light was fading outside; the sun had already set.

Oliver undressed; naked, he ran the hot water into the sunken tub in the bathroom. It was time. The blue eyes were dull. He had already snorted far too much cocaine; with that and the alcohol, he could hardly stand. He fingered his genitals but there was no life there anymore. Oliver was losing it. He went into the bathroom, got into the hot water and took the gun in one hand. He slashed one of his wrists and with the other hand, he cocked the gun and shot himself full in the mouth. The blood seeped out of him.

His last thought before he died was of his stepdaughter, lying by the pool in the sun, naked except for a little bikini bottom. She was just ten years old, his lovely, adorable goddess

Casey, his darling forever. He remembered every line and wrinkle of her delectable body, his forever, or so he had thought.

It was a day later that Fabian received a call that Oliver had taken his own life. His blue eyes were still open when he was found; one delicate, perfectly manicured hand, mutilated by an ugly slashed wrist, lay resting on his genitals.

Fabian also received a call from the hospital that Oliver had attended. He had the numerous tests. He had been told that there was nothing to be done. Oliver was told that he had terminal cancer of the bowel. It was said quite clearly to him that the cancer had metastasized to his brain and liver. He had been given just three months to live. But Fabian had paid off the doctor. There was nothing in fact wrong with Oliver, except some problem with his digestion, which was the only reason he had lost weight. But Fabian knew that this lie, a diagnosis given by a doctor, would tip Oliver over the edge and Oliver would take his life. He hated any kind of illness and would have wanted to have ended it all. Fabian's plan had indeed paid off. One day the truth would come out, but it would take years to uncover what really happened.

Fabian hushed up the news of Oliver's death for at least a week, paying the press inordinate sums. He fabricated a story that Lord Oliver had met his death in a car accident just outside Montevideo. Fabian had spun a double lie and when the news broke and it was in the papers, everyone believed it. People mostly believe what reaches the press and the newsrooms. And Fabian made sure that things went his way.

# 24

"Can't I get out here?" asked Stephanie. They had just passed through the entrance to Farlingham Park. The heavy iron gates stood open. The pillars were tall, Corinthian, and topped by ugly-looking gargoyles; they had their long tongues hanging out. Justin could see the ivy had recently been cut back from the gates.

"It may be a long way to the house. Why do you want to get out now?" Anna asked.

"I just want to... to walk into the woods. I'm tired of sitting in the car." Stephanie didn't say why she really wanted to get out.

"Well, all right. I'll go to the house and then walk back for you. How's that?" said Justin, slowing the Mercedes down to a stop. Stephanie got out and started walking towards the woods. Anna got into the front seat.

"Isn't it a bit risky, Justin? We don't even know the place." She was worried; it brought back too many memories of Giles.

"Oh, she will be all right. She has antennae as big as those people in *Star Trek*. She would sense someone coming from miles away. She probably has one of those stun guns that render other people powerless," said Justin.

It was unlike Justin to joke like this; he never spoke so lightly, especially about Stephanie. Usually, he was too preoccupied with her safety. Anna looked at her husband. He looked tired, she thought; it would be good to get away for the weekend. The car continued slowly up the driveway. A green passageway of trees lined the avenue; the rhododendrons were in full bloom, mauve and white.

Anna, of course, recognized the driveway and then the house. After all, it was where she had lived and died in her other lifetime. She felt a wrench, as though a wind was pushing her back in time; the horrors of that lifetime were upon her now, dim but visible to her. She could say nothing of this to anyone.

"I wasn't expecting quite such an ancestral home," said Justin. "It's a good thing we came early. It will give us some time to adjust before the big event tomorrow. I can't imagine what the Countess of Rigby is like. Do you know anything about her, other than Sidney's tales of horror?" He was still joking, so unlike him. When he is like this, thought Anna, he is usually deeply preoccupied.

"No, I know as little as you do. I must say, I will be as glad as Stephanie to get out of this car. It's really been quite a journey. We should have stayed at Jane's house; she did offer, you know; it's only five miles away." Anna stretched her back against the seat.

"Look at those, quite amazing." Justin was looking at two stone sphinxes facing each other along the avenue. Anna didn't answer; there was something about them she didn't like. "Certainly to Jane's taste though, our resident closet pyramidologist." He was sensing Anna's dislike of him and his brutal humour for the last hour. In truth, he was so deeply upset with Anna and their marriage that he did not know how to cope.

Anna's betrayal of him, her secret sexual relationships of which he knew nothing, his own impending sense of doom and feeling that the life he had no longer belonged to him – none of this made sense. He did not want to live in a fluid world; he wanted certainty, to know where he was, like when he was suturing a wound. Now he was aware that the world was constantly changing and that what he experienced as the truth yesterday was no longer the truth today. It was like a circus. He could not even believe in himself anymore.

Justin was used to Stephanie talking in riddles about a world he could not understand. Yes, a few minutes ago, he had pulled the car over to the side of the avenue and let her out. He had waited for a few minutes as he saw her in her white dress, hat and shoes walk away from them. Soon, she had disappeared from their view completely. He felt sadness in his heart; it was always like this; she was always going away from him to a world he could not understand at all. In a way, she was like Anna, always retreating to a place where he could not follow, where he was excluded.

It had not occurred to him before how alike Anna and Stephanie were; they even wore the same hats these days. When he had mentioned the visit to the Countess, Stephanie's eyes had lit up in a way that he had never seen before. Of course, Stephanie had never told him that in the nether world to which she belonged, she was Smira, daughter of Anubis, and her mother was Thrat. She was of that world, not this. To her, this world was but a delusion. Anubis was again at war with Seth; the battlefield this time was the world. Seth was the opponent of everything that gave life; he sought only chaos and destruction. It was said that Anubis was the son or nephew of Seth. Anubis was the god of the transitional zone between the world above and the netherworld. He was god of the dead and funerals, securing passage to the afterlife for mortals. He was the arbiter of human souls.

At the same time that Seth and his minion, The Jester, were seeking chaos and destruction for Anna, Justin and all their friends, Anubis was trying to save them from the curses of Seth and what was being planned as their final destruction. Farlingham Park was outside of time and space, it was full of witchcraft and ghosts from the days it was built. Both demons and angels stalked its corridors.

Justin had no idea how enchanted or bewitched the place was. As he entered the gates of Farlingham Park though, something made him feel that it was no ordinary place. He had covered his feelings with his jokes and made light of everything, but he was on his guard. He did not know what to expect. Then Anna said something that came as a complete surprise to him. She was obviously having her own thoughts.

"Justin, this place has a certain energy about it; it's peaceful, but at the same time, I'm afraid of it. I fear it will take you away from me somehow. It's as though anything could change here. I felt it as soon as we entered the gates, and now Stephanie has gone." Anna spoke softly so as not to disturb anything. She felt that if anything was too loud, it would tear her life apart. "The gates of hell," she thought. "Who is going to ferry me across to the other worlds?" She had been promised this by her family, that by surrendering and giving her innocence to the males of the Fraternity, she would like them, gain everlasting life. All the years of pain that she had borne, the gynaecological surgeries, the endless infections – there had been times when she had wanted all her female organs to be removed. Something rotten, evil, lived within her. She could not get it out. Then last night, she had experienced a dream, of taking a knife to cut her arm, till blood flooded to the surface. Yes, in the dream she wanted to get something out, something evil, something poisonous. After the dream, she felt hours of immense anger at what had happened to her, that her family was not like other families. But Anna was still in the dream; she was imprisoned in it as though forever.

"It's because you are still recovering from the accident, it makes you have heightened sensitivity. I have noticed this so often with patients." Justin spoke with authority, trying to convince himself of reasonable explanations; he did it all the time. He wanted so hard to believe that the world was real. Anna looked at him with affection, but she felt no passion. It surprised her that she didn't feel it. Justin was so good-looking, but she couldn't feel what she felt for Fabian. That passion was killing her and she knew it.

"You know, Justin, I keep thinking of the experience that I had after the accident. I was away from my body so long. At one stage, I felt that I was living in someone else's body, but it is so indistinct now that I can hardly remember. It did give me a sense of having a separate reality from the body; the whole idea was very freeing."

Justin, for the first time, told her about the experience he had when he was operating on Stephanie; that he had seen a woman standing over Stephanie and after that, her heartbeat had returned. "You know, Anna, I asked her once about her experience of living; we had had all sorts of conversations before that. She said, 'It's all blue, Justin; it's all so simple; everything is made up of blue energy that surrounds everything. It's the first thing I see when I look at somebody, the light that's around them. I come and go in this light all the time; It's my only real home. I don't spend as much time on the planet as you do; I go elsewhere as well. It's nice coming and going, in a way.' She went on like that, saying that she visits other places, and saying that one day soon, she thinks she will leave for good. Her idea of death is so different from ours. It was amazing, really, coming from a ten-year-old little girl."

"Justin," said Anna. "I want to have another baby." So, she thought, it was finally out.

Justin didn't answer, at least not then. He saw the house in front of him and it took his breath away. At the beginning of the drive, he could only see a small part of it. It was like a Gothic cathedral, its flying buttresses shining in the sunlight. Somewhere, he had seen it before, but he didn't know when or how. He had no idea that he had once owned the house in another lifetime as Sir Ashley Cooper and that his wife Amelia, (Anna) had been murdered here. Justin had none of the knowledge that Anna had about past lives. If you asked him, he would say that he did not believe in such things. Anna knew that they had been married before, and in the same lifetime, she had again been unfaithful. There was no end, it seemed, to the cycle of life and death. Their roots and sins went back centuries.

Stephanie found herself in the forest by a stream. She felt tired, having walked so fast through the trees. She was so sure that she had seen someone. She just felt such a tug in her heart when she had seen that person. It was then she knew that she had to be with it, wherever it was. It was like the blue light and the figure were somehow connected. The feeling of tiredness was getting stronger. She saw a large log and sat down and closed her eyes for a few minutes. There was just the sound of the stream, and the darkness behind her eyes. Then she opened them again after what felt like just a few minutes. When they were open, she seemed to be in a different place; everything had changed.

But then she knew that she was in the same spot; there were no leaves on the trees, and icicles were hanging down from the branches above her. She was sitting on the same log, but the ground was covered in snow; there was mist around the trees, and she could only see a few feet in front of her. Staring at her was a deer, just a foot or two away, its breath coming out in clouds against the freezing cold air. The deer was looking into her eyes; it just stood there motionless for minutes, and then it turned and walked away slowly.

"Stephanie, Stephanie." She heard a voice crying her name from the mists. She couldn't bring herself to answer. She looked down at herself. She didn't have on her white dress, but a thick red coat. She looked at her hands; they were older than her own. Then a man appeared from behind the trees. He saw her and was running towards her, his arms flung open. He ran fast, spurred on by the heat of his love for her. She stood up as though to greet him. Out of nowhere, another figure appeared from behind a tree, a tall dark-haired man, a soldier. He took his rifle and aimed it at the man running towards Stephanie, firing one shot. It hit its mark, and the man fell on the spot just twenty yards away from her. His blood ran into the white snow. She recoiled in horror at the brutality. The soldier ran on towards her, not satisfied with only a rifle shot. He was up the hill in no time, racing towards her, his great coat flying in the wind. He slipped and fell, but then he was up again. Stephanie was rooted to the spot. Finally, he was upon her. She tried to fight him off. He threw her to the ground, one hand around her throat. Stones were pressing painfully into her back.

"Bitch," he cried, "you bitch, get out of our country; you are like pigs, you people; worse, vermin! Get out, get out, or we will kill you!" He stood above her. He took his bayonet and plunged it headlong into her heart. She felt her spirit leave her body in the snow. She opened her eyes one last time and saw a figure wearing a hat with bells; it had three peaks. He ran down the hill, his laughter filling and shocking the trees with its sound.

Farlingham Park was full of spells and magic after all these years. Powerful energy would bring up a past life memory in the blink of an eye. The house was not governed by normal laws; the past was present; the present was future. For all who entered here, there was massive confusion, accessing the other lifetimes; for Stephanie, it was immediate.

Her past life had been in Nazi Germany. She was a Jewess, her lover killed, and the soldier's bayonet piercing her heart, giving her a physical weakness in this present life, the seeds and roots from other lifetimes entrapping, holding her in patterns as yet unknown. These mysteries of Farlingham Park, darkness turning to light, were held above the earth in a matrix of unending threads of connectivity both inside and outside time.

Stephanie opened her eyes. It was summer. A figure stood before her. She wept and clung to the figure, her arms around his knees. The figure was thin, only love left inside its frame. Stephanie hung on as long as she could, imbibing the love and the bliss. Her father Anubis, seeking to comfort his daughter, had entered the earthly plane. Then her arms came together into nothingness and the figure was gone. She fell into a deep sleep.

# 25

"Vince, where are you?" Jane was on the phone; she and Anthony were having a late breakfast in her house in Shropshire. She was deeply concerned about Vince, about Anthony, about the whole situation. It felt out of control; Richard's death was a complete mystery, especially not being able to find the body.

"In Cairo, trying to resurrect the movie and deal with all the legal problems arising out of Richard's death. I miss you, Jane, more than I can say." Vince was in his suite at the Adelphi. A lot of the crew had returned to Los Angeles, not wanting to stay; they thought the movie was doomed. Things were not happy in Cairo, and it was unbearably hot. There were demonstrations, and there had been a minor but disruptive earth tremor.

"I miss you too. Anthony is here. He's much better but still very weak. Would you like to speak to him? Are you coming over soon?" Jane was nervous. She felt so close to Vince. She didn't want the relationship to threaten her marriage, but she was pulled without doubt. It was as though something had taken up residence in her belly, deep down, a cord between them. From where did it come? She wondered if they had shared other lifetimes together.

"Yes, put him on. No, I don't think I will be coming. There is too much to sort out here." He waited for Anthony to come on the line. Jane felt let down, but it was probably for the best. She was a married woman with responsibilities to Fairfax.

"Anthony, it's bedlam here. The authorities are kicking up a real stink with the movie. They don't want us to continue. Besides, they are now saying they do not think Richard's death was an accident. Apparently, his wife had no idea he was in Egypt, and he has received huge payments into a bank account in Switzerland that cannot be explained. It's really a mess. How are you, anyway? Are the doctors happy?" Vince sounded troubled. Anthony was concerned but felt so removed from the situation. He mentioned nothing about Richard's death.

"I wish I could suggest something, Vince, but just keep trying. We raised a lot of money to do this, and I want to see it through." Anthony did not sound convincing to himself or to Vince. He felt that the moment had come and gone for the movie, slithering to another river, another time. The energy that had been tied up with the pyramids seemed to have burnt up in his experiences. He just wasn't there anymore. His life was going in a different direction. He continued talking to Vince, saying that the doctors wanted to keep an eye on him in England; he still had unusual neurological signs.

They were lounging around the breakfast table in the kitchen having coffee and toast. The sun was shining through the open door into the garden. Anthony's hair was cropped short; they had shaved his head twice. He looked like a Buddhist monk instead of a film director. The cheeks were hollow, and he had lost over five kilos. Jane had bought him new clothes during their stay in London. His eyes were very brilliant, and he carried himself with a consciousness that he'd never had before. He noticed that his powers of observation were greater, and there was more peace in his heart. He wondered, but only to himself, whether he would ever direct another movie. He felt his life was ebbing away from its present melody to something else. He loved Jane's house; he would sit in the old swing seat in the walled garden and watch for hours the birds feeding and the bees entering in and out of the wild flowers. His meditations grew deeper, and he often only stirred from his seat when Jane reminded him that it was time to eat. They shared their experiences of Kundalini and the exciting but sometimes perilous journey to the upper regions of their conscious being. To Anthony, it was all new; Jane was a big help in giving him the understanding that he so desperately needed.

"Do you want to go to Farlingham Park today? Justin and Anna will be arriving, and we could have a look around before the crowds come tomorrow. I think we are going to stay over there tomorrow night, if that is all right for you," said Jane, still wearing her old corduroy dressing gown. Cedric was sitting on the floor chewing the rubber bone they had bought at Harrods.

"Well, I guess we can go. Sometimes, I feel so tired that I just don't want to do anything at all. I really wonder what is in store for us all at Farlingham Park. It all seems so familiar sometimes, a sense of déjà vu, and then I remind myself that I don't really know that place or the Countess at all." Anthony wore a white kaftan this morning, making him look even more like a monk. He had bought it in Cairo; he liked the feeling of the soft Egyptian cotton and the looseness of the garment.

Spreading a last piece of toast with marmalade, he looked across at Jane. She reminded him of what he always thought Tudor women looked like – the perfect violet eyes, the eyelashes hardly visible and the cascading red hair that in those days would have been caught up in a net of pearls and pulled away from the face. Then there would have been the stiff colour standing high up from the neck and shoulders. She would have worn a unicorn's horn to ward off the plague and perhaps a coral necklace to ward off witches and evil demons. He was lost in thought. Period movies were his lifeblood; he was sure he would have felt more comfortable living in another century.

She was an amazing woman, but she had compromised her life somehow; she did not fit into the Chiswick or even this Shropshire world, but where else could she live now? He had noticed the difference in her since she had met Vince, a highly intellectual and very spiritual man.

"Jane, are you in love with Vince?" The question was unexpected; Anthony often asked questions out of the blue like this. But Jane took it in her stride. She fingered the blue china mug that held her coffee and looked at him.

"Yes, in a way, I am I suppose. The day we were at Claridge's, we nearly ended up in bed together, but I ran away and went to find Fairfax. It's just that, well, somehow, I feel so close to Vince. We have so much in common; see things the same way, like being in love with oneself. I'm also very attracted to him. But I could never leave Fairfax; we are so different, but he adores me. It would break his heart. We have made a kind of life together. He doesn't understand the serpent power, or deeply spiritual things; he is just not interested. The closest he comes to it all is going to mass once in a blue moon."

"Anna is not happy, is she?" said Anthony. It was a statement rather than a question. "I feel she has a secret life, as though she belongs somewhere else and to someone else. She is so beautiful, but Justin does not stir her passion. She is like a unicorn that needs to be set free. Her life, I think, is a burden to her." He continued watching the look of surprise on Jane's face.

She replied, "I really think she loves Justin; they have been together for years. She never really talks about her life before her marriage." Jane was thoughtful. She had known Anna and Justin for so long; it was odd to have a stranger make a comment about them, as though he knew their innermost secrets.

"Maybe she doesn't want to remember what it was like; there may have been someone else. I feel that her childhood was hurtful and confusing to her, as though she has a tear in her heart that will never recover. Her son disappeared too, didn't he?" Anthony was helping to clear things from the table as they talked. Cedric was jumping up and running around, wanting to be in the woods and run in the morning sunlight.

"Giles went when he was nine years old. I wasn't around then, but Anna was ill; she ended up in the London Clinic because of what happened. Justin gave her so much love and helped her through it. She would never think of leaving him after they had been through that together." But Jane doubted her own words as soon as she had spoken them.

Richard's death was creating a great many legal problems for Fairfax who was assisting Anthony in all the legal matters. The police wanted to talk to Anthony about the accident. It was just routine questioning, said Fairfax, but Anthony wondered what was really going on. Egypt was an unusual place; it may not turn out well for him. Suppose he had to appear as a witness, if there was a court case? It would bode very badly for his film career. His thoughts were heavy, as he and Jane walked out into the garden. He sighed; he wished he could stay here forever in this idyllic place.

"Yes, Jane, let's go over to Farlingham Park later this afternoon and see Anna and Justin. Maybe there will be some other people there as well." Anthony stretched and yawned in the sunlight. As he breathed in the air, he felt his life open up before him, terrible events and situations that would take place for them all. He was being allowed a sneak preview, and it was like falling into a bottomless pit filled with a nest of vipers. Jane looked at the shadow that passed across his face.

"What in heaven's name was that?" she asked, concerned.

"I felt I saw the future, my future, your future." He turned away and went back into the house and up to his room. He lay down; his body shivered as though he had the flu. Covering himself in a blanket, he eventually drifted back to sleep.

It wasn't until later in the day that he awoke to Jane knocking on the door, to say it was time to get ready. He felt refreshed from the sleep, as though someone was looking after him. At last, he felt ready for Farlingham Park.

# 26

Fairfax sat at his desk in Lincoln's Inn Fields; he was one of the most gifted barristers of his time.

A dossier was on his desk, one of the most serious he had ever received in his career. Someone had come forward wishing Fairfax to prosecute the Hexagon Club and its members. It had opened up a Pandora's box of such enormity that it would have ripples globally. If Fairfax took on the case, both him and his wife could be in the gravest danger. Yesterday, Lucille Carrington, Anna's mother, had unexpectedly come to see him. She was living in the darkest horror and was afraid now not only for her own life but also for that of her daughter.

Lucille had sat with Fairfax for some hours. She told him everything, about their family, what Anna had been subjected to as a child, the evil and perverse sexual practices that had been observed in their family for generations. She talked of the mind-numbing grooming that each daughter had been through. And now, there had been a death from such practices. One of Anna's youngest cousins had been heavily programmed and trained in the sexual and occult arts. This young girl had been only nine years old, a beautiful and exotic child. One of the Fraternity had drugged the child and taken her to the Hexagon Club some weeks ago. Things had got out of hand. Casey's stepfather, Lord Oliver Pemberton, was responsible for this young girl's death. Things had gone too far. He was quite out of control, and the girl had had a heart attack and died. She may have overdosed on the relaxant that they frequently used at the club on young females who were too tight, too frightened.

The death was, of course, covered up, and Lord Oliver's own doctor in Harley Street took care of things as instructed, removing the girl's body from the club. He wrote a certificate to say that the heart attack had happened at the cinema, although he did a thorough examination that showed the bruises on the young girl's body, the tearing between her legs and the presence of semen in her anus and vagina. But all this was hushed up by Lord Oliver's cheque book. It had been a costly sum to buy this silence and of course, Fabian had been informed of her death. Lord Oliver had been through scraps like this before. But the death of a minor, that was something else. The police were informed but were guided only by the doctor's certificate.

Somehow, Lucille had got to know about the situation and found out that the young girl had in fact died at the Hexagon Club after being savaged by Oliver. This was enough for her to break her decades of silence. All her years of pent-up anger had come out in Fairfax's office, all the rage at what Oliver had done to her own daughter when she was nine years old; Anna's complete lack of memory of these events, being treated like an animal by Fabian, the rapes of Anna by his friends. Lucille felt she would break apart. After she had recounted everything, she broke down in sobs.

Fairfax excused himself from Lucille's presence at that point and left the room. He made his way to the gents and vomited into the nearest basin. The sickly stench of Lucille's account of the most demonic and evil practices that he had ever heard of produced another vomit, this time of his own bile, before his body could settle down and find peace with itself. His whole being felt disturbed. He was afraid for Jane and his family who had been mixing with these same damaged families for years. No wonder Sidney had felt that he was onto something and had expressed his concerns. Fairfax was shaking with shock and disgust.

Lucille's story made so much sense to him; the agonies of Anna and Casey, their mutilated lives. It was as though a thousand-pieced jigsaw puzzle fell together to form a picture so heinous he could hardly look at it. He went back into the office, excused himself to Lucille for his delay and saw how pale she had become; her eyes were red with sobbing. He felt enormous compassion for her, the terrible life she herself as a child had had at the hands of the Hexagon Club. He pulled the cord in his office, summoning one of his staff to make tea for both Lucille and himself.

Lucille had brought some of the huge journals she had kept over the years, documenting Anna's childhood, the grooming and how Fabian had taken her at sixteen, tormented her, and finally had turned her into a high-class whore, compulsive with a severe sexual addiction. Lucille spoke more about Anna, Oliver and Fabian. She broke down yet again. Years of tears and tension welled up, as they both stared ahead in horror at what had happened to generations of young girls. It was the worst kind of sex trafficking that Fairfax had ever heard of, and in the highest echelons of society, all covered up by the worlds of wealth and privilege in which all these men lived.

"I want them to face justice, all the fathers, and most of all, Count Fabian Roth. All of them should face trial; all of this; years, generations of lies, should find the light of truth. Everything should be documented and exposed to the public." Lucille's voice was breaking, her beautiful face ravaged by her tears.

"You do know, Lucille, that Lord Oliver is dead?" Fairfax was not sure whether she had heard the news.

Lucille bowed her head in answer. She already knew. Now she would never have her revenge, and Oliver would not receive the punishment that she wanted him to suffer. She felt that she could kill him barehanded herself, but now it would never happen. She felt defeated sitting in Fairfax's comfortable but austere office.

"You do know that you yourself could face trial, Lucille, for letting these things happen, turning a blind eye to your husband, to the club, not protecting your own daughter Anna, who has suffered so much?" Fairfax was aware that she could face years in jail for her complicities.

"I don't care, Fairfax. I have made my choice; this cannot go on, the lives of young girls treated like cattle to fulfil the cravings of grown men. You know that Lord Oliver raped Anna when she was only nine. She does not remember; she was always hypnotized and drugged in order that she not remember, but I saw her when she came back that day from tea with him. There was blood and semen on her pants – nine, Fairfax; she was only nine; I could smell him on her and in her. She was half asleep for the rest of the day. He must have drugged her and done it to her when she went to see Casey. And what about Casey? What he did to her for years, her mother used to tell me every week when we met – what was going on. Every night, he was going to her room, Fairfax. I think it went on for years; Casey, like Anna, was quite addicted to the violence and the sex."

"But why did you and Antigone not do anything, go to the police?" Fairfax was finding it hard to control his rage. What had this woman been thinking of when Anna had been violated in this way? And Casey's mother, what about her?

"I was under a spell; I had also been subjected to the mind control. We were also sworn to silence; there would have been endless punishments for Anna and myself; she would have suffered even more. You have no idea what it has been like to live with these men, these monsters." Lucille, with tears spilling down her face, told Fairfax how after that, Anna had frequently rubbed herself, frantic masturbation that went on for years, leading to many urinary infections. And then, there were problems in her female organs, infections. Fabian took no care of her at all; he treated her so badly.

One night, Fabian and an American senator took Anna to the stables, tied her up and raped her, even her anus was torn. She took weeks to recover; but by then, she was addicted to sex with him. And then he left her for eight years. "We chose

Justin for her then as a suitable marriage," she said. "Both families were very wealthy; it was a good match. But it did not work, Fairfax; she was too damaged, too addicted to Fabian. Fabian had taken her virginity when she was sixteen, her hymen had been removed." Fairfax raised an eyebrow.

"Oh yes, this was an ancient practice based on the belief that the hymen must not be torn. Their belief is that the vagina, newly penetrated, gives its occult secrets to the penetrator. The removal of innocence of the young girl, the giving up of these secrets, gives the man a gateway to eternal life and to the god of his own universe. Oh, this is their belief. This was also done in Nazi Germany before girls could marry. They all went in the thousands to have their hymens removed. The hymen is an impurity that had to be removed for the secrets to be intact. The master race had to be assured to the Fuhrer. The women had to be cleansed and the hymen removed. This would assure that the babies conceived using special ceremonies would be masters of a new race, all gods within the new German empire. Lots of research on this was done in the concentration camps, things like how those tortured would not have any marks on their skin. Lots of experiments were done on women..." Fabian put up his hand; he could not stomach it any longer.

The story was coming out now. Lucille was in shock. The story was all out of order, but the facts were there, enough to proceed with charges. Fairfax felt the bile coming up again in his throat; he was shocked and pained to hear her story.

"Then Lucille, if you have made up your mind, we will proceed; both of us are sworn to silence. I will have to take council. This is an unprecedented situation. It will need careful handling. We are both in danger, you realize this, and our families too!" Fairfax moved as though to rise from his chair.

Lucille got up to go, pulling her coat around her. She shook Fairfax's hand, both his hands, in thanks.

Fairfax sunk into the comfortable armchair in the corner of his office. His mouth was set into a grim long line. He pulled at his tie. He was going home. It was more than he could bear as a human being to hear this. Now he was worried for Jane's life; she had already warned him that they were in danger, and she was very nervous. Why had he not paid more attention to her? He would go home; but of his work with Lucille, he was bound by silence, a heavy load to bear alone on his own shoulders.

He wrapped his coat around him and ordered his car to be brought around for him to drive home to Chiswick. He locked the dossier in the safe before he left.

# 27

"I simply don't believe it," said Anthony. "We just can't have had the same dream about the same place and as different people; it's just too impossible."

Anthony and Jane were huddled in the Lancia which now stood at a standstill halfway up the drive to Farlingham Park. Anthony felt sick from the memories of the same driveway in the dream where he was pursued by the carriage in the pouring rain. He could still see the heads of the horses in the plumed bridles urging towards them, he himself slipping further and further into the mud.

"But I was in the carriage, Anthony. It was true. I was the woman, and a man sat opposite; and then there was the face of the strange animal-headed man astride the stallion. He had the face of death, his finger pointed at me. It was the carriage that was pursuing you in the mud and the rain. What does this mean? It's strange; it is as familiar to me as though it was my own home."

Anthony put his head in his hands as though trying to remember more, but nothing would come except a kind of agony across his chest.

The Lancia had the roof down, and Jane looked up at the cavernous arch of trees overhead. She thought of the man in the shop who had tried to kill her, the shattering of glass. Cedric was not with them; had gone to the kennels, sadly, with his tail between his legs. He hated going away, but Fairfax had to stay in London on urgent business, and there was no one else who would or could look after him. She wondered what kind of urgent business, but she knew better and Fairfax had hardly spoken to her before she left.

"I have felt for months now that someone has been invading my whole being, watching me and even entering my own dream world. I have a feeling of doom, as though something terrible is going to happen to us all, your family, me and the people close to you, like Justin and Anna." Jane felt waves of fear go over her. There was nothing that she could fight; the enemy, whoever it was, remained invisible.

They saw a figure walking towards them, away from the house along the drive. It was a woman in a white plastic raincoat and blond hair. She was still some distance away.

"Who on earth is that, another ghost? This place already seems spiked with the unreal." Anthony got out of the car and was on his guard. But it turned out to be Casey. She kissed Jane and was introduced to Anthony.

As they caught up with their news, Jane was commiserating with Casey about Lord Oliver's death. Suddenly they heard a movement from the undergrowth coming towards them, and the sound of running footsteps. They all turned to see Justin carrying a little girl in his arms emerging from the undergrowth. So, this is the next scenario, thought Anthony; his own life was becoming a much greater topic of interest for a movie than any other subject he could think of at this time.

Half an hour earlier, Anna, from the vantage point of an elegant white deckchair set out on the veranda, saw Justin running across the croquet lawn and into the forest. Stephanie had not returned, and Anna presumed that he was trying to find her. No one else was out on the veranda with her; in fact, they had seen no other guests at all. A lone butler brought her delicate little sandwiches and a tray filled with china teapots, cream and jam, and finally an impressive basket of scones. She enquired about the whereabouts of the Countess.

"Her ladyship has been delayed. She will not be arriving until late tonight. She sends her apologies and hopes that you will make yourselves feel at home. Miss Pemberton will be joining you for afternoon tea. She has just taken a walk towards the gates. Will there be anything else, your ladyship?" The butler, a man in his fifties, lingered for her reply and then moved back to the house.

Anna surveyed the clipped hedges, the excellent rose garden. The whole feel of the garden and house was Gothic, like an old cathedral. A white peacock strutted this way and that, sometimes looking at Anna and sometimes at the newly erected tents, blue and white, further down the lawns. She thought of this house as it was in the early nineteenth century, closed soon after her death in that other lifetime. She shuddered at the thought. Her ghost must have roamed here for over two hundred years. She was filled with dread at the thought of her own future. Things did not look good.

Justin found himself lost with no path. The light was not strong. There were too many trees, and he had already fallen once on a knot of roots exposed above the ground. He cursed at his bruised shins. He sat down on an old chest kept under a tree for no apparent reason. He opened it, but it was empty. He began wondering where Stephanie was, when he saw an extraordinary sight. Justin moved away from the box and hid behind a thicket of yellow gorse.

A figure had just entered the clearing beyond, dressed like someone out of the Middle Ages. His hat, that of a jester, was topped by three bells. It was the ringing of these bells at intervals that attracted Justin's attention. Justin hid from view and watched the antics of the strange person, or was it an apparition? The figure was dancing in a circle, on the same spot, moving slightly on long, pointed shoes. He cradled a kind of doll in his hands. Then the figure stopped, as though searching for something. He was unbuttoning his tunic. The buttons were now unfastened; there was nothing beneath, as though he had no body. Justin was terrified of this figure. He felt the hair on the back of his neck and arms standing on end with fear. He moved to another spot, afraid that he might be seen. The figure was obviously enraged. He moved towards where Justin had been sitting only minutes before and opened the box. Justin realized now that the box belonged to The Jester. It was a good thing that he had moved.

The Jester put the doll in the box, put on his tunic and with one movement dragged the wretched box into the clearing. He sat on the box, mumbled a few words into thin air; then he and the box, tunic, shoes and costume all disappeared into nothing. Justin felt overcome with exhaustion and vomited into the bushes. He felt the presence of evil in that place, like no other he had ever known.

On a log, now, in the clearing, sat Stephanie, her body slumped forward. The white dress was covered in mud, and on her face and neck, her veins stood out, bluish from the skin. Justin knew she was deoxygenated. She did not recognize him when he picked her up. He carried her in his arms and ran through the undergrowth in the direction of where he thought was the house but instead he found himself halfway down the drive again.

His shirt was torn by the brambles. For some reason, blood had run from his nose, and Stephanie lay motionless in his arms, as he crashed relentlessly on through the forest, heeding neither the brambles nor the upturned trees. At last, he stumbled onto the avenue that led to the house. He stood as though in shock, staring at the red Lancia with its two occupants and Casey standing, leaning against the car. He recognized nothing in his concern for what was in his arms.

"Justin, what on earth happened?" screamed Jane. Justin did not reply, but opening the Lancia door, put Stephanie in and got in himself. Anthony quickly got out and Jane took off at top speed towards the house. Casey and Anthony stood as if rooted to the spot, open-mouthed, watching the car disappear into the distance. Anthony stared at the car as it vanished around a bend and then at Casey, who looked as though she had seen a ghost.

# 28

"I saw a strange kind of man, dressed like a court jester, in the forest; Stephanie saw him too." Justin was talking to Anna as they were dressing for dinner. Anna immediately turned white, the blood draining from her face.

"Why are you so pale, Anna, what's wrong? Do you know something about this?" Justin stared at Anna as though for the first time. Was she hiding something else from him? He had got Stephanie to the house and into bed and was thinking about the shock of seeing this frightful sight. Suddenly, he felt he could trust no one. A view of his life flowed before his eyes like an endless river. None of it made sense, the sacrifices, and the roles that he had played. It all seemed like nothing; even Anna stood before him like a stranger. He thought maybe she had created all the lies in their lives. He felt sure now that someone had placed a curse on him.

"There is nothing wrong. It's just that you surprised me. It's such a strange sight to experience something like this. Do you think you were perhaps dreaming, darling?" asked Anna, meekly. Justin did not answer her.

She sat on the bed and stared out of the window that looked out into the forest. If The Jester was here, it meant one thing for sure; that Fabian was not far away. The two of them were inseparable. Anna was the only person Fabian had ever told about The Jester. She feared him like nothing else she had ever known. She had experienced him in her dreams and about her person as though in some way he had penetrated her aura, like a long, thin needle. The sensation was hard to describe somehow. Fabian and The Jester, she now believed, were one entity.

"We'd better go down now, Anna. They will be waiting for us for dinner in the hall." Anna could see that Justin had changed at the sight of The Jester, as though he were under some kind of spell. Anna felt for the first time that Fabian's words were coming true, that he would take Justin away from her as he had taken Giles.

Later, they were all seated in the great dining hall of the house. It was long and ridiculously thin; the ceilings originally had been painted dark green, full of strange mythical figures; the wooden edges painted in gold leaf. On the walls were Belgian tapestries of outdoor feasts, tables laden with fruits and wines. Figures reclined on benches while cupids shot their arrows into the hearts of would-be lovers. Long windows from the hall afforded vistas of the forest beyond the walled gardens full of summer flowers. The house was a Gothic masterpiece, but even in its precision, it was no earthly place and was ever haunted by strange stories and the past occupants.

They were all seated at the long table, from where their dinner was being served by butlers in full livery. At the head of the table was Justin, Anna to his right. Jane, Anthony, Casey and Randy were close by. At the other end of the table sat another party of people. The table was so long that it did not afford much discussion between the two groups, although Justin recognized the face of a well-known composer. Maybe they would mingle a little more with after-dinner coffee. Justin thought suddenly about Sidney Henderson and his concerns about the family of the Countess and its history. If this afternoon had been anything to go by, Sidney had been right, but it was too late now to do anything about it.

Dessert was now being served. Anthony leaned over to Casey. "How do you know the Countess, Casey? Do you live in New York permanently?" he asked looking into her blue eyes.

"I met her in the South of France a couple of summers ago; she is quite extraordinary. She doesn't mix much socially, even when she has guests. She mostly lives in her chateau in France, but she also has a mansion in Japan, as well as Farlingham Park."

Anthony noticed the sadness in Casey's eyes as she spoke; she seemed lost in some way.

"What are you doing in New York? I was there briefly in the early part of the year; I love to visit."

Casey seemed thrown by the question; it took too much energy somehow. She was aware that she was more nervous and more debilitated than she thought. Surprised at her vulnerability, she thought again of how her own life had been shattered like Maxine's apartment. It had been painful seeing Maxine again, and the wall that had been erected between them had shocked her more than she could say. There was no rudder in her life; everything she had known had broken apart. A personal question even about where she lived was more than she could take. It embarrassed her; she was usually so on-the-ball. Anthony, even with a simple question, was asking for the deepest part of her. She answered the question in a matter-of-fact kind of way.

"I'm just taking a break. I am an artist in New York, but I have shows in Milan and London right now." The words came out in a throw-away tone. She saw Justin looking at her as well, as though he was trying to remember something just out of reach. It disconcerted her, for some reason. Anthony retracted his attention. She knew that he was aware of how she was feeling.

She thought of Oliver, her stepfather, and again felt the terrible grief of his loss. A nagging sickening feeling emerged, showing her that she was far more disturbed by her separation from him than she had realized; it seemed like a terrible dream. The spell was breaking. She would start to become aware of the pain of so many years. But she was not ready; the spell would break like pieces of a mirror. It was to be a slow and terror-filled journey for her. She had been in a trap for almost as long as she could remember.

She looked sideways at Anthony as he was talking to Randy. She wondered why his hair was so closely cropped to his head. It made him look like a monk, and he looked as though he had not slept properly for weeks. Then she started adding sugar to her coffee. She was thinking of Oliver, their bodies bound together for what seemed like most of her lifetime, and the spoon kept stirring. When she came to, everyone was staring at the spoon. She laughed and wondered why they were all here; everyone seemed to be preoccupied with something, as though they were in a kind of mental institution to get cured.

Yes, now Casey wanted to be alone, to explore her own thoughts and to see the house. She wanted to call Oliver, but she realized in shock that he was gone now. She felt confused somehow, as though her mind and soul could not accept his death.

She rose from the table and left the dining room. Anthony's eyes followed her. "Beautiful," he thought. "Such slim elegance, and the fine blond hair and clear eyes." Could he be falling in love? Or was it that he just needed something to divert his attention from the tragedies to come or to have someone save him?'

Randy also left the table to follow Casey; she ran down the hallway, calling after her.

"Where is the other little girl who was supposed to be here? I want someone to play with. You promised there would be someone my own age to play with here," cried Randy, who was bewildered at the size of the ancestral home after the familiar apartment building and doorman in New York.

"Stop moaning, Randy; you will see her in the morning. She wasn't feeling very well today, and the doctor told her to go to bed. So just be patient." Casey wondered whether she should have brought Randy at all.

"Which doctor put her to bed?" asked Randy, determined not to be put off by Casey's irritation.

"Justin put her to bed. He is a doctor," replied Casey.

"What kind of doctor? Is she going to die or something?" Randy took Casey's hand as they climbed the stairs.

"He is a heart surgeon. No, she isn't going to die; she just needs to rest. Randy, that's enough questions for today. I have a headache." Casey mounted the stairs.

"You always have a headache," retorted Randy.

"It's past your bedtime," said Casey.

"I don't have a bedtime. I go to bed when I like." Randy stuck her bottom lip out. She looked like Alice in Wonderland with her straight hair and the headband.

"You are going to bed, Randy, whether you like it or not. Otherwise, you will go back to America." Randy had arrived a few days before with a tiny suitcase that had practically nothing in it and no clothes. Casey could have wept. She had to take her shopping in London to buy her some things. Randy was delighted; it had been a long time since she had anything new.

Anthony also excused himself from the table. He was feeling tired and went up to his room. The butler had already unpacked his things. The room faced the rose garden that backed onto the stables. He wondered about Sean. Where on earth was he? No one had heard of him since Anthony and Richard had gone to the pyramids – vanished, it seemed, into thin air; his pay cheques returned to the film studios; the money unused.

He looked out of the window and saw Anna and Justin walking in the rose garden. They seemed to be arguing about something. Anna wore a suit of white linen; her dark hair was tied back from her head. She reached for Justin's arm, but he pulled away and walked off towards the lake, leaving her alone. Anthony wondered why he was together with all these people, with most of whom he had little in common but somehow felt he had met them all before. And this house, it was too familiar for his comfort. Again, he felt a sense of foreboding. Anthony also did not realize the true meaning of Farlingham Park.

It was midnight and Casey still tossed and turned in her bed. She could bear it no longer. She got up and decided to walk around the house. A high wind, unusual for summer, was blowing around the house; it was whistling through the windows and doors.

Casey took a back staircase up to the top of the house; all the lights were still on. She came eventually to a long corridor;

it was like walking into a previous century. There was a room with the door standing ajar. She stepped inside; the walls were yellow with age. A tapestry stood showing scenes of a deer being pursued and then killed by hunters. Casey was transfixed to the spot, riveted by the sight of the blood from the deer. A single but large bed stood at one end of the long room; otherwise, the room was empty. It was a long room with casement windows at one end. A white gown lay on the bed as though waiting for an occupant to arrive, but Casey felt that it had been many years since someone slept on that bed.

"You are right. No one has slept here since the death of the first Countess of Rigby," said a woman's voice from an alcove inside the room. Casey jumped with fright at the voice.

Emma sat facing her on a very upright chair; it was probably made of cedar wood, the back of the chair exquisitely carved. The uppermost part of the carving was of a dragon's head, twisting this way and that and breathing flames down on the souls beneath with upturned heads that faced its jaws. Parts of the chair, the backs and the arms, were carved as the feet and claws of the dragon. The chair had once been the pew of a famous French bishop, but its real origin was in a monastery at the foothills of a mountain in the far reaches of Tibet.

Casey knelt next to Emma.

"I have been here before, haven't I?"

"Yes," answered Emma. They spent the next two hours together. Casey felt she had known Emma forever. Emma explained that in the first lifetime they were all together in the Hyksos Dynasty in Egypt. Emma was careful not to tell Casey about the lifetimes of her cousin Anna or their friends. She merely told Casey that in Egypt she had been Tarsa, Salitis' wife. Salitis was the political advisor to King Khamudi. Emma recounted there had been great danger, and the Pharaoh's magician had come bearing an asp pretending it was time for King Khamudi's death. But the Pharaoh had been warned in a dream that this would happen. He had the magician shut in one of the chambers of the pyramid where he himself would be buried. The Pharaoh left him there to starve to death; unfortunately, he was not aware that the magician had extraordinary powers and would utter a curse on King Khamudi, as well as his friends and family, for lifetimes to come.

But who was Anna and who were Justin and Anthony? Emma remained silent. She could not reveal to Casey anything ahead of time. Each person had to understand their own predicament at the right time. They were all in the gravest danger from The Jester and Seth. They could all lose their lives. They were all under a curse.

"I can tell you about one more lifetime where you have still been cursed, Casey. In King George IV's reign, you were Charlotte, cousin to Amelia, the first Countess of Rigby. She was wife to Sir Ashley Cooper, physician to the King. The magician from Egypt had already incarnated as The Jester to King George and was slowly killing him. Somehow, he prevented Sir Ashley from having access to the King. The Jester eventually let the King die through neglect. He also killed Amelia, Countess of Rigby, at her ancestral home, at Farlingham Park – yes, Casey, this very house. Her husband was Sir Ashley. The Jester killed Amelia because she was Nehesy, the wife and first consort to King Khamudi in the Egyptian life. Any one close to the King would carry forward the curse imprinted in their karmic patterning. During this life, you were away living in Paris. Eventually, the magician found you and killed you in a hunting accident. You were still only a young woman, Casey. By then, Amelia had already been murdered by Sir John Hargreaves, her lover and her husband's brother."

Emma was watching Casey very closely to see how she was reacting. Emma was aware that Casey had suffered great trauma in her childhood from her stepfather. She knew that even Casey did not know the extent of the damage she had endured. The spell and trap were still intact. Emma knew that she had to tread very carefully; she had heard about Lord Oliver's death, the real circumstances and his evil intent. Casey was carrying an inner karmic pattern that almost matched Oliver's. His pattern after death would be de-programmed so Casey was in grave danger of losing her own existence and life on the earthly plane. Her hold on life already was quite thin; it could break at any time.

"But who was Amelia, I mean, which one of us was Amelia in that life?" Emma gave her no answer. She could not reveal these things now. The light in the room was starting to dim, and Casey knew that it was time to go with her question unanswered.

# 29

Fabian's mind was made up. He picked up the phone and called his London office.

"Please arrange with our police contacts here and in Cairo to have Anthony Jackson arrested for the murder of Richard Abrascus. I'll fax you all the details in a few minutes. We have enough evidence now to nail him. Make sure Anthony is arrested on Monday at the house of Jane Crosby-Nash in Shropshire and not at Farlingham Park." Fabian's in-house phone at the Ritz was ringing.

"Maxine Cleveland has arrived at the hotel, sir. Shall I show her to her suite now, sir?" asked the manager.

"Yes, that will be fine. Tell her that I will be with her shortly." Fabian put the phone down. He was perspiring. His hand gripped the receiver as he spoke to Russell again.

"Sir, will Miss Cleveland be wanting the chauffeur tomorrow? It is Saturday, and I think you wanted her to go to Shropshire?" Russell waited for the reply.

"Yes, yes, send him at nine-thirty in the morning. She needs to be driven to Farlingham Park." He could not bring himself to say 'Emma'. It still caused too much pain.

Maxine was already in her suite. There was little view from the window, which was covered with silk screens. Fresh flowers stood in their vases all around the room. The bed was a four-poster covered in black, matching the sofas and the lounging chairs. The maid unpacked her things and then left. She was alone. She knew that Fabian would have been immediately told of her arrival. She went to the bathroom and ran hot water into the tub. The water came from the base of the sunken tub. Noiselessly, it filled; she added her own essences, the ones that he liked. Slowly she massaged the milky lotion onto her breasts as she lay in the hot water.

Fabian's entrance was silent. He looked at her without speaking. He picked up the phone and demanded that no calls be put through until further notice. He sat on the edge of the bathtub and asked that she elaborate on every detail of her life since he had last seen her. It was like a storm of inquisition. And then he stopped.

"Maxine, I have missed you so much; it's been lonely without you," he said, He looked into her eyes, holding her attention. She saw the black pools of his eyes and again as in France, she felt herself fall into an abyss; darkness enveloped her mind. But this time she knew more; she had learnt how to stay conscious in the presence of his power. He realized that she had become stronger; she had carried out several tasks that he had assigned her from South America, with excellence. She had duped the people she had met and concluded a deal for him worth thousands of dollars. He was pleased with her. And now she let him make the moves, as he liked.

Then she lay naked across the bed, he had carried her to their room. A chasm was created by the absence of her soul, Fabian's own being moved into her; she was his. He knew exactly how far he could take her each time, and then he would stop. Each time, he took more and more of her. She gave him everything; her body, her mind, the cells of her being, and even her soul. Still, it was not enough for him. Her tongue involuntarily curled up on the roof of her mouth.

Then he pulled away from her; she maintained her silence instead of crying out. He went to his briefcase and took from it a box wrapped in tissue and ribbon.

"It's something I want you to wear when we make love. It's very old and special," said Fabian smiling at her.

She opened the box and found a black silk cord among the tissue inside. There was also a long piece of black cloth about six inches wide.

"Show me, show me," she cried excitedly, fingering the smooth silk before he took it from her.

First, he tied the cord around her, over her left shoulder and down between her legs. Then he told her to close her eyes as he tied the black cloth blindfold around her eyes. She became silent, aroused by the feel of the silk. She felt the sense of ceremony.

"It's called a sacred thread. When you wear it and make love, it makes it easy for you to enter the world beyond, the Nirvana. Here, see this tiny clasp? It will tighten around you and it will heighten your senses beyond belief. In the heaven you visit, you may visit the gods and the goddesses, and all your desires will be granted. This physical world is nothing compared with those worlds beyond to which you will now have access. Today is a special day, Maxine; today we will be properly mated. You will feel how different it will be then." He whispered in her ear the sacred sounds that she should repeat. He put the clasp between her legs and tightened it, pulling the black threads. She was totally in his control. Her climax would be in his control.

"Try to pull the sexual energy towards your head. That way, your soul can exit through the top of your head. Visualize your skull opening out." He touched the top of her head; she felt something inside pulling apart.

In her darkened world, closed eyes behind the mask, her senses were heightened. He lay by her side and moved his hands along the length of her body. She felt the black thread caress her back and the silky sensation of it between her legs. The clasp was tightening; she felt a strange sensation of something like a snake entering her. Then, suddenly, she lost all body consciousness; she was nowhere, struggling with floating in a black void. There was no longer anything of herself; she had completely merged into Fabian and there was only one figure swimming in the strange liquid. The figure moved up towards the nether regions and the fires of Kronos, the land that lay beyond the first gate of the dead. They moved together entering the bliss of other worlds, their bodies mating. Each time, she moaned his name over and over, lost in her sensuality but also her ecstasy in reaching the higher regions of her soul.

Maxine was gone for hours. Fabian was unable to rouse her all that afternoon. Later, she woke briefly and stared at him with a new awareness of their union and in a different state of consciousness. For the first time, he stayed with her that night, not returning to his own room. But she wanted more.

That night, The Jester came to him in a dream. The sour voice became louder and louder in his head until it was like thunder. In his sleep, Fabian put his hands over his ears and mouthed his defence to The Jester, but no words would come out of his mouth. The Jester was not happy with his actions. Fabian falling in love with Maxine was not on the agenda. He was to impregnate her while she was wearing the sacred thread; the clasp would be released. During her pregnancy, she would be sent away and abandoned by Fabian. There was to be little contact after the child was born. The child would belong only to The Jester for his own ends. The child's training would be carried out in South America; it would join all the other children there.

The Jester's eyes pierced Fabian's being until his flesh crawled in his sleep. Later that night, he dreamed again. He was himself at Farlingham Park, centuries ago at the top of the house. He saw himself kneeling in front of Amelia. She was naked save for a black thread that lay across her body, tied around her shoulder. Someone was forcing to make an incision in her body, to insert the eye of Osiris. Then her blood spilled over him. The hooded ones left, disturbed by another entry to the house. They had not performed the opening of the mouth ceremony. Quickly, they offered her soul to Seth. He remembered that he was Sir John Hargreaves, brother-in-law to Sir Ashley Cooper. Amelia was his mistress.

"No ..." A long howl emitted from Fabian's mouth as he realized The Jester was coming for Maxine. He was going to impregnate her this time. His worst fears were about to come true. His evil seed would be inside her. It would be a child of Seth, doomed to a life of servitude.

Maxine was deaf to his cries. She found she had left Kronos and the wonders there and was lost in a forest. A strange man approached her, dressed as though for a fairground. She was so attracted to him that she could not resist going towards him. His energy hypnotized her beyond the point of choice. He took her hand and led her to a secluded place. She lay down on the ground and felt his hands reaching for her; she was enveloped in bliss.

He drew closer to her. His face had such great beauty that she was unable to move away; her desire for union with him was irresistible. She wanted him more than even Fabian. He lay over her, caressing her and moving his fingers this way and that. Then he was inside her, moving quickly. As his black seed came within her, she broke her hold with the earth forever. She had never felt such physical passion. She rose up through her skull laughing, holding his hand. Still locked together, they sported back to his universe. But when she looked at him again, his face was like a hideous skull. Black wings flapped around her then, frightening her, the feathers lashing her face.

"A man dressed as a court jester came to me in my sleep." Maxine turned to Fabian as they lay together in the morning. Fabian buried his head in his hands, unable to say a word to her; tears fell silently from his eyes. The Jester would steal Maxine and now The Jester's baby from him forever. He had won; Fabian would never get away now; it was to be certain death for him. He saw that it was written this way, with no escape for him.

# 30

It seemed as though a thousand cars moved in and out of the gates of Farlingham Park that Saturday afternoon. BMWs, Rolls-Royces, Mercedes and the Range Rovers of the younger set who sought to join the throngs in striped tents and rest their bodies on sofas and reclining chairs all over the mansion. Some were curious; some knew that to miss this event would be to miss out on one of the major events in the season's calendar.

The Countess, as she was known to most, moved effortlessly through the groups who held their champagne glasses to their lips in her honour. At a glance, she took in the whole scene and in that moment, she knew their thoughts and intents. Many were afraid of her, sensing the power and energy behind her position and person. One or two people spoke of diplomatic troubles, others of personal tragedy. A word here and gesture there somehow brought ease to the troubled mind. She was dressed in white, a silk suit cut cleverly with a twisted uneven hem to the long jacket, curved long at one side, short at the other. She wore, as did many of the ladies, a hat. It was broad-brimmed and trimmed with pale damask silk roses to one side. She was, of course, beautiful, with her blond hair and eyes the colour of cornflowers. No one ever was able to really get near her or invite any kind of intimacy. She remained always charming but impersonal, as though she had gone beyond to a wider world where to be too personal with anyone would distract her focus. There were individuals at the gathering on whom the Countess kept a close eye. Her enemies, both visible and invisible, were around both her as well as those whom she had chosen to protect. Nothing went unnoticed by her, as she worked ceaselessly and silently that day.

Later in the day and totally unexpectedly, Sidney Henderson arrived in a hired chauffeur-driven car, without his wife. He had received a late invitation and was quick to join in the extravagant gaiety of the afternoon.

Sidney took one look at Justin and drew Anna aside. "What on earth is wrong with Justin? He looks as though he has seen a ghost or the Devil himself. How long has he been like this?"

"Sidney, he's been like this since we arrived, or almost. He said he saw something in the woods. It's as though he has had a personality change. He is quite a different man. I hardly dare mention it to anyone; I trust it's not permanent, just a reaction or something," said Anna.

Sidney had other ideas about what might have happened to Justin, but he wasn't going to discuss them with Anna. Instead, he went about his own business. He had read up further about Farlingham Park; the entrails of debauched living still hung in the air for Sidney. He had read up on the Hexagon Club and had been deeply shocked. But he had no idea that it was still going in the present time. Sidney was indeed uneasy, but he could not fathom what it was that troubled him so deeply. He had been in Fabian's presence and had only just escaped being entrapped himself. Now he was afraid that his friends would share a similar or even a worse fate.

Later that afternoon, Anna and Jane sat away from the crowds on the other side of the house looking down over the fields. It was quieter here.

"Are you all right, Anna? You seem so distracted. Is it Justin, darling?" She slipped her arm through Anna's who did not pull away, as she so often did.

"I feel that I'm losing Justin. It's not just down here; it's been happening for a while. He has lost interest in his life somehow. It's not enough for him; he says he wants to know who he is, I mean, who he really is. Someone once said that Justin would leave me." She pulled a strand of dark hair away from her face as she spoke; in the breeze, it just blew back again.

"You see, it's like this strand of hair that keeps blowing with the wind. There is a destiny here, and Justin will eventually go where he chooses or where the winds send him. There is nothing I can do about it." Anna sighed.

"You have lost so much, Anna; I can't bear to think of you without Justin. Is there anyone else, Anna? I have always wondered – that time when you were away, and you came back looking so sad." Jane fell silent as Anna looked away. She could see she was struggling with something. But Anna's mind was still set in grim determination not to reveal anything to Jane about the charade which was her life. She was beginning to have troubled dreams again, dreams of being trapped, raped and worse. Waking, she felt confused as though she did not know who she was and what she was about. And Lucille was silent and had not contacted Anna for weeks. She wondered what on earth was going wrong. Lord Oliver's death had, it seemed, rattled them all. Things were falling apart. Casey was beside herself about losing her stepfather and hardly spoke to anyone; they were surprised that she seemed to be talking with Anthony. They had met on the driveway up to the house.

"No, not really, it is just too hard to explain. Anyway, let's talk about something else; it's all too morbid for me on an afternoon like this. Look at those two kids down there with the sheep, chasing them around. I wonder what they are talking about." Anna looked away, down the hill.

Stephanie and Randy were in the far fields away from everyone else and alone with the sheep.

"I don't like this place very much. Everyone seems so on edge suddenly." Randy voiced her opinion to her friend.

"The energy is strong here; it brings up people's feelings and makes them wonder why they are on the planet at all," said Stephanie, stroking one of the rams under its jaw.

"What do you mean 'why they are on the planet'? Where else would they be?" asked Randy irritably. She found that Stephanie pressed all her buttons; it made her angry.

"People have to be here for a reason. This is one of the few places where it's possible to make a relationship with God and to know your past lifetimes; we are under the laws of time and space here. But there are parallel universes. This house was shut for a long time and before that, witches lived here. Strange things were going on; Anna was part of it; she lost her life here. The others too are connected to this past lifetime at Farlingham Park; they are all going to have to figure it out. And they are all under a dreadful curse," continued Stephanie. She thought that Randy would not understand at the moment but in time would need this information when she herself had gone from time and space.

"In some ways, Farlingham Park does not really exist at all. One day it will probably just vanish, like the bodies that come and go here. To have a human body is very precious. There isn't only Earth; there are many other places and planets where people live. In fact, I spend a lot of my time on one of them," said Stephanie, sucking nonchalantly on a blade of grass.

Randy stared incredulously at her; she did not understand what Stephanie was talking about. Then she said, "Once, when I was breathing deeply in and out, I felt myself leave my body. Is that what you mean?" asked Randy earnestly, trying to keep up with Stephanie.

"Yes, I suppose so. Have you met God?" she added.

"Not really. Where is he?" asked Randy.

"Well, he's everywhere, really; in the animals, the sky and the trees. Then, well right now, he's in a New York sewer playing cards. Yes, that's where he is," said Stephanie, thoughtfully.

"Does he often play cards in the sewer in New York?" asked Randy.

"Yes, of course, he does; what a silly question. Anyway, I want to go back and see Emma. I like her so much. See you later." And with that, she ran back to the house, leaving Randy open-mouthed and feeling like bursting into tears. She hadn't seen Casey for hours, and anyway, she always seemed to be talking to Anthony. She felt totally alone, and she missed her mum so much. She felt that she had no one now. Wondering what would happen to her, she walked towards the fountain and the lake. There were roses around it and statues of mythical figures; it was very beautiful but it unnerved her. The whole place and all these people scared her.

# 31

They had all had dinner at Farlingham Park. There had been little conversation that night and still only the two small groups of house guests at each end of the table. Sidney Henderson had dispatched himself back to London, his invitation not having been extended for the weekend.

Casey found herself taking the back staircases to the top of the house. All the doors were closed. She tried one, but it was locked. In the dim light, she could see a few cobwebs high up on the ceiling. This area of the house was obviously rarely used. On the walls hung a few paintings, and there were also spaces where some had been removed at one time and taken elsewhere. The house had always had royal connections. This showed in the choice of portraits; some of the artists of the Tudor and Jacobean faces that looked out at her were familiar names to Casey.

There were one or two pictures of the first Countess of Rigby and her husband. One of them held her attention for a minute or two. She was very beautiful. Then Casey moved on along the corridor. Another group of pictures drew her attention; a portrait of George IV, and next to it a much smaller picture. The writing to the side of the painting simply read 'Jester to the Court of George IV'.

She always thought of a jester as full of fun and smiles, but this man looked grave and sombre with a bluish hue to his skin. His eyes looked away from the artist to the left. He had on a traditional jester's hat that ended in three points and bells. Casey had read about the life of George IV. Now from what Emma had told her, she understood why she had been so fascinated by these times in England; of course, she had had a lifetime there. But The Jester, he was something else.

She remembered that Oliver had taken her away from the boarding school in Scotland after two years, not being able to bear his life without his beautiful stepdaughter; he longed for her. She remembered that she cried for a year when she first went to the school, bereft without him. After she returned to the house in Cambridge, he had come to her bedroom then almost every night, at the back of the house, like the old days when she had been so young. Again, they shared their sexual secrets, but he was kind and tender to her then, only playing with or teasing her body. He felt she was too young, too immature for anything more serious. He did not want to make the same mistakes he had made by forcing his way with Anna, even though she had been drugged. It had been a disaster. But he and Casey were close again, at last. Antigone was rarely at home.

But Oliver was dead now, his beautiful body lying in a grave somewhere in South America. He should have been brought home to be buried in the family tomb on their property. Fabian, who was all gracious on the phone, spoke of a terrible car accident, a fire, and there had not been anything left. Where was his spirit now, she wondered? It seemed dark in the corridor, as Casey moved away from the picture. Somehow, she did not believe Fabian.

Casey found her way down to her room at last. She looked in on Randy who was fast asleep with one arm lying around her teddy bear. The bear was so old that it was nearly bald. It had belonged to Randy's mother. Randy missed her more than she could bear. Casey thought again of the corridor upstairs and the story that Emma had told her the night before. It was strange, she thought, that the rooms on that landing were locked.

Everything had seemed so open when she had walked along the upper corridor and found the room with the tapestry. Casey was surprised that Emma has not mentioned Oliver's death; she had talked of everything else.

On the floor below Randy's room, Anthony tossed and turned, burning with a fever, and a sense of dread pursued his sleep. The Countess was aware of it all, but there was nothing she could do to avert the tide of destiny and personal karma that was to flood over Anthony in the next few months. She could only offer support and protection while he went through it all. She had watched over Anthony's life for some time now and she would continue to do so. He was in danger and so were Justin, Anna, Jane and Casey, but especially Jane and now even Fairfax. There were threads of karma too complicated to unravel; they had to experience it.

Emma had lived in India for many years as a young woman, trained in the occult arts and astrology; she was also psychic. She had never married. The incident with Fabian had been too dreadful in her teens and in a way, she had never got over it. He had done dreadful things that night to her mind, body and soul. He had taken her to a very dark place, and it had taken her years to understand what he had really done. Her parents had cast evil over both her and Fabian. Somehow, she had managed to escape the evil spells.

She knew that Fabian's soul was a bound one, taken over by the evil entity of The Jester, an entity that had no material body in this universe but sought to entrap everyone on whom the curse from Ancient Egypt lay. He was immensely powerful. But behind his power was Seth.

Anna lay awake beside Justin. Somehow, she just couldn't see her life going forward anywhere. It was as though she were standing in front of a brick wall. She also had feelings of dread about all their immediate futures. Already she knew they would all be overcome by ghastly events.

Justin slept lightly. He dreamt during the night of Stephanie. He was racing through the forest trying to find her. It was dark, and the branches and leaves were obstructing his path. It was snowing, and the ground was white. His steps were laboured;

his shoes slid on the ice. He could see her face ahead of him, the damp hair clinging to her. She looked anxious. He kept calling her name, but she could not hear him. She walked in the opposite direction. Now she was in the avenue. A black carriage drawn by four horses was approaching her. It stopped in front of her and the door opened. A hand swathed in black reached out and helped her up into the carriage. Then the horses galloped on, throwing up the snow as it disappeared. Justin sank down and drew his cloak around him and wept. He knew that he would never see her again.

Farlingham Park was steeped in silence; all the occupants were asleep. The moon was bright; in fact, it was full. If you had been standing in the driveway, you would have seen the beauty of the house, the Gothic, cathedral style and the long windows reflecting the moonlight. The smell of the roses in the night air was haunting. Anubis, the God of Death, could be seen in that light. Why would the God of Death be standing there at this time? Who knows what his vision of the house would have been or of its occupants? Did he smell the flowers and see the moon? He did not linger; someone had summoned him, but it was not their time or his, at least not now. It was not time for funerary rites. The Divine Embalmer turned on his heel to go, knowing that his wife Thrat, in her earthly form and his daughter were still within the house for now, living out their earthly karmas on the physical plane of existence.

And Seth, the dark-winged god of evil and destruction, still paced the floors of Farlingham Park. He would have his way again, stealing people's souls, their hearts and minds. He of all the gods, knew that the world of sexual practices that had their heyday in the former life of the house, were only a prelude to his taking possession of them all, lured by their sensual addictions into his net once more. These human beings were deluded. They did not know the power of sexuality, how in the floodgates of sexual demonic power, it created access to other planets and universes. No, the human beings had no real understanding of sexual power and its gateways to hell. His time would come again. He would wait. Everything would happen according to his plans. Everything was in place.

He himself was an embodiment of all power. His own sexual practices and rules in Ancient Egypt were the very basis of the Hexagon Club that lived on in all its glory. The trapping of innocents and the renewal of the great Gothic ghosts all belonged to him. It was he who had real power in the universe. He would live forever, offering his chains of delusion to all humans who would follow and obey him. To them he would give all the sexual delights, but they would never know those secrets like he did. He thought back on his own exploits, his tongue hung out and then he licked his lips and savoured his memories.

# 32

Breakfast was in the morning room. Justin was reading the colour supplement as he stifled a yawn. He was bored with the papers; who cared about all these people flaunting their wealth and success all over the weeklies, day after day; the politics; the scandals; the wars. More extravagant weddings were taking place now, costing millions while people in many parts of Europe were starving. The rich would think nothing of having a birthday party for a young child at a luxury hotel, just a few hours of celebration for twenty thousand pounds in one afternoon. It was disgusting. And then the carnage of animals, fifty million animals a year, worldwide, slaughtered just for the fashion business alone. He threw the papers across the room. He was more than tired of it all.

He was irritable after his conversation with Emma, and sleep had evaded him. They had caught up with each other last evening in the dusk, when the last of the guests were disappearing. He had been standing looking at the lake and the rose gardens. Emma had skilfully managed to mend some of the pain in his heart. The scent of the warm summer roses had filled the air.

For the first time in his life, he was really asking who he was. The shell of his ego was breaking, and it was hard for him to bear. He told her about his fear of The Jester and how he felt about himself when he looked in the mirror. She warned him about the enemies that he had. At one level, he was relieved that she knew. He told her how it had seemed that someone had been watching him for a long time. Then she gave him some advice to do certain things when he returned to London. He would always be grateful for how she came into his life at that time. Eventually, she revealed his previous lifetimes to him, his relationship with Anna over several lives; but that was much later. Now he had to live a new life; he knew not what. The only certainty was that the old one had ceased to exist.

Everyone was absorbed, either in their own thoughts or in the Sunday papers. They all had their own agenda with others in the group and with Emma. She would take time with them all. The world seemed to be in turmoil. There seemed to be no moral codes anymore, and traditional religious foundations were crumbling.

Anthony drew his hand over his spiky hair on the top of his head.

"Coming for a walk, Casey?" he asked nonchalantly.

"Well, I should go and find Randy." She was playing for time. The invitation was unexpected.

"She went with Stephanie out to the sheep again. They are crazy about the sheep, those two," said Anna, finishing her coffee.

"Well, all right, just for a while. Maxine is supposed to be arriving this morning, and I want to get things ready for her," said Casey.

At that moment, the butler came into the room.

"Telephone, madam," he said, looking at Casey.

"I'll take it in the study," said Casey as she left the room. "Anthony, I will just be a moment."

"It's Maxine," said the voice.

"Maxine, where are you? I thought you were coming today," said Casey.

"I am. It's just ... well, I will be late. I had a late night and I'm tired. The chauffeur will be here to collect me soon. I just called to let you know. See you in the afternoon."

"Whose chauffeur, Maxine? I thought you would be catching a train – I was going to pick you up." The line had gone dead. She had a feeling someone on the other end had been listening, but who? And who was driving her down here?

Casey walked out of the study in a hurry and went into the conservatory. At that same moment, Emma was entering the conservatory from the other side. She was dressed in white and looked radiant. She took one look at Casey and saw the cloud of worry over her head.

"I just received a phone call from Maxine. A chauffeur is bringing her over this afternoon." The words were rushing out of her mouth. "I'm worried about her, Emma. I don't know who she is with, and I think someone was listening at the other end of the line. I wish there was something I could do."

"Casey, my dear, it would be better if you didn't get involved in Maxine's life. There are issues at stake here that are far beyond your ability to cope. You are in great danger. If you do get involved, the chances are that Maxine could be worse off than she already is. Just try and understand the situation for what it is. We are doing everything that we can." Emma turned to go.

Casey knew that the conversation was closed. It was like a door shutting quietly. As she went back to the morning room, she felt stunned that she had confided so much to this woman. They all had; it seemed that was what they were there to do. All of them were rudderless boats in the middle of circumstances that were beyond their understanding or control. They needed a guide.

"I just saw the Countess," she announced, as she entered the breakfast party again. Anthony smiled at her as she sat down. Jane looked at Casey and Anthony. She could see the attachment had already started. She was happy for them both. She thought of Vince at that moment. How would he think of this place? But it was not to be; neither he nor Fairfax had been invited.

Anthony and Casey eventually got up and left the house. It was a beautiful summer morning, and there was just a little dew left on the grass as they walked towards the woods. They walked for a while and then sat down in a clearing. Very soon, Anthony was telling her about his experiences in Cairo, the dream of the snake bite, the horror of Richard's death and his incarceration in the tombs. Casey's heart went out to him; she was totally amazed that anyone could go through so much and still live to tell the tale.

"I've never had experiences like that. Sometimes though, when I would lie in my bed in New York, I would watch my breath go in and out. I would hold my breath or push it in and out fast. Then I would experience a kind of deep meditation, as though bliss was coursing through my veins. Randy used to sleep in my bed sometimes. She was good at this breathing. Sometimes, she said she would leave her body. My life has been so strange in the last month. I felt I was leaving New York forever," she said. Casey pulled her hair back from her face as though to tie it at the back. Wisps of blond hair that were too short to be caught fell back onto her face again. She looked at Anthony. He was staring ahead, deep in thought. His face, finely chiselled, was thinner than ever before. His cheekbones showed against the hollow of his face. Suddenly he got up and held out his hand to Casey.

"Time to go; I have to meet the Countess this morning." Casey could see that he was still deep in thought. She walked in front of him on the narrow path. Without any notice, he put his hands on her shoulders. He wheeled her around and held her tightly in his arms. Then he kissed her on the mouth. They were breathing fast, caught in the suddenness of the situation. Then they heard voices from the adjoining path.

She was reminded of Oliver's kisses: invasive, always too hasty, impatient, wanting her, urgent, always urgent. She remembered that urgency when she was just a child. She had never told anyone about Oliver – never. It was their secret, a spell that somehow, she had allowed him to cast over her. She wondered if her mother ever realized what had happened between them.

"Quick, Casey, let's go. Someone is coming." He hastily pulled her over to the side of the path beneath the trees. The thickness of the foliage blocked any view of the other path, but they sat down so not to be observed. The voices were coming closer.

"The Jester could kill again at any time. Your experience, though, was the re-enactment of a former birth. You were the woman that he stabbed; that's why you felt the agony of pain in your chest. But he wants you again; it's the nature of his kind. They kill in one lifetime, but because they are not bounded by time, they seek their victims again and again. It is up to you to understand the connection – why he originally sought you out and what was the original karma. Then and only then can the spell be broken. At one level, none of this exists at all; it is merely a reflection of your own consciousness. You are caught in a web; it's only your existence in time and space that makes it real. So, you have in some way to solve it before you are sought out again. Be careful, he is very clever and has accomplices who are only too willing to do his bidding." Casey recognized the resonant tone of the Countess' voice.

Casey and Anthony heard the footsteps fade off into the distance; and so, they quickly made their way back to the house.

"What on earth was she talking about?" said Casey, still whispering.

"I don't know. And who was she talking with? I think it all has to do with Richard's death. I think we are all under a curse. We are all in danger, and she is helping all of us understand the karma and our connections to the past."

"A curse," thought Casey. She had thought of Anna when John Grey was killed, and she thought of her again. Yes, they were all under a curse.

Justin was exploring the house. He came across a room lit only by a small candle. There were some statues at the front of the room that to him looked like some of the Indian gods and goddesses that Jane had in her house. For some reason, he was drawn to sitting in this room. There were no chairs, but comfortable cushions lay around. He went in and closed the door and found a seat in the far corner on which to sit. He sat cross-legged and closed his eyes. Immediately, he saw a blue dot of light in front of his eyes. It expanded slightly into a large ball of light. It was entrancing. Then it vanished, but he then felt himself sinking deeper and deeper into a black velvety darkness inside him. He didn't shift his position at all. He was totally immersed in the ecstasy of his experience. For two hours or more, he stayed there unaware of the outside world. Emma had started the process within him just yesterday, something that deep down he had wanted for a long time ago.

Maxine had spoken to Casey some half hour ago; the receiver had been replaced. She had heard a click and knew that Fabian had been listening from the phone in his study. She was already dressed but had not yet had breakfast. Fabian came into her suite as the waiter was putting breakfast onto the table in the dining room. She went over to him and kissed him. He drew her into his arms again feeling her longing for him.

She viewed him now from the other side of the table. Fabian's hair was still wet from showering; his face was tanned and freshly shaven.

"What are you staring at, Maxine?" he asked. She was silent.

"Did you sleep well, darling?" This time she knew he wanted an answer.

"I don't think I slept at all. I went somewhere away from my body; it was strange. Yes, it was like living a different life somewhere else with other people. They had different values, and there was no sun or moon. The place was lit by a greenish light, as though from a sulphur mountain. And then there was The Jester." She remembered all too vividly the intimacies she had had with him and looked down at her plate, not wanting Fabian to see that she had remembered her aroused state.

"Don't tell me, Maxine. There are some things that are best left unsaid. You have a life of your own now when you visit these places; but you will have to work hard on keeping yourself grounded on this planet. Come here, Maxine." Fabian's eyes grew darker. The lids closed.

Maxine went over to him on the other side of the table. He whispered something in her ear and she laughed.

"Do you still have the thread on?" he asked,

"No. Should I?" She leaned over and put her hand on his cheek.

"Do as you like." His fingers were running now through her hair.

"Today, you are going to the Countess'. I have so much to do that I'm not going to come with you." He never would have set foot anywhere near Emma's; although, after all these years, he had never once forgotten his love for her and the insatiable longing when she was still so young. He had taken her very soul away from her; somehow, she had broken from him and now she had the power. But hers was the power of light, not utter darkness, like his.

"Why don't you invite Casey back with you tomorrow? She is your best friend, and she could be useful to us when we leave." Maxine felt shocked by his suggestion, as though he had slapped her across the face.

"Casey is best left alone. I don't want her involved." But she found her words melting in her mouth and what he wanted her to say came out instead. It was a strange sensation, as though she was somehow under water and her mouth was no longer her own.

"Yes, I will ask her. She is very clever; there is a lot she could do for you and the organization." Tart words from efficient lips, she thought, as she spoke. Fabian noticed the change in her and the struggle. He approved. The Jester obviously knew what he was doing when he took her away the night before. She was much more pliant.

"We will be moving into the house in St. John's Wood tomorrow. I bought it last year; it has a pool – you will love it. You and Casey can have fun there." He was thinking of the recent digital pictures of Casey that had been sent to him from New York. They had been taken in Jack's studio; pictures that Jack had taken of Casey after they had made love: the sensuous back, shapely breasts, the swollen mouth after too much kissing, her blond wispy hair that she had pulled up above her head as she posed naked for Jack's camera, her legs just a little bit apart – a story between the two of them on that day when the snow lay thick in New York City and people kicked large chunks of ice along the pavement.

"Yes, Casey would do well," thought Fabian. Jack had done a good job, but then he had paid him a tidy sum. That was how the world worked; you could buy anything with money. Now that Oliver was out of the way, thank God, things would not be so chaotic; he had been a danger to everyone.

Yes, and now he thought of Oliver's sweetheart, Casey, their bodies entwined together in a satanic melody from when she was a mere child. She was, of course, still under the spell. Oliver would make sure that she never became aware of what really happened to her. But Fabian would change all that and take her body and soul himself. She would forget Oliver; yes, he would make sure of that. He savoured the thought and again looked at the naked pictures. Yes, she would do very well. Oliver was out of the way now.

"That sounds great. I will invite her," said Maxine, suddenly invigorated by the thought of Casey being at the house in St. John's Wood. "What else do you want from the house today at Farlingham Park, Fabian? It's very important, this trip, isn't it?" She looked into his eyes, the black eyes reflecting the depth of his thoughts.

"It's a vendetta. I suppose you could call it cosmic mafia warfare. These people must go; I want them dead; there is a whole group of them souring my plans. It goes a long way back, so far back you wouldn't believe – back as far as the burial deserts of the ancient pharaohs. You don't have to know all the details. But I want them observed: their habits, aspirations, plans, where they are going to be and when. Check out the house, the upper rooms, and the paintings. Be the observer, Maxine; you are good at that game. See what our dear Countess' guests are doing and thinking."

It was Fabian's way of moving forward; like a game of chess, to have the pieces removed one by one; yes, a game of chess; slowly and carefully. When he was ready, he would move in, and checkmate. He knew what The Jester wanted, and he would secure it for him. There would be a big prize for this. And the great Seth would ultimately reward him, giving him his own planet and paradise. He too would become a God. He would own the world.

"I'm leaving soon; the maid has just finished packing an overnight bag for me." Maxine was on her way out now.

He felt the pang of her going again so soon. It was an ache. The attachment worried him. The Jester was right; it was too close. He ran his hand along her arm, softly and slowly. She had on a thin see-through blouse she was to wear under her suit. Then he let go of her, not wanting her to see or feel his desire for her.

"I'm going down to Windsor to play polo today. Call me later here. Arafat Khan sends you his best wishes. Do you remember him? I'm riding in his team today." Maxine remembered him. He had many years ago tried to rip off her dress and rape her at a party in Connecticut. Fabian probably knew that too; maybe they had laughed about it together. She had met Casey at that party. Yes, it would be good to see Casey again; they had been such good friends. Perhaps it could be renewed now. But it was not to be at all like she expected. With Fabian, you had to let go of any expectations. Things just were not like that.

The limousine, its windows shaded, moved out of Mayfair and onto the M1 going north. She could see out, but no one could see in. This, she thought, is the way my life is; it's me who is doing the looking, moving the universe around. She felt she had become Fabian in a way. She thought like him and sometimes she felt she was him. She now had the power.

On her arrival at the gates of Farlingham Park, the statue of the God Anubis fell off its footing on the desk in Emma's room and broke into a hundred agonized pieces onto the marble floor beneath. "So, the Count's mistress already has the power. He has trained her well," thought Emma, as she picked up the broken pieces from the floor. The jackal head of the statue was still intact.

Everyone was enchanted with Maxine; they were irresistibly drawn to her. During the day, she spent time with each of them, drawing out their secrets. Only Anna stayed aloof; she recognized who Maxine was, and she knew Fabian had sent her. Maxine did not know about Anna or that she had also received the sacred thread many years ago. The two women stayed clear of each other. Anthony, too, knew the power she was wielding and felt the dull ache in his solar plexus. He knew that he must stay away from her. Fabian needed no news about Anthony. As far as he was concerned, Anthony was over and out in this world and the next.

Much later in the day, Anthony was in Casey's room. "I don't have much time, Casey. I know something is going to happen to me. Why don't you come to stay with me at Jane's house?"

"I want to, but I am going to stay with Maxine in London. Please don't tell anyone, especially not Emma. She told me to stay away, but I have my own plans." Casey sat beside Anthony on the bed.

"My life has changed beyond all recognition. It will never be the same again. Casey, I don't know where I will be, so give me a number where I can reach you. I'm due to go back to Cairo to finish the movie in two weeks' time. Vince called today; he says I must go back, or it's all over as far as my filming career goes. Someone has been stirring up a lot of trouble for me in Egypt." He took Casey's face in his hands and looked at her for a long time before he let her go.

# 33

It was early Monday morning. All the guests had now left Farlingham Park; it was being closed up for the winter. The Countess had already left.

Anthony stood at the window of one of the guest rooms at Jane's house. He had a view of the driveway; he was watching a grey Ford come slowly up the drive. He couldn't hear the engine; it was so quiet. Eventually, it stopped in front of the main entrance to the house. Anthony already knew that he was going to be arrested and he had everything ready. He did not want Jane to get involved any further. Two men got out; one was much taller than the other. He heard sounds downstairs and Jane talking to the men; her voice was raised in agitation. They were not leaving. A few minutes later, Jane, white-faced, knocked on Anthony's door.

"Anthony, it's the police. They want to talk to you," she said, surprised that he was already dressed and packed.

"Stay out of this, Jane; you would only get hurt, please!" he said, gathering his things. The men were waiting downstairs in the huge hallway with its flagstones. As he walked down the magnificent staircase with his small suitcase, he saw their heads look up at him. It was a scene that had been enacted in so many movies, he thought.

"Are you Anthony Jackson?" asked the taller man.

"Yes, I am he."

"I am arresting you for the murder of Richard Abrascus." He spoke those agonizing words.

"I am Inspector Rawlings. We would like you to accompany us now to the police station. You will not be returning here; you should bring all your possessions," said Rawlings.

"I would like to call my lawyer," said Anthony, who knew his rights. He would call his father in California.

"You can do that from the police station." They didn't handcuff him but led him to the car. He did not say a word to Jane. He kissed her and held her hands in his, then turned away. She watched the car move down the drive and then went back to bed. She pulled the covers over her head and sobbed; she couldn't bear it. All day she stayed there in the shock and misery of seeing Anthony taken away. She made no phone calls except to Justin to let him know what had happened. Then she did not stir until much later in the day.

Anna, too, was at home. She was exhausted from the weekend. Justin left as usual for the hospital. He had a full schedule of surgery that day. He looked awful. Later, Anna went into the garden and made a gesture at pruning the roses. She missed John who often used to look after the garden. She thought about the shaft of the steering wheel sticking into his solar plexus. Mostly, she remembered his eyes looking uselessly towards her trying to warn her. Now he was gone. She wondered if he had had any idea that he was going to die that day. Had he dreamt of the event? Probably not; John wasn't the dreaming sort. She had wondered why he had died. He may have found out something for which someone wanted him dead. Fabian was ruthless enough to take anyone's life, if they got in the way or put his operations into danger.

It was getting dark now, and she prepared to take the basket and shears back to the house. She heard the phone ring, but Julia was away for the day. She could not be bothered to answer it. She walked along the crazy paving to the house. It was so quiet; even the birds were silent. It was nice to be alone; it had been such a strange weekend; it would take weeks for her to make any sense of it at all. Her body longed for Fabian in the sweetness of the evening. She knew that he was still in England, but she had a feeling somehow that she would never see him again. But she was wrong.

Anna was wearing blue jeans and a white cotton shirt. A scarf was round her neck, something she had found in Liberty's after she had spent the last time with Fabian. She thought of Maxine: so young, thin, with long well-shaped limbs, her face, the full lips and gorgeous eyes. Yes, Fabian would find a match for his passion in her, Anna thought. She didn't feel jealous; the pain was too great for that.

Upstairs, she went to the bedroom to look for a book. It wasn't there. She climbed the stairs to the next floor where she had her study in the attic. Three rooms had been knocked into one. She had designed it herself three years ago. Sidney had advised her on the decor; she wondered whether the unanswered phone call was from him. He would be anxious about the weekend. No, she decided that she did not want to speak to anyone. The Countess had talked to her mainly about Justin, but some of the things were directly relating to her own life and past incarnations. She had already known most of it, but there were a few surprises. Emma had warned her to make the most of her life, not to waste time. Anna already knew about her own death at Farlingham Park.

The study held some of the finest books in the world. Anna's father was a collector of fine books on all manner of subjects and had given her many of his books on occult practices. He had been a cold father but made sure that Anna had been groomed well for her presentation to Fabian, all those years ago. He had insisted on exclusivity in this relationship with Anna. His coldness created a longing in her which he then took advantage of by taking her away on dates, having her dress up, and there were endless gifts and visits to her room late at night.

He carefully watched her development; there were times she was drugged when he took her to clubs. She would attend the parties, be seated next to her father to watch porn on a frequent basis and was carefully kept from any other male that might approach her. Anna had no memory of her childhood. She was subjected to mind-numbing programming and mind control in which all club members were experts.

In school, she was not able to learn mathematics. It was as though she were in a permanent fog, unable to remember how to work out problem-solving formulas. She had developed a terror of numbers and calculations, something that existed her entire life. It was as though she had dyscalculia, but it was from the programming of her mind.

Anna had met Justin at Cambridge where he studied medicine as an undergraduate. They had dated, but there was nothing serious until much later, as she was mesmerized by Fabian. She married Justin after he had completed his hospital internship in London. He never knew about Fabian; no one really did, except the Hexagon Club and her immediate family; however, he was rarely out of her thoughts.

She heard Justin's car coming up the driveway. She had a feeling that something was wrong; she should go down to meet him. Justin came into the hallway, as Anna reached the bottom of the stairs on her way to greet him. His face looked grim.

"Anna, I just had a call from Jane in the car. Anthony was arrested this morning at Jane's. He has been charged with the murder of his co-director, Richard Abrascus. Jane is dreadfully upset; she spent the day in bed. I said I would call her later. I don't like her being up there alone at the house, not with all this going on." Justin took off his coat and flung it down on a chair. He held Anna in his arms, but it felt mechanical, with no feeling behind it. He still seemed cut off from her in a world of his own. She thought to herself that perhaps she shouldn't have talked to him about having another baby. Maybe, this was the cause of his behaviour at the weekend.

"But why would they arrest him? He is such a nice man. He can't have been responsible for all this," Anna said, still holding Justin.

"Well, it seems that Richard was not only a movie director; that was just a front. He had been involved in many arms deals, trafficking. No one really knew who he was working for, except that he had a sizeable bank account in Switzerland. It is said that Anthony was tied up in the same business. They are saying that Richard had access to information and was threatening to leak it; and this would have meant ruining a huge deal that Anthony was about to tie up in South America. They say the deal was worth millions to Anthony, so he murdered Richard and he had planned the pyramid journey just to make it look like an accident." He had in fact got all this information from Fairfax who was trying to help Anthony, although he was encountering so many obstacles. Justin went into the drawing room to pour himself a drink. Anna followed; she wanted to change the subject.

"You know, Justin, I really think we should get away from all this. There is always something; it's as though we are all under a spell or something. I hate it. Can't we go and spend some time at the villa? It's so long since we have been there, and you haven't had a real break for over a year. We need to stabilize our lives a little. I feel we are drifting apart."

"I know it would be good to get away, but my surgery lists are so full – not just routine but emergency work." Justin looked down at the Martinis he had just made for them both. His hands were shaking. She had never seen him so agitated.

"Why can't someone cover for you? You are always the one on call, Justin. You can't keep on like this." Anna felt herself flush with anger.

"The only time that I can really schedule to be away would be in early August. The lists close then, and it's a natural time to take a break. Why don't we do it then? Go ahead and make the arrangements." Justin looked at his wife, wondering why on earth she wanted another baby now; he couldn't figure out her sense of timing. Somehow, it felt too late; both their lives had gone beyond it. He hated her now for the infidelities, for her lies; and the black thread that she used in her sexual exploits was always on his mind. He thought one night he would pull it out of the drawer and challenge her, but he knew he never would and so there was a wall between them.

They went their separate ways after dinner; Anna went back to her study and Justin walked along the length of the drive; he didn't feel like being inside. The moon was very bright. He wondered about Anthony; he really liked him; Anthony was linked to his future; he felt it. He couldn't believe the inside information that he had been given by Fairfax. He thought about Stephanie and missed her. He knew he felt envious of her relationship with Emma, always sitting at her feet, the two of them in a world of their own to which he had no access. God, what a life he was leading. How long could it go on like this? He needed to take action to make some changes. He felt as though he was living a dead role, one that was no longer his anymore. Was he trapped? Would there be a means of escape?

The gravel crunched under his feet. The night air was magnificent after the long journey from London and the operating theatres. "Too much blood, I'm seeing too much blood every day," he thought, as he smelt the evening air. And it seemed that things had not been the same since Anna pierced her finger with the thorn. Perhaps the strange spell on them both had started then. He took a deep breath, turned on his heel and returned to the house. He could see their bedroom light on. Yes, it was time for sleep. It would be another long day tomorrow, and he still needed to call Jane in Shropshire. But he didn't call. It was too late by the time he returned to the house and Anna was calling him. Allan Greenberg was on the phone. An emergency had cropped up at St. John's. Greenberg needed his advice, as it was one of Justin's private patients that had somehow found a way into the public hospital. It was a total nightmare, and the patient was now threatening to sue. It was one o'clock in the morning before he got to bed.

# *34*

Jane sat alone in the living room. She had spent the day in bed and had heard nothing from the police or from Anthony. But then, she did not expect that she would.

She sat on one of the new sofas she had ordered up from London. It was covered in a burnt orange floral material; a border of off-white piping ran around its contours giving it a very fitted appearance. Her body was motionless; her fingers picked at the piping. Although it was July, it was unusually cold, and Jane had thrown some logs into the grate and stuffed some paper and kindling in the same direction. Now red-hot ashes cascaded onto the hearth stones beneath. She watched the glow. The telephone stood next to her on a small trestle table. She had called Justin at home earlier in the day and then Fairfax in New York. Her hair, uncombed, was pulled back into an elastic band that she had found near the freezer in the kitchen. She was wearing an old navy-blue skirt; she had pulled on an old cashmere sweater – it had a hole under the right arm. Round and round in her mind she played with the pieces of destiny, trying to fit them into a sensible shape. But events, words and people continued to float around in her brain. Tears brimmed again in her eyes when she thought of Anthony. She had tried to contact Vince, but he had apparently left Cairo. The

Hotel Adelphi was closed because of the sandstorms, and there was no forwarding number.

The light was fading fast; she had kept the curtains open to the wildness of the garden. She liked to see the unpruned trees and the creepers on the windows. The garden in Chiswick was so tamed. But Jane wasn't really thinking about the garden; her thoughts were on Maxine. For some reason, she could not get her out of her mind. She felt Maxine was wielding power that was not her own. Who, thought Jane, was she working for? Oh yes, she was captivating and clever, but there was something robotic about her, as though she had been taken over by something or someone. She and Anthony had discussed it for hours the previous evening. He described the pain in his solar plexus when he was in the presence of Maxine. It was debilitating and drained his spiritual energy.

Anthony had told her that Emma warned Casey not to get involved with Maxine, but she had made her own plans despite the warning and was going to stay with Maxine in London. Anthony was worried; he felt Casey didn't know what she was doing and had already fallen under Maxine's spell. They were, after all, close friends. Jane had shared her experience of the shopkeeper in the village beyond Farlingham Park with Anthony. They had driven back to see it on the way home from Farlingham Park, but whichever way they drove, they couldn't find the village or the shop. The people they spoke to on the way said they had never heard of it, and there had not been a shop in that area for over forty years.

It was dark now in the room, but she didn't reach for the light. There was so much light from the fire, and she wanted to hide with her thoughts in the warm glow. She rubbed her eyes and stretched on the sofa, putting another cushion behind her back. She felt cold from the fear of it all. There were forces at work that she simply did not understand. They were so subtle that it was impossible to arm oneself with any defence.

Jane jumped as the telephone rang like a thousand jangled bells beside her on the table.

"Jane?" said the voice. It was a man's voice.

"Yes, who is this?"

There was silence. She could hear breathing and then the phone went dead on her. She put it down. Then she ran to the windows and closed the curtains. Suppose someone was peering in at her? The phone rang again. This time she picked it up slowly, hesitantly.

"Jane, are you all right?" It sounded like Justin's voice on the other end of the line.

"Oh, Justin, thank God, it's you! I am scared out of my wits up here. The phone just rang; it was a man's voice. He called me by my name and then there was just silence – after a while he hung up. I am so frightened; I don't know what to do." Her voice shrank to a whisper.

"Now, listen, Jane. Do exactly as I say. This call may relate to Anthony's arrest," said the voice.

"You know, when they took Anthony I thought they would take him to London. But Fairfax said that in a case of this sort, they would send him back to Cairo to face trial." Jane's words were running into each other.

"Stop thinking about all this. First, call the police and ask them to come over. Tell them about that call. Ask them to escort you to the motorway; then you will be fine. You should come over to us. It's a long way, but at least you will be safe here." The voice was very matter-of-fact.

"I'll shut up the house now and go. Thanks, Justin, and I'll see you later." Jane felt relieved. She almost called the police there and then, but she decided to wait. Maybe it wasn't necessary. Instead, she went upstairs. Things were in some disarray from the chaos of the morning. Only Anthony's room was orderly and neat. He had folded the bedsheets and placed them at the end of the bed. She switched on all the lights to calm her nerves. She wished Cedric was with her, but he was still in the kennels in London.

At last, she had everything packed and she again went back into the living room. She took a bucket of water and doused the flames of the fire. It hissed, making everything smell acrid. The room looked bare and cold now – all the warmth was gone. She picked up the phone to call the police. The line was dead. She ran to the study, then the kitchen, but the same thing. The line must have just been cut. Her mobile did not work and the computer would not even start up.

Knowing that she must act quickly, she turned off all the power in the house and closed the side door. There were no sounds, but she had the feeling that someone was watching her. Slowly and silently, she made her way to the garage. Carefully, she entered the Lancia and breathed a sigh of relief, as she let it roll down the slight incline. Then she started the engine. All was clear; her breathing became easier. But at the end of the driveway, to her horror, she saw that the gates had been closed. Someone had closed them. She got out and slammed the door of the car and ran to open the gates. They were padlocked from the other side; she took its details. A bright light shined into her eyes. She reeled away in terror.

"I told you that I had been waiting a long time for you. Not so fast. Find the big house with the urns, did you?" She could not see the face because of the light, but she recognized the voice. Then someone grabbed her from behind. In her mind, she saw a picture of the first Countess of Rigby falling to the floor in the attic at Farlingham Park, the glass shattering to pieces as it hit the floor.

# 35

Casey was floating on her back in the pool set in the basement of the house in St. John's Wood. Fabian had had the basement renovated and the new pool and the Jacuzzi were surrounded in white marble; spotlights beamed under the surface making the water appear a luminous aquamarine. She was alone and had been there for an hour or more, soaking in the hot tub and then swimming laps. Someone had given her a massage late in the afternoon using sandalwood and fragrant aromatic oils. Fabian had sent in the oils to help her relax. A door opened at the other end of the pool complex and in he walked. He sat down, looking at her. It was an awkward moment. Maxine had told her Fabian never returned before seven, and here she was naked in the pool. He was looking at her as she hastily turned over on her stomach. Her long legs sent up a cascade of water to hide her nakedness. She hoped he would get the message and go, but he didn't. He wanted to tease her.

"Pass me my robe please, Fabian," she cried from the pool, not wanting him to see her embarrassment, maintaining a cool exterior.

"Here," he said, bringing the robe to the side of the pool. "Is this the one you wanted?" He stared at her. She held his eyes for a moment; it was like looking into an empty mirror. Something moved across her line of vision.

As best she could, she climbed out of the water. He condescendingly turned his back, giving her time to put on the robe. Then he moved towards her. She felt a strong energy encircle her but she didn't cry out. He put his mouth lightly onto hers. She caught her breath, as his tongue moved inside her cold lips. Then, as though he had another thought, he moved away from her and left her alone again in the poolroom. Her heart was beating fast and she felt giddy, as though a wind was pushing past her left temple. She thought she could smell camphor. She took the elevator to the third floor to Maxine's rooms, and, without knocking, burst in.

"I thought you said Fabian did not come home till seven," she blurted out to Maxine.

"Yes, that's right. Why?" She gave Casey a cold stare.

"Well, oh, it's nothing. I thought I saw him at the pool." She sat down wearily on the white silk bed. Pillows were scattered at the other end.

"He wasn't in the poolroom, Casey. He just called from the office to say he would be home very late tonight," said Maxine, eyeing Casey.

"I'm so tired all the time, Maxine. I can't understand it. Do you think I'm ill or something? Last night I had another bad dream. I woke up in a total sweat." Casey still had on the white towelling robe. Her blond hair was drying now in the warmth.

"What was the dream?" Maxine was offering her some hot tea that the maid had just left. Casey felt comforted. She didn't know whether to tell Maxine in detail about Fabian in the pool. Maxine might think she was crazy. Casey recounted her dream.

"I was at Farlingham Park. I saw a body lying on the bed. A woman had been stabbed several times and the knife was still in her. It looked like an Egyptian embalming. Some of her wounds were filled with things, like the eye of Osiris. On her little finger was a ring with a picture of a man's eye painted in enamel. There was a long implement, which I have seen in a museum; it is the opening of the mouth ceremony in Ancient Egypt; it was so horrible. Then I was at the gates of Farlingham

Park. An old man in a woollen cloak was closing them. He could not see me. He dragged the gates closed against me. I was locked into the house and grounds forever."

Casey saw Maxine looking at her with a strange expression. She couldn't make it out. Her eyes were closed to her; it was impossible to read her thoughts. Casey felt the giddiness come over her again. She had lost her sense of place and time. She sat on the bed and sipped her tea; she felt weak. Maxine came and helped her lie on the bed, the softness of the cushions supporting her. Then she went to get something from the next room. She gave Casey a small phial of liquid.

"This will make you feel better. The energy in this house is strong; it has taken me some time to get used to it. This will help you regain your balance, take the edge off things." Casey emptied the contents of the phial into her mouth and lay back against the white pillows. She felt the smoothness of the silk and then she started to feel a slight tingling in her hands and feet, and a calming warmth spread through her body. Nothing worried her now. She looked up at Maxine, thankfully. She remembered that earlier, Maxine had been wearing something different, but now she had on a saffron robe, and her black hair was loose, falling around her face.

It was hard for Casey to focus. She heard something of what Maxine was saying but not everything. Then she felt the robe being touched. Maxine's fingers were softly caressing her face and feeling the contours of her mouth, Maxine lay beside her on the bed. The light went out, and Casey found herself floating away, far away, as she felt her body being moved and caressed until she couldn't remember any of it anymore. The next thing she knew, she was lying in the guest bedroom again and hearing hysterical laughter from a room beyond. But she was so tired that she fell back to sleep again. She saw in her dreams a large vessel sailing on the sea. It was her ship and she watched with interest. It swept over the menacing waves, breaking into other boats but keeping the race and holding its own in the water. Sea spray enveloped her, as she sank again into the darkness of the ocean.

The next morning, she awoke with a pounding headache and heard a clock striking the hour in one of the rooms downstairs. The chimes were calming, reminding her that she did indeed exist in time and space. Her room was at the back of the house. It was a sumptuous guest bedroom with Chinese lacquered furniture, expensive rugs and mirrors everywhere. There was a knock on the door. Casey pulled the duvet up to her chin.

"Come in," she said, cautiously.

"Good morning, Casey, did you sleep well?" Fabian had entered the room wearing silk pyjamas, covered with a dark blue robe of matching material. He looked like any other man at that time in the morning, save for the energy around him. "He carries so much power," she thought. Already, she could feel her body tingle and the sensation of excitement replace her sleepiness. A maid entered, bringing in a feast of a breakfast.

"So, what did you do yesterday, Casey?" he asked.

"I..." She absolutely could not remember a single thing she had done, either on her own or with Maxine.

"Did you go to the pool yesterday? I asked the masseuse to come over." He looked at her, checking her reactions. She wasn't remembering anything.

"The pool, no, I don't think so; for some reason, I can't seem to remember what I did yesterday. I think we just rested most of the day. I have been feeling so tired since I got here." She felt stupid. He and Maxine seemed so kind; she felt ungrateful and mindless.

"Morning, Casey. Sleep all right last night?" Maxine came into the room, already dressed in jeans and a striped shirt belonging to Fabian. Casey felt overwhelmed by all this activity so early in the morning. She looked at her watch.

"It's ten o'clock, Casey. Do you want to come to the West End? The car will take us in an hour if you want." Maxine put her arm around Fabian. Casey was suddenly jealous of the intimacy that they shared.

"Yes, that would be nice. We could go to the gallery and see my pictures, if you like," said Casey, cheering up at the thought of something familiar.

"Your pictures?" asked Maxine. "What pictures?"

A trickle of fear started to run very faintly and then more strongly in the region of her solar plexus. Wasn't she an artist, or had she suddenly got it wrong? She felt unsure, as though she could not remember. Fabian's eyes were boring into her. She couldn't take her eyes away from the gaze somehow. She was lost for words.

"I'm sorry, I must be muddled, or something. I thought I had a show, or something. I guess I must have been dreaming. Sorry, you must think me very stupid." Casey poured some coffee for herself, hoping it would wake her up.

"Casey, you have been working for Fabian for two years now, you know, at the place in Mayfair. You are having a few days off, don't you remember?" said Maxine, sounding irritated. The fear in Casey's belly was worse. She couldn't remember working for Fabian.

"What was I doing at the Mayfair place?" Casey asked, not knowing or understanding anything.

"Casey, I think you must be ill. You were entertaining the clients. One of them roughed you up a bit. It's all right; it won't happen again. You are still shocked; you will get over it. You just need some rest. Perhaps you should stay here today. It sounds like it is too soon for you to go out. The weather is really cold now," said Maxine, buttoning her blouse up to indicate somehow the cold day.

"But, it's the middle of summer. Look…" But she realized the windows were shut and so were the shutters beyond.

"Casey, it is the middle of winter. Fabian, I think we should let her rest some more." With that, Maxine and Fabian left her. She went back to sleep, not wanting to face another moment of her chaotic world.

Later that day, she woke again. She had no idea what time of the day it was, because of the windows being shut, but her watch said two in the afternoon. She went and showered. The mirror that she gazed into did not reflect her image back to her. She shrieked in shock, examining the back of the glass to see if it was a mirror. It was. She remembered that if someone was very evil, a looking glass never reflected the image; either that or she was dead. No, she did not feel dead. She showered but had little or no body sensation, not being able to tell whether the water was hot or cold. Sensation was gone, her image gone. What was left?

A slow dim anger started to explode inside her. She had to fight this. She had to fight what was happening. She grabbed some clothes and fled out of the bedroom. The house was lit only by electric light; all the shutters were closed. Was it the same house that she arrived at a few days ago? She simply could not tell. The rage still boiled inside her. It was the only thing that was going to get her out of the wilderness that her mind had become. She went into each of the rooms; then in front of her was a locked door. She heaved into it with all the force of her anger. She couldn't feel her body. The door did not move but after some pounding, it eventually gave way.

Inside was a dark office, a curious affair with odd pictures of men hanging upside down on the wall, pictures that were old from another century, and a few chairs of black leather. There were pentacle signs all over the wall. Then in the corner, she saw a case of glass.

Gingerly, she went over, wanting to inspect the contents but sensing that a power emanated from that part of the room; her body didn't like it. Yes, inside the glass was a large hat made to fit the head of a man, the hat of a jester but so old that the fabric was worn and faded. Tarnished bells were at the point of each peak. Once it had, she thought, been livid red with yellow inserts.

"Jester," she thought. She had seen the picture of a jester somewhere. But where? She could not remember at all. She turned away, heading for the desk; she opened the drawers, photographs falling out onto the floor. She stopped, shocked by what she saw.

The photographs were of her: a picture of herself naked, her hands holding her hair up from her head, her breasts thrust forward in a pose, legs a little apart. But she could not remember anything. Pictures streamed through her fingers – pictures of her stepfather, Oliver, standing next to Fabian years ago when she was just a child, leaning against a station wagon, the Alps beyond; then pictures of her at fourteen with her stepfather, lying on the beach, Oliver with his hand on her back as she lay on her stomach; then photos of her in Chelsea at art school. Fear knotted in her stomach again.

She looked at another envelope. It was sealed. She ripped it open, her hands shaking. The coloured photos spilled onto the carpet. She was on her knees in the pictures, Oliver naked behind her; their nakedness, caught by the camera with a close-up lens, showing their lovemaking; then Maxine lying next to her, also naked, her hands on Casey's thighs, her head and hair hanging over Casey's face as she kissed her, laughing, Casey on her back. The photo was faded; it must have been a few years old. She could not remember anything.

Nausea gripped her again as she saw herself in pictures that she would have preferred not to see – Fabian in the marbled swimming pool holding her from behind and then a picture of Fabian with his arm around her when she had been at primary school. Why could she not remember? Then there was a new collection, pictures recently taken of all the weekend guests in their group at Farlingham Park: Anna, Justin, Anthony, Jane, Stephanie and Randy. When and how were these pictures taken? Then there were photographs going back years showing her with her stepfather, his obvious sexual interest in her.

One picture was tucked away inside a book. A sepia image this time of Anna sitting on Oliver's lap, in his study, her back to the camera, her legs apart, straddled over him. That was the day Casey had nearly died in the bog; but who had taken the picture and why did Fabian have it? It was horrendous; she slammed the book shut. What had Oliver been doing to Anna?

After Oliver's death, Fabian had gone to Oliver's residences to find the pictures of Anna and Casey that he knew were in his possession. There were lots of photographs and Oliver's 'signature' of his bestial ways, laying a huge trail for the police to easily find. After the death of the young girl at the Hexagons, there were a lot of unanswered questions. Fabian destroyed most of the incriminating evidence. The rest were of interest to him and he had taken them back to the house in St. John's Wood.

The last picture was an old picture of Fabian with Anna, a headscarf around her hair, holding Fabian's hand outside a chateau in France. Anna looked so young. Casey shoved the pictures back into the drawers of the desk; her head was pounding. She had to get out, but how, she couldn't remember, except that seeing the photographs of the group of men had suddenly brought back some memory.

Casey slammed the office door shut; tears were running down her face, a drugged headache in her head. She found her way back to her room. She was about to collapse onto her bed when she saw the headlines of what must have been a newspaper from some weeks back.

The headlines read, 'Lord Oliver Pemberton's Tragic Death in Uruguay'. There was a picture of a smashed black Mercedes upturned on a dirt road. Fabian had put it there as a reminder to Casey about the dangers of crossing him. But Casey knew of his death already; Justin had taken her aside and told her.

# 36

Justin was in his office at the hospital, sitting at the desk, thinking that finally he was going to say goodbye to his life as a surgeon and this dreadful piece of furniture that served as a desk.

"Are you all right, sir?" asked Felicity. He looked so pale and was staring into the distance.

"Felicity, did you ever receive any calls here from Lord Oliver Pemberton?" asked Justin in reply.

"No, I don't remember any calls from him." Felicity wondered what was on Sir Justin's mind.

"Lady Anna's cousin, Casey Pemberton – it was her stepfather. He was killed in a car accident in South America a few weeks ago. It seems it took an inordinate amount of time for the news to reach London. I find that strange," continued Justin.

Thinking aloud, he changed the subject. "Did you book the flight for me I mentioned yesterday?" he asked. Felicity was shocked by the abrupt change in subject. Yes, it was true; that on reflection, Justin had not been himself for weeks.

"Yes, it's all arranged, a one-way and the reservations at the Hilton." Felicity wondered why he had booked a one-way, but she wasn't going to ask him.

"Don't mention this to anyone. It's a special trip and has to be kept secret." Justin returned his thoughts to the black smoke across the river and Fairfax's call. For some reason, Jane came to his mind. Oh God, he had completely forgotten to call her last night. He was worried, but now he had a meeting to rush to at the London Clinic. The call would have to wait.

Jane had just woken up in her own bed. She could not understand how she had got there, as she remembered lying on the lawn with her hands tied behind her back while the men kicked her. She remembered the agony. Now, as she ran her hands over her back, she couldn't even find a bruise to tell the tale. Anthony swam into her thoughts and the scenes of yesterday, and the police again harrowed her spirit.

And then, the conversation of last night came back to her again. They had accused her of killing their leader and plotting the King's death.

"Don't you remember, Jane, what you did? You would like that, wouldn't you, the high and mighty to whom every knee had to bend. Don't you remember your sins?" They went on, sticking their feet into her, as she writhed on the lawn.

"Yes, we will come and torture you again and again like you tortured us, until you lose your mind. And then one day, we will kill you – just a little accident, nothing too conspicuous." Their voices droned on.

Then she remembered losing consciousness, and she had briefly come around and found someone lifting her up into a car and being taken to Farlingham Park.

Now she was in her own bed with no sign of Farlingham Park. She put on some black corduroy trousers and a white sweater and went downstairs. The smell of the drenched fire still hung in the air. She lifted the phone, which gave the usual dial tone. Then she walked slowly to the front gates; they were open as usual, no sign of anyone tampering with them. Her car was in the garage. Then she heard the phone ringing and she ran back to the house.

"Jane, I'm so sorry I didn't call you last night. We had so many things come up and then there was an emergency at the hospital. Are you all right?" Justin sensed Jane's silence at the other end of the line.

She did not answer Justin's words immediately; her head was swimming with confusion.

"Justin, I spoke with you at about eight o'clock. I told you I had received a strange phone call, then the lines went dead and I was attacked by two men on the driveway. You said that I must drive to London and come and stay with you and Anna." Jane's voice was flat-toned and shocked.

"Sweetie, it just wouldn't have been possible. I wasn't near the phone at that time. Anna and I were having dinner; she can vouch for that. I was intending to call you later, but then there was the emergency at the hospital. You are spending too much time alone. You should come back to London as soon as possible. Fairfax arrived back from New York last night. He was trying to call you as well. Where were you, Jane?" Justin was now seriously worried about her. He was running through the possible symptoms, the paranoia, treating her as a clinician would.

"I am still finding the death of Lord Oliver, Casey's stepfather, very disturbing," he said. "The circumstances seem suspicious to me. He died in an accident on the back roads of Uruguay." Justin heard himself giving her all the details. "Why, Jane? Why does anything happen the way it does?" Justin saw Felicity with the plane tickets for Cairo in her hand.

Jane felt choked, sick. She didn't know what else to say, and she knew that tone in Justin's voice well enough to know that he was thinking she was having a nervous breakdown. And now Lord Oliver, she remembered things about him that she did not wish to think about now. And then there had been that day at Anna's house.

"Justin, I think someone is trying to kill me – not only me, but all of us, all our group that were at Farlingham Park last weekend." There, she had said it.

"Nonsense, Jane, it's just in your mind. We don't even know these other people. Just pack up this morning and go back to Chiswick. I don't know what has come over you and Anna these last weeks, always talking in corners and seeing too much in everything ever since that conversation with Sidney Henderson and his scaremongering." Justin was angry now, but he had his own thoughts and his plans. Those had to be kept secret. He didn't want Jane to know what he was doing; it would only create more hysteria.

Jane replaced the receiver slowly. She wanted to go to Farlingham Park to see if she had been there last night; there must be some tell-tale signs of her car.

Green trees showered light on her, as she spun the car in the direction of the house. She liked to drive, and her red-gloved hands on the steering wheel gave her a sense of being in control. Her hair, loose now, flew back from her head in the wind. She wore sunglasses, her favourite Christian Dior pair with the little monogram on the side. Yes, she felt secure as though her world was real once again. She wondered whether she was being administered a drug that would induce the experiences she was having, or whether it was a drug that would make her forget what really happened.

It was much more likely, though, that this was all happening in a dimension that only one part of her existence was aware of, like the dream state. In the initiation cells of the pyramids, she had had strange experiences like these. She was trying to recall what she had done then. Could it be that she were in two places at once? What about the phone call from Justin? How could she hear that, if it never happened? Either he was lying, or her mental plane was being tampered with by someone who knew how to do it. They were all in danger. However much she fought, there was nothing but an invisible enemy. It was thoroughly impossible. But Lord Oliver, that was something else. And why South America? What was he doing there? How was it connected to their set of friends and how was he put in danger? Was he really murdered? She thought back to their early days at the university, of going to Anna's house when they had been up at Cambridge. Lord Oliver had been there as well, although much older than they were.

The terrifying incident happened one day when she was coming out of the bathroom on the second floor; she was only eighteen then and still a virgin. The corridor was thin and dark and there was Lord Oliver barring her way back downstairs. At first, she thought it was a joke; he was playing a game. But the game had become serious. He had pulled her roughly back into the bathroom, locking the door. He was immensely tall and strong. He pinioned her against the wall, one hand over her mouth, his ice blue eyes staring into her face, the lips already bruising her mouth, his tongue probing inside.

To her silent horror, in one movement he had ripped off her thin summer skirt, quickly moving his fingers inside her panties and roughly pulling them down her legs. And then his body was against hers; she was firmly trapped against the wall. His other hand released himself from his pants that soon fell to the floor. A few minutes later, he would have raped her. She was in no doubt about that. He had already moved himself against her, his length between her legs. It would have only been a couple of minutes. She could not move. The bathroom was in a remote part of the house. He was trying to push her onto the floor to get on top of her.

And then Anna's voice had rescued her, calling along the corridor looking for her, trying the locked door of the bathroom. Oliver swore, quickly adjusted his clothing, opened the bathroom door, walked out and slammed it. Anna saw Oliver and then in the bathroom, Jane, white faced with her skirt torn off and her lovely hair all loose around her. That was the day Anna had warned her about Oliver. She had said he was a menace, a sexual pervert of the worst kind. They never mentioned the incident again.

Farlingham Park, or rather its closed uninviting gates, stood before her sooner than she expected. How black they were! She looked at the strange symbols. They resonated with some psychic space within her brain. She remembered something about the gates, but it was so faint, and she was tired this morning as though part of her was still asleep. It looked deserted; the gates were padlocked and only a small narrow wicket gate was available for entry. She was about to go when an old man on a rickety bicycle came along the avenue towards the gates. He entered the wicket gate and stood before her. He had on a faded green hat that had seen many summers. He had it pulled down over his eyes. His mouth worked on a piece of grass stuck between his teeth.

His baggy fawn trousers sported bicycle clips, thin black circles of metal.

"I was staying here at the weekend. I wanted to see the Countess about something. Would it be possible?" She felt silly somehow in front of this old man. He looked at her for a minute or so, summing her up. "One of those London types," he thought, throwing a glance in the direction of the car.

"No, madam, the Countess left to go abroad. The house is being closed now for the winter. She won't be back now until next year. She'll be at one of her other residences." He had taken the straw out of his mouth, but now put it back again, signifying that the conversation was over. He was mounting the bicycle.

"But, last night..." she said, not finishing her sentence. He didn't answer; he was already riding off down the road. She thought she heard his laugh as he disappeared.

She had no choice but to leave. Another idea seized her. She got into the car again and drove in the direction of the shop. She had not found it with Anthony, but she would try again. This time, she got the direction right. Yes, there were the cottages and the place where she had left the car – the red post box. She stopped then and looked at where she remembered the shop to be.

It was derelict. Once, maybe, it had been a shop of sorts, but it was boarded up and in a state of total disrepair.

She stared in horror. Had she been living a nightmare? What was real, her waking or her dream state? She felt an immense chasm opening in front of her. She was falling into it, unable to stop herself. Perhaps Justin was right; she was ill; they were all ill. Maybe Anthony was just an illusion as well. Nothing made any sense. She drove home slowly feeling the warm sun on her face, but inside, she felt as cold and as perishable as ice.

She stopped at the gates to her own house. She wanted to walk up the drive. Anyway, she would be leaving soon. The weeds on the driveway were getting worse. A huge dandelion had pushed its home into the stones. She must get a gardener soon or her own home would become a ruin, like her life. Just past the dandelion, something bright caught her eye. It was a large new padlock. She recognized it instantly, the one that the men used to secure the gate last night. So, it did happen; she wasn't crazy. This was the one and only piece of evidence that all this had happened to her. She remembered now that one of the men had thrown it on the ground when they had rushed through the gates towards her as she had turned and run, seeking the safety of the house. Even if no one ever believed her, she knew herself that her life was truly in danger.

She danced round in a circle, round and round, a new release flooding into her veins. She wasn't going crazy. Now she had the energy to fight back. She would battle it through, save her life and the lives of her friends. She ran to the house and let herself into the back door. The Countess, she remembered, had warned her of something but in veiled terms. Why had she forgotten so quickly? Everything was going to be all right – yes, all right. Somehow, she felt the Countess was working, too, on other planes, helping with the deep wound that affected them all.

# 37

"Could I speak to Inspector Rawlings, please?" Jane was on the phone now with a renewed vision. Of course, she would find out where Anthony was and go and see him. It would be all right.

"This is Inspector Rawlings here. How can I help you, Mrs Crosby-Nash?" The inspector's voice sounded just the same as the other day, when he had arrested Anthony – the same monotone, a cold voice.

"Oh, please call me Jane. I want to find out where Anthony is. I need to visit him as soon as possible." There was a short but significant silence at the other end.

"You know, to be quite honest with you, Mrs Crosby-Nash, I don't know where he is exactly. Let me offer you a word of advice. As far as you are concerned, it would be much better if you did not pursue this any further. You understand it's in your own interest that I am offering you this advice. Justice will take its own course, and there are people mixed up in this that frankly, you would be better off staying away from at this time." Rawlings coughed. His eyes were on the computer screen that held all of Anthony's details and where he was being held.

"But, he is my friend. You don't understand," cried Jane.

"How long have you known Mr Jackson?" The cold clinical voice was coming down the line at her.

"Well, just a month or so," Jane said lamely, trying to recapture the moment when she had set eyes on him first when she had entered the pyramid.

"You formed a rescue party, didn't you?" asked Rawlings, in the inquisitor seat now. Jane didn't answer. What was he getting at?

"We don't want to have to drag you into all this. Some might start to think you were his accomplice," he said, staring at the computer and lighting up a cigarette, as he smiled to himself. "Little high-handed, inquisitive bitch," he thought.

"There are things that have come to light about your Mr Jackson that you would probably not like to hear. A month is not a long enough time to know someone; and weren't you seeing his assistant, Vince?" Rawlings accentuated the 'seeing' in an insinuating manner.

Jane felt panic. How did he know all this? Rawlings felt the panic at the other end. He went in for the kill.

"It is not the sort of thing a husband like yours would want to know about, is it, Mrs Crosby-Nash? Just be warned, dear, and stay away." He knew Jane had no option now but to back off. Not surprised, he heard a click at the other end of the line. She had hung up.

Jane went to the living room and lay down on the sofa. She closed the lids over her violet eyes; her hands trembled on her knees. Her red hair fell over the face, hiding her fine features. She felt the world was closing in. There were trap doors everywhere. There was no one she could trust anymore, not even Justin or Anna. She was totally alone. At the bottom of all this, there was someone trying to destroy their lives. They were severing friendships, breaking down ties, until they all stood alone in the isolation of events, without defence, without strategy. Psychic attack was the deadliest. The Ancient Egyptian scriptures talked of battles that were fought entirely with mantras, the sacred sounds rending the air and tearing bodies apart. Whoever it was, they knew exactly what they were doing.

Jane, motionless, lay thinking and thinking. Eventually, having not furthered any plans, she drove home to Chiswick. No doubt, the demons, whoever they were, would follow.

Rawlings was still smoking the cigarette as he called the house in St. John's Wood. Fabian was on the line.

"She called, wanting to know where he was. I told her to steer off, not to get involved. The little bitch really got scared when I mentioned Vince. That was a nice little setup; got her by the short hairs, didn't it?"

"Don't waste time, Rawlings, skip the flower. I don't want her going off to Cairo. She will only mess things up there. Keep her busy here; then we can kill her when we want. And make sure Sean stays down in South America. Keep him low, out of the way. We have another pretty little situation here; you had better come over to the house tomorrow and get her out of here, somehow." Fabian was referring to Maxine; she had become pregnant, and The Jester prescribed that the women in question be sent to his headquarters in South America and the babies farmed out after birth to be raised as The Jester's children. "Call me later. I have another call coming through, Rawlings. Put that damn cigarette out, will you? I can smell it over the phone!"

The phone slammed down hard in Rawlings' ear. He threw the cigarette on the floor and ground it to a mass of fibres under his heel.

# 38

"Get our doctor over here, fast. Maxine has fallen down the stairs. Send a nurse over, too!" He shouted at one of the maids.

He had to get out of the house. He could not stand being there a moment longer. One of the maids rushed upstairs, and he gave her instructions to look after Maxine until the doctor came. Then he took a taxi to Mayfair and called the house from the office. Maxine had recovered consciousness, and the doctor and nurse had arrived. He was relieved, but still angry with her. She was taking too much into her own hands these days, and a little power was dangerous. She didn't know what she was really doing. He had hit her too hard this time.

The high-class brothel was tucked away in one of those familiar side streets of Mayfair that hid the inner world of those houses and their occupants from view. Mayfair was a playboy's heaven. Fabian always felt it in the air. It excited him. Was he getting bored with Maxine, he wondered? He was thinking of Casey. Maxine had, of her own volition, reversed the effects of the drugs he had administered to Casey while she was still at the house. He was amazed at how she had known how to do this. Maxine had explained to Fabian that she knew Casey better than anyone and that his methods to secure her into his organization would never work. It was better to let her go.

There were two things that Maxine did not know. First, that Fabian had, by his own methods, captivated Casey. His seed was, in a way, already inside her. She would crave and long for him. He had entrapped Maxine the same way, but she was unaware of the fact that he had done this or how it was enacted.

The second thing, which neither Maxine nor Fabian knew, was that Casey had found ways of stealing and successfully hiding some of the photographs she had taken from the desk drawer in Fabian's study, before they had burst in to drag her away. Fabian could be imprisoned for many years for what he had done: the sexual exploits; the rape of young, underaged girls; prostitution in the Hexagon Club; orgies at Thackeray Hall – many girls, so many of them. It was to be the downward spiral for both The Jester and Fabian, but until then all mayhem would be let loose.

"Do you want to meet with any of the girls today?" asked Sally, one of his assistants. "Mandy is upstairs and Diana has just returned from Germany. No one else is here." Fabian was in his office. It was elaborate, French, fanciful, full of tufted brocade and silks, some of which hung in great sculpted folds as curtains from the full-length windows. There was one black and white picture on the wall of one of Fabian's favourite girls. She was completely naked with her back to the photographer and was astride a little French chair that had come from a chateau they used for one of the overnight, notorious events that Fabian staged on a regular basis.

A balcony lay beyond the open windows, filled with small orange trees and white azaleas. Chairs were laid out and a single red canvas umbrella shaded a round table. It had a grand view of Hyde Park beyond. Wine and champagne were stacked in the refrigerator, ready for the first guests of the day.

Fabian's black, shiny desk was stacked with videos, porn magazines open at their centrefolds and jewellery hanging out of velvet boxes. The videos were of their girls, naked in seductive poses and pulling at their G-strings. The clips would titillate the clients, who after being served champagne and canapes, paid a hefty fee for the booking. Their client list was enormous. If the client was what they called 'dry', they would bring in one of the girls for a little touch and squeeze, just enough to arouse. That usually would do the trick, and the client would pay and leave knowing that there would be more pleasure to come.

Fabian's thoughts this morning were around one issue. He wanted out. He was keeping the game going, but only for The Jester. His constant preoccupation was that if The Jester ceased to own and possess his body, would he have any life at all? If, for example, The Jester's existence terminated, would he cease to exist also? The experiment would be dangerous, life-threatening. The Jester was quite capable of eavesdropping on his thoughts. It took an enormous amount of energy to erect any barrier at all. It was like fighting with the wind; you never knew which way it would be blowing.

"No, not now." He was finally answering Sally's question, "Get me some coffee, will you? I have had a hell of a morning up at the house. Is Angela here?" he asked.

"No, she called to say she would be in later." Sally left to fetch the coffee. Fabian thought she looked tired. She needed a holiday; too thin, waif-like. All these blondes with stringy hair and blue eyes, without a suntan, they look wan. He decided to send her off to the Caribbean and give her some breast implants at the same time. It was bad for business to have wan-looking call girls around the office with drooping tits. The luscious holiday atmosphere had to prevail at all costs.

"One of the new assistants has arrived. Do you want to meet her?" Sally asked, returning with the coffee.

"Yes, I suppose so. Better do it now before Angela arrives and all bedlam is let loose round here. Can you bring in that video of the Russian girl?" Liana was their newest acquisition from Uzbekistan. She had been through the training and was one of their most beautiful girls, only eighteen years old. He could not wait to get his hands on her. He was thinking of what he would do with this one. His personal training of all the girls was the last they would receive before they were sent out abroad or to night parties at some country mansion put together by the agency in the most lavish possible manner.

Fabian drank his black coffee. He was deep in thought. It had been very early in the morning, around seven o'clock, when he had heard Maxine leave her room and go downstairs.

He saw a car pick Maxine up. It wasn't one of his chauffeurs. She was alone. Approximately an hour later, she had returned as though nothing had happened. She returned to her room and did not rise for breakfast with him as she normally would do. She appeared to be sleeping. He had gone to her room and wakened her.

"Why did you leave the house so early?" he had asked.

"Fabian, it was personal business; stop spying on me all the time. I need my own space," she had answered.

"You know so little, Maxine; be careful you don't lose the power that you have.

"Fabian, I never wanted you to shoot the photographs of Casey. Leave her alone, Fabian; let her go back to the life that she knows." Maxine turned her face away from him. She never used to do this, but his eyes hurt her. His power was hers now, after being his for so long. And then, The Jester had come. He had filled her with ecstasy.

"Casey is pregnant, Maxine." He knew it from the feel of her body in the days at their house.

"Whose baby is it?" Maxine was jealous of Casey now, wondering if Fabian had been having an affair with her.

"No one you would know, Maxine." Fabian was sure of the fact that Casey's baby was Oliver's. Since Oliver was Casey's stepfather, he wondered if she would keep it. Only Maxine knew the agonizing depths of Casey's relationship with Oliver; Casey had shared so much with her. Maxine had been very protective of her friend and now this unexpected pregnancy.

"You should never take power into your own hands again, Maxine. This house is charged with a certain energy. If you mess that up or try and change the lines of communication, you could get us both killed." He saw Maxine's eyes widen in disbelief. His fury knew no bounds once it started with her. "But I have been with The Jester now. Surely it is all right." Fabian moaned inwardly. He could hardly bear it that The Jester had enjoyed sexual privileges with Maxine that belonged to him alone.

Maxine got out of bed. She wrapped the black transparent robe around her. He looked quickly at her breasts beneath the silkiness; immediately, he wanted her. His forehead was sweating, the palms of his hands moist. His face showed the pain of a thousand years when he thought of Maxine with The Jester. He would take her from him. He had seduced her; his poisonous seed would now be inside her. It would be the end of everything for them.

She took the comb and went to her mirror; slowly, thoughtfully, pulling it through the long, black strands of hair as she sat down on the stool.

Fabian moved towards her and ran his hand across her shoulders and then down into the opening of the gown reaching for her breasts. She pulled away from him, but she was not quick enough. He leaned forward into her and she could feel him against her back. She pushed into him. She looked at his reflection in the glass. His smile was forced, showing oddly-pointed teeth. His mouth came close to her neck.

Then he pulled Maxine by the arm back to the bed. Roughly, he pulled her white thong off. She gasped with the sensation. He reached for the black thread in its jewelled box on the bedside table. This was their ceremony. He had done this with Anna, all of it.

She lay naked now on the bed and he wound the silk thread around Maxine's shoulder and then it was running between her legs. He knew just how to pull and engage its coiled mouth against her. It was soft and hard at the same time. Maxine loved it. In a matter of moments, she would be beyond arousal. Then, Fabian let the thread hang loose, arousing her again but gently this time.

Then, suddenly, he was starting to be rough with her again. She watched his passion mounting to new heights. But she knew how to pace things with him now, his tastes and what he liked to do to her. He was obsessed by her. Sexually, he could never get enough of her. And then the phone rang at the worst possible time. Fabian screamed at her.

"Was that Casey?"

She hardly heard him. She was already in another world and The Jester had been speaking to her. She did not feel like answering Fabian. She had got up now and was walking away; she trod barefoot along the landing. Her toenails were painted pale pink. She watched her feet as they sunk into the whiteness of the rug. Part of her was enjoying the power.

"Answer me," he screamed at her. "Answer me. I asked you a question." His voice was menacing as he followed her. He did not want to be crossed like this. They had stopped their lovemaking with the phone call but their passions were still high.

Still she did not answer. She watched her feet on the carpet, the measured steps and the black robe. Something stirred in her. It was a thought; some powerful memory was surfacing. It was as though she was still in this body, but there was another time.

Then he had hit her across the face, then across the mouth to prevent the full memory from surfacing. He wanted to break the thread of her thought. He did not want her to remember his acts against her. He hit her again. The next thing she knew was that her slipperless feet had tripped; she stumbled, falling down the stairs.

His reverie about Maxine was over. Sally was at the door.

"Angela has arrived. Shall I ask her to get ready?" she asked.

"Yes, tell her I will come up to her room in about five minutes." He was thinking about something else and looked out onto the red umbrella sitting in the sun.

Angela was now in the hallway. She seemed agitated.

"He wants to see you in five minutes. Take it easy, Angela; he has had a hell of a morning," said Sally. Angela stared at her blankly.

Angela, dressed in a black linen suit, walked up the stairs. She had on stockings with a strong black seam down the back of the legs, ending in little bows that emerged just above the high-heeled black suede shoes. On her ring finger, she wore an exquisite large, pear-shaped diamond, set in heavy gold. She went up to her suite at the top of the house. On the other side of the room was a private elevator.

Fabian left the downstairs office and stepped into the elevator. He went up to the top floor. He entered Angela's suite without knocking and closed the door behind him.

# 39

Rivers of blood ran between Casey's legs. Her left arm bore a gash, one-inch long; it was deep. She feared for her life. She cried out in terror at what was happening to her.

Anna had taken to sleeping in one of their spare bedrooms next to Casey's room in their home. Every night Casey awoke in the small hours of the morning, screaming after yet another nightmare. Anna had taken it upon herself to nurse Casey through the first stages of her mourning for Oliver and to help her to recover from the nightmare of her visit to Maxine. She had been in a dreadful state when she left the house in St John's Wood. Justin thought she had gone completely crazy.

In Casey's dream, Oliver's long beautiful body lay beside her. There was no movement, and his hands were resting on his genitals, as though he were asleep. She turned over trying to wake him, but the blue eyes stared straight ahead of him. He was dead, his body now stiffened. The blood from the wound was running down her arm; she cried out in alarm. She woke up then to her own screams.

This was the sixth night of dreams. Anna and Casey had talked all day, sharing something of their earlier lives in their families. There was an intimacy now that surrounded their relationship. They had always been close but afraid for themselves and each other even before the day that Casey nearly got swallowed up in the marshes when they were both nine years old.

This time Casey told Anna her dream; it was the first time. It was nearly always the same dream.

"This river of blood is flowing between my legs; then Oliver is next to me; he is dead..." Casey's voice faded as she neared the reality, the statement of grief and loss.

"Did Oliver...?" asked Anna. Why was Oliver lying naked beside his stepdaughter in the dream? Anna wondered about their relationship. Of course, part of her knew from that day in the marshes when Casey had said how much she hated her life and wished she could die. Anna knew somehow there was a terrible secret in Casey's heart.

"Yes, Anna. It started when I was six. He would creep into my room at night time and just get into my bed, just holding me at first. It went on for years, he would take all his clothes off and wanted me always to touch him in his private parts. He put himself in my mouth. He masturbated in front of me, both standing in the room and in bed. I was terrified. He would feel into my body, in every place his fingers were there, pinching, probing. It was horrible. I had such bad stomach aches afterwards.

"During the day, he would stare at me by the pool, stare and stare, like he was eating me up. His gaze was always upon me. The problem was that I loved him ever since Mother married him. But he filled me with terror as well. I could not seem to grow anymore; there was no space for me; he wanted everything. He kept saying that I was his best friend.

"On my sixteenth birthday, he came to bed with me and I panicked. Always, there had been this terror of what he could do to me. I was helpless and still so small. For the first time, he had intercourse with me on the floor, on and on; I thought he would never stop. I screamed and cried, but he put his hand over my mouth. He hit me if I did not do what he wanted. It was like being devoured; no space, just him in my face, all the time, nearly every night. It hurt so much. He would do it over and over again. He was huge; it hurt. There was nothing left of me; it was as if he took my soul as well. There was none of me left. He would not allow any part of me to be separated from him. I was never allowed anyone else, to be close to anyone." Casey broke down and wept at what she had never been able to tell a single friend for her entire life.

Anna then decided to break the secret that she had promised to never reveal for eternity. "For me, it was Fabian. He seemed to come along one day; and in our family, we have these sexual rituals; I am sure lots of families do this. Anyway, first I had my hymen removed." Anna looked at Casey's eyes staring at her.

"Removed! But why?" she asked.

"I did not really think about it. That was a kind of ceremony that had been practiced in my family for generations. It was done also in Nazi Germany; it is about removing something impure." Anna found the sharing a huge relief after being shut up in her own mind her entire life.

"I have sworn never to tell anyone this, Casey, but I cannot stand keeping it to myself any longer. Then there was the ceremony with Fabian, the passage of sexual rites. The family was there, and other people who wore masks with long noses so that they would not be recognized. Fabian and I were in a specially prepared bed at the ceremony of my first opening, which is what they called it; everyone watched. I did not mind, as I was brought up knowing this would happen. Lucille prepared my body and told me what Fabian would do to me. I was scared. They played chants, like Gregorian chants but played backwards. I was put in certain positions. Then I forget now what happened. They gave me a drink and I must have passed out." Anna realized there had after all been something very strange about her upbringing. She felt uneasy now, and a kind of fog came over her mind, as if she was not allowed to remember more. She wondered now about the full extent of what had happened to her, what had they done to her.

"Anna, you look as though you have seen a ghost or someone walked over your grave!" Casey was concerned about her cousin.

"It is as though I have told you a dreadful secret for which I will pay. The powers that be do not like me telling you these things. They are supposed to be kept secret. I have never told anyone; I thought this was normal, what was practiced in our family." Anna truly believed that in revealing these secrets, she would in some way lose her life.

"Later, Fabian hurt me a lot. He wanted so much of me and trained me in all sorts of sexual and occult practices. It was expected that he would make me a high priestess; the belief in our family is that taking the innocence of a young virgin secures everlasting life for the man and allows him to be master of his own universe, to become a god. If they trained me to be sexually involved with other men, then these eternal gifts would be multiplied. I became a whore, insatiable sexually. I would go to the clubs that my family frequented. I had to watch porn, rapes; they wanted me to become more and more adept in the sexual arts. I had become the high priestess." Anna felt exhausted now telling all this to Casey.

"I am going to get us a hot drink, Casey, then we can go back to sleep. Do you want me to stay with you?"

"I'm pregnant, Anna." Casey had meant to wait to tell Anna this but somehow in her anxiety and grief, it had come out.

"Oliver?" Anna asked kindly.

Casey silently nodded as Anna left the room to go to the kitchen. She realized she was trembling from all that she had revealed to Casey and all that her cousin had shared with her. Making the hot chocolate for them both in the kitchen calmed her down.

It was the tip of the iceberg for both women. They had little idea of the kind of damage that had actually been done to them; it would eventually take Casey years to be rid of the spells and the memories of entrapment and frequent rapes of which they were both only partially aware. Anna was not to be so lucky. She would remain confused about it all for the rest of her life.

A few days later, it was early in the morning, and Casey lay in her own bed in her apartment in Primrose Hill, the counterpane pulled up to her face. She had been with Anna and Justin for ten days at their home in Kent. She had broken down completely with the grief of losing her lover and the shock of being pregnant with Oliver's baby. But the nightmares had receded, and she felt more herself. The predominant thing she felt was tiredness and the inability to remember anything about her stay at Maxine's, except for a vivid dream of finding someone's body at Farlingham Park. Her body felt sore and there was a scratch on her back and bruises on her right thigh. Perhaps she had fallen, or something. Most of the other things she could remember, especially Anthony and Farlingham Park. There were no messages from Anthony, which she thought was strange. Another very strong feeling surfaced, which scared her, and that was a kind of craving. Was that the way she would describe it? Yes, it was strong. She wanted, above anything else, to see Fabian. It shocked her. She was shocked too about Anna's revelations; she felt dizzy thinking about it and the fact that Fabian had seduced Anna all those years ago. She was getting morning sickness now. How was she going to cope with this baby? Antigone, her mother, would have no idea, and the truth could never be revealed to her.

The force of the river of longing for Fabian became like a tidal wave within an hour, and she found herself reaching for the phone. She hadn't seen him for nearly two weeks. It was like a thirst and it had to be quenched. She had to drink. She remembered that it had been like this with Oliver, had to have him, always addicted, as though she could not live without his touch. She had grown into a woman with him, and she had never been able to let him go. He had enchanted her and now she wanted to be enchanted again. She was completely unaware of how strong this pattern of addiction was within her. If she was not addicted or could not be with Oliver, there had to be someone else. It was like a root sewn within her so early in her life.

She called the number that he had given her. It was the Mayfair brothel. Sally answered the phone.

"Hello, to whom did you wish to speak to?" she asked, knowing who it was, as she had been told to expect the call.

"My name is Casey. I would like to speak to Fabian."

"I will try and put you through, but he is in conference," said Sally. Casey wondered what 'conference' meant.

Sally stalled for a few moments and then put the call through.

"I thought I told you not to put any calls through while I am with Angela," snapped Fabian down the line at Sally.

"It's Casey," said Sally.

"Put her through." He changed to absolute smoothness.

"Casey, how nice to hear from you. Why did you leave us so abruptly? I was getting so spoiled by your company." He spoke softly to her.

"Oh, I just felt I needed to be with Anna and Justin," said Casey, lying. "But I would love to see you, Fabian," she said. "There are some things I want to talk to you about." She felt somehow there should be a reason; she did not want to appear too forward.

"So, we should meet soon. How about this evening at your apartment, around eight o'clock? Would that suit you?" he asked, all politeness.

"Yes, that would be fine." She wondered whether he could hear the desire in her voice, the longing. She had tried to sound matter-of-fact.

"So, the die is cast," thought Casey. "Why did I do that?" She would call Maxine and say she was just having Fabian over for a drink at her own house. But then Maxine would wonder. Why was she being devious? It was not her nature.

But she did put a call through to St. John's Wood. The maid answered and said Maxine could not be disturbed. She was in meetings all day. Casey wondered what was going on.

Casey felt unable to get out of bed until much later that day. She ached all over. She was also experiencing some dizziness as well as morning sickness. She spent the afternoon on the magnificent balcony overlooking the tops of the trees in Primrose Hill. She had been left the penthouse by Oliver; he had left so much of his property and vast wealth to her. She had lived there with him, unable to free themselves of each other. She pushed the thoughts away now of what he did to her there, what they shared of their dark secrets and then the other men that he had brought to the apartment to meet his tempting daughter. She remembered she had been dazzled by them at first and flirted but then, things had got out of hand. But she grew to expect this from Oliver from when she was a young child, his temper out of hand; and then later, when ejaculation became a problem, he would cane her.

She wondered whether it was a good move to stay where she and Oliver had shared so much intimacy; but then, there was the baby now, and they would have their lives together, living in Oliver's memory. So, she would have it gutted and redecorated all to her own style and fill it with her choice of furniture, not his. And so, the place would become hers, and the memories of him would subside eventually. She had the baby to look forward to, Oliver's last gift to her.

The penthouse was utterly different to her New York place which expressed a more bohemian outlook, and was filled with large canvasses and contained a studio in which to work. Oil paint usually ended up in the kitchen and so the whole place became chaotic at times; but it represented a certain inner chaos that she always felt in New York. It was an exciting city, but it often left her frazzled. She felt she often picked up everybody's tension as well as her own. That was how the cat food tins got to be piled up against a wall, and there was little, although tasteful, furniture around. The penthouse in strong contrast, had a completely different atmosphere. It was fastidiously neat, beautifully appointed with Italian antique furniture, and she never painted here – sketching, yes, but never paint.

She came in from the balcony. The light was fading, and it gave the colours of the paintings on the wall a muted look. Most of the paintings were watercolours of Tuscany, the romantic depiction of the coastline; shaded beaches looked out at her. They were all Oliver's.

The penthouse was completely out of bounds to her mother, Antigone, who had no idea that Oliver and Casey had lived here together; she had always thought that he stayed at his club when in London. But she was horribly wrong.

Now and then, Casey felt she must go and visit her mother, buried in the suffocation of the house in Cambridge where there had been too many secrets. Surely, Antigone had realized that her husband had been almost nightly in her room when she was a small child. Why did she not do anything to save Casey? No, Casey's anger was so great that when Antigone had called numerous times, she had carefully and quietly put the phone down.

She spent the remainder of the time, before Fabian was due to arrive, working on the designs for a picture that had been commissioned by a client of the Bond Street gallery that showed her work. She was feeling better, and Anna had been a real friend to her. They had shared so much, it had been so unexpected. She had recovered, would recover. She had little idea though of who she was now, lost in a world in which she no longer belonged.

Later, she wrapped a skirt around her still thin waist; already, it had two buttons missing, but she did not care. Neither did she wear a bra; her breasts were sore, enlarged already. They would be obvious through the thin, see-through sexy blouse; it would arouse him; she could play the game. She knew all the games; after all, Oliver had taught her about arousal and sexual highs. It gave her a sense of power in what had till now been a powerless world. She did take special care to put on a black lacy thong, easing it up over her slim hips, imagining him slowly removing it. She applied more makeup than usual, darkening her eyes with liner, smudging brown eyeshadow. "What am I doing?" she thought to herself. "I feel like a slut."

Oliver had made her feel like a whore, but she was his 'whore', pimped to whom he chose. He had treated her like that for as long as she could remember. In the end, it was who she was – the long nights, how he used her body, how he broke her inhibitions. She even remembered doing dress-ups for him even as a young girl. She had entertained his friends so often in the last years that she had become addicted to the excitement, the frenzy of it all. There was the angel and the Devil inside her. She hated it all but longed for the sexual ecstasy and even the pain.

There was a lot of that at times. Sometimes, she could not tell the difference between the pain and the bliss. She was the prey. The men were the hunters, in for the kill. But she was eternally trapped. It was a wild game, with the trap. She could never get out, would never get out. She had no idea really of the web of lies in which she had been living.

She looked at herself in the mirror. "Ready," she thought. Already, she was feeling more than excited even thinking of Fabian. Her lips were very full, exaggerated with the bright red of the lipstick. She was a whore on her own now. She was free. She had no idea that she was still caught in an ever-tightening noose. She thought of the photos she had taken from Fabian's house, of her in nude poses. That was how men were titillated after all; you had to play along.

There were two sides to Casey, and she did not remember which was which anymore. It was the pearls and twinsets over a pleated demure skirt and then there were the tiny thongs, the painted nails, the lurex, the glitter, the chase, the trap, the toys and then the kill.

At 7:30 p.m. the telephone rang. "I have a message for you from the Countess. She says you are in great danger and that you have put yourself in further danger by staying with Maxine. She advises you to have no further contact with Fabian." She had no idea where the call was calling from.

"I have to make my own way in all this; I know how Emma thinks, but I feel I can't trust anyone. Where is Anthony? I haven't been in touch with anyone, not even him." She wondered why her thoughts had not been on Anthony or anyone else. It was unlike her. All she seemed to think about was Fabian. It worried her. It was like being drunk all the time, or even worse, being drugged. Drugs – a bell went off in her head, but it was too late.

"Drugs," she thought, as the door buzzer went off loudly at the other end of the apartment. "Poor Oliver and his drugs – how desperate he had become over the last few years. Nothing was ever enough for Oliver."

"Casey, it's Fabian." That was all he said.

"I'll buzz you in," equally monosyllabic.

She stood motionless in front of him, almost unable to move. The air seemed electric around him – a magnet, and she was just a small pin ricocheting towards him. Done. She had no life of her own. He was dressed casually in a grey cotton shirt and matching slacks. He wore two gold rings, one held a red jasper stone. She noticed his feet. He was wearing canvas shoes, brown. They reminded her of someone, or something. He looked into her eyes and took her arm, bending it round her back, pretending to pinion her. He laughed. She had never heard anyone laugh like that. It was full of sorrow, that laugh. Then she felt herself falling into space. No resistance. She forgot, it seemed, everything.

"So, you had something to tell me?" He knew that she hadn't, but he wanted to tease her to see her reaction.

He was running his fingers through her pale fine hair. She felt the hardness of the ring against her scalp. Then his fingers lingered around her neck. She could not help falling against him, her belly hard. He could tell she was naked underneath the see-through blouse. He was home. He kissed the now smeared lipstick.

Such a thin neck, he thought. He remembered the photographs he had had removed from Jack's studio. She felt small bolts of energy pushing up her spine. It was ecstatic and very frightening.

He talked to her as they sat on one of the long sofas, of his past, his travels, the knowledge he had acquired. Without touching her, he gauged everything about her, the body, the mind, and the spirit. Yes, she would be perfect for what he had in mind.

"You know, I was once in Egypt. Casey, look at me." He wanted her to see the inside of his eyes, where the power emanated. "I sought out someone there, a famous magician. He lived in a small village near the Nile, miles from anywhere, He was a holy man, very mysterious and powerful. Everyone was afraid of him. I spent months with him. No one else came while I was there. I would bring him his food. He taught me all his secrets.

"One day, he had me sit on the floor. It was just an earthen floor, very late at night, just an old oil light in the corner. Then he held his right foot in his hand. I wondered what he was doing. He told me to look at his eyes. Then he took a long needle; it must have been six inches long. He plunged the needle into his toe. At the exact moment the needle penetrated, a bolt of energy shot up my spine. The Kundalini had been awakened from the base of the spine. It nearly blew my head off. Then my body was filled with a fire that never left me, and all the secrets and powers of the universe started to open up to me. I began to know things I never knew were possible."

The room became silent, as Fabian talked less and less. A faint light came from the streets below. Fabian moved towards her, and he ran his fingers down her spine until he reached the very base. He placed his hand on her still belly; they exchanged looks. She felt already that he knew Oliver's baby lay there in her womb. She felt rushes of energy and sounds within her ears, like the soft sound of a distant drumbeat. She felt on fire with it, as though her whole body was singing. Then she took him to her bed and they lay there together, looking out at the dark trees of the park. He moved his hands across her chest, searching for the sternum, pressing his thumb hard onto the bone. He reached then under her skirt to the thong, his hands moving swiftly.

"Careful, Casey, not too fast, hold the energy inside you." He muttered to her in the dark, saying things she didn't understand, moaning incantations. At the top of her head, he drew a line with his thumb across the bones of the skull, Casey entered into another dimension, as though her skull had expanded outward towards the sky. But he didn't stop, and she suddenly felt a warning inside her, as though someone was trying to reach her, save her.

A strange world started to open. She saw in the corner of a room a kind of glass case. Inside the case was the ancient hat of the court jester that she had seen in his office at the house in St. John's Wood. The hat was pulling her towards it, as though she had no power of her own. Then she saw Emma, the Countess, her white hands hammering with an axe at the case, breaking the glass into thousands of small pieces. As she did so, hundreds of black and hideous crows flew into the room, rushing and circling, trying to get out and beating their wings in Casey's eyes. Fabian was becoming frenzied. His hands were in her blouse, hands were all over her, like the crows, on her breasts, pecking her belly.

Then his hands reached down, his fingers taut, seeking entry. She fought him off, but he was stronger, pinning her down with the weight of his body and pressing his face into hers. His tongue dug into her mouth, circling her tongue. He bit her lower lip hard and at the same time his fingers ran down her body, poking her, the thong gone. He pinched her nipple hard, but Casey pushed him away even though she knew that she was coming fast. Bolts of energy ran through her and her orgasm was nothing like she had ever known, cascading through her.

But the birds were in her face now, warning her and flapping their wings. She shoved him. In a minute, he would not have stopped. She wanted him inside her now like nothing else, but another power was intervening, trying to save her life. She knew that once he put himself and his seed inside her, she would be poisoned forever.

"Don't fight me now, Casey. We are one now. It's finished; you know that; don't pull back now." He breathed into her ear and whispered a sound. She relaxed a little. But again, she felt the fragments of glass from the smashed case and saw the whiteness of Emma's hands trying to free her.

The night wore on relentlessly. Fabian and Casey fought their battle. By the middle of the night, it was over. Silently, he left her apartment and returned to St. John's Wood.

In a small cell in Cairo's maximum security jail, Anthony wept as he heard the first prayers of the morning echoing across the city. He had dreamt he had been tricked and robbed. When he awoke, he found himself weeping; not because of the dream itself, but because he knew that his enemy had come back to kill him again. His two friends, Jane and Casey, his allies, already had been stolen from him. Casey belonged to his enemy; he knew it in his heart. She had given herself to another camp. Now he was entirely alone.

# *40*

Justin emerged from the ocean, a clear blue expanse of the Mediterranean. It was the latter part of August. He had his life on hold. The sea reflected the azure tones of the sky. He stood among the usual crowd that attended the ritual of the small private beach at the same time every year in Saint-Jean-Cap-Ferrat. Hats, swimwear, all portrayed a fastidious taste typical of that part of the South of France.

"Well-dressed by day and by night, the designer-wear society," thought Justin. He remembered reading about the private establishments, like the Hexagon clubs in Europe: exclusive, expensive, for the very rich, seeking highs in their nightly sports with ever new partners, whose members drank champagne at eight thousand pounds a bottle. They even had pools filled with the stuff. They came from everywhere; the oligarchs from Mongolia, where eighty per cent of the population lived in tent cities, starving most of the time. But the super-rich travelled constantly, like wealthy scavengers looking for the next fix, the next sexual partner and a better, more expensive orgasm. There was no end to their greed and wanting more, more and even more.

Now sex and pornography were all over the internet; you could have whatever you liked. Justin had heard that 75 per cent of digital traffic was pornographic. Justin felt the world was becoming one big gigantic sexual supermarket where anything you wanted could be purchased at a price. He wondered if Anna had visited any of these places. He put nothing beyond her now. She was capable of anything, of that he was sure.

Anna was lying at the other end of the beach, asleep in the deckchair under their perch for the day and the exotic, multi-coloured parasol, their lot for the duration. She was completely unaware of Justin's thoughts, although she was also one of the sexual delicacies, that he was thinking of at that same moment, in her own exotic world of sexual playtime. But what she offered came at an exorbitant price. The going rate for the most beautiful prostitutes or escort girls in the world was twenty-four thousand US dollars a night. That was just small change for Anna when she felt like it.

Justin picked up his red towel, put on the rubber shoes that prevented his feet from being assailed by the stones in the water and walked towards Anna. He lay on his stomach next to her. She was still asleep, her skin faintly tanned in the strong sun, her hair in a ponytail. It reminded him of the old carefree days. He wondered why they did not do this more often. If it wasn't for Anna, he would never take holidays at all. It was at her bidding that he came here. The villa was perfect too, no telephone and no fax machine. Now he and Anna were totally alone. He felt, at last, his whole being relax in the sun. Stephanie and Paul had stayed with them for about a week and had now gone to Japan to join Emma. Justin missed having them around.

It had been odd having Stephanie with them after the tension and events at Farlingham Park. He remembered her jumping out of the car that day and running off into the woods. Then he had seen The Jester. He dismissed the thought; it was too horrific to remember the experience of that evil place. He had found Stephanie pale and limp, surrounded by piles of decaying leaves under the dripping trees. Was it raining? He could not remember. She was in another world, hanging onto the fringes of worldly existence. She had given him some understanding of that exotic world, but he was too wary of these things. He knew his life as it was, the world of rational explanation, the root causes of disease. When he looked under a microscope, he wanted to believe in what was there. Justin could not give credence to the idea that life was an illusion. To him, it was rock solid. If he made a mistake in surgery, it would have disastrous repercussions. You couldn't argue yourself out of that. Yes, for him there were certain rules and you had to stick to them. But at the same time, he felt the shifting sands of his life under his feet. Things were not going to stay the same. The thought terrified him.

He felt cold water splashing onto his back. He turned over to see who his tormentor was. It was Anna, looking down at him with her grey eyes, dripping water onto him. Her look was full of wickedness.

"Come on, Justin, let's go. We must drive back to the villa. We are having dinner with the Hendersons this evening." As she spoke, she ran down the beach, daring him to chase her across the sand. She wished they could stay here forever, forget about the past and all the events that had besieged their marriage, But Justin would never be happy here. He belonged in London, spoken for by the thousands of people that needed him. He did not belong to her. Last night, she dreamt that Jane died — horrible to have nightmares like this in such a beautiful place. Why Jane, of all people? If anyone, she was the one who should die; then everyone could get on with their lives.

Justin caught up with her and kissed her full lips. He wanted her, wanted to make love to the coolness of her. He flung a wet towel in her direction, but she dodged. The villa, theirs now for so many years, lay in the hills, surrounded by trees and a high fence; no one could break their privacy. A veranda ran along the front, filled with comfortable chairs and a hammock. The inside was tranquil, filled with the memories of carefree summers.

Justin went to his bathroom and took a long hot shower. His body felt so good after the sea and the sunlight. He looked at himself in the mirror. The lines of fatigue were leaving his face. He regarded the deep-set eyes. "Who am I?" he asked himself, but no reply came. He had lonely eyes, he thought, filled with unanswered questions. Stephanie's eyes were different. They were liquid and sensitive, as though they had become telescopes to God. They were full of clarity, like looking into still blue pools of water. It was peaceful looking into her eyes, no anger, and no fear.

Anna was sleeping again. He wondered why she slept so much; she had always been like that, since the beginning of their marriage. He felt it was an escape from too much pain. He went to the study; Plato was on his mind. He read philosophy or biography on holiday, rarely novels. The study was filled with family photographs, people on lawns of mansion houses, hunting scenes, fishing expeditions and polo teams. It was a den of refuge for him, this room. Strains of a Mozart concerto drifted around the room. The music settled his mind. There were bits of fishing tackle, trophies for polo and fishing; on one of the walls, shelves filled with books: some of Anna's and his own collections, a few paperbacks, holiday novels that guests had left behind, some serious books such as the Plato.

The floor was black stone, quarried locally; white rugs were thrown over it for comfort and warmth, On the other side of the room was a huge hearth filled with logs. Sometimes in the winter, they would come here, bringing a four-wheel drive with them. It was much colder then, and they would fetch firewood from the hillsides, running and shouting in the wind. Then in the evening, they would have a fire, throwing sage and pine into the flames to create a heavenly aroma.

The smell of freshly brewed coffee was coming from the kitchen. Justin had forgotten he had put the percolator on before he had showered. He brought a cup back to the den and sat down on one of the sofas. He opened the Plato; something fell out. It was a photograph, or rather two halves of an old photograph taken of him and Anna. They had been holding hands, a honeymoon shot. The picture was torn carefully in two, separating him and Anna. Justin stared, shocked; the picture used to be in a frame. Who had torn it and put it in the book? A wave of fear spread over him. He turned the picture of Anna over. On the back was written in black ink, 'Your wife is a whore'. So, they were still watching, still interfering in their lives. He put the picture in his pocket. He knew he would never show Anna; he simply could not confront her, exotic, beautiful but so vulnerable. But Anna was a whore, he knew that now. There was no doubt about it and the photograph echoed his thoughts. She had given herself to other men, offering her sexual excesses but never to him. He could not even imagine what she got up to; the black thread for him was surrounded in mystery. That kind of sex frightened him. It could be many men, not just one. He did not want to think about it.

Justin saw the door of the study open slowly, then a hand came around the corner of the doorway. It held a long piece of grey fur.

"The costumes have arrived," said Anna spiriting into the room, excited like a child.

"The costumes?" asked Justin.

"Oh God, did I forget to tell you, darling?" Anna looked perturbed. She was sure she had told him about the fancy dress ball in Cannes that night. Justin knew how Anna loved to dress up in disguises. It was one of her things. He hated it, but he wanted to indulge her and so, he added his humour.

At the Hexagon Club, she would don elaborate long-nosed masks, or sometimes delicate filigree ones, perched beguilingly on her head. Costumes that hid little of the delicate curves and folds of her body, leaving precious little to imagination, clung to Lady Anna. It was the custom at Hexagons. There were few female members and she was always in demand. Her extremes were notorious.

Justin's outfit was exquisitely made – a wolf, or it would be when someone had got themselves inside it. At least it was lined with green silk so that the wearer would not itch frantically all evening. He looked at the wolf's head borne on Anna's upturned fist. It was really ugly. Anna had really gone to town on this one. The eyes, surrounded by eyelashes as hard as bristles, poked out from the head. The mouth was enormous, studded with fine pointed teeth embedded in the body of the jaw. The jaws hung open as though held in a permanent scream, and a large red tongue made of felt and foam lolled out of the gaping mouth. Justin hid a smile. Anna looked at him.

"Do you like it?" she asked sheepishly.

"Of course, it's magnificent. Where is yours?" asked Justin, taking the wolf from her. Anna's was a demure tunic, a red cloak and a lacy cap to hide her head. It tied with two enormous satin ribbons.

"Well, let me guess what we are going as. Could it be as Little Red Riding Hood and the Big Bad Wolf?" Justin's stomach was turning over as he thought of wearing the costume, but he kept a fixed grin on his face.

"I guess I am your big bad wolf tonight," he said, taking Anna in his arms. For once, she did not resist.

# 41

The Henderson's house was just behind the town of Saint Paul de Vence, a magnificent place built into the hills behind Nice. The house was on the outskirts of the town beyond the old streets and with views of vineyards stretched out in a sunset that streaked the sky. There was nothing as beautiful for Anna as these scenes of peacefulness. Acres of ripened grapes and woodlands stretching away down the hills, landing eventually at the white sandy beaches and the azure sea of Nice. The house was open plan, rooms cleverly tiered down, one upon another. From the rooftop, you could look down from the balconies, the whole length, down to the ground floor and the kidney-shaped pool on the patio beyond the plate glass windows. It was breathtaking. No gothic ghosts in Sidney's house; they were for clients only. Sidney was all modern, pristine.

Dinner was served on the patio next to the pool. Moira directed the butler, who brought dish after dish of seafood, then roast lamb, desserts and cheeses.

"Where is the Countess now?" asked Sidney. They had been talking about the weekend at Farlingham Park.

"In my head," said Justin jokingly.

Sidney gave him a sharp look.

"Well, it sounds silly, but I mean it. Oh, she is in Japan with Stephanie and Paul," said Justin, adding a little physical reality, for Sidney's sake. "But yes, she is kind of in my head. I find myself thinking about her a lot. Sometimes, I dream of her and Stephanie, almost as though they are watching over me. It's hard to describe, actually." Justin was aware of Sidney's fear. Yes, you could almost smell it. This was out of his depth, even for someone who designs gothic interiors.

"It's the first sign of possession, thinking about the prophet, the guru, whatever the form. No graven images, that's what the Bible says. Why? Because of the dangers of idolatry and possession." Sidney was serious, deadly serious; Justin wondered whether he really knew about it.

"I knew it was a mistake, you and Anna going to see her. She comes from a line of occultists. They have strange powers, these people. They are all in some way vampires, not in the literal sense, of course, but they feed on the idolatry of others. They take over your mind, then your body, and lastly, it's the soul they want. Read the texts, Justin. Read about the stories of all the false gurus. Then there are the women; they put them through tantric sexual rituals, bring them up to a heightened state, orgasmic states, until they don't know who they are anymore. Then these teachers possess them, take them over and get them to do their bidding. Then there are the cult practices with young children." Sidney folded his arms.

"How do you know all this? I only said that I thought of the Countess." Justin argued now, irritated by Sidney's suggestions.

"No, you did not. You said she was inside your head." Sidney banged his hand on the glass table. His wine glass jumped, spilling the red liquid onto the white cloth. There was a stunned silence, as they all looked at the red stain. Somehow, they felt it was a bad omen, given the conversation.

"Justin, you have no idea what you and Anna are into. Now you are defending the woman!" Sidney glared at Justin. He was remembering his own terrifying experiences with Fabian; he had to protect his friends. But they would start to wonder at his vehemence. This was Sidney's fear now.

"What do you know about it, Sidney? You left on Saturday with all the snobs. You didn't see what I saw. She has so much light around her; and Stephanie is so pure she doesn't even belong on this planet. Leave us alone, Sidney; I know what I am doing." Justin was furious.

"You don't know anything, Justin. What about her brother, the Count Fabian Roth?" The room suddenly went quiet. Anna was ashen. She excused herself and went to the bathroom. She thought her knees would buckle. Sidney was getting far too close to the family secrets. What more did he know that he was not telling? Did he know about her family and that Fabian was her lover, Giles his son with her out of wedlock? Did he know about the Hexagon Club? Had he met Fabian and had some experience of which he was now terrified?

"Her brother?" asked Justin, bewildered by what Sidney was getting at.

"Sidney, leave it alone, will you? They are only stories, rumours. You are just frightening Justin and Anna. All they did was go away for a weekend. Now let's enjoy ourselves and, for heaven's sake, let's drop it. It's time we got ready for the ball." Moira, as usual, was soothing the troubled waters between Justin and Sidney. She stood up, her full height, and leaned over them until they got up and went inside for the coffee and liqueurs. There was a roll of thunder in the distance and spots of rain dashed onto the glass. The pool lights went out, and they went upstairs to change after the coffee.

Anna regained her composure, but her head was swimming. "Emma is Fabian's sister; it can't be possible," she thought to herself. She had to find out. But she mustn't let Justin or Sidney see even a remote trace of her fears. As far as they were concerned, she had excused herself to leave the argument. They all knew she hated arguments.

They all met again an hour later, ready for the ball. Justin stood by the long windows, looking out at the blue, unruffled waters. The light was fading and the moon a mere sliver in the sky. He was head to toe in the wolf's outfit. Anna, in the demure red dress, came and put her arm round him and they all laughed. Somehow, it broke the tension from their conversation at dinner. But everyone was still thinking about what had been said. Sidney rarely came down so hard, and it gave them a feeling somehow that there was cause for alarm.

Sidney, attired sombrely in an executioner's costume, all black with a white embroidered collar, was a little too gruesome for Anna's tastes, and she recoiled when she saw him. He heard her quick intake of breath and turned to look at her. "So," he thought, "she does have secrets." He knew now that she had a lover, had been someone's mistress for a long time. Moira was dressed as Anne Boleyn with the black dress and square bodice worn by the Elizabethans.

"How long are you staying down here this time?" Sidney was keeping it small talk with Justin, trying to introduce a lighter note to the evening.

"Oh, just another week!" Justin was thinking of the one-way flight he was taking in exactly ten days' time, the flight that for reasons best known to him, he had not revealed to anyone except Felicity, and she was sworn to secrecy. Sidney noticed Justin had paused before he answered, another clue that something was going on. He was in a way fearing for all their lives.

"Anna, do you have the tickets for the ball, or do I?" asked Moira.

"Oh, I have them; they arrived this morning, special delivery," said Anna.

At last, they were ready. Anna helped Justin into Sidney's Volvo, packing the tail of the wolf in behind him. It was getting late, and they spun into the night towards the brilliant lights of Cannes. Fortunately, the head of the wolf was not too hot, and there were places for Justin to see out and breathe. He sat in the back of the car and nursed the absurd costume. Anna sat next to him, her mind preoccupied by thoughts of Fabian and his sister Emma. Maybe, Emma had been his first love. That was why they never saw each other, and... Her mind travelled a thousand thoughts into the night.

The grand hotel in Cannes was packed. It was hard to manoeuvre the car into the entrance. Finally, the key was offered into the hand of a waiting valet. Everyone was there, and they were whirled immediately into the festivities of the night. Rock stars, Cannes film people, and American movie stars alighted from helicopters on the back lawns. The press, all the media, stood waiting on stairways and bits of scaffolding, waiting for the best pictures to be sent to all the newspapers and TV programmes around the world later that night.

"Anna, so you came. We did not expect you here. Aren't you going to introduce me to your husband?" Fabian's voice came from behind her; he had quickly traversed the crowded foyer when he saw her arrive. When she turned around, she saw that he had on an elaborate mask trimmed with black eagle feathers. The feathers pointed upwards in a bizarre way. She shivered. Anna could not see the rest of him; her vision blurred at the shock of seeing him.

"Well, this is a surprise. Yes, let me introduce you to my husband," said Anna, maintaining ice-coolness towards him.

Justin raised his eyebrows behind the wolf's head, waiting to hear what the man's name was. But Anna wasn't saying it. She had moved away and then the man disappeared. Justin was being swept along in a big crowd that had just entered the hotel. The music of a heavy rock band pumped the air. It was sweltering hot behind the mask. Everyone, including Sidney and Moira, had disappeared. He left the foyer in search of Anna.

Fabian had swept Anna up by sheer force to his suite at the hotel. He wanted her with him. He held her arm tightly until they finally got the door shut; Fabian slipped off his mask and stared at Anna. She stared back in silence. All the questions about Emma vanished, as the familiar eyes looked into her own grey pools of light.

"I want you with me, Anna. You don't belong to Justin. He will leave you." He pulled her to him, took her long hair into his hands and pulled it tight around his fist. He undid her red riding hood tunic. She did not resist. There was no mind anymore. She had always been his. On her eyes, he tied a thin black bandage.

Anna lay naked on her back; there were no pillows, just an empty bed with even the sheets ripped off. Their clothes were scattered on the floor. She was the prey, he the sexual, lustful act. She had once longed for him in her young, innocent body. Now she was shamed, brutalized and yet she knew that this terrible desire for violation and bestiality was part of who she was now. He tied her up to the bed, so that she was lying on her stomach, trussed, ready for him. He ran a steel rod between her ankles notched to the highest hole, the ties secure and leaving her legs wide apart. He humiliated her then, once, twice; the pain searing her body as his movements became more definite, more perverse. She was trapped. After he finished, spent, he untied the straps, flinging a cover over her quivering body and left the room. He was done with her.

Justin felt he would never pierce the crowd. Then someone moved towards him and held his arm. He thought it was someone he knew. He turned to converse with whoever was trying to gain his attention. Suddenly, the crowd shifted, and he was in a small clearing with a stranger.

The strange man was in front of his face. This was the figure he had seen in the woods at Farlingham Park, all those weeks ago. Then it happened so quickly. A shot rang out into the heavy air. Justin slumped over, as the bullet had sunk straight into its mark, his chest. The figure ran quickly into another descending group of people going down the steps. He was wearing a fancy dress, clothed in the strange costume of a court jester. The bell of his hat had fallen on the ground. Someone picked it up; it was entirely rusty.

Everyone fixed their eyes on Justin; someone screamed. He was lying on the marble floor of the foyer. Blood flowed from the wound at an alarming rate. It was soaking out from the grey wolf fur. It looked horrific to the crowd of onlookers – this man dressed as a wolf, attacked and wounded, with the tongue hanging out macabrely from the parted teeth. For a moment, everything seemed to stand still. No one moved.

Thank God someone had the sense to remove the headpiece before the police, ambulance and press arrived. Sirens rang out all over the streets and the hotel. The evening broke up in complete chaos. Justin was carried quickly to the waiting ambulance. It wailed its cry as it carried its precious cargo to the nearest hospital in the town. When it arrived, the entrance was knee deep in press. Justin was unconscious on arrival and was immediately taken for surgery.

Anna came down the magnificent stairway. She was hardly able to walk; the ties had cut into her wrists and ankles. She felt Fabian still deep inside her, the bruised feeling of forcible entry. She had heard the sirens. Everyone had left; Sidney, Justin and Moira were nowhere to be seen. She approached the hotel manager in the foyer.

"A man was shot an hour ago. They have taken him to the hospital," said the manager when she enquired about what had happened.

"Who was it?" asked Anna, wondering why Justin had not waited for her.

"We don't know yet; he was wearing a fancy dress. He was dressed as a wolf."

At that moment, Anna vowed to kill Fabian and end her own life. He had deliberately taken her at the very time he knew Justin would be shot. It was unforgiveable. She ran up to Fabian's room, but the door was locked and there was no answer. She wanted him dead.

She shoved at the door hard with her shoulder and it opened. The room was empty. There was one envelope with her name on the bed. He must have known she would come back. It contained a small velvet purse; inside, there was a scarlet USB. She placed it hurriedly into the hotel laptop, still sitting on the desk. The screen came to life with the first shot of the back of her head, her head masked. Her body was tied backwards, stretched, arching against the black bedrail; Fabian naked, behind her, penetrating, shoving, his back to the camera.

She saw it all, everything that he had done to her: her cries, her pleading, the scenes of lust and depravity. Fabian standing above her, hitting her, the whips, the coils, the toys, all of it appeared before her. This was who she was, and this was who he was: his callousness, his extraordinary sexual appeal, his cruelty. This video was his last gift to her. She ran to the bathroom and vomited. It was the end, but despite herself, she was ready to orgasm again as she remembered their excesses. She would indeed kill him. They would die together, ending their sinfulness together. She was ruined. She was a desolate, wanton woman.

# 42

Anthony knew he had been set up. As he walked in the prisoners' compound behind the battlements of the Cairo prison, he racked his mind, over and over. Who could have done this to him? Emma said he had enemies from other lifetimes, that the karma was catching up with him. He was not yet ready to know his other lifetimes; this would come in time. She said that all he knew of a secure and successful world would have to go. Everything he had would be taken away. She had been right, but he still didn't understand. She said she would stay in touch with him and help, but that he would have to go through the experience alone.

He was wearing the regulation prison outfit made of dark green cotton. The material was rough. It made his skin sore, and he was used to wearing cashmere and expensive cottons against his skin. Richard kept coming again into his mind. Whose was the hand that pushed him down the shaft and where did the person disappear? It seemed there had been no one there at all. It was September and the high wall of the maximum-security jail had held him in its clutches for at least a month; he couldn't remember, maybe it was longer. He had no visitors and received no mail. It was a life of total isolation, and who knew when it would end.

His head had been shaved again, and the meagre diet had meant his weight had dropped. Alone, he stayed in the isolation cell. It was so small, with only a narrow thin bed, hardly wide enough to sleep on, and a pot for his ablutions. The barred window overlooked the compound where he could walk several times a day. He tried to think of himself as a monk, that he had entered the cell voluntarily.

Each day he meditated and did a repetition of the mantra that Emma had taught him. The hours and days slipped away; he no longer cared. He had let go of the struggle and gone beyond it.

One night, he awoke to a thudding on his door and the sound of keys being turned in the lock. The guards were peering down at him. They pulled him up and took him outside to the compound, across to a low-slung building that housed the offices of the prison. The area smelt of smoke and bleach. The lights were fluorescent. They led him to one of the offices through a green door. He was left alone for some time. The faces of Egyptian presidents looked down at him from their cheap, framed photographs on the wall. The office had a small steel desk. On it was a cigarette that had been stubbed out in a flat tin ashtray. An officer entered the room and sat down. He did not introduce himself and seemed impervious to Anthony's presence. He looked at the papers that he had brought with him.

"Anthony Jackson?" The man had large hands, Anthony noticed. The skin on the index finger of the right hand was stained with nicotine. The room was unbearably stuffy.

"Yes, I am he." He remembered the police in Shropshire and Jane's house. It seemed so long ago now. All these people seemed to have vanished.

"How much did you know about Richard Abrascus?" the man with the big hands asked. Anthony looked at his face. It was expressionless, a face you would never remember.

"We were at college together. After that, I didn't see him for years until we met up in the film industry." Anthony wondered where this was leading. "I invited him to come and work on my current movie. It's about the pyramids." Anthony crossed and uncrossed his legs. The man offered him a cigarette. Anthony refused. It was a chance to quit the habit forever.

"Were you aware that his family had no idea where he was? Strange, isn't it, that they did not know he was in Cairo. Why did he not tell them?" It was not a question.

"I did not know that. I thought he was in touch with them."

"No, he had not been in touch for some time." The office was becoming hot and now full of cigarette smoke generated by his interrogator. Anthony felt weary. The man flung a document across the desk.

"Read that." The man suddenly got up and left the office. Anthony was alone; he picked up the papers.

On top of the documents was a black and white photograph of Richard. As he read the rest of the papers, Anthony went white; sweat stood out on his brow.

The document said that Richard Abrascus had not met his death at the pyramid, as had been suggested. The story had taken them all in. Richard had been sighted in South America, arrested for illicit arms deals, drug smuggling and other criminal offences. His funeral in Egypt was a hoax, and no body was found in the coffin. Anthony had not realised that Richard had another life; that Richard was controlled by Fabian for his arms deals. Anthony now realised that The Jester had conspired against him and staged the entire event.

Anthony's head throbbed. He felt he was in a movie, a bad movie. He started to remember what the Countess had said. The world no longer felt solid to him. It was a play of ghastly shapes and shadows.

"You are free to go now," said the officer who had re-entered the room. "We will escort you to the centre of Cairo, if that is where you would like to go."

Anthony nodded. They let him shower and have a shave and gave him back his clothes. He put on the ill-fitting trousers and shirt. He felt like a scarecrow. Then they put him in a jeep and dropped him off at the front of the Adelphi Hotel. It was where he had requested. Someone, it seemed, had secured his release.

He asked to see the manager when he reached the reception of the hotel. Every word seemed to be an enormous effort. He felt curiously vulnerable, as though his skin had been stripped off.

"The manager has left. He is not available for the rest of the day," said the receptionist. She was turning away to another guest as she spoke. Suddenly, Anthony realized that he looked like a tramp and they were trying to get rid of him. Then he asked for the members of the film crew that he knew by name.

"I'm sorry, sir, we have no one by that name staying here." Anthony felt a strange sensation at the back of his neck. He turned around and saw people staring at him. Slowly, they started to look away, averting their eyes.

"I would like a room for the night, please." Anthony pulled out his credit card.

"I'm sorry, sir, but we are fully booked. There is nothing that I can do for you." The woman was becoming impatient, wanting Anthony to leave.

Anthony knew it was the end, the end of a life as he had known it. Now he was just a nobody, with no roof over his head.

He turned on his heel to go and left the brightly lit lobby. In his head, he heard a maniacal laughter and the tinkling of a bell. He thought he was going crazy. He walked mile after mile through modern Cairo, and then into the older quarters. He found a dilapidated hotel on the waterfront. He showed his money and was ushered in without question. At the top of the rickety stairs was a room. There was only a bed and a chair that had lost a leg. He lay down on the bed with a small bag. Fear, like he had never known, swept over him. He felt like a man without a map. The props of his life had been removed, one by one. He was naked and lost. And someone was trying to kill him, not painlessly and quickly, but slowly, gradually taking him apart, piece by piece.

# 43

The paper slipped unannounced through the door of the house in Chiswick. Cedric barked somewhere deep in the passageways; otherwise, the house and its surroundings were silent. A few minutes later, Fairfax, dressed in a houndstooth checked dressing gown, bent down to pick the paper up from the mat. He thought that he should have some kind of box attached to the back of the door, instead of things just dropping onto the mat. It was just too untidy the way it was. He had a coffee cup in one hand and the paper in the other. He put the cup on a table and glanced at the front page. It was Saturday morning.

There was a picture of what looked like a large wolf sprawled across the floor of a hotel in Cannes. Fairfax read the headline.

"Oh my God, Jane!" Fairfax yelled up the stairs at her. There was no reply. He shouted louder.

"Justin has been shot, last night in Nice!" Fairfax ran upstairs.

Jane was in the shower. The radio was on. It was not the morning news; a vague sound of Bach's *Fugue in E minor* came through the speaker, drowning all but the water running from the shower. Jane was scrubbing with an old loofah. She saw the water running in rivulets down her body, collecting in an ocean at the bottom of the shower. She had a sense that something dreadful was about to happen, that the world before she took the shower was totally different from the world she would inhabit after the shower. At last, she emerged from the water, turned off the taps and stepped out from the shower and into Fairfax's face, a picture of shock, standing in front of her.

"What is it?" Jane stared at her husband as though for the first time. He was mouthing something at her, but it was as though he was under the ocean and she could not hear what he was saying, Oh, the radio was blaring something now at high volume – no wonder she couldn't hear.

"It's Justin, he has been shot!" He put the paper in front of her nose.

Jane drew in her breath. She looked at the picture; she felt oddly detached. She said nothing; there was nothing to say. She knew that this would have to happen; all their lives were being threatened. They had lost against their invisible enemies.

The phone was ringing outside the bathroom in the corridor. Fairfax reached out an arm, still clad in the dressing gown, to answer it. In the other arm, he grabbed Jane, still naked, except for a towel.

"Hello, is that Fairfax?" Sidney Henderson's rather excitable voice was on the other end of the line from France. His words were falling over each other in his nervousness.

"Sidney, I'm so glad you called. We just saw the news. It's all over the headlines. What happened? How's Anna taking it? What is Justin's condition now?" Fairfax's questions came in a rush in his anxiety to know what had happened.

"It's pretty serious. The doctors are concerned that an infection will set into the lung. The bullet, which was a bullet no one recognized, was fired from a gun that was used centuries ago. It was made of silver. No one can make it out at all. Anna's all right. Anna is always all right. She is quiet, blames herself, I think. We couldn't find her after the shooting. She disappeared somewhere, met up with someone she knew, I guess." Sidney's voice was getting faint on the line.

"We will fly down today as soon as we have made the reservations. Give Anna our love. She will probably call us later.

Sidney, I am sure Anna has called Casey." Fairfax was about to hang up.

"Anna is under heavy sedation, Fairfax. I am sorry that I lied just now. I did not want to tell you. With her history, it is the last thing that should have happened. She really felt it was her fault and then she collapsed at the hospital from the shock. Too many things have happened. Justin is still in the intensive care unit. You may not be able to see him. I didn't realize you would come so quickly; I wanted to paint a rosier picture for you; you know how it is. They did get the bullet out; thankfully, it just missed the heart, but it pierced one of his lungs. To be honest, it is a bit touch and go." Sidney seemed apologetic now, as though he had lost face from telling another version of the story.

"It's all right, Sidney," said Fairfax kindly, "I understand. But we do want to get over as quickly as possible." He said goodbye and hung up.

Today was the first day of the weekend. He would go down with Jane and then come back for a business trip to Germany the following Monday. He could handle that, and besides, Jane would need to be with Anna.

"Who on earth would want to kill Justin, of all people? Everyone adores him. I simply cannot understand it at all." Fairfax was hanging onto Jane, still wrapped in the towel; she looked as though she could faint any minute.

"The same person who is trying to harm me. It's true, Fairfax. We have enemies. I told you and I told Justin, and neither of you believed me. If you had, this may not have happened. Now our lives will never be the same again." Jane took Fairfax's arm.

"And Anthony, what has happened to him? Is that still part of the situation you are talking about?" Fairfax looked at her in disbelief.

"Situation? It's not a situation, Fairfax. It's life-threatening. Why do you take this stance every time I tell you the truth?" Jane grabbed the towel, put it around her and walked along the corridor to their room, slamming the door behind her. She was sick of not being able to get through to Fairfax. All he ever understood was the law. He wouldn't understand psychic attack even if it hit him between the eyebrows. She got dressed and walked about the room flinging all the armoires open and pulling out clothes.

But Fairfax had other things on his mind. He was deliberately playing naive with Jane. He had met with Lucille several times; her tear-soaked face always the same, repentant, afraid. He did not know if he could save her. They were amassing a huge amount of evidence about the Hexagon Club and its members including Oliver, one of their main suspects in a paedophile ring. Fairfax suspected that Oliver had been murdered in Uruguay. He was just too dangerous and had become a liability. He also could make no mention of any of this to Jane, especially as she was so close to Anna. No one should suspect what he and Lucille were doing. Already, he worried for the safety of his wife and his own life even amidst such evil and the power of the club and its members. Lucille had told him that the group of men were called the Fraternity. Fabian was appalled. He spent most of his waking day thinking about it. At night, he was having dreams of chasing thieves that entered his house to entrap him and Jane.

He came into the bedroom, having given Jane a little while to calm down.

"Fairfax, did you ever do any of that research on the Rigby family as I suggested?" Jane asked him fully, expecting his answer to be 'no'.

"Yes, I did, as a matter of fact. I haven't had the time to even talk to you about it." Fairfax had to tread carefully, appear to be supporting and working with Jane but having his own secret plans about the law and future arrests. It was a difficult situation to be in. Jane knew nothing really.

Jane looked at her husband, her anger gone, and took him in her arms, He looked so crestfallen when she was mad at him. Now he looked happy again. She knew he had enough respect and concern for the situation that she had found herself in with Emma, that he had gone through the trouble of doing the research.

"I hired someone who is an expert, as a matter of fact. He said that it is one of the strangest histories that he has ever worked on in his career. He went back several centuries; I have the manuscript. We can take it on the plane today with us." Fairfax's mind was already on the plans for the flight.

"I kept telling everyone that I feared for my life, but there are no visible enemies. You simply don't understand, Fairfax, however many times I try and explain." Jane was still trying to convey the horror that she felt to her husband.

Fairfax pulled her to him again. It was the only thing that he thought was possible to try and reach her physically. She inhabited a life that he did not understand.

He was a tall, thin man; in some ways, he looked like Justin, but the features were not so angular and he had dark hair that curled to the shape of his neck at the back. Jane called him 'ram's head'; she thought of the tight curls of the sheep they used to see in Wales. Now they never seemed to go away together for a real holiday. There was always something fraught about their lives. Jane recollected a time when the four of them – Anna, Justin, Fairfax and herself – used to go away to Scotland. They would go on fishing and walking expeditions. It was a carefree time. Then Giles came into their lives, and they would carry him everywhere.

Stephanie had said that she had seen Giles. Perhaps she had; but when he had disappeared, it seemed their lives had taken on such a serious note and had never really recovered. Jane had squashed the idea of having children herself; after Giles' disappearance, she was too frightened to get pregnant. Now she realized that for years she had suspected something was wrong with them all, some insidious malevolence was hanging over them. Even Casey was touched by it. Jane had heard from Anna how Casey was plagued by nightmares and in great distress when she stayed with them. Jane wondered about what had really happened between Oliver and his beautiful stepdaughter.

Jane had never told anyone that Oliver had almost raped her in the bathroom at Professor Richard Carrington's house that day when she had gone to visit Anna. She was in fact glad now that Oliver was dead; at least young women and girls now would be safe from his sexual crimes. His reputation was the worst and if he had not been an aristocrat and protected by his own, he would have been in jail long ago. She remembered the incident of a school girl in the paper claiming she had been abused, but no names were ever mentioned. A huge public relations machine had been set up to protect him, linking him to the role of a philanthropist. It was disgusting, thought Jane, what lurked behind advertising these days.

Later that morning, Jane and Fairfax boarded a British Airways flight that was bound for Nice. They shared the first-class compartment with a selection of holidaymakers eager to make the most of the season. The general atmosphere was in complete contrast to the gloom that Jane and Fairfax both felt. She pulled her hair back with her hands and dragged it slowly into a knot on top of her head, which she secured with a British Airways pencil. This was a familiar gesture to Fairfax; it meant Jane was getting down to business.

"Well, where is it then; let's have a look at it." Jane stuck out her hand for the files that she knew Fairfax had in his briefcase. She nudged him with her elbow. She was irritated. Fairfax knew she was afraid of what lay in wait for them too. He was careful to be selective in the information that he gave Jane.

"I'm glad Cedric will be all right. I'm even worried about him. Do you think someone would kidnap him?" Fairfax gave her a look that indicated he thought she was crazy to even think such a thing. Cedric, who would want to capture a grey-haired wiry-looking dog that was not even a pedigree? But Fairfax was indeed worried about his family.

Fairfax got going with his story, heavily edited, as he was preparing what would turn out to be trial notes. "The family, not always known by that title, of course, can be traced through a direct line. Originally, they were French. The reason they are so well documented is because of their connection to the Royal Family: the queens, kings and their courts. From the thirteenth century, they were astrologers to the Royal Family in France but were already then dallying with the black arts. They were practiced in alchemy and magic. They found great favour with the royal families and were assigned much land and wealth. At times, they were socially and politically visible, and at other times they are hardly mentioned, as though they went into hiding."

Fairfax continued. "One or two members were tried for witchcraft, but the cases seem to have been dismissed. The one feature of the family is a continual occurrence of tragedy – untimely deaths, strange accidents and sudden illnesses, as though they were afflicted with a curse. Their houses were often haunted but were still popular places to be seen socially. We are, of course, spanning several centuries. But somehow, the family always remains intact, strong blood ties, it seems." Fairfax paused; he was trying to get a comprehensive picture across to Jane.

"Go on," said Jane, lost in thought, the pencil tilting at an odd angle from her head.

"The reason that many of the family came over to England was because of the English kings. Some enjoyed the company of the French and found them much more amusing than the English. Anyway, it was arranged that certain families would be brought over for the King's delight. The Rigbys were among those who came over. It was not their first stay. King George conferred titles on them; they were given land to build an ancestral home in Shropshire." Fairfax stopped.

"But Farlingham Park is in Shropshire." Jane looked at Fairfax, puzzled.

"Yes, that's the house," he replied. At least he could give this much away to his wife.

Fairfax yawned. He was tired from all the tension and was thinking about Justin. He continued. "It appears that there was a young man brought over by the court. He had a kind of dalliance with King George IV, or so it was rumoured; George was intoxicated by the young man and his incredibly good looks. The man became the court jester. The court became afraid of him and his influence, and he was renowned for practicing black magic and wielding enormous power. To cut the story short, the Royal Family and the court disapproved of him, and they had as little contact with him as possible. He is called the "Jester" by everyone, never by his given name. Events then took a very dramatic turn." Fairfax had done impressive research.

"Eventually, King George became ill. The Jester was with him all the time and never let the King's physician come near him. Then the first Countess of Rigby was murdered in the most horrible way. The family had been involved in occult groups like the first Hexagon Club. The Countess had a lover and apparently, there were some rather strange exotic parties held at Farlingham Park. One day, she was murdered. They say it looked as though she had even been prepared for embalming. Her husband was also later poisoned, it was thought by The Jester, and several other people disappeared."

Jane was shocked by this but did not show her feelings. She had her own ideas of what had happened. She had memories of her past life as sister to Amelia, the first Countess of Rigby. She and Anna both had their memories, but she could not and would not share this with Fairfax.

Jane put her hand on Fairfax's arm. It was time for a break. He was looking dreadfully tired these days, and she wondered what work he was doing that was draining him.

And then thankfully, their first-class meal arrived, lavish even for British Airways. They enjoyed some red wine, relaxing a bit after the terrible shocks of the morning. During lunch, they talked of nothing but Justin, his life and how unhappy he had looked in the last few months. They had also both noted his shortness with Anna, to the point of rudeness, such a change from the doting, loving husband that he had been to Anna all these years. They discussed the relationship and the strangeness of Anna's family, so shut in on themselves, few visitors to the house and the tension between Anna and her mother. Fairfax could not comment on this and changed the subject several times.

Fairfax continued telling Jane about his research as soon as they had finished their dessert and coffees. "The story goes that after The Jester's death, his hat was taken to France and a tradition of witchcraft and folklore built up around it. Some said the hat contained tremendous power, that The Jester was the Devil incarnate and that he cursed forever those involved in his death. It was said that The Jester was resurrected after death and wandered alone in the world, scheming and bringing down the hearts and souls of men." Fairfax paused. Jane was impressed by the depth of his research into old medieval manuscripts and books.

"That is the first part of the history. Then there is the brutal murder of the first Countess of Rigby in 1820 at Farlingham Park."

"Fairfax, I just don't believe that you did not tell me about this! You let me go all the way there without telling me about the murder?" Jane looked into the green eyes of her husband that she thought she knew. But Jane, of course, already knew, but she was remaining innocent with her husband. It would be dangerous for him to know too much. She and Fairfax, of course, were protecting each other.

"So, you do believe me?" said Jane, totally overwhelmed that Fairfax knew all this.

"Oh, yes, I believe you. In fact, I had you followed in case you came to any harm. I have been making my own investigations. Inspector Rawlings does not, by the way, work for Scotland Yard. He is a freelance detective in the employment of Count Fabian Roth. I had to play ignorant on all this, Jane. You see, I also met the Countess of Rigby in London before that weekend. I called her. She agreed to meet me. She said that you were all in danger, and I was the only one outside the circle. So, I was the one who could investigate in safety."

Jane was already miles away remembering the night that she had been attacked. She thought of words that the man had said to her. He said that he had waited a long time for her. Who was she in all this intrigue? How long had he waited, she thought? Jane dozed off. She was tired and now, this revelation by Fairfax made everything so different somehow.

But Jane, like anyone who has some but not all the information, had put herself in danger. Fairfax had tried to put a safety net around her. Whether it would hold or not remained to be seen.

# 44

In his study at the far end of the house in St. John's Wood, Fabian sat gazing in front of him. Sometimes, his face had the look of a hooded eagle, features dark and silent. The brows were gathered above the eyes in a concentrated gesture. He was sitting at a large leather-topped mahogany desk. The leather was red and embossed at the edges. The sleeves of his shirt were rolled up, revealing the fine hands and arms tanned by the sun. The fingers fidgeted with a long silver paper knife. On the desk was a series of photographs. He held the pictures in his hands. He looked at Anna's image, her face wrapped mid-eastern style with a headscarf, the Swiss Alps in the background. "Anna, darling Anna! Where will you be now without your husband? Why didn't you listen to me?" He spoke out loud as though she were there in the room with him.

Then he saw the photograph of Maxine, sepia tones looking out at him: her hair garlanded with flowers that hung down over her body, the white silk jacket slipped off from her shoulders, the lips of her mouth just a little apart. Then the last images looked out at him. He remembered that extravagant night with Maxine and Casey in his arms together. They had all tasted the elixir of the aphrodisiac. On and on they played into the night, their bodies entwined together between the white sheets and the silk kimonos, the moon beaming its fullness down on them; Casey's face, close to Maxine's, the fine breasts slightly upturned in Maxine's hands. Casey would never remember, and she never saw this photograph locked away beyond the reach of her inquisitive hands. He was quite sure she had seen nothing.

A call came through from Cannes, breaking his reverie. His hands rested on the photographs as he talked on the phone. The voice had a cultivated French accent. "He's in the intensive care unit. They are not holding out much hope. Lady Bowlby has been heavily sedated. She really flipped out when she heard the news. Apparently, she was not at the ball when the gun was fired," the cool voice continued. This killing was the work of The Jester. Their roles were enmeshed, but he knew better than to dictate what the outcome of the shooting should be.

"Keep me informed, especially of Lady Anna." He kept the conversation short and hung up.

If the situation had been totally up to him, it would have been different. Severe action would have followed a bungled killing when the instructions were his own. But now he was under orders. It was The Jester who was to have killed Justin; he wondered what had gone wrong. He thought about the relationship between himself and The Jester all that time ago.

When he had first seen Casey, she was eleven years old. She would never have remembered him, and he only saw her once. It was enough to know that one day he would want her for his own; the same with Maxine. They had formed a small group in France; these men and others who were thirsty for knowledge, for power, for sex. They had performed strange, fancifully sexual and occult practices in those days. They were being trained in the black arts, and it was a very dangerous game.

The practices took away what remained of the men's innocence. Fabian smiled as he remembered the men's faces, young then, when he first showed them what was possible sexually, the girls that he had procured. It was beyond their imaginations. Whatever he told them to do, they would do it. It was a wonderful time seeing the awakening of the force of Seth within them, as they became more daring, more willing to experiment. But at times, it led them into unexpected paths and often unrequited tastes. It was a dangerous game they played.

It was expected and customary in the group for the men to sexually bond together. Some had not tasted this kind of sex before, but Seth's teachings were implicit in all the rules. It was expectation that then became rules. There were many rules and a strict discipline. These forces could be deathly.

Penetration was key in the spells, and semen itself was perceived as a divine entity. It was worshipped. These practices were held in exotic and lavish places: beautiful Italian villas, English country mansions like Thackeray Hall, surrounded by immaculate and manicured lawns, with exquisite food and wines to titillate their senses. They felt at these times there was no other world but theirs, a sexual playtime in magical paradises. The men developed tastes that were sometimes unrequited, which gave them an ever-growing hunger, so that in the end they were not just the enjoyers but became controlled and dominated by their own sexual appetites. Their addiction to pornography fuelled the fires of their sexual longing; nothing was ever enough and they wanted more. Fabian supplied them with recreational drugs and stimulants. All of them were on a permanent high, and they used everything in their power to tip over the edge to erotic and psychic power. But in the end, it was to lead to their ruin and disintegration of their lives and souls.

Fabian saw all this. He was, after all, adept in developing sexual power and appetites in others; Anna, Casey and Maxine – his special women and their fathers, picked to be his. And the young girls, trained already by their families to offer pleasure, were mind-numbed with drugs and programmed only to be sexual objects for the men. Many of them were handpicked by him to work in his porn industry, at the brothels and Thackeray Hall. They all seemed to have a good time; sometimes there was a tragedy or an overdose, but it was a rare occurrence. They were trained and brought up to serve the sexual needs of men. It was what they expected of themselves.

There was a knock on the door and it opened slightly.

"Can I come in?" Maxine's voice came softly through the door. She had learned never to enter his rooms suddenly. She had often been shocked by what she had seen. Sometimes Fabian was undressed or waving his long arms at the altar in front of him. There was a stuffed black crow in the corner. Taxidermized by Fabian himself, he loved the crows as much as Anna hated them. Sometimes, Maxine thought that he was completely mad, but she now shared this shadow of madness.

"Maxine, I didn't know that you were even here. Are you feeling better?" He touched the rounding of her abdomen with his hand. Always, he demanded intimacy from her. She thought of the baby inside her now, The Jester's seed and hers growing, embracing in her womb. Fabian took his hands and cupped her face. He ran his index finger across her lip. They both remembered the night the baby was conceived when she had met The Jester, the black cord still tied in a love knot around Maxine.

Fabian pulled her towards him; her body soft and pliant. These were the times that he loved: no one in the house, no Jester, no calls. He wanted her and her alone. In those moments, even Anna vanished from his thoughts. But they had little time left. The Jester did not want her to stay with Fabian now that she was pregnant. He had always indicated to Fabian that they were too involved. He wanted her away, in South America, or anywhere where the foetus was not linked to Fabian; she would have to go, be farmed out. The baby was The Jester's and he wanted the child to himself. Fabian had not yet told Maxine of her imminent departure. Probably, he would not say anything. This was their last day together. Tomorrow, they would find themselves on separate planes, going to entirely different destinations.

They moved out of the study, along the passage, to her bedroom. They always used this room when they wanted to be close. He pulled the blinds and ran hot water for her into the sunken bath. He added some essence of lavender and watched her silken skin as she bathed. He sat in a chair near her, watching, waiting as she began the ritual of which he so liked to be a part. A small candle burned at the side of the bath.

"Where are we going tomorrow, Fabian? Casey called me today; she is not well, with her stepfather Oliver gone. How did this happen, Fabian? How did he really die, surely not in a car accident?" Maxine found Oliver's death perturbing.

"He killed himself. He was asked to leave England. He had become too dangerous and crazy. He was diagnosed at the hospital with terminal cancer. That was it. It tipped him over the edge." Maxine looked at him, wide-eyed.

What Fabian did not tell her was that the diagnosis was a fake, that the doctors had told him a pack of lies. But it was the only way to push Oliver to end his life. In a way now, he felt responsible for Oliver's death. But there was no other way; soon Oliver would have been arrested and then the club and its future would have been in great danger. There would have been police raids, trials. He had managed to side-step all this in other countries. To have it happen in England was unimaginable; no, it was never going to happen. The men were too high up the social ladder, men who were the so-called protectors of the law. No, he had a safe seat with no Oliver around.

The problem was that Fabian no longer knew who he really was. He was his own personality; he was also The Jester, who seemed to have taken him over, to drive him. The part that was left behind wanted to destroy the hideous world that he had created. But how, that was another question. Fabian felt that he, like Oliver, was going out of control. What he had done to Anna in Cannes at the hotel was horrific: the brutal sex, the coldness. He should never have done that and then leave a video clip. She would never forgive him. Yes, he was out of control. They were all out of control, ruled now by a world of demonic gods way beyond their understanding. He, even he, was starting to panic.

"Should I stay in London, do you think, darling?" Maxine looked up at him from round eyes with their dark, delicately shaped eyebrows.

"I don't know yet; I'm still waiting to hear." It was true; he had not heard from The Jester for days. This trip was planned for weeks ahead. There was no way now he could reach him. He wanted to spend the last night with Maxine. The Jester may come though, if they were together. A plan started to form in his mind, a sinful thought of insurrection. But the outcome of a thought and action could be terminal, so he put it aside. He had told Maxine only a part of what he really did. She did not really know anything about The Jester, the real secrets, the cruelty and the loss of life.

After he had taken her, like a child, from the bath, he carried her to the bed and placed her on the sheets. He buried his head in her stomach and caressed her over and over. Maxine remembered the night when he had first abducted her to the chateau in France and had come to her in the middle of the night. She remembered with a stab of pain what had happened. Then later, he had carried her to his own room and she had sunk into some unknown space unguarded by time.

Now it was happening again, like the first time he had entered her. She felt drawn into a web of delight, dangerous and tantalizing, beyond words. Her body flowed like the torrent of a river towards him and then was engulfed by the banks of his body. She ceased then to exist at all on the physical plane but went beyond the veil of orgasm to the light and space beyond. For the last time, she saw Seth in his magnificence and the eyes of the sphinx upon her. She was being pulled into the darkness of Seth's world.

This night he stayed with her, but when she awoke, her body aching from their excesses, he had gone. She lay across the bed, her knees curled up to her stomach. At 7:00 am, as usual, she had the chauffeur take her out.

"Mea culpa, mea culpa, mea maxima culpa," she repeated and again, feeling she had sinned. Incense filled her nostrils as she said the words, praying for their magic. She was in Jesuit territory here in Mayfair, alongside the fancy prostitutes and the gay bars. She looked at the Virgin Mary and then behind at Christ on the cross, dying for her sins. In the distance, a blue stained-glass window shimmered in the early morning sun that strained to gain its entry. She walked forward and took the wafer from the priest in her famished lips. The wine followed.

As she sat down, she put a hand to her small but swelling abdomen. As she rested her hand there, she felt the memory of their lovemaking, the night that she had worn the black thread around her body for him. Now the seed of The Jester was bearing its fruit. But who was it that was already dwelling inside her? Fear welled up like a grey thing, surrounding her thoughts. A stab of pain went through her as she stood up. She must be more careful in the future of her thoughts. Her overlords could be watching them. She was trapped, a mindless prey in their strong deft hands.

# 45

The Jester stalked the woods of Farlingham Park. It had been his abode for as long as he could remember. He was the keeper of the gates, the guardian of the spell he had created himself, out of his own magic, in the pyramid. Alone, he walked into the depths of the overhanging trees, immortal trees that guarded the portals of hell from the onlookers and the greedy ones. In his stature, he was tall, dark and lean. On his head, he wore a hat; the colours were starting to fade; it was so old. There were reds, greens and yellows, merging into each other. Three points came from the hat, carefully sewn and stuffed, but now they sagged a little. At the end of the three points, three bells sat. They were not as bright as they used to be, and if you looked at them closely, they were a little tarnished from the wind and the rain. After all, nothing lasts forever. His tunic, though, was still fresh and fitted closely to his wiry frame. One leg was clad in a yellow stocking and on the other, red hose. His feet tapered off into pointed-toed shoes. The ends curled up as if to reach the sky.

The Jester stopped in his tracks, as though hearing something that he did not like. But it was only the wind in the trees. With the point of one of his shoes, he started moving a small pile of leaves aside so that he could see the ground. It seemed that he waited for someone. It was a damp, cold day; mist surrounded the trees making visibility difficult.

In truth, The Jester was looking for his physical body. What he occupied now was only an illusion. He wanted a real body. The Jester knew that he had lost it somewhere a long time ago. Confusion overwhelmed him again. He had a memory of his body, but it was painful in the extreme. He shuddered as it came into view. His former life reeled in front of him, Jester to George IV. The bitter taste of revenge was still on his lips. Now he was only a ghost, reaping the deaths of those who had created his downfall and his own terrible death in the pyramids. Would his thirst for their blood ever be assuaged?

The Jester was now dictator living out his lusts and revenge through those he had taken over, by exerting his power little by little in their lives. And then, there was still his life in Egypt. That was where, in secret chambers of reincarnation, he had made a wax image of himself so that he could recreate himself anywhere and in any era that he wished. Khyan was the chief architect and the temple magician. He had served Seth in the 'opening of the mouth ceremonies'. On the appointed day, he had taken the asp to the reigning pharaoh who had reached his allotted time on this earthly plane. It was the magician's job to make sure death became available at this time. But he had brought the date forward for his own greedy ends.

Indeed, he had tricked the Pharaoh who had then turned on him and incarcerated him in the death chambers of the pyramid that he had himself built. There with the wax, before he took his last breaths, he fashioned first a crocodile that would take a form to kill the Pharaoh, and then an image of himself that he breathed on and filled with his own life force. It was well that he did, because the Pharaoh had broken and mutilated all the images of him from the city, making the sound of his name and his life form cease. He cursed those who had had any part in his death.

The Jester raked the leaves, back and forth, with his foot and then walked away into the depths of the forest. He was deep in thought. Going to the shelter of the trees, he took off his hat and placed it before him. Out of his pocket, he took out a black book and wrote down the day of Justin's death. He was mumbling something. Creating a small hole in the ground, he descended through the hole to another plane in time. From a distance, Anubis had been silently watching him from behind the trees.

# 46

Justin awoke to hear the rain on the roof of the hospital. He felt the pain of the nasogastric intubation tube at the back of his throat on the way to his stomach. He hated the feel of it. It was cold in the room, not so much from the temperature but from the waves of chilly thoughts that ran around his brain. It was true. He was really afraid, and the ramblings of his mind landed continually on one object of thought – the thought that he was going to die.

A suction machine was draining excess fluid away from his lung cavity. Tubes, wires and needles ran at various points away from his body, hooking up to various machines and bags. Where was Anna? He did not want to think about it. He moved his body with some difficulty across the bed to relieve the pressure. It was after nine thirty at night. He could see the green then red flash of digital numbers that were closest to his bed.

"Sir Justin, I need to take some more blood." The English nurse, who had been hired specifically to look after him, stood by the side of the bed. Justin seemed unresponsive to her, the eyes half-closed against her intrusion. He had heard her voice, but not really what it said. Hearing was difficult, speech was impossible.

Sometimes, his vision was blurred and he found it hard to distinguish one person from another. He tried to focus and move again, but a cry of pain came from his closed mouth. He sank back again into a reverie, preoccupied solely by the thought of death. His whole life played before him like a movie. Who wanted him dead? Then he felt his arm being moved and the high-pitched pain of another needle entered him.

In Justin's more lucid moments, he knew that he had been singled out and shot. It was a strange unknown feeling, knowing that someone wanted to kill him. It somehow gave life a totally different perspective. He wondered if in some way he had drawn this experience to himself deliberately to save his life or rather his soul, or it was a curse going forward from his lives a long time ago. Emma had not mentioned that he would be shot. Maybe it was not up to her to say it, although she may have seen it. She had been there to mend the pain in his heart, the pain of Anna.

His failed marriage loomed before him like an unending movie. He remembered all the times she had gone abroad, with her cocktail dresses, the high-heeled shoes and the red lipstick. He had never guessed then what she was about – always too pre-occupied with his surgery lists and being at the hospital. Now, he thought about how Anna had looked on returning from those trips; always on a high, cajoling, pretending that she had missed him and could not wait to come home. What a liar she was and what a lie her life was in their marriage. They would go out for dinner, her eyes just a little too wide, her laugh just a little too loud.

Justin had felt at times as though he couldn't stand the well-articulated but dramatic life that he had been leading; hanging over bodies every day with his scalpel, opening them up, doing what was necessary and sometimes, in the end, useless. Then there were deaths post-surgery; he was haunted by the screams and tragedy of the spouses and families left behind.

To the outsider, he had a wonderful life: all the usual trappings of success, a brilliant career and lots of money. On the surface, it was perfect; people would give a lot for such a life. But for him, it had become a hollow thing, a role that he no longer felt was his. The problem was, though, how to exit gracefully. How do you just leave a life? It was the thought that had, in a moment of recklessness, pushed him towards buying a ticket to Cairo. Justin had quite simply wanted to disappear. He also had wanted to find Anthony. For him, Anthony had become a figure of his salvation. He felt that by finding him and rescuing him from whatever circumstances he was in, he would in turn find himself, find the life that he wanted. And as for Anna, she no longer belonged to him. For him, she was a high-class whore who had trapped him into a sterile marriage — a marriage in which he had completely lost his own identity as a man, lost his confidence, his ability to love anything, gone forever. The bitterness was like the bile that he tasted now in his own throat, day after day.

"Sir Justin's vital signs are not good. It's a mystery, almost as though something is sapping his energy at some level. He's not really responding to the treatment. Also, there is an infection that has set in to the healthy lung. We've isolated it, but it's an unknown strain, and we have not got a good rundown on the antibiotic sensitivities. I really hope he pulls through, but I do have my doubts." Jeffrey Devlin, the eminent pulmonary specialist, had just flown in from England and was on the phone to Fairfax. He was speaking in one of the doctor's offices off the ward.

"I'm also very concerned about Lady Bowlby. She's had many tragic incidents in the family. She is very distraught. I wonder what she might do in the face of Justin failing to respond to the care here," said Fairfax.

"We are doing absolutely everything that we can, Mr Crosby-Nash. None of us are happy with the situation. It's mysterious, the whole incident. Has there been any success in finding the man who fired the shot?" asked Jeffrey Devlin kindly.

"No, nothing. He ran back into the crowd. Some say that he was dressed like a Jester — you know, part of the fancy dress ball," replied Fairfax.

Inside Justin's room, the nurse went over to the bed once more. She sat down and held Justin's hand. There were bruises on the front of it from IV penetration. She leaned over and put her hand on Justin's damp brow. The blue eyes were open but staring into the distance, as though he couldn't focus and was in a deep world of his own.

A few days later, Anna was back at the villa, allowed home from the hospital where she had been sedated. She was told to rest and was not allowed to see Justin until she was stable. She didn't know what they meant by stable, but she assumed it meant she was pretty near the edge and they did not want her to go over. She herself was past caring.

She paced around the villa at a loss. It was so silent without Justin. She had abandoned her marriage vows to Justin for nearly the whole duration of their marriage. Her husband was shot while she was with Fabian. She had abandoned herself once again to the devastating pain of his arousal inside her, his cruelty, his excesses. At the point of his semen entering her, she had felt a desperation, so intense, she wanted to die. Somewhere in her brain, she heard Justin calling her. She knew something had happened to him. She had now just one thought and that was how to kill Fabian for the miserable life that he had given her.

She had run from the room in the hotel on that night, having dressed again so hastily, a shawl wrapped around her outfit for the masked ball, down a hundred stairs or more. She dared not use the elevator in case she was recognized. Then she arrived to find that everyone had gone. Sidney came back later to fetch her. He did not ask her where she had been, but the look on his face made her think that he knew about her. Sidney had always known; he had penetrated the dark secret. He knew that she belonged to Fabian, and Sidney did not want the others to be affected by the sin that had touched her own life for so long. She would never forgive herself; and she knew even if Justin recovered, which was unlikely, he would leave her. One way or another, Fabian would have his way. It was true he had promised to take everything from her. Slowly and surely, his words were coming true.

Now that she was back in the villa, she went into Justin's study in search of something. When she was there, she forgot what it was that she came for. In the large mirror that stood over the fireplace, she saw a shadow of herself. Her hair hung in limp strands around her face, which was deathly pale. Dark rings ran under her eyes which seemed to have retreated into their sockets. Anna sat down heavily in a chair, shocked by her appearance. She looked at Justin's briefcase that sat closed on the couch. She had no idea what chaos would be reigning at the hospital without him. Felicity had called and told her not to worry about anything. "Felicity," she thought, "has absolutely no idea who Justin is really married to." Life suddenly felt as though it wasn't there anymore. It was like standing in front of a brick wall and there was no door, no way through.

# 47

Casey stood on the balcony, wearing a wide-brimmed hat. It was almost autumn, and she never knew what to wear in this season. She had, however, chosen the hat and a navy, pin-striped suit that reasonably satisfied her. It was the first day that she had really gone out since Fabian had left a week ago, and it seemed that Oliver had died only yesterday.

She went in, then took off the hat, tears running down her face in endless rivulets of grief and shame. Sitting on the edge of the double bed, covered in the same blue counterpane that had been there for years, memories flooded into her mind, great gates of memory opening to things long forgotten, covered in cobwebs and for the first time seeing the light of day. She had buried it all; the hideous thing that had been called her childhood, stolen from her. And now she re-lived it all as she collapsed on the bed that she had shared with her stepfather for so many years – years of degradation and humiliation. She had been his plaything, his prey, a trapped life for what it seemed forever.

She remembered even now, the sound of his slippers, as he walked in his long strides along the passageway in the night, and sometimes even the day, to her bedroom, starting when she was just a child: his endless gifts to her, his demands that

329

she was his exclusive property, the dates in London at expensive restaurants, the games, the dress ups, long drives in the country in his beautiful black Jaguar, his hand resting on her knee. She had been always terrified of him, bound to him forever, a childhood removed from her, seeing things that fragmented her understanding and her mind, broken. She only reported to him and him alone.

And then finally when she was only just becoming a woman, she remembered how in the middle of the night, he had come to her room, pulling her roughly by the arm onto the floor. He took her there, amidst the screams that no one would ever hear, in swift ruthless movements, expertly, shocking her, the terrible pain between her legs, the blood, the mess, his impatience, the hardness of the wooden floor scrapping her back, her nightdress ripped off, the entry to her secret passageways taken at last, secured, removing any semblance of her own reality or space, any hint of privacy gone. On and on it went through the night, her cries, his hugeness, the violence. And then it came, at last, her complete surrender to him. It was finally over; his body slumped beside her, satiated on the cold floor until the next time. It was as though he had even taken her very soul as well as every part of her body.

After his almost nightly visits, there was little left of her own sense of self. She belonged to him then, a slave; he beckoning to her; she would fulfil all his wishes, whatever he asked. He owned her completely, mind, body and soul. Finally, when he thought she was ready, he took her to the Hexagon Club and introduced her to a few members, who quietly and firmly took her body and did to her whatever they chose. Oliver would make her watch porn movies, train her, coach her, show her how it was done and then he would reach for her, using her, getting her to pretend that she was the star of the movie. She would imitate all the moves. She was besotted now with Oliver and all his wicked tricks.

The last years had been the best and worst; the best because they had become so close but worst because Oliver at times had been unable to ejaculate. He would become enraged at her, ask her to do things to him that sickened her, and yet she had no choice. She was his to do his bidding.

And now, Fabian, it seemed, had stepped into Oliver's shoes. It was the same sexual narcotic for her. She did not realize that he was the sole owner of the Hexagon Club and carried the same sexual power of Seth that Oliver had wielded when he was in bed with her.

She had to now fight off the longing for Fabian, which was like trying to fight off the drugs. She was still not sure whether she had won. She was on a slippery slope, and she knew it. Something had happened to her while she was staying in the house in St. John's Wood, but she had no memory at all of her four-day stay. She could guess what had happened. Fabian had planted something inside her, but she didn't know what it was except that she wanted more of it.

The memories stopped. She did know who she was anymore. She was afraid. They had all told her 'never to remember'; it was like an incantation. She feared now for her life. What was the spell that had been placed upon her, arresting her development? Now she was afraid that if she did remember what had happened to her, would they let her live?

She had found a photograph in one of Oliver's jackets. It made no sense to her, and she had no idea why it was in his possession. It was a picture taken years ago, of her stepfather and Fabian, leaning against the side of a black Porsche. Her head reeled again.

She still had the photos of her naked, aroused, in colour, stolen, taken by Jack after their lovemaking. She had removed them from the desk in Fabian's office at the house in St. John's Wood. What had he and Maxine done to her? And what had been Fabian's relationship with Jack? Had Fabian set the whole thing up, introduced her to Jack, paid him to make sure he had made love to her repeatedly? And Jack always took a lot of pictures of her; it had been weird, she thought at the time, although he was a photographer. Now, she had few facts and a lot of fear to go on.

Not only photographs, but she found videos of Oliver naked at the Hexagon Club, the young beautiful women, lying down, their arms reaching up to him, waiting, longing. She had believed for years that she was the only one he loved, that there was no one else. She was shattered by the endless footage of his carnal acts. She could hardly bear his deceit and disloyalty to her. And then at last, there was the terrible anger welling up inside her.

She had stayed inside her apartment, had evaluated the situation, and set her will against Fabian. It was a dangerous thing to do, especially since he probably knew that she was doing it or, maybe not. She had little idea what was truth or fantasy anymore. That night, she had gone into a space quite beyond her body. Fabian was clever, but she did not know how far he had gone with her physically or what he had done to her soul.

For two weeks, she had refused to answer the phone, and the answering machine declared an abrupt departure to New York with no promise of return. Now, today, she bolted the doors against any possible intruders and went onto the street to hail a taxi. Her mind raced as they headed along Regent's Park Road. She was on her way to a special library in London. She wanted to confirm her suspicions. Jane had told her about this library that she herself had used in her occult studies, which housed esoteric books. Not many people knew about this institution; it was not generally open to the public.

While she was in the taxi, she looked at her notebook. Recalling New York, she remembered the time Maxine first went missing, then the visit to the apartment where everything was in chaos. Then there had been the invitation from The Countess.

One day, Maxine just showed up with a string of excuses about where she had been. When she saw Maxine, it looked like her, but she seemed like an empty shell filled with another person's energy. Casey realized then, or soon after, that Maxine had been taken over. It was not hard to believe from the one night that Fabian had been with her. It was like diving into the ocean and being swept along by a current far too strong to resist. The drop must merge with the ocean. He had said it. They were one now. Perhaps her stepfather had been one with him as well. Perhaps other hands had robbed her of her innocence when she was still too young to understand. She shuddered at the feelings. What had really happened to her in the dark, magnificent house in Cambridge?

The house in St. John's Wood was next in the notebook. She remembered some of her dreams. There was the body of the dead woman at Farlingham Park, her face frozen. A black thread caked in blood was tied around her.

"Is this where you want to get off?"

The taxi driver looked concerned; Casey looked so tired.

"You don't look very well. Have you had the flu?" He spoke again, wanting a reply to his questions.

"Oh, I am all right really. I just had a shock, that's all, thank you." Casey did not want to linger and walked quickly up the steps to the library. She did feel terrible, the morning sickness, the fear of the pregnancy.

The special section that she wanted was on the second floor, where the books were very old. Long corridors led off into anonymous libraries where she would never enter. At last, she reached the right room. It was small in comparison to the main libraries. Going upstairs with the galleries of portraits of writers, artists, and past directors of the library, reminded her of the attics of Farlingham Park.

Finally, the call came through for the books that she wanted. The suit was a good idea. They would not think her too weird browsing around in this section that probably never saw the light of day. She took the books to a small readers' private room and remained there for the next few hours. Some of the books were hard to read, but she had working knowledge of Old English. One of the books was several hundred years old. No wonder they kept them under lock and key.

She felt somewhat embarrassed as she took them back to be held for a few hours while she took a break. The young man at the desk eyed her curiously, although he tried to hide his curiosity. But she read his thoughts. How did she learn to do that? She never used to be able to do that. She knew the young man was wondering why a young woman like herself should be reading books on the manifestation of demonic power, possession and witchcraft in the fifteenth century.

A world was starting to fall into place. Now she had some idea what may be happening to them all. The Countess had warned her to stay away. Now she knew why, but she was too deep in to retract now. She thought of returning to New York, but the demons would find her there just as they had found Maxine.

She went out into the fresh air and, on a whim, decided to take a taxi to the Dorchester Hotel to really refresh herself with some afternoon tea. The pages of the books were circling menacingly around her head.

At the Dorchester, sinking into the rich sofas, she became reassured by the sheer opulence of the place. She watched the waiter pour her tea from silver into the delicate china that sat before her on the table.

"Casey, I can't believe that you are here," a voice with a strong Italian accent wafted over to her from behind the sofa.

"Bruno? What an amazing coincidence. What on earth are you doing in London?" She tried to sound relaxed, but her mind was running in overdrive. She realized that she was somewhat paranoid. Had Bruno been following her? Was he tied up with Fabian in some way? But their conversation revealed to her that he was not the enemy; in fact, he may be the friend that she needed desperately.

"Bruno, I hardly recognized you. You have changed so much." The afternoon she had met with Bruno and Flo in New York swam before her mind as they continued to talk.

"You seem tired, Casey, out of sorts. Is anything wrong? I am so sorry to hear about your stepfather." Bruno was genuinely concerned about her.

"No, I'm finding his death very hard. I was with Justin and Anna for a while before they went away to France. I was in quite a mess," added Casey,

"Oh, it was terrible to hear that Sir Justin was shot in Cannes at the annual ball." But then Bruno realized suddenly by her reaction that Casey did not know.

"Shot?" Casey fell back against the cushions on the sofa. Her face was pale. She could not take it in at all. It was as though she had not really heard him as Bruno described the circumstances of the shooting and told her that Sir Justin was in intensive care.

"Bruno, I am in danger – a group of us here, terrible things have happened. Someone I care a great deal about has been injured." The words were out before she had the strength to stop them.

"You know something, Casey; I knew something had happened. You look as though something has taken up residence inside you. It's hard to describe, but something in your eyes tell me that not all is well with you. At the very least, you should go and see a doctor. Physically, you look as though you have been through the mill. This man will take care of you; do some routine examinations." Bruno gave her a card.

"Casey, consider me as your friend. If there is anything I can do, call me, day or night. Is there anything that you want to tell me now?" Bruno searched her face for a moment.

They drew to the side of the lobby and sat on some easy chairs.

"Bruno, I can't make it out. I stayed with these people in St. John's Wood. The strange thing is that I cannot remember a thing about it all, except for a few dreams. I saw the death of someone at Farlingham Park." Casey paused as Bruno frowned. "Farlingham Park is the place where the Countess of Rigby invited us during the summer. It was a heightened experience for me; spiritual energy was strong there. I felt that I had lived there before – I mean, in another lifetime or something. Anyway, Maxine came to join us on the Sunday. She was indescribable. I have never seen anyone change so much. You would not have recognized her. She was my best friend, and I hardly recognized her – empty, somehow, with glazed eyes. They are living in St. John's Wood." Casey paused for breath.

"They?" asked Bruno.

"Maxine and Count Fabian Roth." Casey looked scared when she saw Bruno's expression. He realized Casey was in a mess; nothing was making much sense to him.

"Why are you looking like that?" she asked.

"Fabian Roth is Emma's brother. They never see each other, of course. It is rumoured that he raped his sister when she was fourteen. Everything was hushed up, of course. My mother knows some of their distant relatives and the word got around. Fabian has a powerful reputation. He is a very dangerous man, in every way. They say he is a black magician. There are countless lives that he has ruined. Mostly, those women never speak out because of fear, but one or two have been brave enough. It's best not to go into it. I don't really know much more, but he has a worldwide organization, headquartered in South America, devoted to his work. He is a guru figure to many people. He is charming. You would never think him evil unless you knew." Bruno could see she was scared.

"How can I find out what happened to me in the house? I found a photograph of my stepfather taken years ago standing with Fabian. What do you think that means?" Casey's questions were flying, but she wasn't going to tell Bruno that she had spent the night with Fabian at her apartment.

"It could be that your stepfather had business interests with him?" suggested Bruno.

"But Fabian had his arm around him, as though he owned him." Casey looked blank.

"Well, it is possible that your stepfather was part of the organization." Bruno knew more, but he wasn't going to tell Casey about the organization or what was rumoured about the abduction of young girls. Casey had been through enough already; he was concerned for her. If she was possessed, it did not yet show in her eyes, but it sounded as though Maxine was completely taken over.

Bruno knew nothing of The Jester. He thought the Count stood on his own in all this.

They talked for another hour about Justin, about Casey herself. She seemed as though she just could not understand or take in the shooting. It was as though he had never told her. She must be in severe shock, he thought. Then Bruno left. They agreed to stay in contact.

Bruno had no idea that Anna was Casey's cousin. For some reason, all this did not come up in the conversation. It was strange in a way. He realized it was true that Casey did not know about the shooting. Oliver's death had been enough for her; she was walled in.

Casey decided, on a whim, to stay a couple of nights at the hotel. She found it reassuring and, for some reason, she did not want to go back to her flat. There were too many memories there; she could hardly handle it. She kept thinking about the shooting of Justin; it seemed like a bad dream. She could not take any action now; she would do something later she told herself. Surely, she should make calls, but she felt as though she was frozen, could not take any action.

Having made her reservation to stay at the hotel, she returned to the library. Back in the study, she browsed again through the books. She felt both better and worse having spoken to Bruno. She took copious notes. Some of the content really alarmed her. She was reading a chapter on ceremonial robes, the use of hats and other regalia. She reached the end of one of the books where she saw a picture of a jester's hat; that made her mouth fall open. It described the full role of the court jesters. It was far more than she ever expected. It wasn't a fun role at all.

Hats were crucial in magic. The black pointed hats of the witches had no idle significance. She knew she had seen a hat. There was a vague memory, but where was it? Where had she seen a hat? Was it a jester's hat? If she had seen a jester's hat, why was it where it was, and who was The Jester?

Her head was reeling as she put the books away. Did her father wear those hats? Had she really been involved in all this since she was a child? Was she suffering from, and had she always suffered, some amnesia? Were Fabian's hands on her too when she was a young girl? She felt giddy. Had she been drugged? The world had ceased to have stability anymore.

# 48

Everyone was in the drawing room at Justin and Anna's villa, taking a break from the vigil they were keeping at the side of Justin's bed.

"They're back," said Jane, making a statement as though into the air.

"Who is back?" asked Sidney who was eyeing Anna curiously. What had Fabian done to her the day that Justin was shot? He shuddered at the thought, knowing what this evil man was capable of in one afternoon. He seemed to be sucking the blood out of her. She looked frail and wan. He cared about Anna deeply, but he couldn't broach the subject. Never was it going to be possible to discuss intimacies with Anna. She would stay in her own cool detached world with the pain going on inside her.

"Emma and Stephanie." Jane looked across at Sidney; she knew of his disapproval.

"I just hope her brother, Fabian Roth, is not coming as well." Sidney's words dropped on the little group like ice cold water. Everyone stared at him. Anna hastily left the room. Sidney found himself still both embittered and terrified, maybe for a lifetime about what Fabian had done to him or had attempted to do. He was indeed lucky to have escaped.

"Her brother?" Jane flashed Sidney a glance of disbelief. She hated Fabian. It was he who had caused the death of her sister Catherine's husband Louis. She just knew it.

"Yes, she has a brother whose reputation is very distinguished, that is, if you like that sort of thing." Sidney's voice was filled with malice.

"Sidney, what are you talking about? Why did Anna leave the room so abruptly?" Jane felt disturbed at Sidney introducing information about the Countess. They had trusted her; now she wondered whether the Countess and her brother were somehow at the root of all the ills that had beset them. She herself had not been attacked or threatened again, but she knew that it may be just a question of time.

Anna came back in. She looked pale and avoided looking at Sidney. He seemed to have become obsessed with their misfortunes, had become tangled in their lives, almost without being invited. Why was he here? What were his interests? She no longer trusted anyone.

"Why did they come here, I mean Emma and Stephanie?" Anna asked.

"Stephanie had a dream. She saw Justin appear to her with blood on his face and calling out to her," Jane replied but with as little detail as possible.

"Did anyone call Casey about Justin? She is still in England you know, after she stayed with us at The Beeches." It had been beyond Anna's ability to make calls over the last few weeks.

"Yes, I have called several times, left messages, sent emails. Nothing – she does not answer. I can't understand it; she is usually so responsive." Jane looked anxious, wondering if anything had happened to Casey. Sidney was silent; he dared not say anything else. It would be construed as invasive. He was already in Anna's bad books.

"She just needs her space; she will call us when she is ready and not before, knowing my cousin." Anna silently worried too about what Casey would be going through – the terrible reality of who she really was and what her life with Oliver had been like, the things they had shared as women and now this pregnancy. Yes, she was indeed worried, but she was not going to discuss this with Jane. Nor with anyone else for that matter.

Jane was sitting on the sofa. She wanted to talk to Anna alone. No one had even heard from Anthony after Rawlings had warned her off. Jane had decided to play it safe and not to make any more inquiries. She missed him and wondered whether she would ever hear from him or know his whereabouts. Perhaps, she should take a chance and try to find him. Perhaps, Justin had tried to do something and that was why he had been shot. It was such a confusing time for all of them.

"I'll be on my way. Moira will be expecting me. We are flying to Madrid tomorrow for a couple of nights to see a client." Sidney edged towards the door.

He looked embarrassed as though he realized he had trodden on some sacred ground. The best thing, he thought, was to put some distance between himself and Anna. She clearly could not take his directness, and she looked like she wasn't going to say goodbye. It was time he left her well alone. He had gone too far.

"Bye, Sidney, see you soon, and thanks for calling us in London and spending time with us here. Give our love to Moira." Jane had gone outside to the front door and waved as the Volvo pulled away.

Fairfax, Jane and Anna remained in the living room. Fairfax had extended his stay to be with his wife. He was glad that he had spoken with Justin's pulmonary surgeon on the phone. It was not looking at all good. It was too much for Jane to cope with Anna and Justin alone. He was very concerned about Justin after the call tonight. He wasn't responding to antibiotics and was visibly weaker each time they visited. They took turns to sit with him. Visiting was restricted, and one person could be with him at a time. Anna was not allowed to go until she was more stable.

"I'm going down to get some groceries; with everyone here, we are going to need more food. I'll be back and then maybe we can go and see Emma and Stephanie." Fairfax headed for the veranda. He knew Anna needed some time alone with Jane.

"Thank God everyone has gone. I couldn't bear another minute of Sidney. Even the maid is getting on my nerves. I just want to be alone." Anna sank down onto one of the easy chairs. She sighed and put her long fingers over her eyes. She had dressed up a little today and worn a light wool dress in black; she had on a thin leather belt with a fancy gold buckle. Around her neck hung a grey scarf with large leaves, designed into the fabric in black and white. She always looked stunning, even when she was at her lowest.

They talked then about Casey. But Anna told Jane nothing about the travesty of Casey's childhood, the terrible things that Oliver had done to his own stepdaughter, and the awful fact of the pregnancy. She would have to keep it to herself. They sat and wondered about Anthony. Jane had heard nothing and then had been warned off by Rawlings. She was too scared after that. Jane wanted to have a more intimate talk with Anna now, but it was not to be. Whatever had been said between them had been spoken. For Anna, there was nothing left that she could share. All had to be secret, like the endless secrets of her family that she had finally shared with Casey. But Jane was of a different ilk. She knew nothing of the Hexagon Club and what both Anna and Casey had endured from their childhoods. No, they lived in very different worlds. It would never work to share any of these things.

"Anna, is there anything you want to talk about? You must talk to someone; you can't bottle it all up. It's so bad for you. You never really talked to Justin, did you?"

"There is nothing to talk about, Jane. I feel I am beyond talking, you know, although Justin and I had such some wonderful times these last two weeks. I felt it was our last time together. I couldn't say why; it was just an intuition. Everything gets taken away from me sooner or later." Anna looked into the distance as she spoke.

"Justin would never leave you, Anna. He adores the ground that you walk on," said Jane reassuringly, but she privately nursed some doubts. Justin did seem to have changed since their visit to Farlingham Park and his meeting with Emma. Jane even wondered if he would continue his life at the hospital; he seemed to have gone beyond it. Maybe another kind of life awaited him. He looked gaunt even before the attempted murder, and far too thin.

"I can't see a way ahead, Jane. It is like standing in front of a wall where there is no door or window. It's a dead end. There is no projection forward. Everyone that I love seems to be drifting away to another world, even you, Jane." Anna looked at her friend. There was no desperation in Anna's eyes, just a sense of harsh reality, as though she knew her destiny.

"Do you ever think Giles is alive?" Jane abruptly changed her tone.

"Yes, I sense he is alive. I think someone took him to another country. But I also know that I will never see him again. But you may. You will all go on without me." Anna got up and went to fetch some soda from the sideboard. Her walk was ponderous, as though she was thinking about something else.

"Anna, this is crazy; you are just depressed, that is all." Jane answered her abruptly, trying to undo Anna's train of thought. Where was Anna going with all this? It sounded as though she wanted to die.

"It's not crazy, and actually I am not distressed or depressed. I am beyond that. It's a sense of detachment. I always felt that I died a long time ago during a summer in France; there was a terrible accident; it was even before I was married to Justin. Since then and the miraculous recovery, I have, in a way, been living on borrowed time," continued Anna, as she went to light a fire in the grate. It was a chilly day and already the cold of September days in the South of France were becoming a reality. The fire blazed up. Anna surveyed the sparks and remembered Justin lighting fires such as this in the years gone by.

Jane was speechless. She had never heard Anna talk like this, never, in a way, seen her so strong. She had taken on effulgence that was almost unearthly. Stephanie had said Anna had no light around her, as though she were dead. Jane decided she would ask her what she meant one day – this unusual little girl, who had entered their lives so sweetly and so suddenly, and who told them she had seen Giles playing in the fields beyond the house. Maybe she had been right after all. Perhaps they were all going to begin a new life.

"Well, once Fairfax is back, we'll go straight to the hospital. I expect we won't be back until later on this evening."

When Fairfax had returned with the groceries and left with Jane, Anna stoked the fire to a blaze. She locked the doors and closed the shutters of the windows. There was no light in the house now, save the roaring of the fire. She stood erect in front of the fire looking into the mirror. She took off all her clothes. There, lying in a full circle around her, was the soft thin black silk of the sacred cord that Fabian had placed on her so many years ago. She had worn it when she had become pregnant with Giles. But it was a night she had lain with Fabian and not Justin. Giles was Fabian's child. Giles belonged to The Jester. He had only been on loan to her.

She slowly untied the silken thread that ran around her left shoulder and down her back. It had made its way then between her legs, a constant reminder of Fabian's privileges of entry to her body. The knot untied and now she held the cord in her hands, as though to say goodbye to its magic forever. She touched the coiled mouth that had given her so much pleasure yet also brought her so much physical and emotional pain. Then without any more ceremony, she threw it into the fire. The flames engulfed and consumed it within seconds. Now, she had only what time remained for her; her borrowed time had been extinguished in the flames. Who knew how long she had now.

# *49*

Casey's mind was reeling from the news that Justin had been shot. She just could not grasp it somehow. It was all too much; after all, she had a job to do. She could hardly bear the shock of Oliver's death, let alone the reality of Justin's attempted murder.

It was like a fist that had hit her in the solar plexus. Had Oliver been murdered? It had not made sense to her at all that he was killed in a car crash on some remote road in the outermost regions of Uruguay. She had not even considered the possibility that he had been murdered. What was he doing there anyway?

At her desk in the library, she was intent. Her study was more focused now, surveying the practices of witchcraft and possession in the fifteenth century. She read more on the use of regalia, the chanting of mantras and hand movements used on the body of a person to entrap them. She thought of Fabian's hands on her skull, the way her tongue had risen like a serpent against the roof of her mouth when he had run his finger up her spine.

Reading the books re-awoke the longing that she felt for him, the dangerous excitement and intoxication as the Kundalini hit her genitals. What wondrous power, and yet used in the wrong way, against the divine, it could be disastrous. Fabian was adept in tantric practices, the transcendent sexual fire. But the fire within him moved powerfully downwards to the base of the spine and the sexual centres, creating a vortex of whirling energy and darkness.

His was not a path to the higher centres, or was it? She remembered how he had seemed to lose control and become frenzied when he wanted to have physical union with her. The books recommended meditation on the space between the anus and the genitals. She had tried it on her own. It was powerful and tantalizing, but then, she was lost again in her longing for Fabian. And then, there was the baby. It was an amazing experience to be pregnant now. She had more choices, something of her own, a sign always that Oliver had been in her life. She put her hands down gently now to rest on her belly while she was reading,

But spiritually, she wanted the real thing now, the path to God and the upper chakras. There was no future in the lower chakras. She wasn't hungry for the sort of egotistical power that Fabian quite obviously wielded. It was like Oliver all over again, and she could not bear that. That kind of sex kept you bound, noosed, always descending into the crust of the earth itself. But for Casey now, it would be a long struggle for her to attain any real enlightenment, awareness or healing; she was too damaged. She would need so much help to unpick the tragedy or her life and to bring herself out of the web of secrets and lies in which she had lived almost an entire lifetime.

Back at the Dorchester, Casey soaked her body in the elaborate bathtub inside the bathroom of her suite; it was embellished with tiny rose buds, hand-painted. Thought after thought tumbled through her brain as she lay in the warmth. She looked at her body which offered no memory of what had happened at the house in St. John's Wood. Her baby bump was a soft round mound of love. She wished now that Oliver had known about this baby before he died.

Afterwards, she went into the sitting room and sat at the desk – a good replica of French antique. "She must develop a plan," she thought. There was no one she could trust. Everyone who had been invited to Farlingham Park was in danger, real danger. The possible consequences were hardly worth considering. Anna had been in a near fatal accident. Justin and Anna's son had disappeared some years before. Anthony had been taken away to goodness knows where. Justin had been shot. They were all under the threat of death. She had to call everyone. She had no idea if they even knew of the dangers. Yes, she had better do something about contacting Anna and Justin. Her head swam; she was rapidly going into overdrive.

She tried Jane's house in Shropshire. There was no reply. She knew that Anthony had been arrested because Jane had told her, but she had seemed guarded and vague at the time. Now she called the house in Chiswick. The phone rang for a long time. Jane ran her hands through the blond strands of hair that fell wetly across her face. She was still wearing the hotel towelling robe.

"This is the Crosby-Nash residence." A woman's voice answered. She seemed in a hurry.

"Mrs Crosby-Nash is away with her husband." The voice gave Jane an answer to the questions she put.

"I really need to have their number. Where have they gone?" Casey sounded anxious. It was not going to solicit a favourable reply.

"I am sorry, but I am not able to give you any information at this time." There was a click on the other end. Casey got up and paced the room. The voice was not the maid, Fiona, no, it was someone else's voice, but whose? It sounded like they had been told not to give any information out about the whereabouts of Jane and Fairfax. "So, that is a dead end," Casey thought.

Now she was on the line to Anna and Justin's house.

"Yes?" No announcement of residence – just a man's voice, and abrupt at that.

Casey was stunned into silence. Then she asked for Anna.

"This is the security guard. The house is empty. Why are you calling?" He sounded as though he was trying to keep her on the line. He was tracing the call.

Unbeknown to her, the call was tracked immediately. They wanted to know of anyone who had any kind of business with the Bowlby household. There were French and English detectives running around both countries trying to find those who were plotting murder; the family had hired their own detectives and security guards. Now the detective Grahams, who had plagued Anna, was again digging up the car accident and the death of John Grey.

Casey tried the Countess' numbers. Casey had not played by the rules or instructions. She was so frightened now with everyone apparently gone that she wanted to speak to Emma, but she was not available. "Where was everyone?" thought Casey. She made a list of all the people at Farlingham Park. Randy – of course, she would check on her. Randy was staying with her uncle Ross in California.

"Ross here." Ross never used many words.

"I'm sorry to bother you, Ross. It's Casey. I wanted to know how Randy is now. I haven't had a letter or anything from her for weeks." Casey heard a silence at the other end. What was the matter with everyone?

"Casey, what is wrong with you? You know that Randy is not here. When we got your email and then when Maxine called, we made all the arrangements for Randy to go to Switzerland. Maxine told us that you were staying with her and wanted Randy to join you. She sent a lot of money for clothes and everything, so we assumed it was all right. Randy knows Maxine really well," finished Ross.

Now it was Casey's turn to emit a cold silence.

"Casey, is something wrong?" asked Ross, sounding worried now.

"Oh, it's all right. I didn't realize she was leaving so soon. I'll call you later." She had made a snap decision not to tell Ross. It could make things even worse for Randy. She could not believe Fabian and Maxine could do this – steal Randy away. She was only ten years old. What on earth would they do with her? Casey was now feeling out of her depth. She had taken on too much. A huge net was falling over her world and there was no way she could struggle free. Sooner or later, the net would draw tighter and tighter.

Now it was her turn for the phone to ring. She slowly picked it up.

"Miss Pemberton, this is the Kent police. We are tracing all calls to the Bowlby residence. What was your reason for getting in touch with them, please?" A man's voice sounded pleasant enough.

"Why shouldn't I call them; Lady Bowlby is my cousin; they are friends of mine? Why, what is wrong? Why are the police involved? They don't usually have police answering the phone." Casey was losing her temper. She tried to restrain herself, but it was getting the better of her.

"You are not aware that Sir Justin Bowlby was recently shot in France? He is in a critical condition at the hospital," continued the voice.

"Oh, yes, of course, I forgot." Casey sat down near the phone, her hand pressing the receiver tightly, as she heard again the dreadful news. It must have been all over the papers. It was starting to sink in, but she had not been out in ten days, watched TV or read the newspapers. She had not answered her phone, and her mobile was turned off. She had not wanted to be disturbed. Bruno had told her. It did not register, still had not registered.

"Which hospital?" she asked, expecting an answer.

"I can't tell you that. We would like to send one of our inspectors round to talk with you. His name is Inspector Rawlings. Would you be available this evening?" The voice was starting to irritate her.

"Yes, I suppose so." She was immediately on her guard.

The arrangements were made. She hung up, plunged into an even deeper gloom. She felt totally alone.

Casey dressed in what she had purchased in Oxford Street, in a pair of black velvet pants and a long grey cashmere sweater. As she was brushing her blond strands of hair into a bun, the phone rang. Earlier, Casey had left a message on her mother's answering machine in Cambridge.

"Why are you there of all places? Are you all right, dear?" asked Antigone.

"Yes, of course I am all right," replied Casey.

"Then why are you staying at a hotel when you have a perfectly good flat up the road?" Her mother started the familiar interrogation.

"I don't know. I needed a break, needed to think. I was upset about the news, I mean about Justin; it is hard to believe." Casey was at a loss. How did her mother find her at the hotel?

"Mother, did you or Daddy know a man called Fabian Roth? I mean, it would be years ago." Casey found herself asking a question that she never intended.

"Oh, I don't know; your stepfather was away a lot. He had so many friends. He visited France often. Don't you remember, he used to take you too?" said her mother.

"He did what? Alone?" Casey sat up in the chair, not believing what she was hearing.

"Yes, he would take you off there, sometimes for two weeks at a time. Don't you *remember*, Casey?" asked her mother. Antigone remembered Oliver taking her everywhere he went. He wanted her with him all the time and in the nights; and when Oliver left their own bedroom to go down the corridor to be with her daughter, she had to let him go to her. This was the way the Hexagon Club worked, and she could do nothing to prevent him from going to Casey. It was often not until the early hours of the morning that he would return to their own bedroom. She always pretended to be asleep, never confronted him. The Fraternity could never be confronted; it was the rule, and their house was no exception. The men did what they liked.

"You let me go to France with him alone? How could you do that?" Casey's anger was surfacing again.

"What on earth do you mean? He was your stepfather, Casey." Antigone was all pretence now. Had she found out? Had she remembered the first few years of her childhood and what they had done, their experiment on Casey? "I'm surprised that you don't *remember*."

The clever word '*remember*', it was a trigger word in the grooming. Casey would not be able to really *remember*; they had made sure of that. "I went once, I think. Yes, maybe the name was Roth. It's so long ago. He had a magnificent chateau in the South of France. It had a green roof and an ornamental lake. Oh, yes, and peacocks on the lawn, very beautiful. I really can't understand why you don't *remember*, Casey. You were ten years old; that is old enough to *remember*." Her mother's voice bore into her. Antigone was scared and kept using the word '*remember*'. It was a trick word designed to make someone forget. Casey had read that the age of ten is a significant age for witches to abduct a child. Her mind went ricocheting on and on into webs of thought. A cold sweat formed on her brow, as the realizations started to dawn.

"I just cannot talk about Oliver's death. You do understand that, dear, don't you?" Antigone could not believe how much hatred she felt for Oliver, but she was feigning that her grief was too great. Casey did not answer.

"Casey, are you there?" her mother sounded anxious.

Why had her mother not protected her, saved her from France and what had taken place there, in god knows what violation of her private being?

"I have to go, Mother. I'll talk to you later." Casey sank onto the bed and folded her knees up to her chest. God, she would have to tell Antigone that she was pregnant. She would never tell her it was Oliver's. That would be the last straw. No, there was no need to tell her. She would go away, say the baby was adopted. Anything to keep Antigone at a distance and out of her life.

Antigone quietly put the phone down. "Thank God," she thought. Casey had been drugged and hypnotized so much of the time as a young child. She could not possibly remember what had happened. At first, Antigone was a willing bystander but then she also had become involved in the Hexagon Club. She was a hard-looking woman, robust, strong physically, chiselled features, her blond hair cut very short in an Eton crop and a beautifully sculptured body. She was attractive to men, but she was described as a 'sadistic' lover. People were just a little afraid of her.

Her membership at the club had really been her undoing and doubled the guilt about her own daughter. At Oxford, as a don, she had a lot of access to young girls; it was very satisfying to her to travel down to London and show them the sights, but it has gone further than this. She had introduced some of the girls to Oliver and other members of the club. A few of them, very pretty girls, ended up there, leaving their university studies behind, for the lush life with lots of money, posh cars and all the designer clothes that they wanted. It had given her a kind of vicarious pleasure to be a bit of a bystander and to be a witness to some of the parties and the sexual orgies. All the girls seemed to have great time. It was a wonderful everlasting party for them. Antigone had also started to enjoy her own voyeurism and dallied on the edge of the scandals. She had become very emotionally involved with one of the students, a pretty young girl. It was sad that she eventually had left the club and it seemed had completely disappeared. Years later, they found out she had committed suicide. Antigone had thought it was such a shame.

Somehow, she felt Casey instinctively knew that there was something evil about her. Yes, Antigone even felt herself to be evil. She understood the Hexagon Club and its sexual rules, the purity of purpose in breeding and the grooming of daughters as young girls.

Antigone had travelled to Berlin; her first husband was friend to the Third Reich and they had mixed with the higher echelons of society. Some of the more deviant sexual practices, Antigone and her first husband brought back to the Hexagon Club in England and trained the girls there – a club that was satisfying the perverse sexual needs of officers and government officials in the war party. And then, her husband had been accused of being a spy. He had been found to have homosexual tendencies, then so unpopular in Nazi Germany. He was exterminated in one of Hitler's concentration camps. Antigone had wasted no time in remarrying and finding someone who would couple with her again in her lascivious interests.

Lord Oliver Pemberton fitted the bill exactly, with his title and vast wealth; and so the mansion in Cambridge became an experiment and Casey was that experiment. They had developed a clever programme for her, and they wanted to know how it would work. Antigone sat and remembered the grand days in Germany, the infinite possibilities, the corruption, bodies sold for nothing. Yes, she was no innocent bystander; she had been Oliver's accomplice all along, giving him easier and easier access to Casey during the long nights and dark days. She had gone away much of the time so that her husband and Casey had time to be alone. Even members of the Hexagon Club would come to the house, including Anna's father. They were all at it, these men. They all sullied Casey and the other young girls that they brought with them. She had her jealousy and rage; there were days when she hated them both as they continued fornicating in Casey's little bedroom.

An hour later, the hotel front desk called through. Casey had agreed to see Rawlings in her suite. It was too public downstairs, and someone could recognize her.

"Come in, Inspector." Casey was aloof. She was too shocked by the revelations of her mother to involve herself in conversation. She was also aghast at the news about Justin. She went through the motions of offering him a chair and a drink. The first he took and the second he declined.

Inspector Rawlings got down to business, not waiting a second. He asked her several questions about Sir Justin and Lady Anna Bowlby. How long had she known them? Then he started on Lord Oliver's death and finally he asked Casey about her own relationship with her stepfather. Rawlings knew of course about her incestuous relationship; he also noted the baby bump. This he carefully avoided; after all, it was not strictly now his business about how and why Casey got herself pregnant. Fabian would see it as interfering.

"Let's go through this again. Why are you staying in a hotel when you have a flat nearby? Don't you think it is a little odd?" He badgered now for answers.

"Well, it's funny you should ask that; my mother just asked the same question. I will give you the same answer. I wanted a change, time to think," she finished.

"Time to think about what? Why can't you think in your own place? It's big enough, I mean, not exactly a studio." He felt annoyed at this woman's attitude, felt his authority was being undermined. "What is your relationship to Sir Justin Bowlby?" He asked her again, and he chewed the words in such a way that it gave the impression that she was a bit on the side. She was beginning to hate this man.

"His wife Lady Anna Bowlby is my cousin; we grew up in Cambridge together." She got up as she replied; she didn't want to sit opposite him. It was airless in the room, and she was starting to feel slightly faint, as though her energy was off balance. She went to the drinks cabinet for some tonic water.

Rawlings was noticing her legs in black velvet pants. She started to feel uncomfortable. She knew he was staring at her. Things felt like they were getting out of hand. He was between her and the door, a big mistake on her part. Why on earth had she not seen him downstairs? What on earth was she thinking about?

"At which police station are you based?" she asked, wondering if he was really who he said he was. She also wanted a chance to put him down, ask him a few questions, and get her own back.

He looked at her coldly. "I am part of an international department. We are based in many places. We are private police; we work closely with the police force of many different countries.

"Do you know Count Fabian Roth?" The question came suddenly from her lips. She didn't know why she had asked it, but suddenly she was making connections. It was something about Rawlings' shoes; they were the same as the pair that Fabian had worn one day at the house in St. John's Wood. She remembered he had said he had them handmade in a shop in the back streets of Rome.

"No, I have never heard of him." Rawlings lied, knowing she was perceptive enough to know that he was lying. How did she know? He felt the perspiration on his forehead; this was not going well. He knew that if he bungled this, it would show later. The Count would know.

He continued to ask her questions that would elicit facts about Casey's life, her business, friends and plans. She still gave the same flat unresponsive answers that were sometimes lengthy but gave no real information at all. In the end, he gave up. But he did have a genuine position as a detective, and he could make life difficult. He could detain her if he wanted. At this point, he did not choose to do that.

"Is there anything else I can help you with, or can I show you out?" She stood up deliberately, ending the interview. She felt she had won this round, but next time, the game could go differently.

Then Rawlings did a strange thing. He walked casually over to her. He stood right in front of her, pushed his face as close to hers as possible, then he held her eyes for a few seconds. He did not touch her, but a whirling noise started in her head. She felt she was falling into space.

"Just stay within your limits. It would be a pity if you stuck your pretty neck out too far. There are people involved in this you know nothing about; nor do you have any idea of the dangers involved." With that, he let himself out, much to her annoyance; after all, it was the door to her own suite.

Rawlings cut an attractive figure, dressed in a dark suit with a thread of white through it. He made his way through the lobby, running long white fingers through his ginger hair. His green eyes surveyed the space and, finding nothing of interest, he made his way out to the car parked outside for him. He got in and drove quickly to Fabian's offices in Mayfair where Angela was waiting for him upstairs.

Meanwhile, Casey still experienced the noises in her head. There were rhythmic words that played repeatedly. The words were strange, almost an incantation of sorts, rising to a crescendo. She felt now she was so far into these mysteries that she had to get to the bottom of it. But how?

Firstly, she wondered where everyone was. She knew where they were not; and Rawlings was, she realized, clever at not revealing anything at all. Tomorrow, she would do more research. She would have to scan everything she could find. Then she would probably have to join the enemies. There was no other way. Suddenly, she thought of Anthony. Where was he now? There was no way she could find out. Her way to him would be through devious routes. She would have to play a role. She realized now that she had not asked Rawlings anything about Justin. It was probably safer that way. There was nothing she could do about it anyway.

And now, she would plan somehow to go and find Justin and Anna in the South of France. She was horrified at what had happened and why. The hospital must be close to their villa. She had been there many times. It would be easy to find. But in the end she never went; her destiny took her elsewhere.

# 50

Justin had been given the last rites. Only Anna had been in the room, alone with the priest. It looked as though Justin would die that night, or perhaps the next day. His face looked more angular than ever. His hair now seemed darker, and it clung in wet tendrils to his forehead. Occasionally his breath came in short gasps. Many of the tubes and needles had been removed from his body to give him the chance of a more peaceful death.

It was quiet in the room and the evening was at last giving way to night. Justin was so ill that he no longer had any real thoughts. He felt himself removed from worldly affairs; nothing held any interest for him. He was merely aware of his own existence.

Later that night, Anna had left. His condition had not deteriorated, and she felt that it was safe enough to get some sleep. It was ten o'clock when the door opened and Stephanie entered. Her small frame was silhouetted in the door. Justin was immediately aware of her and rallied his strength a little. She was alone. He wondered how on earth she had managed even to get in to see him.

Stephanie was silent with him and just put her hand in his. Tears flowed down her cheeks, as she realized the pain he had been in for the last three weeks. His face seemed grey to her, hair pressed flat to his forehead. She knew something was very wrong; Justin was not being allowed to recover; the life force was damaged wilfully by an external force. She wished that she had been able to get here much earlier; maybe there had been something she could have done.

She noticed a quick movement behind her. It was slight; she nearly did not notice with her attention so focused on Justin. She turned slowly around to see where the movement was coming from. There, in the far corner of the room, stood an old man. He was dressed in the garments of a court jester. Stephanie had seen pictures of such people. Then she remembered him in the woods at Farlingham Park. But she also knew that this man's body was summoned by will, out of magic.

He had no real body; he had fashioned it himself out of the cloth of space and time. Stephanie took in every detail. He was standing open-mouthed, tantalized by her great beauty. He was spellbound by the young child. Mortals did not generally see or hear him, but he knew that she could see everything. Then he knew that he wanted her, like no other thing he had ever seen.

"You are taking away Justin's life, aren't you?" she asked, staring at his face.

"It had to be that way. He robbed me of my life. He incarcerated me in the tomb in Egypt. This is the end that he now justly deserves." The Jester moved closer to her. He wanted to see her more clearly.

"Is there anything that would change your mind?" She spoke kindly to him, as though she loved him; she always treated people like this. She only saw the goodness in things.

"Yes, now that I have seen you, I would take you instead. You would die instead of him." The Jester came over to her and put his thin hand on her back. He touched the fair hair that fell to her waist. She felt his power, and she shivered.

A long silence fell upon the room, as she considered the implications of what he was saying. "Yes," she thought, "Justin should live; I should die."

"How many others do you want to kill?" She knew his mind.

"That is my business. All of them must go. I have planned their deaths. A life for a life is all that matters. If you come with me, I will let this man live. He will never be touched again by my curse. The others will die. That is the end of the matter." She knew that she couldn't bargain any further.

"Yes, take my life and save Justin's. I have decided." Stephanie stood facing the horrible spectre.

"Then leave the room. Get out of here and I will come and collect you when I want." She ran from the room, realizing that time was short for Justin. She hoped it was not too late.

The Jester stood in the corner and then he walked slowly towards Justin's bed. He passed his long hand over Justin in a series of movements. Justin stirred and opened his eyes. It was as though he was awakening from a dream in which he had been dying. He did not see The Jester, he saw nothing.

Stephanie walked slowly along the hospital corridor, having said goodnight to the nurse and telling her that Justin would be better soon. The nurse was astonished. On and on, Stephanie went along the corridors. She knew Emma was waiting for her. Would she ever make it? She was starting to feel as though she was fading already into nothingness. As she rounded a corner on the approach to the chapel, a statue of the Virgin Mary stood before her. It was the last thing that she saw before her body hit the black and white tiles of the entrance to the chapel.

A few minutes later, a doctor who turned the same corner came across her body lying face down on the floor. Her eyes were closed. The vital signs had gone; there was no breath. From some distance, he heard running. He saw the figure of a beautiful woman. It was Emma. She was too late. Stephanie had gone. Anubis' daughter was gone, leaving only his wife behind on the earthly plane.

# *51*

The Gulf Stream private jet, worth a tidy thirty million US dollars and powered by two Rolls Royce engines, landed with its precious cargo quietly and unannounced at Ezeiza International Airport in Buenos Aires.

On the same day in September, there were several protests around the world, about the ongoing global financial crisis and in Argentina; there were pot-banging demonstrations all over the country about the rising inflation that year as well as escalating violence in Syria. Some of the operations were escalated and paid for by Fabian and his organization. The pay-offs were huge. He transported guns and drugs worldwide now, doing the bidding of The Jester. He opened new branches of the Hexagon Club; this time, he became involved in sex trafficking. It was endless, the devastation of young women's lives. Fabian was becoming less and less willing to lead this life that had been designed for him. But finding no way out, he was forced to continue.

Maxine, dressed in an immaculate pale blue suit, the short skirt just revealing her baby bump, descended down the steps and onto the tarmac. It was windy and hot, typical weather in Argentina at that time of the year. After the grey skies, and the brief, cold early morning encounter with Fabian, it was a relief.

Her shoulder-length dark hair, blown back by the wind, showed her face to be thin and gaunt, with none of the blush and blossoming one would expect for an expectant mother carrying her first child. Her life with Fabian was taking its toll.

Adjacent to the plane was a grey, five-door Mercedes SUV. The rear door was opened by the two men waiting to escort her to the Sierra de la Ventana mountains and Count Fabian Roth's Estancia Villa Stephana, the mountain base for his special operations in Argentina.

Maxine had travelled thirteen hours already, and there was a three-hour drive ahead. They stopped briefly at The Saddle Club, a fancy restaurant on the outskirts of Buenos Aires, frequented by members of the Jockey Club. She was escorted to a table close to the windows overlooking the pool. All eyes had turned to watch her as she made her way to the table; behind her, Fabian's bodyguards. A glamorous, tall woman, obviously pregnant and entering a fancy restaurant full of men, alone with two security guards, was enough to get one's imagination going.

She had removed her jacket and beneath was a see-through flimsy blouse that hardly hid the firm and now swelling breasts of motherhood, pushing upwards from the lacy bustier beneath. Fabian spared no expense on provocative underwear for Maxine. And she loved it all. She looked exotic and their eyes fell on what could be their next prey. She was aware of their looks, as they devoured the sight of her.

There were mostly men in the restaurant and as they feasted their eyes on her, their dicks hardened at their carnal fantasies before returning to table talk with their male companions. It was the breeding season now. Stallions were ready to have their mares. Everyone was on a high and the buying and selling of livestock was bringing in the millions.

She ate alone, picking at the food. And then they were gone again. Maxine rested her head on the soft white leather seats of the SUV, wondering why Fabian had not called her. She could not call him. He hated intrusions. And so, she had to wait for him to initiate a call. Climbing upwards in the SUV, they passed by escarpments and jutting cliffs. She gazed on the scenery with many miles of purple-topped mountains, deserted valleys and trees. It was too rocky for much vegetation, but occasionally there was the surprise of sunflower fields. The yellow densely packed heads of the flowers turned towards the blue skies and white fluffy clouds.

Surely, Fabian would be here in a few days. He had promised. She caressed her growing belly and remembered the night of conception when Fabian had come to her and wound the black silk thread around her, embracing her with his love and his manhood. And then grief coiled up within her heart like a stinging, searing pain that would not leave. It was soon to be her constant companion for the next few days, although she did not know this then. She was alarmed at the intensity and depth of her longing and attachment for him. He was never far from her thoughts, and she was bereft without him, even for a few days.

The car took a turning off the main road and suddenly, they were on a tree-lined road. They passed the massive gates that guarded Fabian's residence. The road wound around for the next two miles lined with Argentina Oaks, the strongest trees in the world, and Pinius Burgeana trees standing fifty feet tall with their curious barks mottled with greys and greens. Soon, the ivy-clad mansion framed with two turrets stood before her in the fading late afternoon sun.

"Madame Cleveland," said the voice, as Maxine stepped from the car onto the gravel drive.

"Oh, you must be Catalina," replied Maxine. "Count Fabian has mentioned you many times."

Maxine remembered all of Fabian's instructions. Catalina was the manager of the mansion. Under her were many staff members; he had given Maxine all the names.

The two women shook hands. Catalina thought Maxine was probably the most beautiful of Count Fabian's women to have come here over the years. Sad though for Maxine, she thought, who would have no idea of the routine now, or that he would have discarded her now she was pregnant.

"Your journey, so long for you, Madame Cleveland – please come in, and I will show you to our main drawing room where we will bring tea for you." She indicated for the men to bring in Maxine's Louis Vuitton cruise bags and trunks.

Maxine felt at a loss for words. She did not know why she was here or for how long. It was just like Fabian to never tell her anything, and why had she brought all this luggage if they were not going to stay here together. Catalina thought Maxine looked very wan and sought to make the conversation light, show her after tea to her rooms, and let her be. The girls always arrived like this, thinking they were the only ones in Count Fabian's life, sometimes heavily pregnant and expecting the Count to arrive in a few days. Of course, he never came. And when the babies were delivered in the adjacent clinic, they were with the mother for only a matter of days. The girls were packed off home, drugged with anti-depressants, given huge sums of money, and told in frank terms to get on with their lives. There were scenes, hysterics; but mostly, they left happy with the money, with the promise of wealth for years to come, but forever mourning the loss of their offspring.

"Your tea, Madame Cleveland; I will leave you to have some time on your own and then one of the housekeepers will show you to your room. Favia will be with you to help you always. Your supper will be brought up to your suite, and tomorrow I will show you the rest of the house and the property. Please rest well." Catalina walked away from Maxine leading the way towards the stairs.

The staircase wound up in a full circle with a white carpet and gold rods securing the fabric in place. Maxine's room was vast, with great pale rose-coloured drapes at the long windows. There were flowers for her everywhere. Antique sofas, also in damask silk, adorned the room, and there were many oil paintings. Maxine recognized a Stubbs painting of racehorses. She remembered that Fabian's most famous polo companions played here in Buenos Aires twice a year.

Catalina noticed Maxine's interest. She had met Maxine's father once when he brought one of Fabian's mistresses here. But Maxine was not to know that, or the fact that Alistair often frequented the high-class brothel in Mayfair or the special soirées at Thackeray Hall known for their salaciousness. Yes,

Alistair was a paid-up member of the Hexagon Club with all its benefits.

"Count Fabian is a keen polo player, as you know. And the polo grounds are only a few miles from here. There are excellent stables on our property, and one or two of the mares are now in heat."

Maxine did not reply. She was in her own world, and Catalina moved to go from the room.

Maxine wanted to ask Catalina when Fabian was returning, but she knew better than to ask in this austere, beautiful place that ran like clockwork. She could not trust anyone. She would have to wait for everything to happen in their time, not hers. She felt drained and exhausted, and her whole body longed for Fabian. She was completely his now, and the baby was their bond. She could not live without him now, the cord between them so strong. Her attachment to him felt like a dark, thick root inside her that had tendrils flowing through the whole of her body and encircling the baby. She felt that if this root was pulled out, it would destroy her completely. There would be no life left in her.

The room was chaste; there was a king-size bed. But the room was empty without her lover. There was a chill, as though a perpetual draft was coming from an open window, but all the sashes were corded and locked.

Favia came in after Catalina had left. She regarded Maxine with interest, and Maxine thought she saw pity lurking there in the shadow of Favia's eyes.

"Where are you from, Favia?" asked Maxine, wanting to make a relationship with this young woman.

"From Brazil, Madame Cleveland," a short polite answer.

"She is not going to give anything away," thought Maxine. "Too carefully trained."

"Have you met Count Fabian Roth?" asked Maxine lightly, surprised at her question, so upfront with someone she hardly knew. She saw Favia pause, her eyes averted for a moment, and then she spoke up.

"Oh, only in his portrait in the dining room. He hardly ever comes here. I have been here five years and have only seen him once or twice," answered Favia, aware of the surprise and shock that was registering on Maxine's face.

"Why ever not? It is his home, is it not?" Maxine ventured, determined that she would not ask any further questions. A chill ran down her spine. Suddenly she felt exhausted. What was happening to her?

"It is only the ladies who come here; that is all..."

Favia moved away towards the door. Maxine could see that she felt she had already given away too much information. Maxine felt out of her depth and wondered what Favia meant by 'the ladies'. Perhaps they were family relations. She put the thought aside.

"Is there anything further that you would like, Madame? The bathroom is through here, and there is a shower and a bath. There is a further sitting room through these doors. This will be your suite while you are here. I will bring up your dinner at eight thirty. Good afternoon, Madame."

Maxine's clothes had already been unpacked and put away. She opened the door into the other sitting room, a small drawing room with a comfy sofa and folded soft red blanket. This was a much cosier room. There was also a computer and a television.

Sitting now on the sofa, having already put on some loose jogging pants and sweater, she drew her knees up, covering herself with the blanket. Feeling lulled into a dreamy state, she turned on the television with the remote.

Within five minutes, she was watching the BBC news channel. The news was breaking to a new story from this morning. The cameras were in London now, broadcasting the death a few hours ago of Jane Crosby-Nash, wife of the well-known lawyer, Fairfax Crosby-Nash, whose clients were too numerous and too famous to mention.

The murder had taken place in their house in Chiswick in the early hours of the morning. They had only just recently arrived back from the South of France.

Mrs Crosby-Nash had been strangled in the kitchen with a piece of electrician's wire, her throat almost cut through; and her grey wolf hound lay beside her with his throat cut. They did not give the dog's name. The newsreader spoke of a violent struggle with the intruders, as though the victim had valiantly tried to ward of the attackers. Forensics said that the dog had died first. Mrs Crosby-Nash was found in a pool of the animal's blood with bruises and marks on her neck. Her husband had been in New York on business and could not be found for comment.

They then turned to the recent story around Jane's visit to her friend, Sir Justin Bowlby, famous London heart surgeon, and his shooting at the famous, annual masked ball in Cannes. He had survived the surprise shooting after a considerable struggle. He was now safely out of hospital.

No one had yet been arrested for the attempted murder, and Sir Justin, recently released from hospital, had gone abroad.

Maxine could hardly believe what she was seeing. She had only recently met all these people: Sir Justin, Lady Anna and Jane Crosby-Nash at Farlingham Park. It was horrendous that this should happen. She thought of her friend Casey and her Cambridge group. Casey was Anna's cousin, and Jane, Anna's best friend. Getting up slowly from the sofa, shocked and weakened by the news, her cup of tea slipped from her hand. At the same time, she felt a warm wet trickle running down her legs. She looked down to see the gush of bright red blood running in rivulets onto the carpet. Her first thought was of Fabian and that she was going to lose their baby.

In Switzerland, Fabian had just arrived in his castle on the craggy black rocks that bore the huge mansion. Randy was due to arrive the next day, and he had his orders.

His head with the black mane of hair was cupped in his hands. Tears were flooding down his face. He could bear his life no longer. After so many years, he had found love in his heart with Maxine. And he could no longer obey The Jester, who had seduced Maxine in nightly sexual orgies beyond the earthly plane. The Jester had demanded that Maxine now be farmed out in South America to deliver her baby, who would then be snatched from her and reared to be a member of his cult with all the other children that The Jester and Fabian had sired between them. They would lose their child to The Jester forever; the evil entity that had owned and occupied his body and soul for years would have finally won.

Fabian now decided that he would break away from The Jester, even if it cost him his life. He could no longer be part of the evil life that had been created for him. As this thought possessed him, Fabian heard shattering glass. The Jester stood before him wearing the ceremonial jester's hat with his hideous slit of a mouth gaping open. He wore all his regalia over his bony body; on his feet, the famous silk shoes ending in points. Fabian's body went cold, as though his life force was drawing away from him. There was silence in the room, as The Jester stared at him with his sharp black eyes willing death to his accomplice. Fabian felt as though a thousand needles were piercing him, and for some strange reason, he started to have an erection.

"If you continue to disobey me, Fabian, your life will be gone. I can snuff you out in two seconds, just as you controlled Anna and took away her life force and filled it with your own." The pale face in front of him was muttering these words.

"Maxine is in danger now. She is bleeding heavily and has been taken to the clinic in your home in Buenos Aires. Obey me, and the baby will be saved; disobey me, and Maxine and the baby will both be dead by morning.

"And, Fabian, just to let you know, that dear friend of Anna's, Jane Crosby-Nash, was strangled at her home in Chiswick today. We used a wire, almost severing her head, and that damn dog of hers is gone. We cut its throat and made her watch it all. Rawlings and his men took care of it. You are far too pathetic now to take on this kind of responsibility. She deserved it, the little bitch, always pushing her long nose in where it did not belong, messing up my plans. She was responsible, with them all, for my death in the pyramids all those lifetimes ago. My death had to be avenged."

The Jester put out his hideous long tongue. It drooled around the orifice of his wet lips. His eyes watched Fabian writhe in agony. He worked Fabian over, laughing in his high-pitched, maniacal way. Fabian slumped back, gasping, as though he was choking. He could not get enough air, and his eyes rolled in terror. At the same moment, he felt himself ejaculate. He felt the warm semen run down between his shaking legs.

And then, The Jester, his regalia and shoes, were back into the glass case, and Fabian was left alone with the madness.

# 52

A storm rent the hot night in Cairo. Anthony was at the Hilton. For weeks, he had laid sleepless on thin mattresses that were his for the lean price he paid for them. Every few days he had moved hotels, so dilapidated and tucked in among the small town of empty dwellings on the outskirts of Cairo, so that no one could find him.

He was exhausted with moving and wanted to stay put in one place. He only left the hotel once a day to find some food and get exercise. Mostly, he had lain on his bed and schemed. It was a strange kind of scheming, because he didn't have any knowledge about what he was scheming against or moving towards. It was like trying to fight a dark spectre on a hideous night. He had no idea where he was bound. Altogether, it was unnerving. There were some days when he wondered if he was alive at all. He remembered the movies he had seen where people were dead and yet, they didn't know it; they found themselves in a hinterland, lost and groundless.

His hair had grown without design or shape. He also had grown a beard, and so his appearance was very different from a couple of months ago.

Then, one day, he felt a thud in his chest. It was as though an external event had taken place to which he must respond.

368

He looked around the bleak room and wondered why he was there. It was like a shocked person who had suddenly come to his senses and wondered what all the fuss was about. "My God," he thought. "Where have I been, and why am I here in this funereal part of Cairo? The world is still going on," he imagined. The best method of defence, he recalled, was attack. Who would want to come and find him anyway in this place? For the first time, he was aware of externals. He knew he had money and access to his credit lines. He had looked at his clothing and was aware that he was wearing the same pair of Levi's and shirt that he had on the day of his arrest. A few times he has washed them, putting them on the balcony and finding something to put on until they were dry.

And then, Anthony had enacted a transformation so astonishing that no one would have recognized him. He had visited a Western barber, had his hair cut in a short business-like style. His beard was removed, and he was once again clean-shaven. He booked himself into the Cairo Hilton, a high-rise building in the middle of the city. He had visited the tailors at the Hilton shops and ordered an array of new clothes, suits, jackets and other business clothes. He purchased everything that he needed to re-join the world.

He knew that his life as a movie director was over; it just wasn't in him to continue. He had no idea what he would do professionally, but it no longer bothered him. His days of mourning his old life were over, at last. He had set the intention of getting back at his enemies, whoever they were.

His plans involved staying at the Hilton for as long as it took to establish whatever it was that he would do next. For some reason, he felt he should not go looking for anyone, that one day someone would turn up at his doorstep and then things would begin. He spent several weeks getting his body strong, swimming in the pool, playing tennis with the other guests and eating good food to make up the weight that he had lost.

One day, he noticed an old issue of *Time* magazine. It was near the bar at the swimming pool. There was a paragraph tucked away in the back of the issue with a photograph of Sir Justin Bowlby. It said he had been shot while on holiday and was in the hospital in Cannes. Anthony noticed that the issue was over two months old. He was shocked but even more shocked to read in a copy of *The Sunday Times* about the recent murder of Jane Crosby-Nash, wife of the well-known barrister at Lincoln's Inn Fields. The write-up was short, describing the early morning intruders to the Chiswick house and the death of her dog, Cedric.

Anthony almost collapsed and went up to his room. With his head in his hands, he sobbed for Jane, for Justin, his friends. He was appalled and shocked at what had happened to his friends, and most of all, Jane. He was devastated this had happened to her; he had spent such a beautiful time with her in Shropshire, and she had taken such good care of him and been so kind. He had been away from his life and news for over two months. It was sad that this was the way he had to catch up. He had Justin's home number but decided to phone the hospital instead. He got through to Felicity. Justin had given Anthony her number saying that she would always know where he was.

"I'm trying to get in touch with Sir Justin; we met in the summer. I only just heard that he was shot in Cannes a couple of months ago." Anthony was merely direct with her. She responded well and liked his voice. He did not want to mention Jane.

"Well, he is fine now. He made a remarkable recovery," said Felicity.

"He is back at the hospital then?" he queried.

"Well, no, he isn't. It was decided that he take leave for the next six months. He needed the rest and the change." Felicity was a bit concerned that she had given away so much, but she was in the office for days alone trying to sort out all Justin's office work. She was glad to be able to talk to someone.

"Where are you calling from? Can I take your name?" remembering that Justin might want to know who the caller was.

"Well, yes, I would be pleased if you would pass on the information. My name is Anthony Jackson and I am staying at the Cairo Hilton." He was pleased with his performance. He was still able to function and still had a brain.

"Have you been in Cairo long?" she asked.

"Well, yes actually, this time for two months." He was surprised at the question.

She was not allowed to tell Anthony why she was asking these questions. She had promised Justin that the one-way ticket to Cairo would remain a secret with her. "Anyway, I must go, there is another call coming in. I will pass on your message to Sir Justin." The phone was put down abruptly and Anthony did not have time to ask her about Jane; it was too late. But as he thought about it again, he realized it wasn't a question he should have been asking Justin's assistant.

As for Casey, he could not reach her at all. She was not in New York, in Cambridge or anywhere else he could think of. He was getting close to despair. Even Vince and the film crew had disappeared. His life was a real charade of cut-out characters that came and went as they chose.

Anthony lay back on the bed, exhausted. It was his first real contact with anyone for a long time. He felt he had been on the moon. His mind engaged again, wondering whether Justin would try to reach him. It never occurred to Anthony that Justin was looking for him. He wandered the streets again, became tired of the endless tennis matches and the food that was far too rich for him. He thought of Jane often, mourned her passing and wondered again who was behind her murder. He grieved for the long lovely afternoons with her at the house in Shropshire, the breakfasts on the lawns, and wondered if he would be able to reach her husband Fairfax. He found it hard to believe she was dead, the wonderful woman that she was, a life wasted and in vain. There was nothing in the press about any of the Cambridge set – Jane's death nor any mention of Sir Justin Bowlby. It was obviously being kept under wraps.

Fairfax had in fact gone into hiding, not apparently in his offices, nor at home; the house already up for sale. Anthony could make nothing of it. Everyone was either dead or gone underground.

Fairfax was at work; he had taken up new temporary offices, which Lucille visited but no one else. Their total focus was to bring members of the Hexagon Club to trial for an endless list of sexual crimes, almost too horrific to imagine – crimes against young girls and women, the grooming and mind-control. Some names were known to Lucille, and others were leaked by members who had either become frightened or were too dismayed by what the club was turning into.

At the end of the month, Anthony had not received any calls. Nothing was happening. He was in his room one evening when the phone rang; it was the reception downstairs.

"You have a visitor, sir. Justin Bowlby. Will you be coming down?" asked the concierge. How typical, thought Anthony, of Justin not to use his full title, a title that was not inherited but bestowed for the great honour he had brought to his own profession as a heart surgeon.

Anthony went down to the lobby. He was surprised when he saw Justin. He was so gaunt and seemed a lot older than he had remembered him. They shook hands warmly, and Anthony invited him back up to his suite. They closed the door on the outside world.

"Anthony, it wasn't easy to get here. My life is fraught with all sorts of dangers, not to mention social and family difficulties." He could see Anna's face now pleading with him not to leave but to rest at home with her. But home and England had somehow become a prison for him now. "So I apologize for giving you no warning at all. It must seem strange for you to have someone showing up like this," he finished. "I had to do everything in secret; no one knows I am here and still I am in danger. You have no doubt heard about Jane." Tears welled up in Justin's eyes, as he mentioned the name of his beloved friend; his shoulders started to heave. Beloved to both Anna and himself, he wondered if he would ever get over her death.

"No, it's not strange at all, you turning up. I am so sad at your loss of such a dear friend, Jane, I can hardly believe it. I had such a beautiful time with her at her house, I just cannot believe that she is gone. It is so terrible. After I spoke with Felicity a few days ago, I had a feeling that you may come. Somehow, you were the link I needed to get back to some sense of reality," continued Anthony.

"Well, it's a bit like that for me. All those days at the hospital, knowing that I was dying, I thought of you. I knew my life would never be the same again, in my mind, even before the shooting. I booked a flight to Cairo. I was restless and had been since Farlingham Park. I wanted to leave my life the way it was; I just could not go on. It was like living someone else's life." Justin thought about Stephanie. What had she been feeling? He still didn't understand her death. Somehow, it was linked with his recovery; he knew that much.

Anthony was staring at him, trying to gauge his thoughts. "Stephanie died, you know; she had a cardiac arrest at midnight. She had just been to see me, although I was not really aware of it at all." Tears welled up in his eyes, as he continued to talk about his love for her – such loss and grief: Jane, Anna, Stephanie.

"She was a rare flower, always radiant. She loved everyone. In a way, I knew she didn't belong to this world. I wasn't surprised that she went, but I didn't really feel that it was her time. I feel she was seduced away; I must find out. It seemed almost as though I would not have lived if she had not died. Just a hunch, Anthony, one of the things I have to find out about." Anthony was indeed dismayed at Stephanie's death; like Justin, he simply could not understand it.

Justin and Anthony spent the whole night talking. They had so much in common now. They talked about what was happening to everyone who was in the group at Farlingham Park. There was a bonding that had taken place that weekend, as though a cloak of protection had surrounded them all and was still there, in a sense. Together they mourned Jane, felt the loss between them as a growing bond; they were both still in shock and disbelief. Justin too had not been able to contact Fairfax.

"Justin, where is Casey? What's happened to her?" Anthony was anxious for information; his mind was going fast, covering all the news, forming ideas and discarding them.

"Casey had also been under attack for some months now, even before Farlingham Park; and then Jane had also been attacked. I wish that I had taken her more seriously now; it could have saved her life. She kept telling me that we were all in danger; I thought she was being hysterical." Justin could not believe he was talking about these things; he was a medical man, a scientist who believed only in measurable facts. "She went to a shop near Farlingham Park and was hit and thrown on the floor. The scene disappeared before her eyes, as though it had never happened. Then one night she had called me; she said then, the phone was cut off, and she was attacked near the gates of the house. Again, she found herself next morning in bed without even a bruise. I didn't believe her at first, but she insisted it had happened. She had only one piece of real evidence and that was a brand-new padlock the men had thrown from the gate." Justin was starting to get worked up about the events that had affected his family and friends. Jane's death and his near-death experience were taking a great toll on him.

They decided to rest and went down to the reception to get Justin's suite organized. He insisted on not using his title at the reception. They found a suite for him down the corridor, just a little way away from Anthony. They wished each other a good night. Anthony did not ask about Casey again, although he wanted to; but he felt Justin for some reason was avoiding the subject.

They talked for days on end, sharing memories of their past lives that Emma had helped them understand. They had started to re-experience these memories and now had more understanding about the situations they were in. Both knew about their lifetimes in Egypt and the Hyksos Dynasty where Justin had been the presiding pharaoh. He had murdered the magician of the temple and that Anthony had assisted him. This way, they were both in danger of murder by The Jester who was the evil entity behind the disembodied form of the magician from all those lifetimes ago. Their past lives and those of their friends, it was going to be years before they understood the curse that was still upon them, the vengeance still strong against them in this current lifetime.

# 53

Angela Nicholson tapped on the intercom with a newly manicured right index finger. The nail polish was a deep shade of red.

"Patrizia, get up here quickly." Her deep resonant voice found its way to the lower parts of the Mayfair House. Angela was looking at the email from Maxine to Fabian. She saw the entreaties for a return to status quo. Maxine was obviously not satisfied with her life in exile; not only was she not satisfied, she was threatening life itself. Angela thought dryly about the fate of yet another candidate for Fabian's available position of queen of the beehive. Angela had scaled too many heights to have any compassion for those who trod after her.

"Patrizia, get yourself on a flight to Argentina. Maxine needs some attention; the Count has farmed her out. You know how he detests pregnant women. We have to take care of her; she may produce the wanted son. You know he likes to have the babies and children educated at the school. Anyway, you know all the ropes. Make sure she's having all the right treatment; she's on the edge." She looked straight at her.

"Oh, and by the way, please call Mandy. She's expecting guests tonight. She needs three outfits picked up from the designers in Knightsbridge. Order the Rolls for this evening.

They are going to Thackeray Hall in Buckinghamshire. It's an overnight do," she added.

"Is Mandy going on her own, or do you want another girl to travel with her?" asked Patrizia.

"No, there are seven girls already there. That's the arrangement. Mandy can drive up there in one of our cars. I'm leaving for Switzerland tonight. Send him an email, will you? Say that Casey has been poking her nose around the house in St John's Wood. She may be planning to get in. Rawlings wants to know their next move. Also, Sir Justin took a flight to Cairo. I know it's hands off Justin now, but he has just joined Anthony at the Hilton. Oh, yes, and tell him that Anna is back in Grassock Oaks. Sean's drawn up the manuscripts that he wanted on Witches Lore in Belgium, the fifteenth century document. Please send them to me." Angela thrust a large wad of money into Patrizia's hand. "That's for expenses."

She stood up now, away from her desk. Her beige linen suit fitted the willowy figure like a glove. She moved towards the window.

What Angela did not know was that her whole world had already been turned upside down in the last twenty-four hours and more change was to come. Angela did not go to Switzerland. She was warned off, and a little rumour was around that there was to be a police raid at the Hexagon Club. No, things had not gone well for Fabian, the club or anything else for that matter since he had invited Lord Oliver to take his own life at the villa in Uruguay. No one had seen Fabian for over a week, nor was he in contact with his organization anywhere in the world. Randy was also nowhere to be found. Patrizia flew to Argentina but was told Maxine had already gone, with no hint as to where. The staff were tight-lipped and revealed nothing about her whereabouts or that of Count Fabian Roth, their lord and master.

In England, a certain Inspector Rawlings was crossing St. John's Wood Road when a car came hurtling around a corner. He was hit by the car and, although taken to hospital, he did not recover. No one gave it a second thought, just another city accident.

# 54

Randy had been picked up from Zurich with a very small suitcase. She had no coat on for some reason, and her knee-high socks had slid down her legs. Her tangled hair looked as though it had not been combed for weeks, and she also looked extremely hungry. Fabian was furious with Casey for not making sure she was looked after. He had dismissed all his servants for the day, so he took it upon himself to take care of her. He immediately ran a hot bath for her. He indicated the bath, the soap and the shampoo, and then he shut the door and left her to it.

In her room, he had some clothes for her: loose knit sweaters and some pants, socks and underwear. For some reason, he knew how to look after a child.

In the kitchen, he started to make breakfast and place some calls.

"Catalina, please put me through to Maxine immediately," grasping the phone in a vice like grip.

"Sir, I am unable to do that. She is heavily sedated and in the clinic."

Catalina knew Fabian's moods well and was anxious not to get his anger going. Fabian had called many times since The Jester had told him that Maxine could lose the baby. He was beside himself.

"Why was I not called immediately?" he asked, barely controlling his anger.

"It was middle of the night," came the sheepish reply. Fabian had been trying for hours to reach Maxine.

"So, what is happening now with her and the baby?"

Randy was calling out to him from the bathroom. He was worried now that she had slipped and hurt herself.

He told Catalina that he would be back in a moment.

He opened the door and saw Randy completely naked standing in the bath, demanding some help with her hair. The shampoo was running down her face and had obviously got into her eyes. She seemed completely unaware that she was in a strange house, in an unknown bathroom, and was standing there in her nudity.

He told her he was on the phone with an urgent call, to sit down in the water, and he would come to her in five minutes. He saw her mouth tremble then, and tears filling her soap-filled eyes. Her hair was hopeless, and it was going to take hours.

"She and the baby are fine. But, she was hysterical. She was apparently told by one of the maids that you never come here, and so she has been expecting that you would abandon her." Catalina thought it would be better to tell him half the truth. Maxine had threatened to kill herself and the baby, but Catalina was not going to share that with the Count.

"Put me onto the doctor." Fabian had had enough of Catalina's simpering, he wanted the hard facts.

"He has gone to Buenos Aires," she replied.

"Well give me his fucking mobile number then," he shouted. He was beyond livid. "When Maxine wakes up, tell her I will speak with her later, and I will be there at the end of the week, as soon as I can manage to get out of here."

Fabian was sweating profusely; drops of water fell onto his brow and down his face. "God," he thought, "I am a mess," as he rushed back to the bathroom to find Randy playing with the soap, squirting it across the bath and back again. There was no sign of the shampoo. But then, he saw that it was lying on the floor; she had either dropped it or thrown it across the room in her temper.

She was beautiful. He was surprised she had allowed him into the bathroom, but she seemed unconcerned that he could view her body. Her back arched as she held her head back, so he could wash her hair. It was a mass of tangles still. She had overused the shampoo, and the foam was starting to go all over the bathroom floor. "Shit," he thought to himself; perhaps this was a big mistake, bringing this kind of liability into his home.

"What is in that room with the glass case and the weird hat inside? It looks like a Punch and Judy outfit!" Her eyes were shut and her head down, as he put shampoo all over her long hair. She was washing her stomach with soap, completely unabashed.

"How did you get in there? It is usually locked, Randy." He whispered to her, not wanting to frighten her.

"I did not like it in there. I felt all kinds of pins and needles, and then I heard this bell sound. I ran out after that. Don't worry; I am not going in there again!"

Fabian hoped that she would not pursue her original question. But she did, just as he was rinsing her hair and smoothing the water away from her forehead.

"It is a long story, Randy, not a very nice one. I don't like the hat either, or the room, but I don't know how to get rid of it."

Indeed, that morning, he had been wondering how to rid himself of The Jester. Already, he had disobeyed him by calling Argentina; the instructions were not to see Maxine again.

"Well, why don't you bury it into the ground? That is how you get rid of a voodoo doll and its curse. You wrap it in white cotton, rub it in sea salt, go deep into the woods and bury it."

Fabian was wondering how on earth a small ten-year-old knew something as specific as this.

He did not answer her immediately.

The Jester's instructions to him regarding Randy were to entrap her so that later as a mature girl at sixteen, she would come to them and would be ready to be deflowered. They would then take their pleasure with her. His mind slid back to Oliver's death; it was unfortunate but the death of a minor at the Hexagon Club would have been a potential disaster.

Fabian decided there and then that nothing would happen to Randy. He was not going to entrap her, entice her, seduce her or obey The Jester in any way. As he went through these thoughts, he felt a tug in his belly, as though the energy was seeping out of his body.

Randy noticed immediately that some change had taken place.

"You have a curse on you, don't you?" Randy eyed him with her enormous blue eyes.

He could not believe that he was hearing this.

She lay down in the bath on her back, head submerged as in the movies, when one wonders if there will be suicide or a sharp intake of air as the head comes up. But she was just letting all the shampoo run off her hair.

Fabian inwardly moaned at her budding beauty and felt like Humbert with his Dolores Haze in the book *Lolita* that he had read so many times. He knew it by heart. How many times had he read Nabokov's delectable description of this passion?

"You do, don't you? That is why you are quiet." Her head had come up from the water. She pursed her rosebud lips at him, and he moaned inwardly a second time.

"It is complicated, Randy. It is very complicated."

Fabian knew he had an issue that had haunted him his entire life. He loved young girls. He had nursed photographs of these young girls given to him by their fathers, promising favours later. And there had been his own sister, arousing him to the point of despair. It was a terrible life that he had led.

"Time to get out, get those tangles out of your hair, and get your breakfast." He was leaving now, wanting to make a quick exit.

As he walked across the bathroom and opened the door, looking back, he just caught the sight of her eyes staring after him, seeing things he did not want her to see.

He checked his emails while getting the eggs ready for Randy's breakfast.

"Oh, what the fuck?"

It looked like Casey was also on her way here. She was very angry he had taken Randy to stay with him in Switzerland.

The email announced her arrival rather than requested it. Today was Saturday, and she was due to arrive Sunday afternoon.

His life was an insane dance, an endless dance with The Jester. He had no idea who he was without The Jester's presence. He felt that there was no other option now but to finish him off. He shuddered at the thought. He vowed to himself that once he had killed The Jester, he would find out who he really was, get his own life back.

Randy came into the kitchen from the bathroom; she was dried and wore the pyjamas that he had bought for her, a complete miracle.

Immediately, without hesitation, she climbed onto Fabian's knee.

They worked on getting her hair untangled with the use of a huge comb that she brought with her, and the gold hairdryer left over after an overnight party at his brothel. He thought he was finally going mad.

Randy had yelled at him for his incompetent combing, and then dissolved into giggles at his jokes. She immediately adored him; he was so incredibly handsome.

"When did you meet Stephanie?" Fabian asked gently. He did not know whether Randy knew yet of her death.

"Oh, I know she is dead, Fabian. She told me at Farlingham Park that she would not live long. Justin did the surgery and all, but she knew that her heart was not good. She loved Justin so much. They had a special bond."

Fabian thought that Randy had in fact no idea how special that bond was, that Stephanie had in fact bargained her life for Justin's. The Jester fell in love with Stephanie. He wanted her and so he took her to the lands he inhabited above the earthly plane. Fabian had all these facts at his fingertips.

"Stephanie taught me a lot when we met at Farlingham Park. She taught me how to read an aura. She said Anna did not have one. She thought Anna would also die soon."

A jab of pain hit Fabian. It was as though a dark shadow passed over him. His great love, Anna – the last time they had met, when Justin was shot, was unbearable for them both.

Fabian shifted his position in the chair when he thought about it. Randy was half asleep now, nestled into his chest, her now tangle-free hair cascading over his navy-blue Guernsey sweater.

He was deeply sorry now for what he had done to Anna. He had taken her at such a young age, and she had given herself to him so completely. And the last time they met, he should not have ravaged her in the way that he did – videoing the debauchery at the same time. The way he had hooked up her arms, tied her legs, and clamped her open – no, it was wrong of him. She had no control at all, and he remembered how he pushed himself down her throat; then toyed with her; finally fucking her till she was screaming for more. God, it was good, this kind of power! But now he knew the pain that it caused to Anna and others that he had treated in this way. He had taken human lives, caused terrible suffering and disturbance to so many young girls' lives. It was terrible. The more he became aware, the more he shared Anna's suffering and wanted to repent. He could not go on. It had to stop.

But Anna was suffering and had suffered for a long time. He felt sad now that he had taken so much of her life at such a young age. She had had no chance to have her own life. She did not know who she was at all. Her marriage was in ribbons, all because of his lust and greed.

Fabian was becoming human; he was feeling things like love and compassion. It frightened him. It was all new to him; before it was money and power and sex, but now something else seeped into his soul. How had he gone on so long?

Randy shifted, fully awake now. Maybe she had sensed his thoughts; she looked into his deep black eyes. Somehow, she was floating and finding that she was drawn into his magic. His hand was on her back, and she put her bare foot along his other leg. She was almost on top of him now, breathing gently while she rested.

"Randy, we need to get up now. I have to put some logs on the fire."

"I don't want to move. I like being here with you." She pouted at him. "I want to stay here with you forever in your castle and be your princess. You can buy me lots of dresses and take me to fancy restaurants."

"It is time you got dressed for the day; take off these pyjamas. Then, we can eat breakfast by the fire, if you like, and I will tell you some stories of far-off days and the kings and queens of this land in the mountains."

Randy was successfully distracted by this and went off to her room to put on some of the items Fabian had prepared for her.

Fabian went out for some logs. He noticed the open door of the room where the glass case held The Jester's talisman. He heard a sound and was about to go in, but on second thought, he slammed the door shut, locked it, and put the key in his pocket.

After a day of innocent reverie, Randy had finally gone to her bedroom to sleep without argument. Fabian sat on the leather sofa in front of the fire. He was cold and depressingly weak. The embers of the fire were dying. He sat there. Eventually, he put another log on. Though drained, he was far from wanting to sleep yet.

He lay back drinking another scotch and soda and thought of Jane. Tears again started welling in his eyes, as he thought about her murder as it must have been, in the kitchen in the afternoon. It was horrendous to think about it and the thought of the dog with its throat cut in front of her very eyes. She had adored Cedric; he went everywhere with her.

He had first met Jane at Anna's house, or rather her father's house, in Cambridge. He was a very celebrated Emeritus Professor in Law for many years, then had become the dean of his college. This must have been twenty years ago, when Anna was fifteen years old, the year before he had taken her virginity and she had become his forever in that strange ceremony, in the house that had too many secrets. She had had no idea of what went on and had been heavily programmed from such an early age. Fabian grieved now for her, that she had lost any kind of proper childhood and had been groomed entirely for him. She had been so delectable, so beautiful that he having enjoyed her wanted to share her sexual secrets with his friends. It was a terrible thing to do, and she was so open and trusting of him. She always did what she was asked.

Anna's father had promised Anna to him and had kept her under very strict watch to make sure her dates were much prescribed. Then, Jane and Anna were just schoolgirls, flirting with dons who graced her father's table. Her mother Lucille had been a debutante and reminded him even then of Lauren Bacall, mysterious and looking at you with those half-closed eyes, those full lips somehow smiling as she looked at you. Whether she was aware of her husband's sexual exploits abroad, Fabian did not know, but he knew she was aware that he himself had entertained designs on her daughter for a long time.

The house was a paradise, set in wild parkland on the edge of Cambridge, with deer and a lake. There were stables and outhouses. It was all too idyllic. The Cambridge crowd would gather at the weekends, playing tennis and having drinks on the terrace overlooking the woods beyond.

Jane, always a little wan with her long red hair flowing down her back, would come often to spend time with Anna. Already, she was brilliant and destined for the university and a double first.

Her death was an agony to him, as well as Anna suffering. He hated himself for what he had become. It was really his fault and callousness that had caused Jane's death.

Now he had cut himself off from the power of The Jester and vowed to destroy him, even though he knew that may have meant the end of his own life. He had to take the risk; there was no other way. Love had taken over his heart. He had found Maxine. He wanted to be with her and their child forever.

# 55

Justin had been in Cairo now for two weeks, to be with Anthony and to go back into the pyramid. They were conspiring to rid themselves and their circle of The Jester and prevent any further killings. Justin had advised Casey not to come; in fact, he had forbidden it. She was in too much danger herself, too wrought about her stepfather's death. Justin did not know it but there was worse to come for Casey, as Fairfax was getting closer to exposing the vast Hexagon Club and Lord Oliver. Casey would find herself revealed as the victim in the terrible deeds of Antigone and her stepfather.

Justin hated Fabian now, as he had tricked and duped him, taking Anna from him. Anna had been Fabian's mistress now for so many years. Justin had finally talked with Sidney about his suspicions. They had taken a long walk on their land at The Beeches one Sunday afternoon after lunch. It was a windy day, cold and damp. For some reason, Justin had found himself bringing up the whole terrible subject of his marriage to Anna. It was so out of character for Justin to do this but he had reached a point of complete despair. In the long walk and the silence, Sidney was ready for him. He could see that Justin was close to exploding. It was better Justin let himself go with him rather than in the operating theatre. And so, Sidney, who knew a great deal about Anna and her lover Fabian, gave Justin an abridged version and nothing about her trips to the Hexagon Club and illicit affairs. Justin had asked if there were other men but Sidney knew his friend would not be able to take this. He assured him it was just Fabian. Justin believed the lie. Now Justin thought to himself, "Let Fabian keep his whore; he had no further use for Anna in his life." He still found it hard not to think about the black thread that he had found in its sequined box in her drawer. He thought about the years of infidelity, the wasted love, the passion that he had felt for Anna that would never be satisfied.

He was drumming his fingers on the table, as he sat opposite Anthony. They were in total silence except for the sound of the aria *Un bel di vedremo*, from Puccini's *Madame Butterfly* wafting out of the room through the elegant windows that were flung open, embracing the breeze from the Nile. The hotel was expensive and luxurious, and they were in Justin's penthouse suite.

The room was heavy with their grief at losing Jane. Justin had known Jane since the early days of Cambridge. He was thinking about her young years, only eighteen and headed for a successful career. She was always lovely, with her very red hair pulled behind her in the famous pigtail. She wore some eccentric clothes in those days, was outspoken and full of fun, attending the many parties. Now, it felt as though a requiem should be sung for her short life. He shuddered at the thought of the murder at her home in Chiswick and that of Cedric, her beloved dog whom she adored. It was unthinkable. They had not seen or heard from Fairfax for weeks, and there were no answers to any email or phone calls. He had obviously gone to ground in his agony. It was as though they had all vanished into the thin air.

Justin felt that Jane had never found herself in the world after Cambridge. She was so other worldly and found it hard to connect with real practical things; going off to Cairo had unsettled her, and she never talked about the magic she had studied there among the tombs. He felt she was a lost soul, as lost as Anna had been. Maybe this is why they had been such close friends; in some ways, they had understood each other's universes. But then Anna had a secret life and had successfully duped them all; except, of course, for Sidney Henderson, their interior designer and friend. He had guessed Anna's secret and had tried to warn them all about the dangers they faced. But none of them had believed him until it was far too late.

"Anna..." said Anthony moving to a more comfortable chair away from the table.

"Yes, I am thinking about her, all alone at The Beeches. There is no one for her now – too much loss, the end of our marriage; her son gone; and now, Jane, her close friend; if she ever really enjoyed closeness with anyone," he added sarcastically.

How could he have been so stupid, even as a doctor, not to realize that there had been something wrong with Anna; a vacant expression, too much beauty, a denial of the sexual side of their marriage? She had a strong inclination to take tranquilizers; he should have seen the warning signs. But he never could see her difficulties because he fell in love with her and had come under her spell, always longing for her but never reaching her shores. She was always remote and unavailable, enticing and enchanting, a woman of the deepest secrets.

And now this revelation, that all this time she had really been a mistress to Fabian, a man he never wished to set eyes on. He was the Devil himself and had ruined Anna for any normal kind of life. But Justin did not know the half of it. He was unaware that Casey's stepfather had sexually awakened Anna at nine years old one rainy day in Cambridge. No one knew what Anna had to bear in those long young years of her early life.

No one knew that there were times in her marriage when Anna would take any lover; it did not matter who or where, although she was always careful. It was her secret entirely. She was out of control when she felt these strong sexual appetites, and it led her into dangerous places. She would travel, stay in five-star hotels, incognito, just to be away and take a lover. She carried the thread with her and the blood-coloured whip. Men would be only too happy to join her in her suite for a night of entertainment that even they could not have imagined. And then, she would return home with some excuse for Justin about her work and how she had to do research in Europe, as though nothing had happened. It was true; Anna was a high-class whore. And she always took great wads of notes from the men. It was part of her game with them. It was just as well Justin did not know even half of it all. It would have broken him to know the realities of the woman with whom he shared his life.

"Justin, we have to go into the pyramid tomorrow." Anthony could see Justin was still lost in thought. He still looked very pale, and his cheeks had dark hollows that matched the lines under his eyes.

"What exactly are we going to do? Are you hoping that we will find the entrails of The Jester?" Justin's humour was at its worst.

"He has a presence there, a residence for a being that does not really live on the earthly plane; it is a feat in itself. He lives, I am told, at the very point of the pyramid. If we find him, we can make sure that he leaves the earth and no longer has any power." Anthony was in full swing now with his ideas.

Justin stared at Anthony in some disbelief. For Justin, who was used to stitching people's hearts back into their chest walls and who had lived in a completely logical and predictable universe, this was quite an intellectual leap.

He remained silent; his now longish pale hair flopped over his face, the long, pensive and drawn face which, as he bent over the glass table, was reflected back at him. His life had nearly ended at The Jester's bidding; his wife was no longer in his life, and he had passed the life of being a heart surgeon. It had vanished into thin air. He had enjoyed all the privileges of society and rarely questioned his own existence. But now, he had experienced shock after shock, which had finally led him to question who he really was.

His blue eyes focused on Anthony, as he went to shut the doors to the balcony. It was the end of the day, and it was getting cold; the bright Egyptian sun was starting to recline on the coming of the moon.

"It is really hard to explain all this to you. I spent months, even more than a year, researching the secrets of these pyramids. It is a tricky science and involves more than one-dimensional thinking." Anthony saw Justin's eyes narrow in a kind of disbelief, but he said nothing.

"All I know is that Sean and Vince had found out amazing things about this multidimensional existence." Anthony persevered with Justin, trying to explain things to him in a language that he would understand.

Anthony had knowledge now of the chambers and their secrets in the upper reaches of the pyramids. The burial place of 'Ka' was set on the same course as the North Pole's celestial spheres. The Pharaoh, once dead, ascended to heaven to join the inextinguishable stars. Sean had worked out that the spells they had found in the sacred papers connected to the evolutionary cycle of the pharaoh's afterlife. Anthony had yearned for the magic of the magician, for the pharaoh who had been buried in this same pyramid. Anthony guessed that The Jester was a reincarnation of the magician who had tried to take the life of the pharaoh before it was due.

"Where are Sean and Vince now, Anthony?" asked Justin, as though he was reading Anthony's thoughts. He drained his glass of wine. They had enjoyed drinks and canapés that had been brought up to them an hour ago.

"I don't know. I have no idea. They could just have been a figment of my imagination. Maybe all this stuff never happened. The mind conjures up things just to invent the self." Anthony was lost in thought. He knew not whether his dreams in the night were imagined or his daily life.

"The self?" asked Justin, raising his eyebrows high in his forehead; disbelief was written all over his aquiline face, the thin mouth drawn now into a hard line.

"We are facing the question of karma here. If karma is upon a person, then that which comes into existence between the body and self dissolves into its own source and drops its form. When there is no sense of 'I', then there is no longer any karma." Anthony sounded sure, but Justin felt as confused as ever.

Anthony was trying to work out why The Jester couldn't inhabit a body on earth, yet still had a life. He had not taken over Fabian entirely. Anthony simply did not know enough to figure it out. All he wanted to do was go back into the chambers of the pyramid and find out where The Jester had been and to get rid of him.

"You have lost me, Anthony. I have not the slightest inkling of what you are talking about. It is hard for me; my mind is so much on Jane and Anna, it is hard to be speculative or to understand these esoteric things. But I will come with you; however, it will be you who finds the way for us." Justin's words gave Anthony some comfort. He was grateful that Justin was here. Otherwise, he would have been entirely alone.

Justin felt as though he was in an isolation tank. Emma had explained some things to him, that each person was re-incarnated from another lifetime and that he had been the Pharaoh in the lifetime when his consort Nehesy had been the mistress of one of his principle advisors. This advisor had been Fabian who was enjoying his own former lifetime. In another incarnation, he himself had been also the physician to King George IV, and his wife was the mistress of his own brother. The Countess of Rigby, Amelia, was Justin's wife in that life and this. The Jester hovered around them hoping to vanquish them forever as revenge for when he was incarcerated in the tomb of the Pharaoh as punishment for taking the poisonous asp to the Pharaoh before his allotted time. Justin could just not take this on board at the present time. He was too involved in his own grief and loss. He also experienced himself as a rudderless boat. There was no sense of going anywhere but into his own being.

At dawn the next day, the jeep was ready to take Justin and Anthony to the tomb and the very pyramid where The Jester had been incarcerated in his former life as the magician.

The door was open, but as they walked in, the sun was already strong on the doorway and they did not notice the two horned vipers, often seen by the Egyptians as the Devil incarnate.

"Get back, Justin!" cried Anthony as he saw the snakes. Justin was just about to step into the small pit in which they lay entwined.

Justin moved back quickly. Anthony took his measure of the snakes; his sharp eyes calculated the danger. The snakes were asleep or dozing and he indicated to Justin to walk around the pit, in this way not disturbing them. It was a horrible omen to both and already they felt the danger.

Soon they were in passages familiar to Anthony, and he measured where the corridors were to the upper recesses. This way, he took a different turn and had the maps that Vince, not Sean, had drawn up for him.

In two hours, they had reached the top of the pyramid and stood outside a wooden door. It was locked. They sat on the steps, weary from the climb.

A bright light came on, and around them they could see cameras and movie projectors as if from nowhere. It was as though they had entered a movie set and strangely, they were unable to move from the steps.

A screen stood before them, and they saw Farlingham Park as it was in 1820. It showed the hallways of the mansion and the great pentacles that had been drawn across the floor to represent the magic and erotic practices of the era. The Countess was dressed in the costume of the times, and she was indeed alluring in her beauty. She seemed to be alone in the house, but there were guests and their orgies on that night. Then shots were taken of her in the upper chambers and the long room with the casement windows where she had been found after her death.

The scenes were dreadful. Justin and Anthony were visibly distressed as they watched The Jester and two other men set upon the Countess, tying and gagging her before they took their sport with her. You could see their long penises entering her naked body from all angles. She was hung up, and beaten till she breathed no more. In the beginning, it had been a game with her lover; in their excesses, they had not seen The Jester and his men appear through the door. Then, once dead, they made the necessary incisions on her body to prepare for the opening of the mouth ceremony and the preparation for her burial.

The last shot was of her hand hanging down, one finger adorned with the ring on which was painted a tiny picture of her husband's eye. That year, it was the rage to have such a ring created and to be worn for all to see.

Justin and Anthony were in darkness again. They sipped some water they had brought with them. All this time, Anthony was calculating how to bring down the wooden door that was at present locked and barring their way. Justin was clearly dazed.

Then the lights came on again; the same screen came on flashing tiny pictures that they could not read. This time there were pictures of Fabian; pictures of him with Anna in her young years; photos of Casey with her stepfather; then pictures that neither Anthony nor Justin could bear to see, of young girls being assaulted by older men. They did not recognize any of the people, but it made them ill looking at them.

Anthony got up and went to hit the screen with his cane, but the cane went straight through the screen as though it hung in space with no physical form. He then went for the cameras but again they had no physical being; his cane was hitting out at nothing at all.

In front of them, they heard long maniacal laughs and the tinkling of bells. The Jester stood before them laughing, but he had only half a body, as though his existence had been eaten up. He was losing his power. Justin and Anthony did not know that Fabian and Casey had buried his hat and regalia at the house in Switzerland, but because of this he only had half his power and half his body.

Anthony lit a match and a long taper he had brought with him. There was nothing there and no sound.

"There is nothing, Justin, just nothing. These movie screens were in our own imaginings. There is no Jester. He does not exist. It is the poison or spectres within our own minds," screamed Anthony as he banged the locked door. He set the taper to it to burn the door. But instead the door simply vanished.

There was nothing in the bleak room with its whitewashed walls save three pictures on the wall in black and white, carefully and elaborately framed. The pictures hung in a row. There were spotlights in the ceiling that highlighted the pictures and their artistry to excellent advantage. The floor was made of light oak floorboards. The room was obviously newly renovated.

The first was a photograph of Anna in her twenties. She was sitting on Lord Pemberton's lap in his study at his home in Cambridge. It was like a portrait of the lord of the manor and the mistress of an aristocratic family. Anna's head was held high, as she posed for the picture. Both Anna and Lord Pemberton were completely naked. Anna sat astride him with her back to the camera. Her arms were above her head, in the act of tossing her long mane of dark hair. She was leaning forward slightly, the camera catching her in the act of kissing her lover.

The second portrait was of Casey, a woman of some beauty, standing by her stepfather. The picture had been taken in the woods. Both figures were again naked. Casey wore only a black suspender belt; one leg bore a black fishnet stocking attached to the belt. A leather 'O' choker was around her slender neck. Oliver had on a medieval long-nosed mask.

The third picture was of Fabian, also naked with his hand on the alluring and youthful buttocks of a young African woman; she was tied by the fingers to a narrow iron metal bed.

There was nothing at all in the room besides these three pictures.

Justin and Anthony stared horrified at all three pictures. As they looked, Lord Pemberton's face started to peel away, revealing the face of a hideous man with a slit of a gaping mouth. Fabian's face in the photograph was also melting, and there before them also stood The Jester. He had eaten away the lives and souls of both Lord Oliver and Fabian.

Then, as though by magic, everything around them disappeared; the pictures, the room and the pyramid were all gone; a strong wind blew their bodies here and there, and they lost sight of each other in an ocean of space.

They had been pulled into The Jester's universe, and it was his face alone that was behind the serious and entrancing face of Lord Pemberton and Fabian. They were in the nether regions of the world from where there was no escape. Once again, he was the master of their minds, which existed now only in the chaos of their own imaginings.

But once again, Emma rescued the two of them from the spiralling karmas of The Jester's world. He was the master of treachery and the author of all that was demonic on the earthly plane. Again and again, he could conjure and confuse anyone to the point of insanity, which is what he intended to do with Anna, Justin, Anthony and Casey. Jane was already dead.

But now, he only had half a life and half a body. Somewhere he had lost his power, not realising it was buried deep with his Jester's hat in the soil of the mountains of Switzerland. Love for Stephanie had destroyed his evil etheric being and his form was dissolving, the karmas releasing from his being forever, until he no more roamed the earth in revenge.

And so, he continued to half stab and half confuse in the darkness of despair. Anthony and Justin had lost all contact with themselves and any kind of reality in previous surroundings. They were caught in a centrifugal net, an ever-tightening dimension of space and time.

Emma held them as they were buffeted this way and that for three days and nights. She had the power to transcend even this evil. With her husband Anubis' help, she severed the net from its mooring, allowing them to fall out back into the realms of space and time, to reach the earth's surface once again. They would never remember the dark chambers, the film of the Countess' death, nor the pictures on the wall. It would be all gone. All these things, after all, had been illusions created by The Jester. It was time for The Jester, the greatest illusionist of all, to go.

# 56

At Zurich Airport, which was always clean and silent at the busiest of times, Casey went through customs and looked for Fabian's chauffeur at the exit.

She wore a charcoal grey trouser suit, short jodhpur boots, and her blond hair, now quite long, was tied back in a ribbon. She was here to do business. Her anger with Fabian knew no bounds. Her jacket did not quite do up and her baby bump was visible.

The chauffeur was there to greet her in the ridiculously large black Mercedes with its shaded windows of smoke screen glass, Fabian's signature of power wherever he went.

She was settled on the back seat with a TV, magazines, and DVDs, whatever she would require for the four-hour journey they would take to the upper reaches of the mountains beyond Zurich, mountains that were all year covered at their tips in the whitest of snows.

She drank the coffee that had been put in a thermos for her but had not touched the croissants on the silver tray.

Soon, she was looking through the DVDs, but that really held no interest for her. She examined one of the few drawers near the back seat, and there in a black cover was a single DVD; on the tiny side strip, there in small writing, was "Thackeray Hall – Part 3."

She had no idea where Part 1 and 2 would be, but it aroused her curiosity. And so, she slid it into the player and found the remote.

She thought it must be some promo from Sotheby's for Fabian in his quest for further homes around the world. The first shots Casey saw were of an orangery, then paddocks and the stables of an exquisitely preserved Elizabethan house with numerous outbuildings. The entire feeling of the place was Tudor, and beams were part of the roof structure in every room. She wondered where this magnificent property was in England. It did not look unlike Jane's house in Shropshire. Poor Jane, she was the one who had really paid for all their past sins, whatever they were. It was tragic and terrible that she should lose her life so young. All the deaths had come one after the other; Oliver, Justin's near death and then the news of Jane from Justin who had called her just before he had left for Cairo. And then Stephanie was also dead. Focusing again on the DVD, she saw that in the garden all the trees were cut back in curious designs. The designing, cutting, and training of trees were obviously practiced as an art form here. Casey was intrigued.

Then the DVD went blank, quite black. She was about to signal to the chauffeur that the player had broken down, but within moments of her confusion, new images started to emerge.

The camera was now obviously in the house; the rooms were lit by huge candles, lamps and chandeliers. This was a totally different atmosphere; it was now night time.

Here on screen was a brief view of the wild blue eyes of her stepfather. His head was curiously bobbing up and down. Chills ran through her, but she was unable to pull herself away from the screen for any of the hour-long footage.

The camera moved slowly downwards, beneath the bobbing head, and lingered on Oliver's dallying with a very young woman. Casey gasped as the camera moved to a close-up. The girl's long, ash blond hair was strewn over her shoulders and down onto the bed beneath her, where she had sunk on her elbows and knees. Lord Pembroke's immaculate hands were working the young woman's buttocks as he knelt behind her. Casey was sickened.

Casey was, from her childhood, used to the shocks and pain that her stepfather had inflicted on her. She was inured so much that she always had delayed reactions. But she could not help her own disgust and at the same time arousal at seeing her stepfather seducing another woman. She was groomed by him to have certain responses; and after all these years, she was unable to undo her reactions. She did not indulge in watching or reading porn, but when it came to her unannounced, she was unable to tear herself away. She was filled with both shame and longing. But in all honesty, she wanted to see more.

As a child lying with her stepfather, when he had come to her in the beginning, there was at first the horror of his sexuality. And then, the actual act of intercourse and what he had done to her was shocking – the excruciating pain and her terror. In time, it had turned to pleasure and excitement knowing that it was wrong. Then, there was the thrill of knowing that at any moment her mother could come in and Casey could yell at her that her stepfather belonged to her now. It was as though she took on Oliver's evilness. He kept the door of the bedroom securely locked against such intrusions. And later, when he had inflicted a lot of pain on her, the fastened door came with the territory. Then, there was the hatred for her own mother with whom she had to share him, and the never ending and impossible longing for him to be hers and hers alone, always.

The camera not wishing to linger further, moved on to the next room. This time an even younger woman was lying completely naked, tied to a bedpost while two older men were forcing her into different positions. Again, the camera took advantage of its magnifying lens.

The next scene further captured Lord Pemberton, lying in a deck chair licking strawberries and drinking champagne out of an elegant eighteenth-century cut-glass flute, waving his hand at the camera, His great eyes were protruding now, as he stuffed his mouth with strawberries and then sugared cream.

Then there were hors d'oeuvres served: skewered oysters, caviar, and salmon crepes with sour cream. Close-ups of all the food were shown on the screen, ending with the strawberries and cream, some of it finding its way onto the still naked party goers.

All these scenes, Casey presumed, were filmed as a travelogue for the next overnight event. Casey was horrified; she knew Oliver was a philanderer but not this bad. She was aware of her own programming, the reactions, the grooming she had gone through. And after all of it, she still adored Oliver, dead now and buried. And now, there was the child inside her. It was a travesty of any purity she had left, and she knew it. She instinctively put her hand to her belly and the baby inside her.

As the tape played, Casey heard the chanting, almost like an incantation in the background. Otherwise, there was complete silence. You could not hear the screams, the cries of ecstasy, or the simple pain that must have emitted from those female lips caught in the net of sexual games. Most of the players were masked.

Casey fast forwarded to the later images. Her father seemed to have disappeared.

She remembered, as a child, the first time her father had tied her hands to the bedpost, having turned her first on her belly. Without any warning, he used a flogger on her. He was gentle at first, but at times he was out of control, and she suffered terribly. Later, it was much worse. He would get angry and use a tightly braided cat on her buttocks and back before he penetrated her. Other acts inflicted on her contained for her the worst psychological scars, those of guilt and self-recrimination.

Inside the pain, like a sheath, as she got older, there was the ecstasy of repeated orgasms. And as he trained her, she taught herself to submit; give him the ultimate pleasures and assist him to control his madness for her. Ejaculation was always a problem for him. He had to be stimulated in certain ways that were often at the door of her physical suffering.

Eventually, she became his submissive and he her dominant. It was months of torture before he was able to use her completely in this way, when she submitted to anything. It seemed now that she was forever lost in his space.

This time in the video, there were shots of the awkward and hard angles of the topiary. Fabian was showing two young men around the garden. Cubes, obelisks, cones and tapering spirals of the trees were everywhere, and seemed to be mirroring the contortions and twisting of those people who were occupying the house itself. The trees, like the women, were trained to form strange shapes, to bend and twist in ways that were not really natural to them.

Casey shut the DVD down. She looked at the mountains, the snow capping ahead of them. She was as silent as the snow itself.

# 57

"You will have to bury it in the ground, Fabian." Randy's voice spoke with some authority.

Randy had no idea what she was dealing with; but from the naivety and purity of a child's perspective, she knew something was wrong and that this jester's hat and the other regalia had enormous power over Fabian. His ashen face told her that something was very terrible, a force draining his energy, and she could see the fading blue light around him.

Of course, Randy had never seen him as he was before, wielding the power of The Jester, wearing his hat ceremoniously, imbibing its great power over him. Thrilled with all that, The Jester would give him, by way of power, wealth and endless sexual titillations. She saw him as he was now. His actions had cut himself off from the power of The Jester.

The great oak doors of the castle were flung open on Casey's arrival. Fabian almost fell down the steps in coming to greet her. She was horrified to see how he looked.

As they climbed in the huge hallway, it was apparent that he had lost a considerable amount of weight. His skin was sallow, almost yellowed, and he had none of the energy he usually carried. His presence was one of gauntness, and there was no feeling of evil or predatory sexuality. Casey was very confused as to what had happened.

"Tell Casey that she has to come in here right away, Fabian! She has to help us!"

Casey could hear Randy's authoritative voice giving out orders from the back of the castle. Fabian quickly took Casey through the long dark hallways, oak panelled, towards Randy's voice. She saw Randy leaning over something on the floor. With all her might, Randy was dragging The Jester's hat along the carpeted floor.

"Randy, don't you dare do that on your own! You have no idea of the danger you are in by touching it, let alone dragging it along the floor!"

"Fabian, we cannot waste any time at all. We have to get it into the hole!" Randy screamed at him.

Earlier, Randy and Fabian had dug a hole in the garden almost on the cliff edge itself. There was a drop of hundreds of feet, and the faint hue of the blue, snow-topped mountains beyond.

Casey came out of the veranda doors and viewed the hole. She laughed for some peculiar reason. She could not stop. On and on she went. Fabian and Randy watched her open-mouthed.

All the tension of the journey; seeing Oliver having sex with so many women on the DVD, then arriving at the mansion and seeing The Jester's hat being dragged along, and then the huge hole. It was too much for her. Her laugh was becoming maniacal, building to a crescendo. Her eyes were too wide. She started choking. Her body was running back into the house, into the room where the hat had been. She started rolling on the carpet. Fabian was noticing her baby bump.

"It's The Jester," yelled Randy. "He is starting to possess her."

They ran for water, putting salt into it, as they both knew. They threw it over her and prayed.

Gradually, Casey calmed down, but there were shards of glass from the broken cabinet in her hands.

"You have to get every piece out, now! It will all be contaminated with the evil," insisted Randy. And she and Fabian took a good hour trying to do just that. Randy had been right; the glass was impregnated with the demonic moonbeams of The Jester; created to wreak havoc if they ever entered a human being.

Fabian gave Casey a sedative, took out every bit of glass and bandaged her hands, carrying her to the spare room.

It was apparent to both Randy and Fabian now that together they would have to drag not only the hat, which had become the weight of lead, but all the paraphernalia that Fabian had kept as part of the rituals of bondage and servitude to The Jester. There were chalices, bones, blood, masks, ropes, and candles. It was endless, the stream of things that they collected from that room. Then, every single piece of glass had to also go into the hole. Salt was added. Finally, earth was thrown on the top and the hole was sealed over with small rocks that they had collected.

It was done.

They sat and waited on a small bench, watching the stones for an hour or more. But nothing happened, and it was curiously silent.

The sun went down over the vast crags. They watched the small wind-blown trees and mountains, but still nothing stirred.

In the evening, Randy noticed that Fabian was becoming increasingly weak and started to have a fever. By nine o'clock, it was worse. By then, Casey was up; and she and Randy took Fabian to his room, laid him down on the huge bed, and covered him with a rug; as one minute he had a raging fever and was crying out in a delirium, the next he was shivering with cold.

They kept a vigil all night. They never left him and took no food of their own. They lit candles, said prayers over him, and rubbed salt onto his hands and feet, hoping to remove the evil from his body.

The next day, he was much improved, and they all went out to the garden to look at the pile of stones covering the tomb of The Jester's hat and all the magical tools and implements. The sun was out, and they just sat there looking at the stones, each with their own memories.

"Where are you going next, Fabian?" Casey was concerned for him, concerned that The Jester would find him and kill him. Fabian had so little strength now, all the evil and malice having drained from him.

"I am now in the process of selling up everything. All the arms business, the places in London; I want none of it anymore." Fabian was speaking to them quietly, afraid, in a way that his dreams of being with Maxine and their baby might not come true. He did not tell them about the Hexagon Club or the brothel, but he knew that Casey was now aware of Thackeray Hall.

"Well," said Randy, "I want to live with Casey and you, Fabian. I haven't got anyone now. I want to go away to school and have all my clothes brought from Harrods. I want a dog from Harrods, too." Randy went on and on, but they listened to her. She too had lost everything. They wanted her to know that she was being heard.

"What do you want, Casey? Are you in love with Anthony?" Fabian was gentle with her and put his arm round her.

"How did you know that?" asked Casey.

"Unfortunately, I know everything. I know that right now Justin is in Egypt with Anthony, and that they are going to go back to the pyramid to find out what really happened to Richard. The Jester's plan and my orders were to kill them both in the pyramid. But now, I am refusing to follow orders. So, I am probably going to be the one that is killed with them." Fabian put his head in his hands once again.

"But I can't be with Anthony now because I am pregnant," sobbed Casey. "You know who the father is, don't you Fabian?"

He was silent.

"How on earth did you get so entangled and taken over by this demon?" asked Casey, curious as to how this quiet, simple man sitting next to her had been turned into a monster.

"It is a long story, Casey, longer than you think." Fabian paused a moment. "I come from a strange family of occultists." He did not want to tell Casey about his parents, the famous

Hexagon Club, the vipers' nest of the Nazis nor that they were eventually murdered by the post-war Reich. He would just tell her about The Jester.

"One night I was in my bed going to sleep, and there was suddenly a figure standing in front of me. I was aware that gurus and saints could project themselves at will into someone's house or room. But I could tell that this man was no saint. However, I was strongly attracted to his energy, but it was not good energy. It was tantalizing and titillating. He said that he knew me well from other lifetimes. He enchanted me as a boy of five years old and he offered to bring me all sorts of gifts and powers. I wanted power, as I saw my parents able to do many things.

"Over the years, he had an increasing power over me and wanted me to do things for him, little things at first and then much bigger things. Then he would stay away. I would long for him in a way. I was very lonely as a child, with only my younger sister and no friends, so he had also become my friend.

"Later, in my twenties when I had been sent away to the United States, The Jester came and told me that in a past life he had murdered the first Countess of Rigby and that he and several men had raped her, then killed her preparing her for an Egyptian burial. This was in George IV's reign. The Jester told me that he was the son of Seth the Egyptian God and had been killed by one of the pharaohs. The Jester revealed to me that Justin was, in a past life, this Pharaoh and Anna in this same life was his queen or consort. He told me that I had been totally involved in the murder of the Countess, who apparently was my mistress. Anna, the queen of the pharaoh in the past life, was also my mistress."

Fabian seemed so weakened by this revelation to Casey that she again urged him to go and lie down and rest. Fabian went back into the house, and it was dusk before he started to talk again.

Casey thought about what he had told her and was shocked beyond belief with all that The Jester had developed within Fabian and how evil he had become. He did not want to confess to her the sexual crimes of which he was guilty, his exploitation of women, and the endless ring of sexual secrets around the world where women were bred and raised for the sexual gratification of men. He would not describe the incest between daughters and their fathers and how he had made these arrangements, how he had had Anna in his control completely from the age of sixteen. Casey had only been aware of the sins against her but had no idea that Lord Pemberton was part of a much bigger ring of sexual activity.

Later that evening, when Randy was fast asleep, Fabian and Casey spoke more about what had happened.

"And my stepfather, what about Oliver? I saw a DVD of him at one of your orgies in the car, on the way here."

Fabian looked at her. He lied to her. He could not bear to tell her that Lord Pemberton was one of the most notorious paedophiles in England. Nor could he bear to admit to Casey that he himself had the same kind of tastes for the 'Lolitas' of this world.

But Casey did not pursue this about her stepfather; instead, she talked about herself as a young girl.

"Anna's father was a very strange man, but my own stepfather was really my world. I hated and loved him. We were sexually involved with each other from when I was aged six. He just came to my room one night. Later, he was completely depraved when I was a bit older; he taught the best and worst forms of sex. It was terrible, most of it, and I was constantly in pain. But one becomes addicted in a way to what one thinks is love and of course even at a young age, he knew how to bring me to a climax. He knew every single part of a young girl's anatomy."

"And the baby, Casey, it is Oliver's, isn't it?" He could not bear to think of her carrying this evil man's child. He had arranged it that Oliver had committed suicide, a fact that he would not tell Casey, but one day she would find this out.

"I don't know what to say to you, Fabian. I miss Oliver terribly; the baby is the only thing left of what we had together." She shuddered at the memories; they were starting to surface again. She was shocked.

She did not tell Fabian everything, but it was a relief. They were both relieved to share what had happened to them. Much was left unsaid and then Fabian told her that he planned to go and see Maxine and take her from South America to California and build a house there for them and the baby.

Casey said that Anthony and Justin had not invited her to Egypt; it was just too dangerous. They had no idea then about the baby, but she was planning to go back to New York for a while and have the baby there, well away from Antigone. Randy would go with her as she needed to be with someone who loved and knew her. The rest would happen as their destinies unfolded.

Fabian took her in his arms and kissed her forehead. "I am so sorry, Casey, sorry for it all. I wish all this had never happened." He truly wished he had never met The Jester and had to lead this terrible life for over three decades.

In a few days, the house would be empty again. They were all on their way now to different parts of the world to live out what was to be their new lives.

That night, Casey took hours to get to sleep. Her room was at the edge of the long castle. She thought of Oliver, their long years together, the strange circumstance of his death and the video at Thackeray Hall. The dreadful realization was dawning within her, the realization of who her stepfather really was. She was restless and agitated and then slept. But she awoke again a few hours later, and there it was, as in the nightmare, her hand cutting into her arm, the cut to get the poison out of her, the poison it seemed of a thousand years. It was Oliver's face then in front of her, laughing at the huge joke of her life; then the crumbling of the face before her very eyes and underneath the hideous mask of The Jester. There was no Oliver any more, only this apparition, the same apparition that had impregnated her. And then, the dream that she had had when she was staying with Anna and Justin became a reality, of the fresh blood running between her legs. It was there, flooding out of her; the sheets were already stained with the redness of it.

And then, there was Fabian suddenly next to her bed, with tea, hot towels. She was silent for a long time, as Casey realized that she was losing the baby, the contractions coming rapidly, the frequent trips to the bathroom. Fabian took care of her until the early hours of the morning. She was spent, blood everywhere; the final cramps came, and she doubled up; the foetus left her body forever. Fabian took care of cleaning everything up and put her back to bed.

They talked for a long time, Casey's face pale in the small bedside light that he had put on for her.

"Casey, you could never have had Oliver's baby; it was a dream, a nightmare in which you were living for years. To have the baby would have meant that the spell would never have been broken between the two of you. It would have been a monster inside you, just as Oliver was a monster." Fabian was not going to spare her now. She had to know at last, the truth; it was the only way she would heal.

"No, I don't want to know," Casey screamed at him. "Leave me something of my life with him!"

"There is nothing you can keep, Casey; you have to let it go. Oliver was one of the worst paedophiles in England. You have to know this, Casey."

She held her hands over her ears and pulled the covers over her. She was shaking now with the shock of losing the baby but also from what Fabian was telling her. He was lancing the boil of her life, the poison at last coming out, poison that she had wanted to get rid of for years, within her system. She felt that she was rotting from the inside out – putrid, stained.

Anthony at that very moment had recollected the picture of Casey with the single fishnet stocking and her stepfather in the pyramid; Oliver, naked beside her in a pose, entrapping his prey. He heard her cries, saw it all and in that very moment Casey too thought about Anthony, and the danger that he was in.

And then she got up, collapsing into Fabian's arms, her sobs convulsing her whole body as she let go of the only thing that would have kept her chained to Oliver forever. She was free at last; but it had cost her dearly. She would mourn the lost years, the terrible years of her life, never to be returned to her.

The next day was a silent day. Randy stayed in her room, and Fabian and Casey sat together in front of the log fire, watching the first fall of snow covering the stones and the earth in which the regalia and hat of The Jester were buried.

They experienced the tragedy of both their lives; it was too ghastly to speak of, both possessed and tormented by souls that their beings could not withstand. Fabian sweated and shivered as The Jester started to leave him; the shell that was left was too frightening. He did not know who or what he was anymore.

# 58

"Fabian, where are you?" Maxine screamed from the edge of the cliff. She had been running after Fabian in a game around the park and grounds of the house. He had collected her and pledged himself to end his empire. Their house was at the cliff edge. This was to be a new life. He had sold the chateau and the castle, wound up his affairs and set his heart to giving his love and money to the world. But little did he know that in defying The Jester, his own life was now in jeopardy. He had tried to leave Maxine and obey The Jester, but his love for her was too strong. He also, for the first time, wanted to marry and be a real father to his children.

In the light of his love for Maxine, the blackness of his deeds and those of The Jester became repugnant to him. Wanting to make amends, he brought Maxine to a safe place in California.

"I'm over here. Come over to the cliff and see the ocean," he cried out to his wife.

As he reached the cliff edge, he tripped over something sharp jutting up just before the view of the beach and rocks below. He tried to regain his balance, but he keeled over and fell the full drop. His body was like a dark shadow as it fell, as though it was not a body but resembled a black crow.

Maxine looked over and saw his body on the rocks below. She ran down the path, a scream forming on her face, the features distorted. There he lay, as handsome and precious as when he was alive. She watched his face for several minutes. She saw, to her horror, it starting to change; a mask peeled from his face, revealing the hideous face of The Jester. Her screams ran across the cliffs and down into the ocean, until someone came to help her. By that time, Fabian's body had crumbled and disintegrated to such an extent that it was unrecognizable.

"This decomposition is unusual. The only time I've seen this before was when I was working in one of the museums." A police officer, who had come quickly to the strange scene of Fabian's death, was talking to his mates, macabrely, shocked out his skin.

"They brought over these mummies from Egypt, yes, Cairo it was. We had to unwrap those things. It was for experimental purposes. Well, as soon as we did the unwrapping, there were the original bodies, as though they had only died yesterday; but within one hour, at the most two, they looked like this one, totally withered away. Makes you think, doesn't it? The forensic boys will be interested in this case; I can bet you. It will start a whole investigation," continued the police officer. "Here, someone needs to look after the lady. She's pregnant and in shock. Get her to the hospital; anything can happen after a shock like this," he continued, finally looking in Maxine's direction.

But Maxine had already gone. She had walked and then swam a long way into the ocean. Only her head was visible, then suddenly it vanished, and then there was nothing.

# EPILOGUE

## TWO YEARS LATER

The driveway to The Beeches was shrouded as was the countryside beyond in the early and unexpected snow of the winter. The trees were bare of their usually russet-coloured leaves and the previous night had seen a severe frost, so that the twigs on the branches of the beech trees each carried a small burden of ice.

Jane had walked slowly up the path to the house, her progress slowed by the snow and the pregnancy with her first child. The great joy of her marriage with Fairfax — she remembered the long years of summers that they had all enjoyed together at the house, she and Fairfax, Justin and Anna, cocktails on the patio, bridge and dinners in the evening. Then there had been Stephanie's party and she herself accompanying with the cello, Anna on her new piano. She had been lost in the closeness of the company and the long strands of melody that flooded the drawing room with its soft lighting and warm comfortable sofas. Now, it seemed so long ago. And now she half expected Anna to come down the drive, in search of some holly and mistletoe, as it was soon to be Christmas.

But Anna had died just a few days after Fabian died at the bottom of the cliff in Santa Barbara, California. She had been walking in the garden; she was just mounting the steps to the bridge over the stream when she collapsed and was taken to hospital. Anna did not survive; it had been a massive aneurism in her brain that caused her passing. She had never known how long she would live, once Fabian was gone and The Jester with him. Her life had been always sewn up with magic; she had never known real freedom and she herself had known that she was living on borrowed time once she had burned the black thread in the fire.

Before her death, her mother had come to see her, bringing with her all the journals that she had kept about the Fraternity and the Hexagon Club, warning her that there would be police raids at the club and at Thackeray Hall. Anna had broken down at the realization of who she was and how she had been captured as a young girl in the terrible skeins and threads of suffering. She had broken partially free when she had burnt the black thread that day, wondering how long she had now. It was unbearable to her. She had asked Lucille to leave and never come back.

Maybe she no longer wanted to live without Fabian or Justin in her life; maybe she felt that she could not bear to endure the hours of interrogation from the police, because she had been privy to the secrets, had been part of the Hexagon Club. It was bound to come and so, she chose to die, her suffering going with her to her grave now that the spell had been broken within her. Her mother Lucille would not be so lucky.

And Jane, who has been so miraculously saved from death by the cleverness of her husband and the police, had been living in a safe house in Canada for over a year. The police, with the help of Fairfax, had uncovered the plot to kill her at their family home in Chiswick. They had been at the house when the assailants had arrived and had arrested them and got them to report to The Jester's gang that the murder had happened. With the assistance of the BBC, they had staged the murder, and got it onto the news and in the papers, so that everyone believed it. It was heart-rending to hurt their friends in this way, but there had been no alternative; Jane's life had been in danger for a long time. On her return, they both came out of hiding. They sold the house and moved to Richmond, to an even larger house with a river front view. There, they had conceived their first child. The baby would be due in April.

Antigone and Lucille were both arrested. Antigone was given a fifteen-year sentence; she was sent to Broadmoor for her crimes, for procuring young girls for Oliver and the Hexagon Club and for failing to protect her young daughter Casey from her husband who had committed horrific sexual crimes against his stepdaughter. Had he himself lived, he would have served an even longer sentence for his sexual crimes as a paedophile. Lucille had a shortened sentence, but she was charged with not protecting her daughter from ritual sexual abuse and for not reporting the fact that Anna had been twice raped, once at the age of nine by Lord Pemberton, and when she was sixteen in the stables at the family home by Count Fabian Roth and an American senator.

The much bigger hearing would have gone on for months for the main player, Count Fabian Roth. His crimes were endless. Not only had he run an illegal establishment, the Hexagon Club in Mayfair, where young girls were offered as playthings and toys for the wealthy, but he had owned such establishments all over the world and was guilty of sex trafficking. He kept brothels in all the major cities. His involvement with drug running and arms deals would have added to the weighty list of crimes for which he would have to account. But his body had lain at the bottom of cliffs in California and then had strangely disintegrated in sight of the crowd that had surrounded him.

Jane was sitting alone in the garden now and thought of all the other arrests, of men from inside and outside the club; and now many women coming forward, telling of the sexual abuse they had experienced from their own fathers, employers, uncles, brothers and the Hexagon Club. The world was glued to the news, staggered by these terrible revelations.

When the police teams arrived to raid the various Hexagon clubs around the world, the magnificent buildings were always empty; all the furniture had been removed, even the light bulbs had been taken. No one was there. Someone had tipped off the clubs' managers. The Hexagon clubs had gone into hiding, as they had done in 1820 after the death of Amelia at Farlingham

Park. Whole families went underground, left the countries they inhabited, taking their strange culture and sexual practices with them – who knows where. These families and the Fraternity were immensely wealthy, could cover their tracks and pay large sums for people's silence, even the police. Many dossiers on victims and perpetrators went missing. It was thought that the abusers were too high up in society, men of real power, and the documents had been stolen and destroyed.

Jane thought of Casey now; she had a complete breakdown once Antigone had been sent to Broadmoor. She was in a London hospital and then at a private clinic for over a year. Justin came to see her when he could, although he was now living in Kashmir. But he would come for weeks to London to be with Casey. She took a long time to heal, her body shaking continuously when any memories surfaced. She was given a lot of drugs, but she remained silent, pale and listless. Justin wondered if she would ever recover from what Oliver and Antigone had done to her in their terrible experiment with their daughter. So much had been uncovered in the trials.

And then Justin decided to take Casey to India, away from London, Cambridge, Antigone, Oliver and all the pain. He took her to be with him and Anthony in Kashmir. Already, Justin was treating patients with Ayurvedic medicine, but this was not really working well for Casey. Whatever he gave her made little difference.

Justin had emailed Jane from India to say that Casey had decided to go away on her own to travel, to make a pilgrimage around India. She was depressed and the memories of Oliver still haunted her. She was still far from well. It seemed as though no one could help her heal from the ghosts of her past.

Jane walked back to the car at the end of the drive. Fairfax was waiting for her; he opened the door. Then they drove back to the house in Richmond. Catherine and the children were coming today, so she had a great deal to do.

"How was the house?" asked Fairfax.

"Just the same as ever. It's hard to imagine that Anna isn't going to walk out of the house towards you with a pair of shears and a bunch of roses," she added.

"Yes, I suppose it is," said Fairfax.

They were silent for the rest of the journey, each caught up in their own thoughts. Fairfax was glad Jane was by his side now; for so long, she had been in a world of her own. Now she was involved in their life together, their friends, dinner parties and holidays away. She was pregnant now with their baby and had put on some weight; she looked much better for it. The car made its way towards London and was lost from sight in the fading winter light.

Justin and Anthony bought a large house at the foot of the Himalayas; it was surrounded by verandas on the outside which gave way to gardens that they beautified over the years. It was a paradise and Justin had set up a small medical practice which was well attended by local people. Being a keen scholar, he also studied Ayurvedic medicine. Truly, he was a gifted man. He thought little about the life he had left behind and hardly ever went back, except to see Casey when she was in the clinic. This was his life now; his heart was full of longing for God. All the years of questioning were over for him. He was content to work the medical practice and tend his orchids. After eventually finishing at Oxford, Giles often came to visit Justin in India.

Justin made a final visit to England on his own; he wanted to mourn Anna and to see her grave. He then went to Shropshire to take a last look at Farlingham Park. He drove along the lanes in the evening dusk. At last, he came around the final bend of road. The gates of Farlingham Park were open; they looked so timeless. Ivy clung to the black iron, and the gargoyles still stood atop the gates. The avenue was overgrown, and brambles had grown around everything. There was no house beyond the trees that lined the avenue. There was simply nothing there at all. Not a single clue that there had ever been a Gothic mansion beyond. Justin simply could not believe that it had gone.

Anubis had gone long ago, taking his wife Emma and daughter Stephanie to other worlds. Seth also was far now from the earthly plane. Whatever original purpose they had to be here was now over. Justin and his friends were safe now. Fabian and The Jester were no more and would never re-incarnate to this world again.

# APPENDIX

## *LIST OF MAJOR CHARACTERS*

## 2010

| | |
|---|---|
| Lady Anna Bowlby (née Carrington) | Justin's wife, Count Fabian Roth's mistress |
| Sir Justin Bowlby | Heart Surgeon at St John's Hospital in London |
| Giles Bowlby | Anna's son by Count Fabian Roth |
| Professor Richard Carrington | Anna's father, Cambridge Professor |
| Lucille Carrington | Anna's mother |
| Jane Crosby-Nash | Anna's friend from Cambridge University, Egyptologist |
| Fairfax Crosby-Nash | Jane's husband, a barrister in Lincoln's Inn Field |
| Casey Pemberton | Anna's cousin |
| Lord Oliver Pemberton | Casey's stepfather, Antigone's 2nd husband |
| Antigone Pemberton | Casey's mother, Oliver Pemberton's wife |

| Maxine Cleveland | Casey's friend, journalist, Fabian's mistress |
| Alistair Cleveland | Maxine's father, US Senator |
| Sidney Henderson | International interior designer |
| Moira Henderson | Sidney's wife |
| Count Fabian Roth | Industrialist, The Jester's puppet, Occultist |
| Emma, Countess of Rigby | Socialite and Occultist, Fabian's sister |
| The Jester | Reincarnated Magician from the Hyksos Dynasty |
| Anthony Jackson | Film director |
| Stephanie Arnold | 10-year-old, Justin's patient |
| Randy | 9-year-old friend of Casey's from New Yor |
| John Grey | Anna and Justin's chauffeur |
| Richard Abrascus | Co-director of Anthony's film in Cairo |

# King George IV's Reign   1820

| Amelia | First Countess of Rigby |
| Jane Cavendish | Amelia's sister, living at Farlingham Park |
| Sir Ashley Cooper | Amelia's husband, chief physician to the court |
| Charlotte Brooks | Amelia's cousin, living in Paris |
| James Wetherby | Editor of a medical magazine |
| Sir John Hargreaves | Amelia's lover and brother to Sir Ashley Cooper |
| The Jester | to King George IV |

# The First Life – 1640 BCE Family Seat at Avaris, Egypt

*The Royal Family of the Seventeenth Dynasty of the Hyksos Kingdom*

| King Khamudi | Fifth Hyksos King or Pharaoh. |
|---|---|
| Nehesy | 'The Great Wife', the Pharaoh's chief consort |
| Anat-Har | Ruler of the Temple and Temple libraries (House of Life) |
| Ya Qub-Hat | The Pharaoh's magician |
| Salitis | Political advisor to the Pharaoh Khamudi |
| Tarsa | Salitis' wife |
| Khyan | The magician's brother and chief architect |
| Anubis | God of the Embalming and the Afterlife |
| Seth | God of Evil and Destruction |
| Thrat | The God Anubis' wife |
| Smira | The God Anubis' daughter |